# Love at First Sight

After several very happy years as a bookseller, Jessica Gilmore moved into the charity sector and now works in the Arts, living out her Noel Streatfeild dreams by walking through the Stage Door every morning. Married with one daughter, two dogs and two dog-loathing cats, she lives in the beautiful Chilterns, where she can usually be found with her nose in a book. A lover of a happy-ever-after, Jessica loves to write emotional romance with a hint of humour and a splash of sunshine.

As day dreaming is her very favourite hobby and she loves a good happy-ever-after Jessica can't believe she's lucky enough to write romance for a living. Say hi on X at @yrosered or visit sprigmuslin.blogspot.com

# Love
## at
# First
# Sight

## JESSICA GILMORE

ORION

An Orion paperback

First published in Great Britain in 2024
by Orion Fiction, an imprint of The Orion Publishing Group Ltd
Carmelite House, 50 Victoria Embankment
London EC4Y 0DZ

An Hachette UK Company

1 3 5 7 9 10 8 6 4 2

A CIP catalogue record for this book is
available from the British Library.

ISBN (Mass Market Paperback) 978 1 3987 2243 9
ISBN (eBook) 978 1 3987 2244 6

Typeset by Born Group
Printed and bound in Great Britain by Clays Ltd, Elcograf S.p.A.

www.orionbooks.co.uk

For Mum and Dad, love always x

Paris, 28 June 1995

Bonjour Maman et Papa.

Paris est très très très bon. I should have paid more attention to French in school, you were both right as always, but that is okay because the waiters speak English to me before I even open my mouth! I am going to give up on going to university, get a garret in Montmartre and paint. Or maybe write books. Or compose. Something artistic that means I will wear a beret and all black and be effortlessly très chic! Zut alors, Paris has my soul!

Miss you. Love you always. DON'T WORRY.

Lottie xxx

I

# Chapter One

'I mean it, I am *done*.' Nora Fitzgerald folded her arms and looked defiantly around the table. She could see why her friends looked sceptical. Her more recent romantic choices had been questionable to say the least. 'No more dating. No apps, no set-ups. None of it. D.O.N.E. Done.'

'Hear, hear!' Ana held up her glass in a toast. 'I'll drink to that. Dating *sucks*.'

Nora clinked Ana's glass. 'Exactly! It really *really* sucks. Here's to the end of dating. No more being ghosted by a man who still lives with his mother, no more being the rebound fling before he decides to propose to his ex.'

'No more finding out he's married with a baby on the way.' Ana grimaced. 'Or watching him cry at his university girlfriend's wedding.'

'No more standing in sweaty rooms watching *terrible* guitar bands week after week, only to find him snogging someone else behind the drum kit.'

'To be fair, you should have known not to trust anyone in a band called *Hooray Henry*,' Felix said with a slight shudder, looking up from his intense perusal of the menu from the other side of the table, although, as they came here nearly every week, he probably knew it by heart. 'And they were *really* terrible. No offence, Nora, but I for one was delighted when you broke up with Lee. He should have paid *us* to turn up at those gigs, not charged us for the experience.'

Nora cringed. It was bad enough that she had wasted half a dozen weekends dutifully attending gigs in the back rooms of pubs in the outer reaches of London, but worse she had begged, cajoled and bribed her friends to join her. 'I can't believe I put you through that. I am a truly awful friend. And I actually thought I was heartbroken for a good few weeks after I finally dumped him. What was I *thinking*?'

'We did wonder.' Felix's husband, Dai, nudged her. 'But we all kiss our fair share of frogs before we find our prince.' The smile he gave Felix was so tender it almost . . . *almost* . . . weakened Nora's resolve.

'Well. I for one have kissed my last frog,' she said. 'No more awkward first dates where they don't ask me a single question about myself or eat all my food. No more sitting awkwardly while everyone in the bar knows I have been stood up. No more commitphobes. No more foot fetishists. No more unsolicited dick pics from random strangers.' She thumped her fist on the table. 'It's time to say *no*. Applications are closed. Frogs need not apply.'

'Go, Nora!' Grace tossed her long braids back as she broke into applause. 'I'd love to say I'm in, but I'm weak. I don't want to be single forever.'

'You've haven't been single for as much as a week since we started Year Seven,' Nora pointed out affectionately. 'You just have to lift a finger and men fall into line. Besides, you *love* the dating game.'

'True, and I am not ready to stop playing yet. But that's because I know not to take it seriously. I'm not the romance nut here, Nora. I don't believe in soulmates or a happy ever after. When it stops being fun, I'll stop and if I've found someone I'm compatible with, then great, and if not, then that's fine too. But *you* want the fairy tale. You always have. I just don't see you settling down with a cat and your

4

knitting and a nice box set.' She grinned at Nora. 'Not the way you knit anyway.'

'Oh, I am not giving up on finding Mr Right,' Nora said. 'It's *dating* I'm done with, not love. I still want to fall properly in love, to get married and maybe have children and all of that. But I'm not getting anywhere dating, so I have decided that I need to stop trying so hard, and I just have to trust that it will happen for me the old-fashioned way.'

Her friends exchanged amused glances.

'The old-fashioned way? To join together two grand estates?'

'Newspaper adverts?'

'Becoming a governess in a spooky Yorkshire mansion?'

'At a ball?'

'No, idiots.' Although a ball would be rather cool. '*Fate*. When the time is right, I'll meet my soulmate. I just need to trust in that.' Nora took a gulp of her Prosecco and avoided four sceptical pairs of eyes.

'Honey, I hear you, but sometimes fate needs a helping hand,' Dai said. 'Look at me and Felix. I had to drink an obscene number of flat whites before he even noticed me, let alone started flirting with me.'

'Oh, I noticed you,' Felix said softly and Nora's heart twisted. *This* was what she wanted. Not the combat of dating, but to be settled. She wanted pyjamas and a takeaway on a Saturday night, long walks across Hampstead Heath talking about nothing and yet finishing each other's sentences. She wanted a perfect fit. *Her* perfect fit. And recent experiences were proving that she was unlikely to find him on an app. She shouldn't be surprised – after all, hadn't her mother raised her on classic romantic films? If they had taught her anything, it was that you didn't find love, *it* found *you*, often in the most unexpected places and at the most unexpected times.

5

'I love the idea of a soulmate, but I just don't trust my hormones not to lead me astray,' Ana said. 'I swear, I can tell each month when I ovulate because I get *obsessed* with procreation. I sit on the tube and look around and think, if we get taken through to another dimension, who here will be the best hunter-gatherer and I find myself trying to catch their eye in this intense way. I can't stop myself. The evolutionary instinct is scary stuff. If I trusted in fate, I'd be married to some hulking rugby player with no emotional intelligence but fabulous upper body strength.'

Nora couldn't help laughing at the image of six foot, leggy Ana hunting down her prey during rush hour like some kind of leopardess on the prowl for a mate. 'OK. I'll just make sure I still feel it's right when I'm *not* ovulating. All I know is that I need to trust in what my mum always said, that when I meet the one I'll just *know*, like she did when she met my dad. She said that the universe has a plan for all of us, I just have to stop trying to *make* it happen and *let* it happen.'

'But I thought you didn't know who your dad is?' Dai snagged an olive from the bowl sitting in the middle of the table. 'Have I got that wrong?'

'I know *who* he is,' Nora said, immediately defensive, although she knew Dai was just interested. It couldn't be easy for him as the newest member of such a tight-knit group, friends who had known each other so long there were no secrets, no unknowns. 'I just don't know *him* – and he doesn't even know I exist. My mum met him in Italy, in Florence – isn't that the most romantic thing you ever heard? She was interrailing the summer after her A levels and met him at a gelato shop – he knocked hers right out of her hand and insisted on buying her a new one. It was the ultimate meet-cute.' Nora sighed. She could picture it so clearly, her mother, hair in plaits, adorably freckled nose, the gelato falling to the floor. Her father, tall, handsome and apologetic. 'They spent a few perfect days together; it wasn't until she got home several weeks later that she realised she was pregnant with me. But the point is, the moment she saw him she knew he was going to be in her life forever – and through me he was.'

'But they didn't stay in touch?'

Nora shook her head. 'No social media in those days. Not even email, not for most people. Mum didn't even know his surname. They were both heading south so parted in Rome with the promise they would run into each other again, but somehow it didn't happen. She had other relationships, of course, later, a couple pretty serious, but no one else made the same impact on her. You know, right until she died, I think she hoped she would see him again one day, if only to tell him about me.' She blinked, her eyes suddenly hot.

It was nearly the fifth anniversary of her mother's death, but Nora still missed her all the time. They had been unusually close, partly because of her mother's youth, but mostly because of the kind of person her mother had been – warm, impulsive, empathic. Every time she returned home from another failed date, she wished her mother was there to envelop her in a hug, make her a cup of tea and cheer her up by putting on one of the nineties romcoms they both adored. Who could stay sad while watching Tom Hanks and Meg Ryan find each other on the top of the Empire State Building?

'That's incredible. It's hard to imagine a time when you couldn't just add someone on Insta and they would still be there long after the tan has faded, liking every cat picture.' Dai took another olive. 'Do you know anything about him at all?'

'I know that he was Swedish, planning to study architecture and called Erik and that's it. Luckily, I do have a couple of photos, so I at least know what he looked like in his late teens or early twenties.' She looked down at the table. 'I was doing some tidying the other day and I came across Mum's diary. Well, it's more a collection of postcards and letters, so I don't feel like I'm intruding reading them. Seeing their time together through her eyes makes me feel like I know him a little better.' She blinked, remembering the way her mother's expression would soften whenever she talked about the brief time she and Nora's father had spent together. Finding and reading the postcards made her feel like her mother was still here, for a few moments at least, her voice so vivid and alive. Nora was doing her best not to rush through them, reading them one at a time, in those moments when she really missed her mother.

And if her mother were here, she knew she would tell Nora to stop trying so hard to meet someone. To trust in fate. Finding the postcards and letters felt like a sign to do exactly that.

'At least you have a name,' Dai said. 'Can't you use that to track him down?'

'Do you know how many Eriks there are in Sweden?'

'Er, a lot?'

Nora took a sip from her nearly empty glass. 'There are around sixty thousand males called Erik in Sweden. I can discount any aged under forty-five and over sixty, but it's still too wide a field and narrowing the search area down to architecture hasn't helped. Besides, even if I did track him down, he might not want to know me. He might not even remember Mum or he might have a family of his own and not want the complication of an adult daughter wanting to play happy families.'

Nora had told herself that many times, but it didn't stop her trying to find her father. Didn't stop her spending especially lonely evenings on social media, search sites, using photo recognition software, searching architecture firms around the world, the crumpled photos by her side, looking for any clue, any man of the right age who might have been in Italy at the right time. What she would actually do if she did ever find him, she wasn't sure. Her dream was to be part of a family again, the reality might be rejection.

'If anyone can find him, you can,' Grace said loyally. 'You're the best in the business.'

'It's not quite the same.' But Nora couldn't deny that part of the reason she enjoyed her job working for an heir hunter firm was because, even if she was missing part of her heritage, she got to reunite other families. Yes, her job was all about money, but the people she tracked down often inherited more than just cash and assets, they found a family history and sometimes an actual family as well.

For someone as alone in the world as Nora was, that was the biggest prize of all.

To Nora's relief, the waitress turned up at that moment and Dai's questions ended as they got down to the important business of ordering. Nora had been friends with Grace, Felix and Ana since school; there was nothing about her life they didn't know. Well, almost nothing, they didn't know how lonely she was, that fact she kept to herself, not wanting their pity. They'd already steered her through enough tragedy. They knew she wanted to find her soulmate but they didn't know how much of that desire stemmed from her longing to be part of a big, bustling family. To come home to noise and chaos and love, not an empty house where her footsteps echoed forlornly around the hallway and just two coats hung on the hatstand meant to hold five times as many.

Dai reached for the Prosecco bottle, but when he lifted it up, it was empty. 'Have we finished it already? There's the red we brought, but I'm still in the mood for bubbles. Anyone else?'

'I'll go and get a bottle,' Nora said, getting to her feet. Their favourite tapas restaurant was a bring your own, which made it surprisingly affordable even in trendy Hoxton. 'I meant to grab a bottle before I got here, but I was running late. No, honestly, Dai,' she insisted as he tried to dissuade her. 'It's my turn and there's that lovely wine shop just over the road. I'll only be a few minutes. Just leave me an olive – and if the padron peppers arrive, do *not* eat them all!'

Grabbing her bag Nora made for the exit, glad of the opportunity to clear her head and get some air. Dai's innocent questions had stirred up a lot of feelings she tried to keep dampened down and, she realised, as she swayed in her too-high heels, she had been swigging the Prosecco more quickly than usual as she had responded.

Her shoes, like many of her clothes, had belonged to her mother. Since her teens, Nora and Charlotte Fitzgerald had shared a wardrobe as amicably as they had shared a house. Even better, her packrat mother had thrown very little out, leaving Nora with a plethora of original eighties and nineties outfits to choose from, in addition to some gems from her grandmother's wardrobe. Tonight, she wore a silk slip dress of her mother's teamed with the black-laced ankle boots. They had been her mother's favourite shoes and wearing them always made Nora feel closer to her. It didn't hurt that they also added three inches to her diminutive five foot two height.

As Nora left the restaurant, she turned to look at her friends framed in the window. Ana's often stern, sharply cut features relaxed in laughter at something Grace had said, while Dai and Felix leant close to each other across the table, lost in their own world. Who would have thought that Felix would be the first of them to settle down? Dai had softened some of his more cynical edges, made public his romantic side. They were the perfect example of two people who were just meant to be together. And they had had the perfect meet-cute. If Felix hadn't decided that following his father into the city wasn't for him after all and opened up a coffee shop instead, if Dai hadn't taken the wrong exit off the Heath, if he hadn't been so smitten with the handsome barista that he had continued to take the wrong exit day after day, then Dai wouldn't even be part of their lives. It was almost terrifying how much had hinged on that wrong exit and a flat white. Thank goodness fate had brought them together. OK, fate with a bit of a helping hand from Dai. Regardless, the pair had everything she wanted for herself. They were proof that her soulmate was out there waiting for her.

Lost in thought, Nora stepped out into the road, only to stagger and nearly fall as, instead of landing on hard tarmac, her foot sank down. Had she snapped a heel? These were Gucci ankle boots! Her mother would kill her, no matter that she herself had been dead for five years!

The moment of dark humour took away from the discomfort of the misstep and the humiliation of nearly falling flat on her face in the street. *Not* very hipster Hoxton cool of her.

Nora straightened carefully, flexing her ankles and knees to check for damage as she did so, and looked down to see what had happened.

A grate. A big grate right by the pavement and she had gone straight through it. At least, her heel had. *Idiot.*

She lifted her foot. Except it didn't move. What the actual? She pulled again, but no, the heel was obstinately and definitely stuck in the grate. Another tug, harder, the effort squeezing her ankle and bringing sudden tears to her eyes.

'Damn it.'

Nora looked around wildly, but all she could see was a taxi a few metres away with two men standing beside it, one holding a bag. Besides, what could she say? 'Please help me, my vintage and horribly impractical boots are stuck in a grate.' What could anyone actually do? The only option was to unlace the boot, take it off and try to wiggle it free when it wasn't encumbered by her foot.

Right. A plan.

Only, of course – *of course* – it was starting to rain, the wind whipping up. It was early May, but the weather clearly hadn't got the springtime memo. What had she been thinking coming out without a coat? Her dress might be an original Ghost 90s slip dress, but it was still silky, skimpy and now increasingly damp. As for her hair, she could actually feel it starting to frizz, to rise like dough on a warm windowsill.

Nora bent down and started to tug at the laces. These boots had seemed oh so cute at home, with their hooks and the way they laced all the way up her calves, but, as her fingers numbed, she was bitterly regretting not pushing her feet into her flat fur-lined boots and choosing practicality over style. And had this lace *knotted*? Damn. It. She tugged again, only to realise she was making the problem ten times worse. The rain intensified and she swore under her breath. If only it would stop raining. If only she could see! If only her fingers would work . . .

One of the two men standing by the taxi called out sharply in her direction. '*Attenzione!* Look out!'

Nora whirled round, wrenching her ankle as she did so, and saw a motorbike coming towards her at what seemed like an impossible speed, lights blaring straight at her. Desperately, she tugged her now painful foot, tears of vexation, pain and fear mingling with the rain running down her face.

'I can't get it free!' she cried out and heard running footsteps before a hand grabbed her shoulder.

Nora looked up, dimly taking in a tall slim figure, a glimpse of wet, dark hair and the impression of razor-sharp cheekbones. She gave another tug. 'It's stuck.'

'*Cavola! Accidento,*' the man muttered, before slipping an arm around her shoulders and holding her tightly as he gave a sharp tug and, with a moment of exquisite pain, her foot was pulled free from the drain, the motorbike roared past and, for the first time in her life, Nora Fitzgerald fainted. Right into the arms of her rescuer.

Vienna, 1 July 1995

Mutter und Vater,

Oh, Vienna! With your boulevards and tea rooms and cakes! I even went to the opera the other night – can you imagine? I am so very cultured now.

Anyway, change of plan. I am going to move here instead of Paris and waltz and eat sachertorte and have a little dog who I will walk through the park before another coffee and more cake.

You will be very happy to know that, so far, all the hostels have been clean and safe and the trains nearly all on time. There are loads of backpackers with huge rucksacks and little money on the post–A level pilgrimage, it's funny to see the same faces in different cities. It's not just the Brits though, I am meeting lots of interesting people from all over the world. Miss you though!

Your Lottie xxx

# Chapter Two

Nora knew three things. One, it was still raining. Two, her foot really hurt. And three, she was propped up against a wall, her eyes closed.

'What happened?' she murmured like some kind of film heroine, the effort of opening her eyes somehow too much, but still uncomfortably aware that her dress was soaked through, her hair dripping. Woozy as she was, she couldn't help but worry that her mascara had ended up halfway down her face.

There was no answer, but she could hear a rumble of male voices speaking Italian, one indistinct, the other a deep, gravelly voice that was somehow comforting. More, familiar. Safe.

She tried to open her eyes but couldn't make out much more than a blur before she had to close them again, the throb in her ankle drowning everything else, before drifting back off into that strange twilight world.

'Nora? Nora!'

'Is she hurt?'

'Do we need an ambulance?'

'Nora, honey, are you OK?'

'Give her some air.'

'We need to move her inside.'

'Should we? What if she's hurt?'

'But she'll catch pneumonia if she stays out here!'

It was nice that her friends were so concerned, but Nora wished they weren't quite so loud. Her shoulder was throbbing, her foot was still doing something that made throbbing seem like a benign activity, she felt faintly nauseous and she'd gone from wet through to absolutely soaking.

She managed to open her eyes and this time keep them open and blurrily made out Grace, Ana, Felix and Dai standing over her. Behind them, looking concerned, were Tony and Elena, the restaurant owners.

'I'm fine,' Nora croaked, but nobody seemed to hear her.

'No ambulance,' she tried again and this time her voice was stronger.

'Nora! She's awake.' Ana crouched down by her. 'Are you sure? What if you have concussion?'

'I didn't hit my head.' Nora touched her head doubtfully. Surely, she would feel it if she had? 'A guy caught me.' Nora suddenly felt bereft, missing the strong arms around her, that strangely familiar feeling of safety. 'Where is he?'

'What guy? Are you *sure* you're not concussed?' Ana looked even more concerned.

'There was a guy,' Grace said excitedly. 'He stepped away when we all came out. I think Dai spoke to him? Dai? Who was the guy?'

'Nora's knight in shining armour? No idea.'

'He was Italian, I think. A real hero. He saved my life. Or at least he saved me from a nasty accident. Tall, dark . . .' Nora caught herself. Maybe she *had* hit her head if she was blurting out every thought.

'Tall, dark and heroic. Maybe fate is telling you something,' Felix teased. Then he turned serious. 'Nora, I think we should call a paramedic and get you checked out.'

'I'm fine,' and she increasingly was, the ache in her shoulder receding, the pain in her ankle lessening. She looked around. 'I just wish I could say thank you. Did he take off?'

'Once we were here and he knew you were OK,' Dai said.

'Oh.' Nora wasn't sure what her sudden swoop of disappointment meant. 'Well, I'm just glad he was here in the first place.'

'So are we,' Dai agreed. 'Oh! He asked me to give you this.' He held up a small business card. 'In case you need a statement for insurance or anything, he said.'

'Thank you.' Nora used Felix's proffered arm to get gingerly to her feet and test her ankle. It twinged as she put weight on it. Possibly sprained, she decided, but definitely not broken. 'Let's get out of the rain, I want my patatas bravas even if you don't. I didn't make it to the off-licence though.'

'Don't worry about that.' Felix put his arm around her and helped her limp to the restaurant door. 'I'm still not sure we shouldn't get you checked out, let alone feed you alcohol.'

'I wouldn't turn down some ice for my foot, but otherwise I'm fine.' Nora wasn't being brave, with every step she really did feel better. Oh, her ankle ached, as did her shoulder, clearly a little wrenched from when the stranger had grabbed her to pull her back, she was beginning to shiver as the wet fabric of her dress clung to her skin and she wasn't sure she dared check her boots for damage, but for all that, she felt strangely excited. It was almost as if she had recognised her rescuer, even though the whole thing had taken seconds, she hadn't even spoken to him and she had never seen him before. It was just like her mother had described meeting her father. Looking up and just *knowing*, despite the driving rain and the fact she could barely make out his features. And even though, in this case, the hero of the story hadn't stuck around.

*

17

Despite everything, Nora managed to enjoy her dinner, gratefully accepting Elena's offer of a towel and a sweatshirt and tracksuit bottoms to change into and sensibly sticking to water rather than any more wine, but she found it hard to concentrate on her friends' conversations, instead replaying the events of the accident over and over. The whole thing had probably taken less than a minute, and yet every milli-second was stamped on her brain. The shout, the rescue, the strength as he had hauled her to safety . . .

'Did he say anything else?' she asked Dai as she ensured the precious business card was safely stowed away in her bag after sneaking a look at it.

*Gabriel Catalano*. Catalano . . . *Just like Jordan*. She and her mother had curled up together and watched every episode of *My So-Called Life*. 'This will teach you everything you need to know about being a teenager,' her mother had told her, and she'd been right. Nora had lost her thirteen-year-old heart to the monosyllabic, guitar-playing Jordan just as hard as Claire Danes had. She'd even affected dressing in big plaid shirts and tried hennaing her hair that summer in the hope that she'd find a Jordan of her own. It couldn't be a coincidence that he had the same surname of her teen crush. It had to be a sign.

'Just that he was sorry, but he was already running late and he hoped you were OK. Why?'

'No reason,' Nora said as nonchalantly as possible, but Felix's brown eyes gleamed.

'You seem very invested for *no reason*.'

Nora's cheeks heated. 'I just thought I ought to thank him, that's all.'

'You have his card. Why not get in touch and offer to take him out for a thank-you drink?' Dai grinned. 'He's around our age and very handsome, if that's what you wanted to know.'

'No, not at all,' Nora protested weakly, her cheeks hot.

Dai was right, the normal thing would be to get in touch. But taking him out smacked of a first date. Paved the way to awkward silences and a quick summing up, of ready-made excuses and inevitable disappointment. And Nora had turned her back on all that, hadn't she? She was leaving her life in the hands of fate. If Jordan – *Gabriel* – Catalano was who fate intended for her, then she would see him again. The universe would make sure of it. Wouldn't it?

At 3 a.m., Nora admitted defeat. It wasn't just the throbbing in her still swollen ankle or the bruising in her shoulder, or the spicier than usual patatas bravas keeping her awake. Every time she closed her eyes, she relived the incident, the lights bearing down on her, the deep gravelly voice, the moment she was hauled onto the pavement and to safety.

Nora got out of bed and pushed her feet into her slippers, shrugging on her fleecy dressing gown. The house was chilly, bordering on down right freezing, and as always preternaturally quiet for a house in London. Quiet and empty. On the one hand, she was lucky – what other twenty-eight-year-old owned a three-storey Victorian terrace in Hampstead, just a few minutes' walk from the Heath? On the other, she would happily live squished into one room in a crowded flat share, moaning about the price of renting, to have her grandparents and mother back again. It was a surprise sometimes, how much that knowledge still hurt, still overwhelmed her, leaving her bent over and gasping for breath. She hadn't realised how physical grief could be, not until she was swamped in it.

Switching on the landing light, Nora made her way down to the big kitchen diner at the back of the house and flicked the kettle, picking up the card Gabriel Catalano had left with Dai off the kitchen table. Of course, he might have left the card for Dai, not her. He might be married or have taken a vow of celibacy or be in a polyamorous relationship and Nora was not judging, but she knew she wasn't cut out for sharing and . . .

*Nora Florence Fitzgerald, stop getting ahead of yourself.*

The thought was so clear she could almost see her grandmother, always calm, always wise, padding around the kitchen dispensing love and tea in equal measure. There had been no one better during a crisis of confidence.

Nora looked over at the three framed photos she kept on the sideboard, her constant companions. The first was of her grandparents on their wedding day in the late nineteen-fifties, so very of the era with her grandmother's bouffant hair and her grandfather's dapper suit, both wearing wide and hopeful smiles. They had needed that hope, waiting nearly two decades for Nora's mother to come along. Maybe that's why they had taken her unexpected teen pregnancy in their stride, offering their daughter and her baby a home without a murmur of reproach as far as Nora knew, giving Nora the happiest and most stable of childhoods despite their unorthodox situation.

The second photo was of her mother, Charlotte, on her last day of school. Impossibly young, yet less than a year from becoming a mother, wearing tie-dyed dungarees, her hair in two long plaits, posing in huge sunglasses, little knowing that in just a few weeks she would meet the man who would change her life forever.

The third photo was of them all on Nora's sixteenth birthday, her grandparents now white-haired and wrinkled but still recognisably that young couple, their smiles wider than ever, and both still effortlessly stylish, her mother looking little older than Nora herself, the pair often mistaken for sisters thanks to their resemblance, with their strawberry blonde hair and green eyes, matching smiles and slight build.

The photo had been taken just twelve years ago. Now Nora was the only one left.

Nora made herself a mint tea, taking it and her laptop over to the battered sofa by the patio doors, where she curled up, pulling a blanket over her for warmth. In the dark days after her mother had died, she had often slept down here, needing to be in the heart of her home. She took the card out of her dressing-gown pocket and examined it. A name, an email address, no more, no less. That was fine, she could and did work with a *lot* less.

But would researching her hero be cheating?

On the one hand, the universe might have given her the card as a clue. A push in the right direction. But, on the other, looking him up did feel a little dodgy. Verging on stalkerish.

She shut her laptop and put it down on the sofa. She had actual real paying work to be getting on with, she shouldn't be wasting her time with this. And if fate had really catapulted her into the path of a speeding motorbike so that Gabriel Catalano could rescue her, then fate would make sure she met him again.

Luckily, Nora was too busy over the next couple of weeks to give her rescuer more than one or two – or ten or twenty – passing thoughts, thanks to a breakthrough in one of her more obstinate cases tracking down the heirs of a million-pound-plus estate. Her trail had led her to Devon, which meant a trip out of London, and by the time she returned home, weary and still with only part of the puzzle solved, she was ready to admit she had gone a little overboard in her reaction to the incident.

So, she had looked up and felt a jolt of recognition? She'd known at the time that adrenaline had been racing right around her body, creating all kinds of strange feelings. Gabriel Catalano was saving her life; she would have connected with anyone right then regardless of age or sex. No, it was nothing more than an understandable reaction to nearly getting run over. She had made a vow and she was sticking to it. Her love life was to be left in the hands of fate and that was that.

It had been a long day, with more than one cancelled train, and she was too tired to cook, but Nora was an old hand at batch-cooking and she found a lasagne portion in the freezer saved for exactly this scenario. She put it in the microwave to defrost and poured herself a glass of wine before preparing a side salad. She'd just rinsed the lettuce when her phone pinged and she looked down to see a mysterious message from Grace.

*Have you got it? What are you going to do?*

Typical Grace, expecting Nora to read her mind.

*Got what?*

*The invitation!*

*Invitation to what?*

There was a long pause before two words appeared.

*It's Jake*

Right. Jake.

Nora took a bigger gulp of wine than she had intended, her stomach churning.

*What's Jake?*

Another long pause. Nora could practically see Grace, face screwed up typing and deleting.

*He's getting married.*

Then, quickly: *I can't believe he hasn't invited you.*

*Jake's getting married?* But as she typed, Nora realised what she really wanted to ask. She bit her lip, unsure she wanted to hear the answer as she typed the more important question. *Who to?*

*No idea, I didn't even know he was seeing anyone. You know he stopped doing all social media.*

*Probably to stop me tracking him.*

Nora was only half joking. After all, there had been a time when Jake had known her better than anyone. He knew exactly what she could do with a name and a social media profile. But if he thought she was going to waste her time researching *him* then he was . . . well, he was probably right. Damn him.

She sucked in a deep breath, the smell of the defrosting lasagne making her nauseous, folding her arms around her middle as if she could physically keep her feelings locked in. Jake had been the boy next door. Literally. Nora didn't know a time when he hadn't been there on the other side of the garden wall, a year older, annoyingly superior, half teasing and half ignoring her, depending on his mood. She, in turn, had half idolised and half hated him. Until one day she didn't hate him at all.

She grabbed her phone, flopping down on the sofa.

*It's not fair. Why is Jake getting married and I am enduring a purgatory of horrendous dates and even more horrendous*

23

*short–term relationships that should never have got past*
*the first date?*

*I thought you were done with dating.*

*I am. But that's not the point.*

*I know, babe. You're right. It's not fair. You deserve more.*

Of course, Grace knew. She'd had to endure the *I think he likes me oh no he's ignoring me* sixth-form stage, the blissfully loved-up part that followed, when every other sentence started with 'Jake says'. She'd been the first to accept Jake into their tight-knit group, even used him as a confidant for her own eventful love life . . . And, of course, she'd been there at the end.

Grace more than anyone had picked up the pieces he had left behind. Helped Nora put herself back together. As far as Nora knew, the two were no longer in contact, which made Jake's decision to invite *her* friend to *his* wedding feel strangely personal.

Unless he had invited the whole gang including her, after all, she hadn't opened her post yet.

Nora stood up and walked numbly over to the sideboard to check the small pile of post waiting to be recycled or dealt with, but she already knew she hadn't overlooked anything; she'd have noticed if there was anything personal among the typed envelopes.

She picked up her phone, typing where she stood.

*Nobody wants the ex hanging around like a ghost of relationships past. I'd have had to find a reason to decline anyway, even if he had invited me. You have to go, though. I want every detail.*

*I know what you mean about ghosts, but you're more than just an ex, you are part of the family.*

*Were. They moved, we split up. It's fine.*

It was fine. Now. Kind of. But it still stung. Jake's family had always been there, Christmas drinks and summer barbecues throughout her childhood, then practical, kind and supportive after first her grandfather, then her grandmother died. Later, an endless source of comfort and practicality during her mother's illness and after her death. But then Jake had accepted a job abroad and it had been horribly clear he didn't see her in his new future. Nora didn't blame him, not rationally. Grief had changed her, made her smaller, more exposed. He wanted to get out there and live and she wanted to curl up and hide away. It had been messy and hard and drawn out, but maybe they would have come to some kind of way of being around each other if his parents hadn't sold up and moved to Hampshire. Now the people who had been her second family sent her cards at Christmas and impersonal and absurdly expensive candles for her birthday and she wasn't invited to the wedding.

But that was fine. Jake had moved on and so had she. She actually barely thought about him. Nora *really* wanted him to know that.

She flopped down on the sofa, moving a notebook to the side as she did so, and as she picked it up, Gabriel Catalano's card fell out and onto her knee.

Maybe this news *was* fate giving her a nudge, telling her to take matters into her own hands. Maybe it was time to see if lightning really did strike twice.

*Florence, 12 July 1995*

*Ciao Mamma et Papà.*

I take it all back. Italy is where I am meant to be —
and oh, bella Firenze! I am Lucy Honeychurch with a
room with no view but a mind and spirit waiting to be
awakened. I didn't know anywhere could be so perfect
but oh, Florence really, really is (as is the ice cream).

*Tutti amore,*

*Lottie xxx*

# Chapter Three

People often confused Nora's job with that of a private detective, but the two professions were very different. Most people were delighted to hear from Nora for a start; she brought good news, often involving money. She also spent more time following paperwork than people and had never yet had to change her appearance.

And she was very good at what she did. So a work email address was laughably easy.

A few seconds later, she was on Gabriel Catalano's work's website – some kind of investment banking company. She clicked on the About Us tab and there it was, a comprehensive staff list. 'Thank you,' she muttered.

In less than two minutes, Nora had a professional profile. Gabriel Catalano was a partner at the firm and, according to the brief biography, born in Sicily, educated first in Milan, then at LSE, with a year at the Sorbonne. There was an accompanying picture. Nora sucked in her breath as she took him in. Dai was right, he *was* handsome with perfectly cut dark hair and the beautifully defined cheekbones she remembered. Nice: brains *and* beauty.

Nora grabbed her notepad and scribbled down the details. Now the work began.

Two hours later, Nora had switched to herbal tea and was munching on her half-finished lasagne cold on the table, as she finished her initial profiling, using the most obvious tools: the electoral register, social media profiles, googling to build a picture of her rescuer. He lived in swanky apartment in a converted warehouse overlooking Regent's Canal near Hoxton, liked to ski and surf, hike and climb, had run at least one marathon and clearly enjoyed good wine and expensive meals. She could work with that. Not the marathon part and she wasn't a huge fan of climbing, but she was fond of beaches and liked the idea of the après part of skiing. Most importantly, he seemed to be currently single, the elegant dark-haired beauty he had posed for many photos with disappearing from his profiles around the New Year.

Nora put her notepad down and took a sip of tea. If this was work, then the next step would be to pick up the phone and arrange a meeting. She bit her lip as she reread the profile she'd compiled. Was it a bit *underhand* to have researched him so extensively based on nothing more than a feeling and a brief encounter? When she carried out research for work, it was for the other party's ultimate benefit, although, of course, she was also paid. The obvious, sensible thing to do would be to email Gabriel and suggest a thank-you drink, just as her friends had urged her to do.

Nora opened up her email and tried a few drafts, at first formal, then funny, followed by flirty and, in the end, more than a little filthy. She read through her last attempt, blushed and deleted it.

No, an email wasn't going to cut it. Besides, she didn't want to set *up* a meeting, she wanted something natural.

Wanting was one thing, though; deciding how to achieve it something completely different. She spent several evenings turning various situations over in her head, each one increasingly implausible, until she knew there was only one thing she could do – head out on a reconnaissance mission and see if she felt anything when she saw him again.

The next morning, Nora was up early and, although she wasn't planning to actually *talk* to Gabriel, she made sure she was the best version of herself. Her hair shone, loose on her shoulders, waving at the ends thanks to a lengthy session with the curling tongs, and she chose a flattering pair of black trousers and a blouse she knew brought out the green in her eyes, teamed with her mother's cropped leather jacket to add a little interest, her make-up carefully minimal for that glowing, *I am naturally a morning person* look. Finally, she grabbed her laptop. Time to look busy.

She joined the morning commuters on the tube and, one line change later, exited Bank and headed to a side street. Her research had indicated that Gabriel Catalano liked to buy his coffee at a small independent coffee shop and bakery close to his city office and often breakfasted there.

Nora nonchalantly crossed the road and examined the menu in the window, clocking a round table by the counter perfect for her needs. She breathed in, trying to quell her nerves and caught sight of her reflection. What was she *doing*? This wasn't normal behaviour! She should just walk away, go home and get on with her life, accept this was a moment of madness in reaction to the Jake news. Trying to manipulate fate never worked well; she had done Classics at school, and knew it usually meant an ironic and sticky end.

Embarrassed and relieved no one knew she was here or why, Nora turned to leave, but at that moment, someone left the café and an intoxicating scent of warm bread and perfectly brewed coffee wafted out. Her stomach rumbled – a reminder she had barely eaten last night and hadn't had any breakfast yet.

Breakfast didn't count as stalking, surely? Besides, Gabriel had probably been and gone. Curling her hair had taken longer than she had anticipated and bankers always had early starts.

What harm could breakfast do? It was the most innocent meal of the day. Mind made up, Nora went into the café and ordered a flat white and a brioche with a berry compote, taking up residence at the round table and opening up her laptop. She might as well get some work done so the morning wasn't a *total* bust.

The door opened again and a tall figure stepped in. Nora could have sworn time slowed as she heard a deep laugh, a fast-paced conversation in Italian. She risked a peek over the top of her laptop and her heart thumped painfully, her breath momentarily leaving her body. It was him, Gabriel Catalano, even more handsome in person than in his posed headshot, leaning casually on the counter as he chatted with the barista.

Panic hit her. The truth was, he was unlikely to recognise her. After all, last time they'd met, it had been misty, raining, her hair plastered over her face, mascara running down her cheeks, her foot stuck in a drain. In a way, it would be insulting if he *did* recognise her. But *if* he did, surely he would put two and two together and realise she had deliberately set out to find him. He worked in a bank! He could add up!

Hastily, she closed her laptop and shoved it into her bag, then, head down, she grabbed her coffee and headed towards the door, unable to resist one sneak peek as she left. Adrenaline shot through her as Nora found herself meeting a pair of dark, long-lashed eyes.

She halted, unable to move. Should she smile, say something, leave? To her utter mortification all she could manage was a squeak, so quiet she hoped he hadn't heard it, before she managed to tear her gaze from his and launch towards the door and half tumbling through it.

Nora had barely caught her breath, when she heard a voice behind her. 'Signorina? Miss?'

What? He was coming after her? Would he want an explanation? A restraining order?

'Miss?'

She stopped, resigned to her fate and turned.

Gabriel Catalano was staring right at her, his brow slightly creased in query as he held out an object.

'You forgot your phone.'

'I forgot my?' Her phone! What an utter idiot! 'Oh! Thank you.' She smiled, half in relief, half in amusement at herself, and her stomach jolted as he smiled back, revealing gleaming teeth.

'You're welcome, I know how annoying it is when you lose your phone,' he said, then paused. 'You look very familiar. Have we met?'

'Have we met?' She was squeaking again. 'Erm . . .'

'I'm sure we've been introduced.' His brow creased in thought. 'I know! It was the opening of the Thame Gallery!'

The what now? 'I don't think so,' Nora said truthfully, mind whirling. Should they play guess the place for a while and hope he remembered or, as fate had quite clearly intervened and justified this whole mission, should she remind him? 'Oh my goodness,' she said before she could think better of it. 'Surely not!' Overdone? She felt a little like she was back in her primary school play overacting for all she was worth. 'It wasn't you, was it? The man who saved me from the bike. In Hoxton a couple of weeks ago?'

'The man who . . .' he repeated, almost as if he was wondering himself. Didn't he *remember*? Was the event that had taken on such symbolism for her forgettable for him?

Did he go around doing heroic deeds every day? To her relief, he brightened. 'Ah, si, Hoxton. Of course. In the rain.'

'And now you have just saved me again. It's terrible how much of our lives are in our phones, isn't it? I'd be lost without it.' She took a step back. 'Anyway, what a coincidence. I've been wanting to thank you ever since it happened, I'm glad I saw you again.'

'Oh no, there is no need to thank me,' Gabriel protested. 'It was actually . . .' He paused. Nora could sense him giving her a thorough once-over, sense the warm approval softening his eyes, his mouth softening into a sensual curve. 'It was . . .' he said again, almost absent-mindedly. 'It was nothing,' he finally concluded, although she couldn't help but think he'd been going to say something else entirely. 'How's the ankle?'

'All good now, but it was sore for a while. My pride was dented, and the boots a little worse for wear, but it could have been a lot nastier if you hadn't been there.' Her shiver wasn't feigned. She still saw the headlight bearing down on her when she tried to fall asleep at night. She held out her hand. 'I'm Nora, Nora Fitzgerald.'

Gabriel enfolded her hand in his and a shiver ran up her spine. 'Gabriel Catalano.'

'Nice to see you again, Gabriel.'

'Please, my friends call me Gabe.'

*Gabe*. It suited him.

'So, what brings you to this part of London, Gabe?' Nora laughed, embarrassed. 'Sorry, that sounds like the cheesiest pick-up line in the world.'

'Not when you say it.' Was he *flirting* with her? 'My office is just around the corner, and so I usually breakfast here,' he gestured to the café behind them. 'This is the closest thing to home I found in London.'

'Where is home?' Nora felt a little like a fraud, she knew this already, but now she was on the stage, she had to follow the script.

'Sicily.'

'Oh, how gorgeous!'

'You've been?'

'No,' she admitted. 'But I am a real Italophile, I kind of have to be – my mother met my father in Florence. I've always wanted to visit Sicily.'

'You should, there's nowhere quite like it. How about you, Nora?' She liked the way he said her name, the elongated first syllable making her prosaic name sound exotic. 'Do you work around here?'

'No,' she said quickly. 'I was just passing. I work in probate, from home mostly but I . . .' She thought desperately. 'I, er . . . have a meeting not far away. I was early and fancied a coffee and here I am. I can't believe I bumped into you here, I have been wishing I had a way to contact and thank you.' Too much? Would he remember giving Dai the card and start to think it all a little too convenient?

Apparently not. 'Coincidence?' Gabe's dark gaze held hers. 'Or fate?'

Excitement beat a rhythm as her pulse sped up. Did he feel it too? This connection? 'I . . .'

At that moment, Gabriel's phone beeped and as he glanced at it, it was as if whatever spell was keeping him standing in the street talking to her was broken. '*Mi scuzi*,' he frowned at his phone, then replied to the message, thumbs moving rapidly. 'Nora Fitzgerald, I am very pleased to see you here safe and sound, but unfortunately I have to go.'

'Yes. Of course, don't let me keep you. It was lovely to meet you properly while not semi-conscious. Thank you again.' *Please ask for my number*, she begged silently.

He didn't move, frowning thoughtfully. 'How long is your meeting?'

'My what?' Of course, the fictional meeting. 'Oh, that. Just an hour. Hardly worth coming all this way or at all, in these days of Zoom. Apart from the coffee – and bumping into you of course.' *Shut. Up. Nora.* She'd never been a good liar, always overembellishing.

'Because I was wondering if you wanted to meet me for lunch? I know a good Italian restaurant not far from here. I think you might like it.'

*Lunch.* On the Very Same Day. Gabriel Catalano was clearly both spontaneous and romantic. It was perfect. *He* was perfect. Just as she had dreamt he would be. *Thank you, fate.*

Nora smiled. 'That sounds wonderful. I'd love to.'

'OK, then. Lunch. And I have no meetings afterwards, so I don't need to worry about time, if you don't?'

'I can always make time for a good lunch.' It wasn't strictly true, Nora was still working on the large estate and if she wasn't successful, she didn't get paid, but she could make up any lost time this evening. 'It's a date.' Surely, in these circumstances, her no dating rule could be bent?

His eyes gleamed with amusement. 'Ah, but, *bella*, this is not a date, is it? It's fate.'

To assuage her increasingly uneasy conscience, Nora headed for the nearest library and put in as good a morning's work as she could manage. There was usually something about libraries that soothed her: the smell of paper and polished wood, the murmurs and low-voiced chats. She was the only person of her age she knew who actually had a library card. In another life, if she'd studied English Literature as planned, then she might have followed in her grandmother's footsteps and become a librarian herself. But for once the library failed to work its magic, Nora's emotions a mix of guilt and doubt, tinged with excitement and anticipation.

To her relief, Gabe was already waiting at the restaurant when Nora arrived, standing up as she approached the table and leaning in for a double kiss. He smelt amazing, if different to how she remembered, spicy and expensive, the embrace assured and natural. Not just his embrace, Gabe himself was so assured and natural that Nora soon forgot her doubts and found that she was enjoying herself.

He took charge, of the meal – 'Are you vegetarian, any allergies? No, in that case, shall I order for you?' – and of the conversation so easily, she was swept along as he talked her through each of the dishes – all simple, all utterly delicious – the wine she agreed to order even though technically they were both working afterwards, the conversation flowing so effortlessly, she barely noticed the other tables leaving, the staff starting to set up for the evening service.

At one point, after their mains had been cleared, Gabe excused himself to make a call. 'I've taken the afternoon off,' he said simply as he returned. 'Some things are more important than work, don't you agree?'

Some things, by definition, clearly meant spending time with her. Nora could only nod, almost numb with shock that everything was not just falling into place, but better than her wildest daydreaming. She couldn't remember the last time things had felt so easy.

By the end of the afternoon, Nora was confident she would score pretty highly on any quiz about Gabriel Catalano. As she had deduced from his social media, he was active, a lover of adrenaline sports, whether on land or water. He loved cars, his beloved Naziunali Siciliana – who knew Sicily had its own national football team? – and yet was clearly equally passionate about the arts, inviting Nora

35

to a gallery opening the following day. Music, he told her, was part of the Italian psyche and, horrified that she had never been to an opera, he offered to remedy the situation at once. He was refreshingly up front about his last relationship, telling her it had lasted for just under two years and simply run its course. He was open, enthusiastic, everything the last couple of years of sinking in the dating cesspool had told her not to expect from any man.

True, Nora hadn't volunteered *quite* as much information, she hadn't really had the opportunity, but that was OK, she enjoyed hearing him talk, saying the word *we* so naturally. We must, we will, wait until we . . . there was an assured assumption of future time spent together that was a balm to her lonely soul. She was sure there was a real connection between them, not a one-sided crush.

His dark gaze caressed her, she couldn't stop looking at him, her own gaze lingering on the curve of his cheek, the vulnerable hollow of his neck, the chords of his wrists. His voice enveloped her, his accent thickening with excitement, low and intimate. She felt new with him, mysterious, sophisticated, the tragedies and loneliness that she sometimes felt defined her firmly in the past.

She liked the sunshine and warmth he promised, the world he inhabited so apparently effortlessly, a world he promised to invite her into. She liked that plans were made for the following evening with absolute simplicity. She liked the way their fingers brushed together as he walked her to the tube, the contact tingling through her. She even liked that he didn't kiss her goodbye, but the way his gaze paused on her mouth left her in no doubt he wanted to. Nora's whole body was fizzing with hope.

'*Grazie*,' Gabe said as they reached the tube station entrance. 'That was the best lunch I have ever had.'

'Me too,' she admitted.

'I hope it will be the first of many. Fate brought us together, who are we to deny her plans?'

A tinge of guilt marred the moment, her conscience reminding her just how much of a helping hand fate had had. She should tell Gabe about her own part in their meeting while things were still new, she didn't want something so right, so full of promise, to be spoilt by dishonesty, but before she could speak, he kissed her cheek and stepped back.

'You're different, Nora Fitzgerald. Special. I am very pleased that of all the cafés, you came into mine, but I think that destiny always intended for us to meet again. *A domani*.'

And with that he was gone, leaving Nora staring after him, the confession unspoken. But did it really matter? She might have engineered the meeting, but not the recognition, not the lunch, not the connection.

She should leave the past firmly in the past and concentrate on tomorrow. Here was a real opportunity for happiness, she would be a fool to jeopardise it in any way. Gabriel Catalano was everything she had dreamt he would be and more. Her mother was right, love was just like their favourite romcoms and here she was, living out her fantasy at last!

Florence, 14 July 1995

Dearest Darling Parents,

As you can see, I am still in Florence! It's the
backpacker's raison d'être (is there an Italian
equivalent?!) to be forever moving forward, but I just
can't tear myself away from this wonderful, gorgeous,
gem of a city.

News! I think I've met my George Emerson (I am
pretty sure he's not a Cecil!). It was molto romantico.
Actually, it was everything . . . He knocked my ice
cream (berry!) out of my hand and insisted on
replacing it and then we had coffee, which turned into
dinner, which turned into supper, and then we went
for a walk and we talked for hours and yet still have
everything to say! I am literally the definition of giddy
whenever I think about him — which makes me giddy
twenty-four hours a day. He is Swedish. I know nothing
about Sweden apart from the muppets but am learning.
Did you know Stockholm is all islands? I told you
backpacking would be educational!

Your Lottie xxx

# Chapter Four

'Who are you? You look familiar, but I can't quite place you.' Grace squinted at Nora exaggeratedly as she opened the door of the flat. 'Come to think of it, you resemble someone I used to know. Nicola? Flora? Something like that.'

Nora held up the bottle of champagne she'd bought to celebrate finally settling the large estate, which meant a nice pay day was on her horizon. 'It's been literally days since I saw you – and I can just take this back home, you know.'

'Nora! That's it. Come on in and bring that bottle with you. Ana's just getting showered, she only got in from New York this morning. You know she always needs several showers to recover.'

'Imagine if she flew cattle class like the rest of us.' An ex-model and now agent, Ana had only turned left on aeroplanes since her teens.

'I'd rather swim.' Ana came out of her bedroom looking remarkably rested for someone who had just crossed over the Atlantic; it just showed what taking the red-eye in first class could do. 'Hi, Nora, I was beginning to think I had imagined you.'

'Again, literally days!' Nora kissed her friend's cheek. 'I've just been busier than usual.'

'Oh we know! And we want every detail.' Grace grinned at her. 'Don't leave any tiny thing out. But first, drinks. Champagne cocktails anyone?'

Nora took her customary seat, a comfortable armchair in the bay window of the spacious flat, and relaxed. Despite their very different tastes – Ana all sleek lines and muted tones, Grace preferring vibrancy in both colour and texture – their flat had a cosy yet coherent feel and Nora always felt instantly at ease when she was there.

'So, how's it going with Mr tall, dark and obscenely handsome?' Grace handed Nora a glass and settled herself on the sofa. 'Oh, this is good. No one makes champagne cocktails like me.'

'So far, so good, but of course it's only been a few days.' Nora felt uncustomarily shy as she took a sip of what was indeed a perfect cocktail, just the right amount of tart balancing out the sweetness. The three of them usually told each other everything, but she hadn't admitted that running into Gabe was anything but the life-changing coincidence it seemed to be. Nora wasn't sure why she was keeping it a secret. Maybe because the truth made her look slightly unhinged, a little desperate? Maybe because she wished so hard that their meeting had been the fairy tale it appeared that she wanted to fool herself that it really was?

'A few days maybe, but you've seen him every night. We're honoured you showed up this evening,' Ana said, with more than a hint of sarcasm.

'Cocktail evening is a time-honoured tradition,' Nora protested. Maybe best not to mention that she was meeting Gabe in town afterwards at a late-night jazz bar. She wasn't too sure about the jazz part, but Gabe assured her she'd love it, and she *did* love being the kind of girl he thought she was.

'As are Felix's weekly late-night sessions, but you missed this week.' Okay, now Ana had gone from a little sarcastic to downright hostile.

'So did you!' Nora countered.

'I was in New York. What was your excuse?'

'I meant to come, but Gabe had this art gallery opening. Felix understood.' She didn't mention Gabe's mock horror at the suggestion they start their evening in Hampstead, which was, he joked, too close to the edge of Zone Two. 'Why do you care so much whether I was there or not?'

'Because this is all too typical. Suddenly you are all art galleries and swish parties. With Lee, you were rock chick girl. With Ethan, you started watching rugby and you *hate* sports . . .'

'I don't *hate* sports,' Nora protested a little weakly. 'And what's wrong with taking an interest?'

'It's more like a complete personality change. It's like you were a total recluse after your mum died and Jake left and we understood why.' Ana ignored Grace's increasingly frantic attempts to shush her. 'But since you started dating again you've become *that* girl.'

'What girl?' Nora glared at her friend.

'The girl who lets her friends down and becomes a clone of her boyfriend.' Ana sat back and folded her arms.

Nora mirrored her, then, when she realised what she had done, hurriedly uncrossed her own arms.

'I do not.' But Nora knew there was enough of a kernel of truth in Ana's accusation to make her squirm. She just wanted to fit in, to be liked. Was that so bad?

'You are enough as you are, Nora, I wish you could see that.'

'We'll be at the next one, promise. I really want you all to meet Gabe, and he can't wait to get to know you. Gabe is different, Ana. You'll see when you meet him.'

'*We* already, is it?' Grace was clearly relieved to find a change of subject. Her smile was sly as she sat forward expectantly. 'OK, let's get to the tea. How much of a caveman is he on a scale of one to ten?'

'Grace!'

'You can tell us.'

The three of them had coined the term 'caveman' a few years before when Grace had been dating a man who was perfect on paper but had clearly got all his lovemaking skills from porn.

'I feel like a failed pancake at the end,' she had complained. 'Battered and flat. I keep trying to show him what works, but he obviously thinks foreplay is Chris Martin's first band.'

Nora couldn't remember which of them had had the idea first, but someone had remembered her mother's novels about a cavegirl who had invented medicine, pets and, in the end, the patriarchy, and the steamy love scenes they had pored over as teens (as, judging by the well-thumbed pages, had Nora's mother). Giggling, Grace had photographed them and sent some of the choicer examples to her boyfriend, reporting back with some satisfaction that the lesson had been absorbed and acted on. Since then, they had always graded their lovers on the caveman scale.

Nora had never minded sharing before, but this was different. Besides . . .

'I don't know,' she admitted.

Surprised silence.

'Variable?' Ana asked, a little grudgingly; she was clearly still annoyed with Nora.

'No! I'm not sure because we haven't . . . Because we're taking it slow.' Please leave it there, she silently begged them, but of course there was no way they weren't going to interrogate her further. Nora would if the situations were reversed after all.

'Taking it slow?' Grace echoed in disbelief. 'But you spend every second with him.'

'Not *every* second.'

'Then why? The man is gorgeous. Nora Florence Fitzgerald, explain yourself,' Grace demanded as if she were still in her classroom and Nora a recalcitrant ten-year-old. 'I know it's not been long, but you have been out with him every single day, passing the hallowed third date days ago. The rules of dating dictate you should have got horizontal by now. Or vertical – whatever you prefer.'

'There's nothing to explain. Like you said, we've only just started seeing each other. It's just . . .' Nora took a deep breath, knowing Ana was regarding her sceptically. 'Gabe is *it*, my soulmate. I knew it the moment I saw him. And he feels the same way. We have our whole lives to be together. I just want to enjoy every second. Not rush any of it. We kiss for hours, like teenagers. It's . . . it's romantic,' she finished almost defiantly. It really was, she loved how Gabe wasn't rushing her, that he seemed to want her company just as much as her body.

'You really think he's the one?' Grace asked, eyebrows raised so high they had almost left her face.

Nora took a deep swig of her cocktail, more embarrassed by admitting how quickly and deeply she had fallen for him than she would have been by giving Gabe a caveman score. Not that she had any doubt that he would be a ten when they got there. His kisses were incendiary enough and left her in no doubt that he knew exactly what he was doing.

'I know he is.'

She didn't miss the look her friends exchanged, a mix of concern and disbelief.

'In that case I'm happy for you,' Grace said, a hint of doubt in her voice. 'But I'm glad you're taking it slow and getting to know him properly.'

How could Nora explain that she *did* know him? That she had known him the moment she had heard his voice, looked into his eyes?

Some things were probably better left unsaid.

The cocktails soon disappeared, as did the second serving, and by the time they sat down to Grace's famous chilli, Nora was more than a little tipsy. She'd need to drink a lot of water before heading into London to meet Gabe.

'So, still no invitation from Jake?' Grace asked as she set plates of chilli in front of them.

Nora helped herself to yogurt, coriander and cheese from the bowls in the middle of the table. 'No. But I think we all know I would have received it already if I was going to be invited. It's fine. Honestly.' It wasn't. It hurt. But the more she told herself she didn't care, the more she might believe it. Besides, she had Gabe now. Far better to focus on him. On her future not her past.

'I can't believe Jake asked all three of us and not you. That goes against every friend code. You break up, the friends stick with the original party, everyone knows that. He even asked Dai. He has never even *met* Dai.' Ana got increasingly voluble with every word, no longer cross with Nora now she had someone else in her sights.

'To be fair, he gave Felix a plus-one because they are married.' Not that Nora wanted to be particularly fair.

'Not the point. Anyway, we shall refuse to go. In solidarity.' Ana held up her wine glass. 'Friend code and solidarity.'

'No!' Nora was touched by the gesture. 'Don't refuse on my account. Go. Then send me messages telling me that the bride's hair has frizzed and the colours clash and Jake looks trapped, even if none of it is true. *Especially* if none of it is true. Besides, I really *am* fine. I have Gabe now.'

The look her friends exchanged was exactly the same as the one they had exchanged when she had said that Gabe was the one.

Nora put down her fork. 'What?'

'It's just . . . the timing,' Ana said carefully.

'What do you mean the timing?'

'You find out Jake's getting married and then, *ta-dah!* You meet your soulmate. You don't think that's a bit of a coincidence?' Grace asked.

Suddenly her appetite was gone. Nora pushed her plate away, the chilli and cocktails sour in her mouth. The news about Jake *had* galvanised her into tracking down Gabe.

Automatically, she repeated the same mantra she used every time her conscience tried to pierce her happy-ever-after bubble. *All I did was nudge things along. Gabe might not have recognised me, and when he did, that lunch date was all on him. I couldn't have predicted that we'd end up moving so fast. That proves this is real.*

But she couldn't blame her friends for wondering; if Ana or Grace had fallen so quickly for someone, then she would be exchanging concerned glances and asking concerned questions. It was what friends did.

She picked her words carefully. 'I'm sad Jake and I don't have a friendship anymore, after everything we were to each other, went through together, after knowing each other all our lives. I wouldn't be human if it didn't upset me. But I would like to wish him well. I *do* wish him well.' Even though he had walked out on her when she was vulnerable and grieving. But that was all in the past. 'It still hurts that I've lost his family too, I guess I depended on them too much. But it's very understandable that his fiancée doesn't want me there. And Jake *is* the past. Gabe is the future and I am actually really excited about that. He's different to

45

anyone I have ever been with before. He makes me feel . . .' She tried to find the right words. Precious, wanted, but she couldn't admit that. 'His life is fun,' she said instead. 'And I really need that. So be happy for me? Please?'

'We are happy for you. But that doesn't change the fact that if he hurts you, we will end him,' Ana said, waving her fork in a way that showed just how serious she was.

'Understood.'

The problem was that her friends didn't know Gabe yet, so of course they were suspicious. It was up to her to make more of an effort to draw him into their circle, tempting as it was to keep him to herself. It would all work out, she was sure. This was her happy ever after, after all.

'Here's your shirt.' Nora handed the newly washed and ironed shirt to Gabe, drinking him in as he stood there in just his grey linen trousers, chest bare, hair not yet combed into place. He was delightfully rumpled. She loved seeing him like that, he was usually so perfectly put together.

'*Grazie, bella.*' He took the shirt off her and carefully laid it onto the chair before leaning in for a lingering kiss.

Mmm, he smelt so good. Nora pressed closer as his hand slipped down to her hip.

'But I was thinking, we could stay in. Watch one of those old movies you like.'

'So, you can fall asleep again?' Nora protested, slightly breathless as his hand caressed her hip in slow, dizzying circles.

She had been a little disappointed that Gabe had spent most of *Sleepless in Seattle* on his phone, falling asleep before Jonah had got on the plane, but then again, she knew how busy he was, how little time he got to relax. It was silly to be upset just because that film meant so much to her – although she *had* made an effort to watch Italian football and had researched the opera he had taken her to, to make sure she approached it with as open a mind as possible. Not, she told herself, Ana's words still rankling, because she was *that girl*, but because she genuinely wanted to experience the things Gabe liked.

'Besides, I promised Felix we would be there. He puts on a really good night, you know. I think you will enjoy it even if it is in Zone Two. And,' she added slyly, 'his coffee may not be Sicilian but he gets lots of awards. He roasts it himself.'

It was unlike Gabe to pass up the opportunity of trying good coffee – and if she had to bribe him, she would. They might have only known each other for a few weeks, but she was falling harder for him every day, and that meant she really needed to introduce him to her increasingly impatient friends who were all expecting Gabe to be there tonight.

'If it makes you happy, then of course we will go.' He nuzzled her neck and Nora closed her eyes, her nerves and hormones whirling in a dizzying happy dance. They still hadn't slept together, and every kiss, every touch was full of anticipation. She loved this sweet courtship, this lack of pushiness, although she was more than ready to take the next step. She just wanted it to be really special, memorable when they did. Gabe had been talking about a weekend away soon, just the two of them. It would be the perfect time.

'I was thinking,' she said, reluctantly stepping back as Gabe reached for his shirt. 'If you are going to spend more time here, keep coming over straight from work, then maybe you should have a drawer here.' She scanned his reaction nervously. Was it too soon? 'That way, we wouldn't need to do quick post-work laundry sessions, fun as they are. After all, I have plenty of space.' Not that her grandparents' solid mid-century wardrobes compared with Gabe's vast cedarwood walk-in closet filled with expertly tailored suits, handmade shoes and designer clothes for every possible season and activity. Even his walking clothes were stylish.

'A drawer?' His almost-black eyes were full of laughter, caressing her.

'If you want. I know we are almost in Zone Three here, but it is my home.' Nora could hear a hint of defensiveness in her voice and tried to soften it. 'I want you to feel that you belong here too.' It was far too soon to think about living together, but she wanted him to love her house. After all, she couldn't imagine living anywhere different.

It was more than just a house to her. This was the home her grandparents had moved into as newlyweds, saving every penny to be able to restore the then dilapidated, neglected house. This was where they had raised her mother, raised Nora, so filled with love and memories, they permeated every room. One day Nora wanted to raise her family here too, to make new memories.

Gabe hadn't said anything, but she could tell that he was a little underwhelmed. Everything in his flat was perfect, chosen to complement the light and space. His appliances were state of the art, his pictures by up-and-coming artists, his sheets cost more than her winter coat. But Nora's house hadn't changed much since her mother had died – and *she* hadn't changed much from her parents' time. The furniture was solid mid-century – once more sought after and fashionable, if achingly uncool through Nora's childhood, but it all needed sanding down and restoring, the Ercol chairs could do with re-webbing, the sofa respringing. The wallpaper was faded, the wooden floors dull, the kitchen almost a museum exhibit. It wasn't that Nora lacked the money to redecorate – she'd been left with a nice nest egg as well as the house – but she loved the house as it was, as it always had been. It made her feel like her family were still with her.

'You know,' he said as they walked down the stairs, 'this place could be stunning. You could put a glass box extension on the back, really open up the space and the light. The floors have so much potential, they just need restoring. If I was you, I'd knock through some of the rooms, replace the staircase . . .'

'Replace it? It's original!'

'It could be a real statement piece. You're wasting a lot of potential here, Nora.'

'I *like* the staircase.' There was nothing she disliked more than houses that looked Victorian on the outside but were modern on the inside, all cornicing and flourishes gone. But if she and Gabe really were the real thing, if they really were going to build a life together, then she would need to compromise. 'I mean, obviously the house needs work. You're right, I can't keep it as a shrine forever.' Although part of her, most of her, really wanted to.

'Do you remember Dominic? We met him at the Serpentine?'

She'd met a lot of people at the Serpentine, all terrifyingly cool and knowledgeable about obscure artists. 'I think so. With the beard?' That was a safe bet. They had all had beards.

Gabe nodded. 'He's an architect. We should get him round.'

Her heart swelled with that casual 'we'. 'That's a good idea. It wouldn't hurt to hear what he thinks.'

'*Bene*. I'll drop him a line.'

Nora led the way to the kitchen and opened the fridge to get Gabe a bottle of the beer he liked and she had immediately bought to have in when he visited. She couldn't deny that part of her was a little disappointed that Gabe didn't appreciate her home the way it was, but then again, why should he? It held no memories for him, he just saw a slightly shabby, old-fashioned house. His taste was so impeccable, of course he would want to put his stamp on it. Making new memories meant making changes, if she was really ready to move on, to make a life with Gabe, then she needed to let go of the past. However hard it was.

Half an hour later, they were on their way to Felix's poetry reading, part of his weekly late-night sessions at his coffee shop. Not only was this the big meet with her friendship group, but also the first time that Dai would have seen Gabe since the night in Hoxton. Nora's nerves were so far on the edge, they were nearly spilling over; she really hoped Dai didn't mention handing her Gabe's card. Gabe himself had not mentioned it, but if Dai said anything, then Nora was planning to pretend she didn't remember receiving it. But she was uneasily aware that there was a fine line between subterfuge and downright deception and she was perilously close to crossing it.

'There's always an eclectic mix of people at these things,' she chattered on to cover her nerves. 'Hampstead literary types, cool poets and people who just really like coffee. Felix puts on a great rolling evening event programme. Poetry of course, open mic nights, even a classical music night – something for all tastes. He's worked so hard since he set this up, we're all so proud of him. Dai will be there of course; he's a teacher, as is Grace, but they teach different ages. Ana is literally just back from Milan, she's there a lot and knows it well, so that's something you have in common.'

*Stop babbling, Nora.* The problem was, Gabe still knew very little about her life and her friends. They had largely skipped the small talk part, the often awkward getting-to-know-each-other part, which meant, as their conversation was firmly about the now and the future, there was still so much to discover.

'How many brothers and sisters do you have?' she asked abruptly. Gabe had mentioned siblings in the plural, so there were clearly several of them, but Nora hadn't been able to get a handle on Gabe's family and his place in it.

'Mmm?' He was squinting at his phone. He turned to her, eyes full of apology, and with a sinking feeling, she anticipated his next words. 'Nora, I am so sorry, but I need to work. A client in the States needs an update tonight.'

'Can't it wait?' she pleaded. 'My friends are beginning to think I invented you.'

'Not if I still want a job tomorrow.'

'Well, why don't you work at mine? Then I can see you when I get back?'

His smile was tender. 'You are very sweet.' He bent his head and kissed her, long and lingering. 'It's tempting, but I need to concentrate. Look, come over tomorrow evening and we can try that new cocktail bar I told you about.'

'I guess.' Nora could hear the disappointment in her voice and tried to pull herself together. 'We can do poetry another time.' She smiled up at him. He was dedicated to his job, in demand, these were good things. And when he let her down, he did always make a real effort the next day.

'You are amazing,' he murmured, pulling her close. 'Far too good for me.'

'If you say so . . .' she teased.

'I do say so. I can't believe how lucky I am. *Ti amore*, Nora. I love you.'

All her disappointment was forgotten as the enormity of his words engulfed her. She knew he loved her, just as she knew she loved him, the intensity of the last few weeks, the feeling of rightness, that fate had played its part and delivered her the soulmate she had yearned for was too strong, but neither had actually said the words yet. Until now.

'You do?' she whispered. 'Oh, Gabe, I love you too,'

'I know I am letting you down. I do want to meet your friends, Nora, just as I want you to meet my family.' His eyes lit up with excitement. 'Let me make it up to you. Prove how much I love you, how serious I am about you, about us. It's my Nonna's eightieth birthday at the end of the month and we are planning a big party for her. Come to Sicily with me. I want my family to know and love you like I do. We could make a proper holiday of it, spend some real time together away from the pressures of work, what do you think?'

'Come with you to Sicily? Oh, Gabe, I would love to.' Here was everything she wanted, she needed. A man who loved her and who she loved, a man who was meant for her, and now she was going to meet his family. Nora Fitzgerald was going to get the happy ever after she had dreamt of after all.

Rome, 20 July 1995

*Ciao bella!*

Guess what! Still in Italy, con amore, but I dragged
myself away from Florence, with many lingering
backwards looks and promises to return. I really feel
like I left part of myself there. But all roads, as they
say, lead to Rome — and here I am at last.

I am so full of culture you wouldn't recognise me. I spent
today just wandering around the Forum and it was like
going back in time, only with more cameras and fewer
togas. You would both love it — we have to come here as a
family, so Dad can tell us all about the battles, and Mum
the stories about which senator stabbed which one in the
back (I know this one, Et tu, Brute!).

George (whose real name is Erik) is here as well, but
he leaves tomorrow. He asked me to come to Naples
with him and I really, really wanted to, but of course
am meeting Julia here. We plan to meet again, maybe
Naples, or Sicily, that's the beauty of the backpacking
trail, we are all heading to the same places. He wants
to be an architect and the way he talked about the
buildings . . . You would like him, I think. I do!

*Tutti amore*

*Lottie xxx*

# *Chapter Five*

'Two weeks in Sicily, you lucky girl,' Grace sighed, looking wistfully at the pile of clothes laid out on Nora's bed waiting for selection. 'Wine, ice cream, beaches, did I mention the wine?'

'There's a perfectly good wine shop around the corner.' Ana folded her arms. 'I still think less than a week's notice for a two-week trip is . . .'

'Spontaneous? Romantic?' Grace suggested.

'Thoughtless. It assumes you have nothing better to do than jump when he clicks his fingers.'

'We weren't going to go for two weeks originally.' Nora picked up a sundress from the pile and held it against her, refusing to let the strained atmosphere between her and Ana dampen her spirits. They hadn't spent any time alone since cocktail night, Nora managing to avoid her during the poetry reading, not wanting any snide comments on Gabe's absence. 'We were planning a long weekend around the party and that's two weeks away, but then Gabe started to talk about all the places he wanted to show me and it was obvious a long weekend wasn't going to be nearly enough. So, a proper holiday it is.' Her stomach fluttered with excitement. This was the opportunity to get to really know Gabe, to see him with his family, away from the pressures of his job and his hectic London lifestyle.

'Doesn't Bruce mind you just taking off like this?' Ana continued.

'Technically, I'm self-employed and I just wrapped up a big estate. Besides, he was the one who pointed out I haven't taken a proper holiday in years. Not that he's one to talk.' Her boss was a workaholic and Nora wasn't sure she'd known him take more than a few days at a time in the near decade she'd worked with him.

'But still.' Grace picked up a straw hat that had belonged to Nora's grandmother. 'Two *weeks* with his parents. That would be a lot if you were married with three bambinos. After not even a month together . . .' She surveyed herself in the mirror. 'I *love* this hat.'

'What do his parents do?' Ana took the hat off Grace and tried it on herself.

'Some kind of café, I think. They're holding the birthday party there. But to be honest, he doesn't talk about them very much.'

Gabe was so open about most of his life. Nora knew all about his ambitions, his life goals, his hobbies and interests, he swept her along in conversation and activities, but he wasn't one for long nostalgic catch-ups. He had the same lack of curiosity when it came to Nora, easily accepting that she lived alone, but never really questioning her about her family and past. On the one hand, it was refreshing, no more poor, tragic Nora, she got to reinvent herself as the kind of fun person who jetted off to Sicily with barely any notice. On the other . . . No. There was no downside. She didn't need to narrate her past to Gabe, just as he didn't need to give her a family tree (although, it would be helpful). They would learn these things in time, as part of their journey together.

'There's at least one brother he's mentioned a couple of times, I think a sister as well, he definitely has siblings plural,' she continued. 'I think the family is quite large.

Lots of uncles and aunts coming to the party anyway.' She tried to repress a shiver, although whether it was one of anticipation or nerves, she wasn't quite sure. Nora's life had been so small these past few years, mainly working from home, hanging out with her safe, trusted circle of friends, a handful of short-lived relationships, that the thought of being introduced to a large group of people who were all related and spoke another language and would no doubt be scrutinising every word and look and gesture was daunting, moving to terrifying depending on her mood. But, then again, only child of an only child, Nora had devoured books about families growing up. She didn't want to be a Potter, she wanted to be a Weasley, not Anne Shirley but one of Anne's children, a March, a Bettany, a Marlow. She devoured stories of crowded tables and hand-me-downs, of sibling jealousies and adventures with longing.

'So, does anything on this bed say suitable girlfriend to you?' she asked. The problem with dressing in an eclectic mix of vintage, second-hand and her mother's and grand-mother's clothes was that she couldn't even picture a capsule wardrobe, let alone put one together. 'It's proper hot there now – mid-June in Sicily is height-of-summer England. We'll probably do sightseeing, sailing, sunbathing, as well as some more formal nights out.'

'You don't need your clothes to say anything,' Ana said unexpectedly. This, for her, was practically heresy. 'They will love you because of you, Nora, not because of the fit of your dress.'

'Who are you and what have you done with Ana?' Nora pretended to faint with shock.

'Look, Nora, there isn't one style you've ever knowingly worn while it was actually *in* style, but that's your look and you make it work. If they don't like it, then that's their loss.'

'From what Gabe's said, his ex was achingly cool. I just don't want to let him down.' Nora stared at the pile of clothes, still unsure.

Ana's blue eyes narrowed as she gave Nora a long appraising look and Nora waited, a little nervously, for her friend to speak. Ana had made her feelings about this trip and Nora's wholesale embrace of her new relationship clear, and she was clearly suspicious of Gabe and his seeming inability to stick to a plan to spend time with her friends. But instead of a lecture or a cutting comment, her eyes softened as she unwound one of Nora's mother's scarfs from around her long neck and laid it back on the overflowing bed. 'You could never let anyone down, but it's my job to tell you that the right clothes maketh the woman, and somewhere on that bed, in that jumble of material, are the right clothes. We just need to find them. Come on, let's start digging for gold.'

An hour and a half later, the three had assembled a wardrobe which, if it wasn't capsule, was perfect for Nora's needs, a mix of casual and smart, complete with a formal party dress for Gabe's grandmother's birthday.

'You could do an entire editorial shoot on your wardrobe – seventy years of fashion.' Ana slipped on a delicate silk shawl and struck a pose.

'Have you kept everything your mother and gran owned?' Grace asked as she helped Nora fold some rejected tops.

'Pretty much. Gran hated to throw good clothes away; her mother was a seamstress, and they didn't have much money growing up. Then Mum liked to wear Gran's old clothes and I like to wear things that belonged to both of them. It makes me feel close to them.' She paused. 'You don't think it makes me look, I don't know, odd?'

'Odd? In what way?'

'Well, you know the way I mix eras. It's a little eccentric, I guess. Gabe is just so put together. I don't want to let him down.'

'Has he said anything?' Ana's expression was fierce. 'Because if he has—'

'No, of course not. It's just . . .' Nora hesitated. It wasn't really anything. Just the way he had admired the effortlessly chic put-together look of a coworker, the suggestions he had made when they went shopping, about beautiful, well-made clothes in taupes and greys that were certainly elegant but a little, well, dull. The way he had checked in with her before a work dinner she had accompanied him to, the laugh in his voice when he suggested she be 'not too Nora on this occasion'. The swift up-and-down and slight frown when she went full-on vintage. She got it, their tastes didn't always align, and she didn't want to let him down in front of his family.

'Look, Nora,' Ana said firmly. 'I work with a lot of people for whom fashion is their whole life and hardly any of them have your natural sense of self. You be you. Don't listen to anyone who tells you otherwise . . . Apart from me and Grace, that is.'

'Thank you. What would I do without you two?' She meant it. Ana might take no prisoners but she, like Grace, was fiercely loyal. Nora knew how lucky she was to have them in her life.

'You'd still be staring at a bed full of clothes and panicking,' Grace said, pulling them both into a group hug. 'You have a wonderful time, Nora, you deserve it.'

Nora hugged them back fiercely, as always feeling like a Lilliputian compared to her friends. She might be an only child, but she had the sisters she'd always wanted in Ana and Grace. They always had her back, and she had theirs.

'Right. We want pics every day,' Ana said briskly, disentangling herself.

'And a caveman score. I refuse to believe you won't seal the deal this holiday,' Grace added as they headed to the front door.

'We're staying with his parents. There might be separate bedrooms,' Nora said, but she was very much hoping that over the next two weeks things did progress physically. She had been a very sensible girl so far, not wanting to rush in like she had in the recent past, to enjoy the moment, to separate what she and Gabe were building from her failed attempts to find love in the past, but she was finding it harder and harder to remember all the reasons why waiting seemed like such a romantic idea.

'He's a native, he'll know where all the secluded beaches are.' Grace's wink was so exaggerated that Nora was still laughing as she waved Grace off.

Ana lingered on the doorstep, her expression serious. 'Have a good time, Nora, but be careful. You've been together such a short time. I don't want you to get hurt.'

Nora's good humour evaporated. She was tired of being treated like a child. 'I know what I'm doing.'

'Going away with someone you barely know?' Ana folded her arms. 'Worrying if your clothes are cool enough? It's not like you. Is it any wonder I'm worried?'

'Look, Ana. If you can't be happy for me, then maybe just don't say anything at all. I'll see you when I get back.' Nora closed the door, but not before seeing the hurt on Ana's face. Her friend meant well, she knew that, she just didn't want anyone to burst this bubble she was in. For once, everything was perfect. And if Ana couldn't see that, then that was her problem.

*

The next morning, Nora was ready long before Gabe had said he would pick her up, waving aside her suggestion she meet him at the airport. One suitcase stood by the door alongside a piece of hand luggage which included a full change of clothes because, as seasoned traveller Ana said, you never knew where your suitcase would end up, and a cross-body bag with money and passport, book, phone charger and phone. She was ready. She just needed Gabe.

Nora sucked in a deep breath. Two weeks with the family of a man she had only just really started seeing. Was she crazy? Nerves fluttered in her stomach and she reached out to the hall table to steady herself. She hadn't been abroad for years, had barely left her corner of London, apart from work. It was all too easy to curl up in her home, in her memories, especially since lockdown.

A confident knock on the door interrupted her as she was on the verge of spiralling and relieved, she almost ran to open it. Gabe would steady her; his confidence always did. She loved his certainty, the way she didn't have to think because he always knew what was right. It was so restful after five years of being so alone, of having to make every decision by herself.

'Hi.' She stood on tiptoes to kiss him, giggling as he swept her up in an exaggerated embrace. 'I missed you.' She also loved this, the lack of games. The lack of playing it cool. He was in – all the way in – and so was she.

'*Cara*,' he murmured as he set her down. 'Are you ready?'

'All packed,' she assured him.

Gabe looked over at the suitcase and raised his eyebrows. 'Don't tell me,' he said. 'It belonged to your mother?'

'My grandmother took it on her honeymoon. It's still in really good condition.'

'It probably weighs so much, it takes up half your weight allowance.' He lifted it and pretended to stagger. 'You know, they even come with wheels nowadays.'

'This one has character and history.' Nora knew Gabe was teasing her, but she couldn't help sounding defensive.

'At least no one will think it's theirs when we get to Catania.'

Travelling with Gabe always meant travelling in style. He thought nothing of flagging down black cabs or hiring town cars and, sure enough, a sleek Mercedes was waiting outside Nora's house for them, a driver taking their cases and opening the car door so they could slide into the luxurious back seat.

The VIP treatment continued once they reached Gatwick Airport, with fast-track check-in and then through security, a swanky airport lounge offering everything from massages to gourmet food, before they were escorted to the aeroplane and their comfortable seats at the front. Left to herself, Nora would never have spent the money on first-class seats for a short-haul flight but Gabe clearly never flew any other way and had insisted on treating her.

'Tell me about your family,' she said, accepting a glass of champagne from the steward with a grateful smile. 'Who will I meet? We're staying with your parents, right?' The nerves fluttered again. The last parents she had met were Jake's, but she had never had to go through a formal meet-and-greet with them, she'd known them all her life. Did Gabe's parents even speak English?

'*Si*, we are staying with my parents, who are going to love you. My Nonna lives with them, as does my youngest sister, Violetta, who is still at school. Nicoletta is married and lives close by and, of course, there is Luca. My brother.'

Nora had been counting. 'There are four of you? Wow. Who's the oldest?'

'Luca, then me. Nicoletta is your age and Violetta is the family baby, she is just sixteen.'

Teenagers to octogenarians and all ages in between. 'Right. Big family.' Just like she had always dreamt of, but now those dreams were turning into reality, it was a little more daunting than she had expected.

'Then there are the cousins.'

'The cousins?' she echoed faintly.

'My father was one of six, my mother four. Some stayed in Sicily, others moved to the mainland, to America, Australia, but, of course, all of my Papà's family will be coming for the party.'

'Of course.' The nerves intensified again, and Nora took a large sip of the champagne before putting it firmly to one side. Tempting as it was to down the contents of the glass, she needed all her wits about her for the hours ahead.

She hoped Gabe would prep her further, but instead, with a murmured apology, he opened his laptop and buried himself in work for the entirety for the flight. Two weeks off clearly meant something very different in banking circles. Nora had left *her* laptop and notebook at home, her only devices her phone and Kindle.

Nora would have been grateful for a less speedy departure from the airport, but the VIP treatment continued and before her ears had really adjusted to the change in language, she and Gabe had collected their bags and were heading through Customs and out to Arrivals.

This was it. Two weeks with Gabe's family. It was a long time, most of her married friends didn't spend that much time with their in-laws!

Nora didn't even know what Gabe's family looked like. Unlike her, he didn't have photographs on display – at least, not photos of other people. There were several of Gabe himself, surfing, climbing, at a fancy party in black tie, but nothing to give her a clue as to which of the smiling groups waiting at the arrivals lounge were the Catalanos.

'Gabe, Gabe, *qui*!' A teenage girl was waving excitedly, flanked by a couple in their late middle age who, as they spotted Gabe, joined in the enthusiastic waving before, as they neared, falling onto Gabe with tears, embraces and loud, fast voluble Italian.

Nora stood back, shy, not wanting to intrude on this family moment.

'Mamma, Papà, Vi, this is Nora,' Gabe said as he disentangled himself. 'Nora, this is my mother and father, Chiara and Antonio, and my youngest sister, Violetta.'

'*Molto piacere di conoscerti, grazie per avermi invitato a casa tua*,' Nora said carefully. She had been practising so hard on Duolingo that she was in the top league, racking up so many points every night that Dai had accused her of using AI to inflate her scores, but she had never spoken Italian to anyone actually Italian before.

'*Tu parli italiano?*' Gabe's mother beamed.

'A little. A very little,' Nora said hastily before she got pulled into a full conversation in the other language. A few prepared sentences were one thing, an actual back-and-forth a whole other ball game.

'Always full of surprise.' Gabe dropped a kiss on the top of her head. 'But honestly, Nora, everyone you'll need to talk to speaks English.'

'I know, I just thought . . .' But Nora didn't get a chance to finish her sentence as Gabe fished his phone out of his pocket with an apologetic look. He had switched it on the second the landing sign had gone off and had spent most of the last twenty minutes replying to emails, despite spending the whole flight working. Nora understood how busy his work was, how crucial – well, she didn't actually understand because she still thought of actual hedges when he said the word hedge fund – but she had hoped he would switch off while he was here.

'Yes? I see. Hmm. Of course. No. Leave it with me.' His expression gave nothing away, his voice was even, but Gabe's fingers were tapping against his thigh, a sign she already recognised as one that showed he was annoyed, or bored. 'No. Not an issue. Send it through . . . When? Fine.'

He clicked the phone off and slid it back into his pocket and Nora tensed. She was becoming an expert on that particular half-apologetic, half *shucks, what can I do* look.

'I am so sorry, but I'm needed at work.'

'Oh no.' Nora tried to hide her frustration; obviously it was worse for Gabe. 'How long will it take?' It wasn't ideal, but hopefully a few hours with the laptop and he would be done.

'I don't know. Several days, I think.'

'Several *days*?'

'And I need to be on site. They need me in New York,' he continued, concentrating on replying to a message on his phone. 'It makes sense for me to get tonight's red-eye from Rome. I'm just waiting to see what flight they book me on from here.'

'*Tonight?* But . . .'

'Oh, Gabe, no!' Chiara exclaimed, her face crumbling.

Gabe's father didn't say anything, but his set expression and folded arms spoke volumes.

'You literally just got here,' Violetta said. 'This has to be a record, even by your standards, Gabe.'

'The boy can't help it, he has a busy job,' his mother defended him.

'We're all busy, Mamma. I'm just saying, when isn't his visit cut short? At least he usually makes it to the house first. And what about Nora?'

The group turned to Nora as if they had forgotten she was there, although they had spoken in English. She wished she wasn't, that she was safely back home.

'I'm sure I can just get a flight back today,' she said, trying not to let her disappointment show. 'Honestly, don't worry about me.'

'Nonsense, there's no need for you to leave. Gabe will be back soon. It's Nonna's birthday after all,' Gabe's mother said, sounding more hopeful than sure.

'Of course, I will, as soon as I can,' Gabe promised, his smile easy as if it was all sorted, almost as if his family's disappointment, Nora's awkward situation, hadn't touched him. 'Two days, three, a week max. Stay, Nora. Enjoy your holiday.'

'But . . .' There were so many buts, she didn't know where to start. But she would be staying with strangers. But they were supposed to be spending time together. But he was going to show her the island he had grown up on. But they were supposed to be making memories together. But they were finally going to have sex and she had packed some new underwear especially.

Before she could pick one of those reasons, Nora found herself pulled into a warm hug. 'Of course, you must stay, Nora. We've been looking forward to meeting you, to spending time with you,' Chiara said. 'You can't come all this way just to leave straightaway.'

'Do stay,' Violetta added her pleas to her mother's. 'Just because Gabe is unreliable . . .'

'I'm not unreliable, just busy,' her brother retorted, as he smiled down at Nora with the look that always made her melt. The intimate, caressing smile that shrank the whole world down to just the two of them. 'You deserve a break. Enjoy it. I'll be back before you get the opportunity to miss me.' His kiss was warm, tender. 'I want my family to know and love you,' he murmured.

'I don't know,' she demurred. 'It's a lot to ask of them. I'm sure they don't want to entertain a stranger for however long.'

'You're not a stranger! You're the girl I am going to marry, it makes sense for you to get to know my family and for them to get to know you. Stay, have fun, relax.'

Nora stared up at him in surprise. *Marry?* They had been heading to that point from the very first lunch, spoke about a future together as if it were set in stone, but neither had mentioned marriage before.

'What was that?' Chiara turned sharply and Gabe laughed, pulling Nora close.

'I told you, Nora's one in a million. Look after her for me.' His phone buzzed and he glanced at it. 'I'm sorry, *cara*, I need to jump in a call and find out my flight details. I'll call you soon.'

Gabe kissed her swiftly, clapped his father on the shoulder, ruffled his sister's hair, hugged his mother, picked up his case and walked away, leaving Nora staring after him, unsure what had just happened, but knowing that her life had just changed forever.

Sicily, 30 July 1995

Buongiorno!

I know, I know, still in Italy! So many countries and cities and adventures (and different foods) await, but it is SO beautiful here, it's hard to tear myself away. Just when I think I couldn't love Italy more, I discover something new to fall for.

I might have been wrong when I said Pompeii was the most evocative place I have ever been to – obviously in terms of tragedy and history, it was unbeatable, but Sicily has it all: ruins galore, stunning scenery and, oh, the food! Let's move here immediately and run a little guesthouse. I can be the cockney signorina.

Love and even more love,

Lottie xxx

# Chapter Six

There was a slightly stunned silence which carried on for far longer than Nora was comfortable with before Gabe's mother evidently collected herself and stepped forward to embrace Nora. 'Oh! You're getting married! Welcome to the family.'

'Not exactly, we haven't . . . I mean, we're not actually . . .' Nora was still shocked. What had just happened? How had she found herself not just holidaying without her boyfriend but with Gabe's family assuming she was engaged to their son? She'd told Ana she could look after herself. Clearly, she had been wrong. How did she extricate herself from this embarrassing farce?

'This is so exciting.' Violetta's hug was far more natural, her face lit with delight. 'I can't wait to tell everyone!'

Nora tried again: 'Like I said, we're not actually engaged . . .'

Chiara shook her head. 'You know, in my day we just got engaged, there was none of this engaged to be engaged and waiting for the perfect proposal, was there, Antonio? It was much simpler, but then we didn't record every moment on our phones either.'

'It's not that, it's just . . .' But she couldn't find the right words, and while she was still searching for them, Gabe's father picked up her case.

'*Bene, vamos.*' His tone might be reassuringly matter-of-fact, but his face gave away his true feelings, creased into lines of surprise and some disappointment. Nora didn't take it personally; she knew a strange Englishwoman was a poor substitute for his absent son.

'*Si*, come along, Nora, is this all you brought? The car is just along here.'

Nora was swept along by Gabe's family and in just a few moments was ensconced in a large car, Chiara insisting she took the front seat, Nora insisting just as firmly she would be more than comfortable in the back with Violetta.

'So, how long have you and Gabe been seeing each other?' The car hadn't pulled out of the car park before Chiara began her interrogation. 'Gabe is so private. I thought he was still seeing that artist until he said you would be coming here with him. Not that we are not very glad to have you here, Nora, or not delighted that you and Gabe are engaged, it's all such a surprise. Lily was very talented, of course, a nice girl . . .' Antonio snorted and Chiara nudged him firmly as she continued. 'But it wasn't easy for her, being teetotal and vegan. Which is why she had such lovely skin, I suppose.'

Nora suppressed an urge to check her own complexion.

'Are you vegan?' Was that a note of anxiety in Chiara's voice?

'No. I'm not teetotal either.' Even if she had been, she might have lapsed. Spending two weeks with her new boyfriend's family was one thing, doing it alone while trying to figure out what Gabe had meant by *going to marry* was definitely going to require something tart and chilled to take the edge off.

Antonio muttered something to his wife and Nora wasn't sure whether to be glad or not that she hadn't progressed to the muttered comment stage on Duolingo – relieved, she decided. Better to not know what they were saying.

'What do you do, Nora?' Violetta asked. She was watching Nora so intently, it was unnerving, her expression speculative and inquisitive. Weren't teens supposed to be surgically attached to their phones?

'Oh, I work in probate.' It was instantly clear that fluent as all three Catalanos' English was, *probate* was beyond them. 'Um, I help track down the family of people who died without a will, so they can inherit.'

Silence.

'It can be really rewarding. I give people a piece of their history that sometimes they didn't know they had lost. Or closure. Sometimes they meet other relatives and form friendships. That's always nice. It's not just about the money.'

'Family is the most important thing of all,' Chiara said and Nora nodded.

'I agree,' she said, so softly she wasn't sure that they heard.

Nora looked around with interest as they headed away from Catania airport, along a dusty motorway, the sun high and bright in the sky. The built-up areas of the city outskirts in the distance were overshadowed by the volcano clearly visible in a way she hadn't expected, the trees lining the motorway mostly palms, a reminder of how close to the southern edge of Europe she was, nothing felt familiar. Yet her mother had travelled through here, all those years before. It was comforting to know she was following in her footsteps, although, with a jolt, she realised she had no idea where they were actually going. Gabe had said so little about his home, his family, beyond mentioning a café – or was it a restaurant? She was heading completely into the unknown. For a moment, fear superseded the nerves.

'Do you live far from Catania?' she asked as the road pulled away from the dusty flat and began to climb through shaded woods.

'Nearer to Taormina, about thirty minutes from here. The vineyard is in the national park, the volcanic soil is the best for the grapes,' Chiara said.

'Vineyard? You make wine, that's so cool.' She didn't hide her surprise and saw Antonio's shoulders stiffen as Violetta rolled her eyes.

'Gabe didn't mention the family vineyard?'

'Well, no.' Had he? Had she forgotten? Of course she hadn't! How could anyone forget a *vineyard*? She tried to defuse the sudden tension in the air. 'But we've been together such a short time really. There's a lot we have still to discover about each other.' She was beginning to wonder what else he hadn't told her.

Antonio muttered something else and Nora didn't need Google Translate to get the gist. He was clearly hurt, and she didn't blame him. She felt uncomfortable about more than having just been abandoned with these strangers. It was that sense of being lied to by omission. Gabe adored Sicily, she knew that, she thought he adored his family – he had been quite clear that there was no way he could miss his Nonna's birthday – but he spoke about them so little. He was so of the present, so out of sight, out of mind. Did that absorption stretch to her as well? Was he wondering about how she was getting on or was he so focused on New York, she had slipped his mind completely?

What's more, he'd always given the impression that he was self-made, that he had climbed his way up from nothing, with casual mentions of what sounded like a humble family café and home. But there was nothing humble about the car they were in, about his family's clothes. His mother's earrings looked like they cost more than everything Nora owned.

The next half-hour passed in relative silence, Nora aware that her ignorance and Gabe's absence were responsible for the tension in the car, but she had no idea what she could say to try to break it, so, she too said nothing, instead looking out of the window with interest, drinking in the landscape which had broadened out again to show the plains and mountains, vineyards and farms and occasional enticing glimpses of the sea.

'Here we are, Villa Catalano,' Chiara said as the car turned through wrought-iron gates onto a long driveway.

Nora took in her surroundings eagerly, her anxiety ebbing somewhat. On either side, vines spread out as far as the eye could see, framed by mountains and hills and . . .

'Is that Mount Etna?' The volcano had been in view for much of the car ride, but somehow she hadn't expected it to be quite so visible from Gabe's actual home.

'Yes, of course. As I said, the volcanic soil is perfect for grapes,' Chiara said, as proudly as if she had shaped the volcano herself.

'Wow, I can't believe how close it looks,' Nora said, more than a little nervously. Was that *smoke* rising from the top? She wished she'd paid more attention in Geography.

'Don't worry, we're far enough away. We get plenty of notice if we have to evacuate.' Chiara clearly meant to be reassuring, but Nora would have preferred no mention of evacuation at all.

It was all beautifully tended and prosperous, the main road better maintained than Nora's own street, without a pothole to be seen.

Antonio headed right as the drive forked, an attractive cluster of stone buildings to their left.

'That's the restaurant,' Violetta said, following her gaze. 'The guest accommodation is a short walk away in the old winery. And just beyond that is the visitor centre and the factory – there, behind those olive groves. That's where the work actually happens. I'd love to show you around if you're interested.'

'Oh, I am very interested. I would love that,' Nora said, but the feeling of discombobulation only increased. *Visitor centre? Guest accommodation? Restaurant?*

They drove on for a few more minutes until they reached a second pair of gates, these guarding the entrance to a graceful stone-built villa. It was impressive, the original house flanked with a wing either side and yet welcoming, with huge flower-filled pots and trees in the front courtyard. The windows were shuttered, giving the villa a fairy-tale feel.

Antonio followed the drive round to the back of the house, pulling up outside a stone-built garage. Beyond, Nora could see a terraced garden leading to a small orchard and, behind the other wing, a pool house and a glimpse of an inviting swimming pool.

'This is gorgeous.' She didn't have to dissemble. If Nora had been asked to draw the perfect Italian villa, she might have come up with something very similar – although without the volcano in the background. Despite Chiara's reassurances, Mount Etna still felt a little close for comfort. London definitely had its dangers, but fire-breathing mountains weren't one of them.

Chiara beamed. 'I am glad you like it. I hope you will be very comfortable.'

'I am sure I will.' But Nora wasn't sure at all. Nothing about this situation was *comfortable*. Maybe, just maybe, she had been just a little too accommodating with Gabe, which was why he thought she would be fine with his abrupt disappearance. She could hear Ana's caustic tones: maybe he just hadn't thought about her at all. She pushed the thought away. He'd invited her to meet his family, hadn't he? That was the most meaningful gesture of all.

73

Stretching out her stiffened legs, Nora climbed down from the car. The afternoon sun was still hot – a shock after the air-conditioned car – and she stood still for a moment, letting the heat soak onto her vitamin D-deprived city skin, inhaling the heady scent of lemons, oranges and greenery tinged with salt – a sure sign that the sea was not too far away.

'Come, come . . .' Antonio had picked up her bags and Violetta looped her hand through Nora's arm, pulling her along. 'Let's introduce you to everyone – everyone who is here anyway. They're all looking forward to meeting you.'

Nora wasn't sure how true this was, considering that no one had actually known of her existence until last week, but she was grateful for the younger girl's enthusiasm.

Both of the wings were at an angle, creating a three-sided courtyard at the back of the villa, a stone-floored space clearly used a great deal. Vines hung from wooden beams overhead, with lights threaded across and along each beam, and a wooden table large enough to seat at least twenty dominated the centre space. A couple of small bistro tables, for more intimate gatherings, were tucked into nooks created by potted plants, with some outdoor sofas situated near the lawn, positioned to get the most out of the incredible views.

'Oh how pretty!'

'*Grazie*,' Chiara said. 'It's nothing special, but we like it.' Her proud expression belied her words – she clearly knew just how special it was.

A woman of around Nora's age was seated at the large, wooden table, a baby in a pram on one side and a small toddler kneeling up on the seat next to her. 'Nicoletta, this is Nora.'

Nicoletta was instantly on her feet with exclamations of welcome, kissing Nora on the cheeks, introducing herself and the children, and it was a couple of minutes before she looked around in some surprise and said, 'But where is Gabe? Did you leave him at the airport?'

There was a moment's silence and her eyes flashed.

'He's not here?'

'There was a call. He had to go to New York unexpectedly,' Nora explained, aware of the same tense undercurrent that had been present in the car.

'Of course he did.'

'Now, Nicoletta.' Chiara broke into Italian and the two had the kind of low-voiced, intense conversation that was uncomfortable to listen to even when you didn't understand the language.

The atmosphere was broken as a woman came down the steps to cries of '*Nonna*'.

Nora hadn't realised how much she had built up a clichéd picture of Gabe's grandmother in her head as a little, maybe slightly stooped white-haired old lady dressed in black drapery and lace. Instead, she was confronted by a tall, slender woman, with expertly dyed hair caught up in an elegant chignon, dressed in what Nora's knowledgeable eye instantly recognised as vintage Chanel.

'*Donde esta Gabriel?*' Her voice was clear and commanding.

'Gabe has been delayed, Nonna,' Violetta said in English, pulling Nora forward. 'He'll be here soon. But Nora is here, Gabe's fiancée.'

'*Gabe's fidanzata?*' There was no mistaking her surprise and Nora cringed. She really needed to make it clear she was girlfriend status only.

'Well, if this isn't just like him,' Nicoletta said.

'No, it's not . . .' Nora tried again, but before she got any further, Nicoletta was kissing her on the cheeks.

'I mean, this is wonderful! Congratulations, Nora.'

She had to hand it to the Catalanos. They were doing their best to make her feel welcome, even if surely – *surely* – they weren't really pleased that their son and brother was apparently marrying a stranger he had literally dumped on them before running away?

But how lovely if Gabe *had* meant it, if a proposal was in the offing one day soon, if that meant she might be a part of this family. Who knew, one day this misunderstanding might be part of the family folklore, an anecdote to be laughed about over wine. A *remember when*, one of many.

One of the things Nora missed most about her family was those retellings of family history, so clear that she could picture scenes she hadn't even been alive for. The day her grandfather finally got the courage to ask her grandmother out after three failed attempts. The time they took her mother camping and it rained all week. The day her mother kidnapped a cat because she was so desperate for a pet. Anecdotes that meant nothing to anyone else, but were part of the Fitzgerald DNA. She wanted to be part of those *remember whens* again. To belong. Gabe was so lucky to have all these people waiting for him. If they were her family, she would never leave.

'How did you and Gabe meet?' Nicoletta asked, moving the toddler to the other side of her lap as she did so. Nora watched for a moment, the way her arm was curled around the small solid body, the way the child leant in, his cheek pressed close to his mother's shoulder, and a sudden almost overwhelming sense of loss swept over her, so all-encompassing, she almost gasped. Part grief for her mother, whom she missed every single day, and partly a yearning she had never even acknowledged before, not so much for a child of her own – although she did want to be a mother one day – but for that sense of family.

As she watched, the little boy shifted, turning and smiling at Nora. She smiled back, her heart aching.

With a jolt, she realised the family were all gazing at her expectantly. Of course, Nicoletta had asked her a question. How she and Gabe had met . . .

She had told a few people about their meet-cute, of course – her friends, Gabe's friends and acquaintances, a couple of her colleagues – and the more she retold it, the less her own part in engineering the meet seemed to matter. After all, Gabe might not have recognised her at the coffee shop, they might not have hit it off. But she couldn't help but feel uncomfortable with so many of Gabe's nearest and dearest waiting for her to speak.

'He said it was fate,' Chiara said softly and, as one, the women sighed. Even Antonio looked slightly less gruff.

Nora felt her cheeks flush. 'Well, it kind of feels like that.' And that was true, wasn't it? Hadn't she recognised something in him the moment she'd heard his voice? All she had done was exercise a little agency, that was no crime. 'The moment I saw him, I just knew.'

'Sounds romantic,' Nicoletta said and Nora couldn't help but return her smile.

'It really was. I got my heel caught on the road. It was dark and there was a motorbike coming towards me. I wasn't sure they had even seen me and they were riding very close to the pavement.' She didn't have to fake the tremor in her voice. 'I heard a shout. Next thing I know, someone had hold of me and was pulling me out of the way, so hard my heel came free.'

'Gabe?' Violetta breathed.

'Obviously I didn't know who he was at the time. I heard his voice, looked into his eyes and then I . . . well, I am ashamed to say, I fainted. By the time I came round, my friends were with me and my mystery rescuer had disappeared.'

'Then what happened?' Chiara asked.

This was the bit it was harder to relate naturally, her own guilty conscience making every word sound rehearsed. 'Well, a few weeks later, I was in the city and stopped in at a little coffee shop. Gabe was there and recognised me. He asked me to lunch and . . .' She smiled. 'That was that.' None of that was an actual lie. 'The feeling I had when I first saw him was still there, only stronger the more I got to know him. I guess you could say it was love at first sight.'

'How romantic! Gabe was right, it was fate.' Violetta's eyes glowed.

'Like something out of a film,' Nicoletta added.

'You and Gabe are clearly meant to be.' Chiara kissed her on both cheeks. 'Welcome to the family, Nora. We are very happy to meet you. I hope from now on you will consider Villa Catalano your home and we your family. Now, let me show you your room. You must be desperate to freshen up. Violetta, bring her suitcase.'

'Thank you.' As Nora followed Chiara and Violetta, the words rang in her ears. *Consider us your family.*

Her once dull and uncomplicated life was feeling more complicated by the moment and yet she couldn't help but feel that she was exactly where she was meant to be.

*Barcelona, 10 August 1995*

*Mummy, Daddy*

*Barcelona is gorgeous and the Sagrada Familia everything I hoped it would be. The whole Gaudi vibe is just totally surreal, like being on Mars or something.*

*And tapas! Why don't we have tapas in England? So very civilised.*

*But Barcelona will be my last stop. There's been a slight change in plan and I am coming home early. Nothing to worry about, I just miss you and have had my fill of crowded trains and hostels. Will call when I get to Dover.*

*Cannot wait to see you both.*

*Lottie xxx*

# *Chapter Seven*

Chiara led Nora into a huge kitchen – a light, square room dominated by an enormous stove, a vast table covered with chopping boards, bowls, spoons and vegetables, and sauce pans hanging from a rack in the ceiling. It smelt delicious, like tomato and basil and lemon, and Nora's tummy rumbled in response.

'I was going to put you in Gabriel's room,' Chiara said. 'But as we don't know when he will be arriving . . .'

Nora fought back the urge to apologise. This was Gabe's own family, and it wasn't as if she had known he was literally going to fly straight back out.

'I am very sorry, Nora.' It was as if Chiara had read her mind. 'I hope you are not feeling too uncomfortable. We really are very happy to have you here and to get to know you. It's just all been rather a shock.'

'Typical Gabe,' Violetta muttered.

'His work is just so demanding,' Nora said, feeling the need to defend him.

'Family is the most important thing of all,' Chiara said firmly. 'And if he is going to be a good husband, he will need to remember that.'

Nora winced at the word *husband*. She really needed to find a way to set them straight without making a big deal of it.

'Now. Gabe's room has been barely touched since he was a teenager. We will redecorate for you, but until then, one of the nicer spare rooms, I think . . .'

'How about the little barn, Mamma?' Violetta suggested. 'We had that cancellation, remember? And nobody else booked in until the end of the month. That way, Nora can have her own space until Gabe gets back?'

'Excellent idea. *Bene.* You must be feeling a little overwhelmed, *si*? The little barn will be perfect. Let me just collect a few things. Now come.'

Chatting all the time, Chiara led the way out of the kitchen into an equally big hallway. It was more of a room than a passage, with a sideboard on one side and a long sofa on the other, a red rug laid over the ceramic tiles. A staircase ran up either side, a galleried landing joining the two. Doors led off and through them Nora glimpsed a grandlooking sitting room and a formal dining room, with wide dark passages leading from the main house into the wings. Chiara continued through the double front door and down the stone steps into the courtyard at the front of the house.

It was an inviting space, shaded by trees in pots and a simple yet elegant fountain at the front. To one side was the drive that led around to the car park, on the other a pretty lemon and orange grove. Parked close to the house was a golf cart and, with a surprising amount of strength for such a slender girl, Violetta heaved Nora's case onto it.

'I love your suitcase,' she said as she did so. 'Is it vintage?'

'Yes, it belonged to my grandmother.'

'Then it is very special,' Chiara said as she clambered into the driver's seat. 'Come, sit next to me, Nora. Violetta, you can go into the back. The little barn is only a ten-minute walk away, Nora. You won't mind being away from the house?'

'No, not at all. So, you rent out cottages as well as make wine?'

'Why yes. Didn't Gabe tell you *anything* about us?' Violetta leant over from the back seat.

'Not really. I think he wanted me to discover for myself.' Nora was trying to be diplomatic, but Chiara's lips compressed and Violetta's snort made it clear what she thought of that theory.

'Antonio's family has made wine here for generations,' Chiara said proudly. 'Father to son, there has always been a Catalano here. He hoped that Gabe and Luca . . .' She stopped.

'Luckily, he has two daughters who are keen to carry on the family business.' Violetta's tone indicated that they had had this conversation many times before.

'Here we are.' Chiara was obviously relieved to change the subject as she drew up before a charming small stone building. 'The rest of the guest accommodation is on the other side of the vineyard, nearer the restaurant and guest facilities, but, of course, you will be at the house most of the time and use the pool any time you wish. You're not a guest, Nora, you are family now.'

The casually spoken words stopped Nora in her tracks. Family. The one thing she wanted and didn't have. She'd spent less than an hour with the Sicilians, but she was already warming to them, getting some kind of measure of them. Antonio came across as a little gruff and silent, but she suspected that was driven by disappointment that Gabe had so clearly rejected the bequest he wanted to hand on as it had been handed on to himself. Chiara clearly adored her children. Violetta was young but not shy or gauche, probably more self-possessed than Nora herself.

She didn't have a handle on Nicoletta yet, nor the disconcertingly glamorous Nonna, who clearly prescribed to the Joan Collins school of not aging, but she was filled with curiosity to get to know them. She wanted to get closer.

To *be* closer. To *belong*. Luckily, the language barrier was much less of an issue than she had feared.

'Your English really is excellent. All of you,' she said to Violetta as Chiara jumped out of the cart, key in hand. 'Which is a good thing, because my Italian is still at the *Donde est la cafe* stage. I'm trying, but I started too late, I think.'

'I'll practise with you.' Violetta brightened. 'We were all raised to speak English and French too. The vineyard deals with buyers from across the world, and what with the restaurant and the holiday villas, Mamma and Papà wanted to make sure we could all communicate properly. We had an English au pair for many years.'

'Your parents were very wise.' Nora clambered off the cart and tried, unsuccessfully, to get her suitcase before Violetta did.

'Come on in, Nora.' Chiara had opened the front door and Nora stepped inside, gasping with delight as she took in the light-filled space.

'What a gorgeous place!'

The cottage was just one big room, but the back wall had been replaced with glass to stop it feeling dark and claustrophobic – and to take advantage of the incredible views across the vineyard to the hills behind. A kitchen area was tucked against one wall, a table perfect for two placed in the corner, while two comfortable sofas formed a cosy L, positioned perfectly to enjoy the views.

'OK.' Chiara turned around from where she had been busying herself in the kitchen. 'The fridge has milk and cheese, the bread is stored here.' She indicated a cupboard. 'There is also some lemon cake made with our own lemons. Lemonade is in the fridge, as is white wine. Red wine is here. The bathroom is on this floor.' Chiara nodded at a door. 'And the bedroom is up there.' *There* was a staircase leading to a mezzanine and, looking up, Nora could see glimpses of a bed. The whole was simply but stylishly decorated – colourful cushions on the sofas, landscapes on the wall. It was a little rustic, but the kind of rustic designed for people who didn't like mud.

'This is really too kind. Are you sure it's OK for me to stay here?'

'If you are happy to. There is room at the house, but I thought you might appreciate your own space.'

'Oh I do, but don't turn down bookings on my account.'

Chiara showed Nora the well-appointed bathroom, with a tub big enough for two and complicated-looking shower, and took her outside to show her a pretty little patio complete with table and chairs and a swing seat, as well as, intriguingly, an outdoor bath. This really was a honeymooner's paradise. If only Gabe was here.

Nora's stomach twisted. This was supposed to be their time. Real quality time away from the demands of his work, his busy social life, his friends. Time to really connect. Instead, she was enjoying all this alone.

'Why don't we leave you to freshen up? You can find your way back?' Chiara interrupted her thoughts and Nora pulled herself together. This was less than ideal in many ways, but she definitely couldn't complain about her surroundings or the hospitality.

'Easily.' The villa was visible from the front door, the path clearly laid out.

'Great, we'll be eating in an hour. *Venti*, Violetta. Ciao, Nora.'

'Ciao.' That was one word she *did* know. 'And thank you again.'

'There's no need to thank me. I meant it. You are one of the family now.'

Once left alone, Nora quickly unpacked, shaking out her clothes and hanging them in the built-in wardrobe. The bed looked comfortable, made up with crisp sheets and cosy blankets, but she resisted the urge to lie down. Instead she poured herself a glass of the lemonade Chiara had supplied and curled up on the sofa with her phone.

There was no message from Gabe.

Nora stared unseeingly out at the view. She knew why. He would have headed straight back through to the departure lounge and immediately started working until it was time to board, where he would work some more. It wasn't that he was thoughtless exactly, he just had no concept of multitasking. She understood and she wouldn't nag him, get upset unnecessarily. From what he had said, his previous girlfriend had needed constant check-ins, constant reassurance. It had suffocated him. But right now Nora could do with a little reassurance herself. After all, leaving her alone in a strange country wasn't the same as blowing off a poetry reading or taking a work call while Nora was his plus-one at a terrifyingly formal dinner party where she knew no one and he'd left her alone on a table of corporate bankers for an hour.

She thought long and hard, aiming for the right tone before typing:

*Your family are lovely, but they are missing you. I'm a poor substitute! Your mum has given me the nicest cottage, but it's a bit lonely for one. Hurry back.*

She reread it and then, with a disgusted snort, deleted the lot. The neediness rang through every word.

OK. Try again.

*Ciao Caro! Your family are lovely, as is the gorgeous cottage they gave me. I am being well looked after but miss you! Hurry back, we have a lot of sightseeing to do.*

That was better. Right. Now the important bit.

*Funny thing. Your family overheard what you said at the airport, you know, the going to marry part, and they think we are engaged, or at least engaged to be engaged. I haven't I wasn't sure We need to find a way to put them right before Nonna's party obviously. Sooner. They are adorable. And so are you. Miss you. xxx*

Nora reread the message several times, gnawing on her bottom lip before finally pressing send. Hopefully Gabe would message his mother and tell her the truth and the whole engagement talk would die a tactful death. For now at least, until they really were properly engaged.

Right. What next? A shower and then she should head back to the villa.

Nora sat for a moment, trying to muster up the courage and energy when her phone pinged. She snatched it up eagerly, only for her heart to plummet when she saw it wasn't Gabe with a solution but her friends' group chat, called The Heathcliffs, after their home and Felix's pre-Dai obsession with surly, unavailable men.

*Grace: How's meeting the fam going?*

*Nora: OK, I think. I met his parents and sisters.*

*Grace: More importantly, any hot brothers?*

Nora: One brother, but I have yet to meet so can't comment on volcanic scale . . . BUT I can see Etna from my window.

Ana: OMG.

Nora: They own a vineyard!

Felix: Bring us back a bottle or two.

Grace: So, has Mamma Catalano put you in separate rooms? Remember when I went to stay with Tom's mum and she gave me the room beside hers with the squeaky floorboard outside my room? Every time I went for a wee, she appeared at her bedroom door to check I wasn't off to defile her precious baby boy.

Felix: From what I remember, Tom didn't need any defiling.

Nora: Actually, we would be sharing a room, but Gabe has been called away unexpectedly.

Grace: WTF

Felix: Sorry, babe, that it is

87

so disappointing. When are
you coming home?

                              Nora: I'm not. I'm staying,
                              I've been looking forward
                              to my holiday and he'll get
                              here as soon as he can.

Felix: But isn't it like super
awkward?

                              Nora: A little. They are
                              really nice though and
                              really welcoming. What is
                              awkward though is that his
                              family seem to think we're
                              engaged.

Ana: OMG

Felix: Ana, is your phone
stuck on those three letters?

Ana: Sorry, on a work call.
Easier to use autofill.

Grace: I agree OMG. What
did you say?

                              Nora: Um. Nothing yet

Felix: Nora!

Grace: Nora!

Felix: You idiot! You should
have sorted it out straight
away.

*Nora: I know! He just said
something at the airport that
made it sound like it was all
sorted and every time I try
to say it's not true, no one
seems to hear me.*

But Nora knew her argument sounded weak. *Was* weak.
None of her friends would have had any problem with
managing to make it clear they weren't engaged, without
making it sound like a big deal. It was just . . . she really
liked how accepting the Catalanos were. Would they be as
warm if they didn't think she was going to be a permanent
fixture in their lives? She just wanted to keep that feeling
for a little longer.

*Grace: Just don't accept any
heirloom engagement rings.
Or try on wedding dresses.
There's something about
putting on a white dress
that finalises things. Don't
you think it's odd when
MIL try to hand over their
old dress? Like they want to
marry their sons?*

*Felix: EW. Grace!*

*Nora: I promise. No rings,
no dresses, and I'll try to
find a way to tell them the
truth without looking like a
prize fool.*

*Felix: It might be a little
late for that.*

> *Nora: Thanks for the
> reassurance. I'd better
> go. There are at least 8
> Catalanos waiting for me
> aged between 1 and 80.*

*Grace: Have fun.*

*Felix: Ciao Bella!*

*Grace: BE CAREFUL.
NO HEIRLOOMS.*

Nora put down her phone with a sigh. Her friends were right. She *was* a prize idiot. All she had to do was say 'Oh, we're not engaged' and it would all be sorted. But she was where she was and all she could do was try to make the best of it.

It was obvious that work call or not, Ana had contributed little to the chat. Nora knew that she owed her an apology for being so curt earlier, but she had no idea how to broach it, especially now Gabe had complicated things by jetting off. Ana was probably feeling completely vindicated in her suspicions.

Checking her phone in hope of a message from Gabe, Nora realised she still had time before she needed to return to the villa for dinner. She needed a shower. Or how about that rather spectacular outside bath on the terrace?

The cottage she was in was clearly designed for honeymooners, from the super king-sized bed to the shower big enough for two. But the crowning glory was the large decadent-looking bathtub out on the terrace. It was screened in with frosted glass so the occupant could look out at the spectacular view but enjoy complete privacy. Nora had also spotted some gorgeous oils in the bathroom. How relaxing would it be to take a nice long soak? Relaxation was something she could definitely do with right now.

Fifteen minutes later, Nora was enjoying the warm, fragrant water, lying back in the comfortable tub and looking up at the clear blue sky. Birds sang overhead, she could hear the faint sound of machinery in the distance, but otherwise it was as if she were completely alone.

She closed her eyes, sinking down as far as she could without wetting her hair, tied in an inelegant messy knot on the top of her head. She could get used to this. Maybe she and Gabe should move here, to this cottage. He could work on the family farm and she could learn to make pasta and . . . But somehow she couldn't visualise Gabe here. He was all about the city, in his handmade suits and his air of busyness. The outdoors for him was a thing to be conquered, with ropes and boats and high-tech gear.

But Nora could imagine herself here . . .

She kept her eyes closed, the sun warm on her face, her body enveloped in water, the world so far away. The birds, the machinery, the footsteps—

Wait? The *what*? There was someone nearby? And she was completely naked.

Nora sank deep down in the tub, holding her breath hoping that whoever was there would just go away. Instead, the footsteps got louder, firmer and were quite clearly heading in her direction.

Her *naked* direction.

She sank down even further, as if she could hide under the water. If you were going to give guests outdoor bathtubs, then people should bear that in mind when walking around the gardens, she thought, eying her towel, loosely draped over a chair a good few steps away.

The footsteps stopped. Nora held her breath. She had no idea why she felt so sure she didn't want the owner of the footsteps to discover her. It was most likely Chiara or one of her daughters checking in. This could, *should*, be the kind of anecdote they would laugh about, the kind of family history she had missed being part of, but somehow, she knew those footsteps weren't Chiara's. They were too firm. Too masculine.

Nora stayed completely still, and then, as soon as the footsteps began to recede, climbed out of the tub as quickly and quietly as she could, wincing as water sloshed over the side, grabbing her towel and wrapping it firmly around her wet body.

Slicking her now damp and tangled hair back, Nora sidled to the corner of the cottage and peered around the edge of the wall. Nobody there. She waited a second, heart hammering, before making a run for it, scuttling on her toes to the next corner, just a few feet from her front door and safety.

Another careful long look, pressed flat against the wall as if she were in Her Majesty's secret service, armed only with a towel, and then round again to the front of the house. She could hear something but wasn't sure if it was the hammering of her heart or the unwelcome return of the footsteps . . .

Phew, safety at last. She reached for the handle and pushed the door.

*What the—?*

Nora pushed again, the towel slipping as she used her shoulder to add some heft. But the front door was stubbornly and indisputably stuck. One hand clutched at the towel, the other pushed and pulled desperately at the door handle, but nothing gave.

'Come on,' she muttered desperately. Was there a knack she was missing?

'You did remember to put it on the latch?'

Nora didn't mean to scream, but somehow a high-pitched noise escaped her as she whirled round, both hands now clutching the towel to her, only to see . . .

'Gabe?'

Her relief was short-lived. The man looked familiar, really familiar, but that was probably because he really did look like Gabe. In fact, the resemblance was uncanny, although there were subtle differences. His cheekbones were sharper, his mouth quirked sardonically, not like Gabe's easy-going charm, his hair falling over his forehead in a way Gabe's ruthlessly styled hair would never dare to do. Nor would Gabe be seen in faded jeans and a short-sleeved crumpled white shirt – although maybe he should if the jeans fit him as well as these fit . . .

'Sorry to disappoint you. I'm Luca.'

'Yes of course. I would offer to shake your hand but . . .' Nora shrugged and instantly regretted it as the towel slid down another centimetre or so and she yanked it up, aware of the amusement in Luca's sharp gaze. Amusement and appraisal. 'I'm Nora.'

'Yes.'

'I don't suppose you know how I can get back in without climbing through a window?'

Unsmiling, Luca held up a key.

What was it with this guy? The rest of the family had been so welcoming, but Luca was treating her as if . . .

As if he knew she was a fraud.

But that was just her unease talking.

93

'Great! if you could just open the door, I would be very grateful.'

Luca didn't answer but strolled past her, so close they almost, *almost*, touched and within seconds the door had swung open.

'Thank you! I really appreciate it. Oh. You're coming in?' It was the most rhetorical of questions as Luca had strolled in in front of her and was standing in the middle of the sitting room. 'Make yourself at home. Stupid, I suppose this is your home. Anyway, I'll just . . .' She seemed to have lost the ability to speak in complete sentences.

Nora took a deep breath. She was fine, this was all under control. If control meant watching all dignity slip away from her, that was.

She gripped the towel so it tightened around her and straightened to her full five foot two and one quarter. 'Anyway, it really is lovely to meet you, Luca, but I promised your mother I would come back to the villa for dinner and I really can't turn up dressed in a towel.'

'Go ahead and get dressed. I'll wait.' He leant against the kitchen worktop as if he had all the time in the world.

'There's really no need.'

'I insist.'

Game and set Luca.

But the match was still to be won and Nora was finding out more about her opponent with every word.

'OK, then. Do make yourself comfortable. There's wine in the fridge.'

Nora managed to prevent herself from stomping up the stairs, not wanting Luca to know how much he had managed to discombobulate her in just a very few yet very long minutes, stifling a yelp when she looked into the mirror. Her usually silky hair was wet and tangled, sticking up at odd angles, her cheeks were flushed, her eyes glittering. She looked like some kind of dryad driven mad by too many bacchanal frenzies.

'It's nice to meet you at last, Luca,' she called down through the mezzanine railings, determined to make nice. 'Gabe has told me a lot about you.'

OK, that wasn't entirely true, but it felt politic to say it. Silence.

'Interesting. He has told me nothing about you,' Luca said finally. 'In fact, when I last visited him, he told me he wanted to get back with Lily.' He paused, clearly for effect. It worked. 'He was talking about proposing to her. And that was just a few weeks ago. And now I hear *you* are engaged to be married.'

Was that true? Gabe had made it sound as if and he and Lily were well and truly over. 'It's been a whirlwind.'

'More than that, quite the touching saga, I believe. Love at first sight, Violetta tells me.'

This would all be a lot easier if, like his sisters, Luca didn't speak English quite so fluently. Only rather than learning his from an au pair, he had clearly been tutored by a barrister in how to cross-examine a guilty client.

'I wouldn't say saga, more like a fairy tale.' Nora deliberately kept her tone both bland and upbeat.

'A fairy tale? Yes, it does seem rather . . .' Another pause . . . 'Unbelievable. You and Gabe just ran into each other, and you recognised him from a couple of weeks before? Quite the coincidence.'

Oh no, no, no. Nora was not proud of her little deception, the manipulation she had used to put herself in the right place at the right time, but it was done. And it had worked! She hadn't forced Gabe to stop and talk to her, to ask her out, to fall for her as hard as she had fallen for him, to propose. Those things were real and they were what mattered and it was wonderful.

Her chin jutted out as she injected some steel into her voice. 'That's London for you. Sometimes you are exactly where you need to be at exactly the right time.'

Nora dragged the brush through her hair, welcoming the pain as it got caught in the knots. *Besides, what was I supposed to do?* she asked Luca silently. *Allow Gabe and that connection to just slip away?*

But of course he didn't answer. He didn't know that she was carrying on a conversation with him in her head, or that his evident suspicions were entirely justifiable.

Nor would he know, she decided, tackling a particularly nasty knot with gusto. Gabe's family were everything she hadn't dared hope they would be. She had spent less than an hour all told with them and she was already falling under their spell.

Nora hurriedly got dressed, not wanting Luca to be left alone for too long – not that he was going to find anything incriminating. It wasn't as if she kept a diary! She pulled on a pair of jeans and a boho top of her mother's, twisting her hair into a fishtail plait and putting on enough make-up to cover the shadows under her eyes.

She stared at herself in the mirror. She was doing nothing wrong. She and Gabe were together, if not actually engaged. They were the real deal, so what good would it serve to tell anyone that their romantic meet-cute was more of a set-up? It wasn't relevant.

But her reflection clearly wasn't convinced, and as Nora descended the stairs to meet Luca's too-knowing gaze, she knew he wasn't convinced either.

Hampstead, 10 September 1995

Dear Erik,

Why didn't we exchange addresses? I was so sure I
was going to see you again, that our routes aligned,
it seemed more romantic to leave our reunion to
fate. Idiot me! So here I am, back in London writing a
postcard I can't send.

I wonder where you are tonight . . . Portugal? Germany?
Or are you back in Sweden getting ready for university?

I have some big news to share, but I don't know how to
say it. I haven't told anyone yet. But I wish you were
here to tell me it was all going to be OK.

Charlotte x

# Chapter Eight

Nora was aware of several conflicting emotions as she made her way along the dirt path that led between the vines towards the villa. Obviously, she was nervous about spending the evening with a host of strangers, and more than a little anxious thanks to her unexpected status as prospective daughter-in-law, but she was excited too. It had been a long time since she had spent time with a large family and she craved the noise and teasing and laughter and even the bickering. The acceptance. It would be nice to spectate. To be part of it. No matter what the man striding just ahead of her thought.

Not that she actually *knew* what he was thinking. Luca hadn't said a word since they had left her cottage, apart from reminding her to bring the key, an annoying smirk evident in his voice and expression.

But maybe she was misreading him and the situation. The truth was that his abrupt manner might have nothing to do with her at all, he might have had a bad day at work, put his back out, put something red in the washing machine and dyed all his towels pink. As Grace told her class regularly, just because they were the main character in their own story didn't mean they were more than a bit part in someone else's. Nora just wished she had been more prepared when meeting him for the first time.

And clothed. Clothes would have been good.

She could feel her whole body heat with remembered embarrassment.

Nora breathed in. The evening sun was warm on her shoulders, the air enticingly fragrant with the scent of lemons and herbs and other fresh smells she couldn't identify but were a definite upgrade on concrete and traffic fumes. The sky was still blue despite the hour, barely a wisp of cloud to be seen, and she was surrounded by acres and acres of vines, green and budding with their valuable crop. Twist one way and there it was, the glimmer of sea inviting her in the distance, twist the other and she could see the awe-inspiring sight of the mighty volcano, currently peaceful . . . but with the potential to fire up at any time. They were *really* close.

Nora shivered, the images she had seen of Pompeii flashing into her head, the terrified mummified bodies, curled up as if they could hide from their fate. She might be standing among carefully cultivated vines, but the view was a reminder that the natural world was just a step away. She had never felt more of a Londoner in her life, Hampstead Heath just didn't compare to this ancient landscape.

'You OK?'

It wasn't until Luca spoke that Nora realised she had stopped, her gaze fastened onto the volcano.

'Yes. Fine,' she said automatically. 'It's just . . .'

'Just what?'

'So primal. The volcano is in charge, we are just insignificant. Ants here for a second while it is eternal – compared to us anyway. I'm sure a geologist would put me right pretty quickly.' Nora hadn't meant to be so openly introspective and winced in embarrassment, painfully aware that Luca was regarding her with some puzzlement, as though something about her didn't add up.

'It's this way,' was all he said. 'This path is a shortcut.'

The path Luca led her down cut through the vines until they reached the other side of the villa, then skirted around the edge of the olive grove and along the side of the inviting-looking pool. A few moments later, they were back at the terrace, where the family were once again sitting around the table, along with a tall man who held the baby in one arm as he chatted to Antonio.

Chiara jumped up to greet them. 'Nora, welcome back. I think you met everyone here earlier, except for Carlo, Nicoletta's husband and our head chef. Carlo, this is Nora.'

'Hello,' Carlo said in careful, heavily accented English with a warm, welcoming smile.

Nora watched with a pang of envy as Carlo shifted the baby to his other arm, dropping a kiss on top of his head. She was a sucker for a man with a baby, and she didn't need Freud to tell her why.

'Lovely to meet you.' Nora turned to Chiara. 'The room is beautiful, thank you again.'

'Although you should have warned her about the lock. If I hadn't come along, she would still be locked out,' Luca added and Nora froze. *Please don't mention the towel.*

'Oh, Nora, I am so sorry.'

'Not at all. I . . . It was no big deal,' she managed, aware her cheeks were scarlet and that Luca was watching her closely, an amused smile tilting his mouth. 'Anyway, I brought you these as a thank-you for inviting me here. I hope you like them.' She proffered the tote bag she had grabbed from the cottage towards Chiara. 'Just a small token.'

Gabe had been spectacularly unhelpful when she had asked him what she should bring. 'They won't expect anything,' he had said. 'Just you will be enough.'

Which was sweet of him, but Nora was sure it wasn't true. It didn't help that anything she would usually bring as a gift was an Italian speciality, from chocolate to coffee. In the end, she had gone to Fortnum and Mason and purchased a ruinously expensive box of sweet biscuits, some fancy savoury biscuits and a selection of pickles, along with a bottle of local gin inspired by the Heath and bottled in Hampstead.

As she had hoped, the gifts stopped anyone questioning her further about how she had got locked out. Instead, she found herself telling them about her home, about walking on the Heath and growing up in London, until it was time to eat and they sat down to a delicious dinner of salade caprese, the tomatoes tasting of sunshine and mozzarella creamier than anything she had ever eaten before, followed by a seafood stew so fresh and aromatic, she didn't need urging to agree to a second helping.

The Catalanos made a real effort to include her and keep to English, but when swept up in conversation would forget and break into Italian. Nora didn't mind, she was just enjoying the whole experience of being there. Of sitting at the busy long table, eating delicious food properly al fresco, sipping equally delicious wine watching the dynamics between the family. They were obviously close-knit, although she sensed a coolness between Antonio and Luca, similar to the one she had sensed between the older man and Gabe, and she remembered Chiara saying he had hoped to pass the vineyard on to one of his sons. Obviously Gabe wasn't interested, but did that mean Luca also worked elsewhere? Hopefully that meant he *lived* elsewhere as well. She was aware of him watching her throughout the meal, that same speculative look she had noticed while walking in the vineyard, as if he couldn't quite figure her out.

He had left her with puzzles of her own. Was what he had said true? Had Gabe been thinking of getting back with Lily just a few weeks ago? That was just before they'd met. Gabe hadn't said much to her about his previous relationships, not that that was surprising. He wasn't one to do deep dives into feelings. She'd tried to tell him a little about Jake, but the conversation had never really progressed beyond a few facts before he kissed her and told her that she had him now and not to worry about it. But that was good, wasn't it? She didn't wallow with him. She didn't mourn the past and all she had lost, there was no looking back where Gabe was involved.

'So, what are your plans, Nora?' Luca asked, and she startled, recalled to the here and now.

She gave him a swift glance, his mouth was curled into a pleasant smile, but his eyes were cold.

'My plans?'

'Oh, wedding plans.' Nicoletta clapped her hands. 'The vineyard is a very romantic wedding venue, I can vouch for that.'

'But maybe Nora wants to get married in London,' Chiara cautioned. 'With her family.'

'I . . . We . . . Gabe and I haven't really discussed it.' Understatement of the century. 'But this would be idyllic. It's so beautiful.' What was she doing? She should be shutting down wedding talk, not practically booking a venue!

'Your family wouldn't mind if you got married here?'

'No.' Nora put down her fork, her appetite gone. 'The thing is, I don't actually have a family. It's just me.'

'Just you?' A horrified hush had fallen over the entire table. Even Luca lost what she was beginning to think was his customary sardonic expression.

'We were a small family anyway.' Nora couldn't help but look around the table as she said it. At the four generations eating together – the son-in-law, the two sisters with their strong physical similarity, Luca, clearly his mother's favourite as she kept sneaking food onto his plate and occasionally ruffling his hair as if he was no older than his small nephew. 'Just me and my mother. We lived with my grandparents until they died around ten years ago and then it was just me and my mother, until she got sick.' To her horror, her eyes were hot, her throat swollen and she fumbled for some water.

'And your father?' Luca asked.

'A mystery. My mother knew who he was,' she added hurriedly. 'But she met him abroad, in Florence, and they lost touch. All I have are a couple of photos.'

'Ah, Firenze,' Nicoletta sighed. 'Such a romantic city.'

'Your father is Italian?' Chiara's eyes brightened.

'No, Swedish. But he and my mother met in Florence backpacking.'

'Have you been to Florence?' Nicoletta asked.

'No, this is my first visit to Italy. My mother and I were going to interrail, after my A Levels; she didn't get to finish her trip because she was pregnant with me. But my grandfather got ill, so of course we stayed, and after he died, my grandmother needed us. She died less than a year later, but then . . .' Then her mother had been diagnosed with her illness and for four years they kept talking about one day, about how when she was better they would go, planning and replanning routes, the things they would see, the places they would stay. 'It just didn't happen. Anyway. I am here now. My mother visited Sicily on her travels, I have a picture of her in Taormina on the beach, so it's great to be finally treading in her footsteps.'

'And Gabe let you come alone,' Antonio grumbled.

'Never mind that, we will make sure you have a wonderful time. You will love Sicily, Nora,' Chiara clapped her hands, 'there is so much to see. But tomorrow you must enjoy all the facilities we have right here. There's a wonderful pool, heated by volcanic springs . . .'

'And a plunge pool right next to it,' Violetta interjected.

'*Si.*' Antonio nodded. 'Tomorrow, enjoy the vineyard and then the next day one of us will show you some of the island. Nicoletta, you are Nora's age.'

'I'm up for showing Nora around tomorrow, but we're really busy at the beginning of the week, I can't take any time off at this late notice,' Nicoletta said. 'Sorry, Nora.'

'No, don't apologise, it's fine.' Nora was more than a little embarrassed. 'None of you were expecting to entertain a lone visitor. Honestly, I'll be fine.' They were pretty rural and she had never learnt to drive, but surely there were buses? Did they have Uber in Sicily?

'And my week is busy too.' Violetta smiled apologetically. 'Not that I can drive anyway.'

'This is not the kind of hospitality we show our guests.' Antonio sounded annoyed now. 'Nicoletta, surely . . .'

'I will take Nora around.'

Everyone went quiet and stared at Luca.

'Not enough to do at your uncle's?' There was an edge in Antonio's tone, matched by Luca as he replied.

'Like you said, the Catalanos are nothing if not hospitable. I am owed a few days' leave. So, I am at Nora's disposal until Gabe returns.' The sardonic gleam was back.

Great. She would literally rather have had any other guide.

'You really don't have to put yourself out for me,' she protested weakly.

His answering smile took no prisoners.

'Oh, I am more than happy. I can't wait to really get to know the girl my brother is going to marry.' It sounded like a threat, not a promise.

*

The next day was as relaxing as Nora had been promised. She breakfasted alone in her cottage after a long, refreshing sleep, fresh bread and fruit left at her door along with a note urging her to come to the villa if she needed anything more substantial. The sun was already bright, and she made sure to smother herself in factor 50; where her skin was concerned, her Irish ancestral genes had conquered all. She had two tones: pale and red. Her hair was tamed in a fishtail braid, and she was make-up free as she pulled on a pair of brightly patched denim dungaree shorts that had once been her mother's, over a sports bra. She looked a little like she was about to head out and milk a cow, but before she could make a decision whether or not to change, there was a rap at the door and Nicoletta and Violetta burst in. The former looked effortlessly elegant in a simple linen shift dress, her younger sister more casual in shorts and a vest top.

'*Buongiorno.*' Nicoletta gave Nora a quick hug and a double kiss. 'I hope you slept well.'

'Really well, thank you.' It was true. She'd expected an uneasy night thanks to Gabe's absence, the engagement mix-up and Luca's obvious suspicions, but between the fresh air, the long day's travel and the excellent food and drink, she had been tired enough to fall into a long dreamless sleep.

'Ready to be shown around the vineyard?' Violetta asked as she accepted a cup of the coffee Nora had just brewed.

'A VIP tour for one,' Nicoletta added.

'You don't have to put yourself out for me.'

'I finished school last week and am spending some of the summer leading tours, so you are helping me out, this is good practice for me,' Violetta said.

'And I have a rare few hours where I am not working or with the children, and what nicer way to spend it than getting to know my new sister?' Nicoletta added.

Looking at their expectant faces, Nora knew there was no way to refuse without being rude; not that she really wanted to. She was far too intrigued by the extensive vineyards and other operations the Catalanos owned, not to mention the promise of a luxury spa, and so she happily put herself in the sisters' capable hands.

The day started with a buggy ride around the vineyard, which was even bigger than Nora had supposed, followed by a visit to the factory where the wine was pressed, fermented and clarified before it was in carefully controlled rooms and bottled.

'No treading the grapes?' she asked as she looked at the complicated pressing machinery and Violetta laughed.

'We always tread the first hand-picked crop at the start of harvest traditionally. But that's just a reminder of our roots and for fun. We don't sell that batch obviously – although we all make sure our feet are well washed!'

There was so much to take in: bottling, labelling, a busy office where orders were taken and marketing done, an enjoyable hour joining in with a tour group on a wine-tasting journey around the island and then lunch in the excellent restaurant. This was followed by a visit to the old winery, now the heart of a small but luxurious complex of charming holiday apartments, before they jumped back in the buggy to head to other end of the vineyard to enjoy a dip in the volcanic springs and a massage and facial at the accompanying spa.

'I had no idea of just what a huge operation you run.' Nora sat back in her padded lounger, positioned perfectly on the shady plant-filled terrace to take advantage of the incredible views of the treelined hills. She had been pummelled into total relaxation and was now wrapped up in a robe as they enjoyed a glass of excellent wine. 'I mean, I knew your family ran some kind of restaurant . . .' She was aware she was dissembling. Gabe had made it sound like a busy traditional café, not the elegant restaurant serving food every bit as good as the Michelin-starred places he liked to frequent back in London, and he had certainly not mentioned that it was set in its own vast estate. 'But this is something else.'

'The family has owned the vineyard for generations,' Nicoletta said. 'And there has been a restaurant on site for many years, but Papà expanded hugely when he took over.'

'Mamma too,' Violetta added. 'She was the one who renovated the winery into apartments, insisted the restaurant be a destination spot and not just an add-on, founded the spa.'

'Oh, nothing would have happened without Mamma,' Nicoletta agreed. 'Papà wanted to make us a wine lovers' destination, and we are, but Mamma knew the value of diversifying and tourism.'

'Do you get many visitors?'

'All year round, but now summer is here it starts to get really busy,' Nicoletta said. 'We are part of several external vineyard tour itineraries and that can mean four tours a day, plus anyone can book in for a bespoke tour or join one of the public ones we ourselves run daily. We also offer spa days with wine tasting and food, luxury weekends and weddings and other special celebrations. The apartments are already booked out for the summer; you were lucky we had a cancellation for the little barn, it's not often available.'

'Obviously tell me to move out if anyone else wants it,' Nora said, not without a pang; she had occupied the bijou cottage for less than twenty-four hours, but she was already very fond of it. 'But, honestly, I cannot believe what an empire this is. It must take a lot of work to look after everything.'

'Papà always says they should have had five more children,' Violetta giggled. 'You can imagine Mamma's response to that. But it is very much a family affair. Nicoletta runs the restaurant and also has responsibility for the gift shop and tours. Papà is in charge of the wine and Mamma the events, accommodation and spa. Right now I am a tour guide, but when I leave school, I will take over the marketing. The university is in Catania and I can do a business degree there and stay at home so I can start straight away.' She tossed her hair defiantly. 'One day Papà will see it's a blessing we are so involved, even if Gabe and Luca aren't. Although neither of us are winemakers and that's obviously crucial. It would be good if Luca . . .' She trailed off. 'Well, he is proud. Too proud.'

'As is Papà.' Nicoletta smiled at her sister. 'Of course I love our father, but he can be so old-fashioned, even for Sicily.'

'I think it's amazing that you both *do* want to be involved. Although, sitting here, drinking the wine and admiring the view, I think it's more of a mystery why your brothers don't want to be.' Nora couldn't help fishing for more information.

'Oh, Gabe was never interested, not in the vineyards anyway. We would be out helping in the fields, and he would be at a computer planning some kind of way of making money from *our* work.' Nicoletta laughed. 'He was the only child I knew who invested his pocket money. He usually managed to turn a profit as well.'

'What about Luca?'

Now why had she asked that? She should have asked for more stories about *Gabe*. She wasn't interested in Luca Catalano. But maybe she should be. It might be useful to get a handle on him and figure out just why he had so clearly decided she was bad news.

'Luca was always the first out into the fields in the morning and the last back at night during the summer, he's as passionate about wine as Papà, as any of us. Gabe was always going to leave Sicily, to live in a city and work in an office and make a lot of money, but not Luca.'

'Then why . . .' Nora began then stopped. It really was none of her business.

Luckily, Nicoletta was more than happy to fill in the blanks without any more prompting. 'Luca is too like Papà. They are both very stubborn, don't always say what they feel, both very passionate. And they both like things their own way. Luca travelled after he finished university, visiting vineyards and winemakers all around the world, and came back brimming with ideas, but Papà was very cautious about implementing any of Luca's suggestions. I don't think he could understand why Luca wanted to change things. Papà thinks the vineyard is perfect as it is. It was very frustrating for poor Luca, difficult for all of us. They argued a lot. In the end, Luca took a job with our uncle in his wine-exporting business. So that's both sons working in offices rather than on the land.'

'But didn't you say that your father introduced changes himself?'

Violetta nodded. 'I don't remember my grandfather, but from what Nonna and Mamma have said, there were arguments when Papà took over too, just like his with Luca. But Papà was still a young man when his father died and he was the only son, so the vineyard was all his.' She rolled her eyes. 'I have no idea how my aunts felt about that.'

'And Luca isn't tempted to return?'

'I don't know,' Nicoletta said thoughtfully. 'Luca is stubborn, like all Catalanos. He may well think he's made his decision and that's that.' Her smile was rueful. 'As a family, we discuss everything endlessly, but not this. Not in front of Luca and Papà anyway! It's hard though, especially for Mamma; they are still cool with each other, even though it's been years since Luca walked away. But even if Luca did decide to come back, he'd soon see that he wouldn't have things his own way. The vineyard is a *family* business, not a father-and-son one.'

'That's right!' Violetta high-fived her sister, while Nora sat back and sipped her wine, mind racing with all the sisters had disclosed.

So, Luca was passionate, stubborn and prepared to go his own way, no matter the consequences for his family. Interesting. And disturbing, because, for whatever reason, he seemed to have taken against Nora, and if that really was the case, then it was clear he would make a formidable enemy indeed.

*Hampstead, 18 September 1995*

*Dear Erik*

*The secret is out, I told my parents last night. I didn't have much of a choice, university starts next week! And I am not going to go. Not yet anyway, and probably not Oxford. Poor Dad, he was so proud of me getting a place there, but he took it surprisingly well. Maybe he had guessed, I've not exactly been full of plans for my glittering future. Don't worry, I'm still planning to be a kick-ass lawyer at some point, but not just yet. Because although it doesn't make any sense, I am going to have the baby. Our baby.*

*How do you feel about that? It's big, isn't it?! Scary! I don't remember teenage single mum being on my top-ten-things-to-do-before-I'm-twenty list. And yet . . . and yet, it feels right somehow.*

*Mum and Dad are in shock, obviously. From Oxbridge high-flier to walking scandal in one conversation. But they are already so supportive. I'm so lucky. But oh, I wish you were here.*

*Ti amore*

*Charlotte x*

# Chapter Nine

Try as she might, Nora could think of no real reason why she shouldn't take Luca up on his offer to spend the day sightseeing, and so she was up waiting at the breakfast table, dressed in a floral fifties swing dress, her hair in a chignon with wavy tendrils framing her face, make-up carefully applied as if her bright red lipstick was armour. It was the kind of look she expected Gabe to make some kind of joking yet pointed comment on, to ask her if she was going to audition for a part in a historic film, for instance. Luca merely raised his eyebrows when he saw her and, for a fleeting moment, Nora could have sworn she saw approval warm his usually (in her experience so far) severe expression.

'Ready?'

'Luca,' Chiara scolded him. 'The poor girl has barely touched her breakfast. Sit down, have some coffee. Be civilised.'

'Honestly, I am fine,' Nora assured her. 'But I am going to second the coffee,' she added, smiling at Luca. 'It really is excellent. I can see why Gabe prowls London looking for something to match it.'

At the mention of Gabe, Luca's expression hardened once again, but he sat as bade after dropping an affectionate kiss on his mother's cheek.

'So, what do I need for today's expedition?' Nora asked. 'I have suncream, comfortable shoes, a hat. Will I need a swimsuit?' She was determined not to let Luca get to her. Let him glower at her, she would just smile in reply.

'I thought we would go to Taormina. Then, if we have time, drive along the coast road. It might be sensible to bring a costume and towel just in case there's an opportunity for a swim.' He sounded amiable enough, but Nora wasn't fooled.

'Words I never hear in London. I'll just go and grab them from the cottage, see you back here in a few. Oh, and Luca?' She held his gaze steadily. 'Thank you. This really is very kind of you. I'm looking forward to it.' There, she would wrong-foot him with niceness.

Nora almost skipped as she headed back to the cottage. The sun was out again, the air pleasantly warm with the promise of real heat and she was on holiday, in Italy at last. It would be silly to let Luca ruin her day.

It was disconcerting just how much he looked like Gabe, though. The same eyes, same shaped, even if he lacked the easy-going charm that Gabe exuded. Even their voices were similar, although Luca's was a hint deeper, darker, slightly more gravelly. Just like Gabe had sounded that very first night. Every time he spoke, despite herself, a shiver of recognition travelled through her.

Maybe today's forced proximity was a good thing, a chance to clear the air. She didn't want to be at odds with *any* of Gabe's family.

Full of good intentions, Nora kept up a flow of chatter as she and Luca drove out of the vineyard and onto the small road that wound through the hills and back towards the coast, Mount Etna behind them. He didn't contribute much, if anything, to the conversation, but she didn't let his silence deter her as she determinedly talked about all the things she had done the day before, trying to provoke him into answering.

Luca remained guarded, his posture tense, eyes hidden behind his sunglasses, mouth taut, replying in monosyllables where possible, but after a while, Nora realised that rather than being uncomfortable, she was rather enjoying the strange duel she seemed to have been drawn into.

'It was great to spend so much time with Nicoletta and Violetta yesterday, they have been so welcoming.' Slight emphasis on *they*.

A grunt in response.

'I still can't believe the sheer scale of the vineyard and of all that goes on there. Before I arrived, I had no idea just how big the vineyard was, let alone the rest of the operation.' To be fair, she hadn't known there even *was* a vineyard, but she wouldn't go into that. 'Seeing so many tours pass through, how busy the restaurant was even at lunch, it's very impressive. Your parents must have worked so hard. You must be so proud of them,' she said guilelessly, as if she didn't know about the conflict between Luca and his father.

Another grunt, only this time his hands tightened on the wheel.

'It's a shame Gabe has no interest in being part of it. Not that I can imagine him out among the vines, not unless there is some designer sportswear especially for grape picking and an adrenaline sport aspect to it.'

Was that a reluctant smile tugging at his mouth? She mentally awarded herself a point. One Nora, zero Luca.

'It's lovely that your sisters are so close, especially with the age gap,' she continued. 'I don't have any siblings, but I do have two friends who are like sisters. And Felix is like a brother too. The three of them have been there for me no matter how dark it has got.' Now why on earth had she volunteered that? 'Are you and Gabe close?'

'What has he said?'

Four whole words. Nora awarded herself four points, one per word. If she got an entire sentence, complete with subclauses, then she would take that as a knockout win.

'Not much. I love Gabe . . .' Luca's jaw tightened and she rolled her eyes, glad of her large sunglasses. 'But he isn't one for . . .' Nora paused, suddenly unsure of where to go with her sentence. It wasn't that Gabe *didn't* talk, in reality he usually dominated the conversation. He just wasn't *introspective*. His conversation was dominated by work, what he had seen that week, his achievements, whether a good gym session or a personal best on his morning run. Thinking about it without being enveloped by his often all-encompassing presence, their conversations seemed rather . . . well . . . shallow. But it was still early days, they were still getting to really know each other. 'Gabe is so of the moment,' she said at last. 'That's part of what drew me to him.' No more looking back, no more poor Nora, no more being defined by loss. She didn't have to *think* when she was with Gabe, that was what was so refreshing about their relationship. 'You're the oldest, aren't you? Did you boss him around horribly when he was a boy?'

'Gabe is almost impossible to boss around.'

Nora laughed. 'This is true.'

To her surprise, Luca carried on without prompting. 'My mother would say we are equally stubborn. The difference is, I stand my ground and he just charms his way into doing exactly what he wants. But, of course, I am sure he is different with you.'

'Well, no, not really,' she admitted. But Gabe's life was so much more interesting than hers. It was harder for him to compromise than it was for her, he got bored so easily – not that she didn't find that obstinacy frustrating, that ability to slide out of things that didn't interest him irritating, she wasn't *that* besotted. Look at their current situation! He'd promised to let her know when she could expect him back and yet all he had done so far was send her a photo of his (five-star) hotel suite, his (Michelin-starred) dinner and told her he missed her and that he would be back soon, but not to worry because *bella, you are my destiny.* Whatever that meant! He hadn't even responded to her plea he sort out the engagement misunderstanding.

Usually, his romantic statements made her swoon. No one had ever called her their destiny before, but right now, she wanted something more tangible than grandiose statements and vague promises. She liked Gabe's family – *really* liked them – they had made her so welcome in an unfussy way, accepting her and drawing her in, but the longer Gabe left telling them the truth, the more awkward it would be.

'No,' she said again. 'He definitely likes to get his own way, but to be fair, I am pretty easy-going.'

Easy-going or a pushover? She knew what Ana would say.

Luca shot her a glance that wasn't entirely unsympathetic. 'I would watch that. Gabe has many good qualities, but he needs keeping in line or he'll walk all over you. That's why he and Lily were always arguing, she wouldn't put up with his nonsense.'

Right. 'Thanks for the warning.' Now she was the one sounding taut. 'But Gabe doesn't walk all over me.' *Didn't he?* She straightened, tilting her chin defiantly. 'We're just very compatible.'

'How lucky for you both.' Was he smirking?

Nora turned and looked out of the window and the admittedly breathtaking scenery. They were coming into

Taormina now and she could see colourful buildings perched on the cliff edge, the town graduating down towards a sea so perfectly turquoise blue, it almost hurt.

'It's almost too good to be true,' Luca said after a moment.

'It is *very* beautiful,' Nora agreed, staring at the scenery in awe. She had never seen anything like it, it was more like a scene from a film than real life.

'Not Taormina, although, yes, it is beautiful. I meant how amazingly compatible you and Gabe are.'

OK. Now they were coming to it.

'I wouldn't say too good to be true. Surely being compatible is the most important thing in a relationship?'

Luca shrugged. 'First of all, there is the staggering coincidence that you just bumped into each other after sharing a dramatic event. Then, once you did, it turned out that you are perfect for each other. So perfect Gabe changed his mind about reconciling with his ex-girlfriend and got engaged to you in record time. Who knew real life could be so like a film? Of course, my brother is very successful. Wealthy. Fortunate for you, I would say.'

Nora's teeth ground together. It wasn't Gabe's money and success that had attracted her! 'My friends would argue that he is the lucky one,' she returned sweetly.

'Of course,' he nodded, 'but surely they would agree with me that things have moved very quickly. Tell me, what is it about him that made you fall so quickly for him?'

That was direct.

'I just knew,' she said before she could formulate a less personal answer. 'Before I knew his name or his occupation or anything about him. That night, when he saved me, the moment I heard his voice, I knew. It was like everything suddenly made sense despite how frightened I was, despite the pain in my ankle. I just knew that here was my person. You probably think I am an idiot . . .'

She waited for a cutting reply, but to her surprise, Luca didn't answer and when she looked over at him he had gone pale, his hands gripping the wheel like they were careering along a motorway, not crawling down a busy street. What was *that* about?

'You are saying you fell in love with him that night . . .' he said finally, almost uncertainly.

'Yes,' she said almost defiantly. 'I know it sounds crazy, but that's what happened. And when I met him again it just confirmed what I felt. My mother always told me I would know when I met the man who was right for me. And I did. Instantly.'

'You've talked with Gabe, about that night?' His voice was as taut as his posture.

'Not much.' She was feeling uncomfortable now, wishing she hadn't brought it up. 'He doesn't like to discuss it, he gets embarrassed by the whole thing.' She stopped, cheeks burning. 'Oh no, I completely forgot that he didn't want me to mention it.' Which she found endearing, humility was so unlike Gabe. 'Please pretend I didn't say anything.'

'I see.' Luca looked lost in thought and they spent the rest of the short drive in strained silence.

By the time he pulled up in the car park of a large stone building on the headland, with spectacular views down the hill and out to sea, Nora had decided that she had had enough.

'Look,' she said as they got out of the car. 'I appreciate you giving up your day for me like this, but clearly you are suspicious of me or don't like me, or both. Whatever. I get it. Just a few weeks ago, you thought Gabe was about to get back with his ex and now here I am. I know it seems quick and it's unexpected. It *is* quick. You're his big brother and looking out for him. But I don't want to spend the day with someone who is trying to catch me out and doesn't want to be with me. I haven't been on holiday for a really long time. This is already not what I was expecting, but really, I'd rather spend the day exploring on my own. I'm fine on my own. I'm used to it.'

Luca didn't answer for one long minute, a muscle beating in his jaw the only sign he had even heard her. Nora waited.

'It's not just Gabe,' he said at last, his voice low and a little hoarse, familiar, tugging at her memory, reverberating through her. 'You have been here for less than two days and already my family loves you. Violetta has raided Nonna's wardrobe and is ordering vintage clothes online, Nicoletta is planning a girls' night out with you. Mamma has said nothing, but I can see the relief in her eyes when she looks at you.'

'That's because I'm not vegan. I think she accepted me the moment she heard that.'

Luca laughed, the sound unexpected – and kind of nice. 'That certainly helps. But it's also because you take an interest in the family business, in the family. You are warm, you talk. You act like you want to be here . . .' He didn't say *unlike Lily*, but the words hung in the air.

'I like your family, I'm glad they like me.' It was a balm to her lonely soul hearing these words.

'Nonna thinks you have grace – her highest compliment – and as for Papà . . .' Luca sighed, raking a hand through his hair. 'He was the only person surprised when Gabe didn't return from Milan and he's never quite forgiven Gabe. He sees you take an interest in the vineyard and I can tell he thinks that you might be the bridge he is too proud to build.'

'Right. OK.' Nora had no idea what to say, what to think. She hadn't considered that Gabe's family might need her. Want her for her, rather than as an extension of Gabe.

'Look, Gabe is my little brother and I love him. It's my job to look out for him, just like I look out for the rest of the family. They are falling for you fast. Just like he has. And if there is any chance they are going to get hurt . . .'

'Not by me. I know the value of family, Luca. More than anyone. And I feel the same way. Like I am meant to be here. If I had been able to go back to London without causing offence when Gabe had to leave, then I would have. I didn't want to be a burden. But your family made me so welcome, have been so kind, are so warm, it's a privilege to get to know them. I mean that.'

'I believe you do,' he said slowly.

'Then can we call a truce? For today at least. But, either way, I am more than happy to explore alone. You don't need to play babysitter.'

'And explain to my mother and grandmother why I abandoned you? I wouldn't be so foolish. But yes. Truce.' He regarded her steadily, his expression unreadable. 'For today anyway.'

'I can't ask for more than that.' To her surprise, Nora felt a warm glow of anticipation at the thought of the day ahead. She'd thought she would prefer to spend time alone, to get away from Luca, but despite his obvious – and understandable – suspicions, she was strangely drawn to him. Now they had come to an understanding, she was looking forward to their spending time together. 'OK, then, where are we going?'

'The first place everyone goes, of course – the Teatro antico di Taormina.'

'Who am I to break tradition? Lead the way. And Luca . . .'

'Si?'

'Thank you. For being honest with me. For looking out for Gabe. For looking out for your family. They are all lucky to have you.'

She meant every word. Luca Catalano had a good heart – and good instincts. Nora needed to be on her guard with him, but how she wished everything was as simple as it seemed to be. That she didn't harbour any guilt about how she had met Gabe, that their reunion really had gone down the way everyone thought. All she could do was enjoy every moment while it lasted. She knew better than anyone just how precarious happiness really was.

Hampsted, 16 April 1996

Dearest darling most perfect Nora Florence,

One day old and already it feels like I have known you forever. That I have loved you forever. All I want is your happiness. I understand that whole Mama Bear stuff now, I would take a sword to anyone who tried to hurt you, would dive into burning buildings and icy lakes and sacrifice myself in a million ways just to keep you safe. I had no idea I could feel this way. This determined.

I wish that things were different, that I could tell your daddy that you are safely here, and so beautiful. So smart, I can tell. The way you take everything in already. I wish that he could know you and be part of your life. But one thing that you must know is that I wanted you, loved you from the moment I realised you were on the way. And although I knew your father for a very short time, I loved him and he loved me.

Your Mummy xxx

# Chapter Ten

The truce was an excellent idea. Nora wouldn't go as far as to say that Luca *trusted* her, but he wasn't as obviously suspicious of her either, and when he wanted to, he clearly had just as much charm as Gabe. He was also a knowledgeable tour guide, filled with love and passion for the charming old coastal town with a history going back to before London had been a glint in Julius Caesar's eye.

'The theatre is Graeco-Roman,' he told her as they bypassed the queues of tourists. 'But the town is much older, dating back to the fourth century BC, although the area around was settled for several centuries before that. The whole island has a long, rich history – we're so much more than Mafia and volcanos.'

'There's the food for a start,' Nora said.

'Our food is justly famous too,' he agreed. 'Good food is paramount for a Sicilian's wellbeing.'

The Teatro antico di Taormina was like nowhere Nora had ever been before, perched high on the headland overlooking the sea, the stone seats graduating down towards the semicircular stage, crumbling pillars and the remains of stone-built buildings framing the stage, the sea an incredible backdrop. It was easy to picture it thousands of years before, filled with people and music and noise.

'And you can still see performances here?' Nora asked.

'Yes, they start soon. A mix of opera, classical and pop, usually – sometimes there are cinema screenings too. They are popular – at the height of the season, tickets can be hard to get, unless you know the right people.'

'Which you do?'

'Which I do.'

'It must be incredible . . .' Nora sat down on one of the stone seats and stared out at the sea. 'To sit in seats that have been used for literally thousands of years, watching people perform on a stage that generation after generation of actors have performed on. What a sense of history. You know, I live in what's considered to be a pretty historic area, but when this was built, my home was probably scrubby countryside. Even a couple of hundred years ago, there were still highwaymen on Hampstead Heath and we were a small village not really part of London at all; my road hadn't even been built yet.'

'Have your family lived there for a long time?'

'Oh, not at all. My grandparents moved there soon after they were married. My grandfather was brought up in Camden, his family were descended from Irish immigrants, while my grandmother was from Shoreditch. She thought her family had always lived in the East End, but when I did her family tree, we discovered that actually most of her ancestors had moved to London from the country when industrialisation hit; she had links to Essex, Shropshire and Kent. There's nowhere like this where I can stand and say, my ancestors would have stood on this very spot and seen exactly what I am seeing. That's really special.'

'It is. That's why we are such a proud nation, I suppose. The world might see us as an island at the foot of Italy, but we know that great civilisations grew and prospered, conquered and were conquered here for thousands of years. That knowledge is in our blood.'

It was fascinating seeing history through his eyes, hearing the pride in his voice. Gabe would call himself a proud Sicilian, but by his own admission he rarely came home. Whereas Luca had travelled the world but returned to his island, to use the knowledge he had gained there. Nora got it. If she had those kinds of roots, she would feel the same. In some ways, she did, look at how she clung onto her house because it connected her to her lost family.

At that moment, a tour guide stopped close by, and they found themselves enveloped by a horde of people, all wearing headphones and serious expressions as they listened to him.

'Come on,' Luca said, and they headed down towards the stage.

The next half-hour was filled with facts and figures, anecdotes and stories, neither of them touched on anything more personal, but Nora couldn't help reflecting that, in one morning, she had told Luca more about her family background than she had told Gabe in the weeks she had known him.

The next stop on their tour couldn't have been more of a contrast, a beautiful garden overlooking the sea, already filled with a profusion of early summer flowers. Winding paths led to ornamental follies and shaded corners, while the wide boulevard looked out over the sea.

'There is no such thing as a bad view here, is there?' Nora said with a sigh, leaning on the balustrade and staring down at the turquoise water. 'What a gorgeous spot this is.'

'You should feel at home here, the gardens were founded by an English woman, Lady Florence Trevelyan. Rumour had it, she had an affair with the heir to the English throne and Queen Victoria expelled her.'

'Really?'

Luca grinned. 'Who knows if it's true, but it makes a good story. Sicily has always attracted travellers; Taormina in particular has been a destination for the rich and the beautiful for centuries, and once here, not everyone leaves. Lady Trevelyan ended up marrying a local doctor and founding this garden.'

'I can see how that happens,' Nora said. 'Not so much the founding of a garden, I haven't met a plant I can't kill with a toxic mix of too much love and benign neglect. My friend Felix says I have the fingers of doom.'

Luca laughed and she felt a small glow of satisfaction. It was surprisingly easy being with him.

They turned back into the garden, wandering down a path shadowed by trees and up the steps into one of the fanciful follies. Nora removed her sunglasses and let her eyes adjust to the gloom.

'I totally get why people stay. It's very easy to fall under Sicily's spell. I've only been here for two days and already I don't want to leave.'

'Maybe you'll be able to persuade Gabe to come home more often, maybe even return here one day,' Luca said.

Nora grimaced. 'I couldn't even persuade him not to jet straight off on a business trip five minutes after landing – not that I tried very hard. Tried at all, in fact. You know how he is.'

As soon as she said the words, she wanted to recall them. She had barely even admitted to herself how annoyed and hurt she was by Gabe's behaviour, the way he did just what he wanted, the lack of consideration he showed her.

But, to her relief, and surprise, there was no condemnation in Luca's warm gaze, more understanding mingled with a pity that caught in her throat, made her chest tighten with a sudden melancholy.

'*Si*,' Luca said softly. 'I know how he is.'

Nora blinked quickly, ramming her sunglasses back on to hide the sudden burning in her eyes. 'Come on,' she said brightly. 'What's next?' She was not going to dwell on Gabe's absence. She had promised herself not to be that girl. Not to cling or be needy, but to be cool and fun, to go with the flow and see where it took her. Gabe loved that about her. She wasn't going to spoil it all by moping now.

She pretended not to see Luca's appraising look before, without a word, he led the way out of the folly and gardens and back into the town.

The next stop was for food, bought from local stalls and eaten as they walked along, freshly made arancini stuffed with mozzarella and mushrooms, and delicious fried aubergine and potato croquettes, followed by granita, crushed ice, impossibly cold and bursting with the taste of fresh lemon. The sun was hot now, glancing off the steep, marble streets and colourful buildings, and Nora was relieved when they wandered into shadier areas with street markets bursting with colour and sound and smell. Gorgeous jewellery, bright fabrics, aromatic spices and an array of food from the myriad stalls tempted Nora. It was easy to imagine her mother striding through these streets, drinking in the sights and experiences. It was comforting, to finally follow in her footsteps.

Nora took note of various gifts she thought her friends might like: a soft silk kaftan jacket for Ana, a turquoise bracelet for Grace, painted crockery for Dai and Felix. Gorgeous as it all was, it was also overwhelming, and increasingly hot, and Nora was glad when Luca suggested they stop for a while in a pretty bar, shaded from the sun, but with yet more spectacular views across the sea. She ordered a refreshing spritz and some water, sitting back, looking out at the vista, absorbing all she had seen.

To her surprise, the conversation continued to flow easily, although she was a little guarded, not sure how far their truce really extended. Luca told her a little about his job working as a wine exporter and his post-university travels that had taken him all over the world.

'Where was your favourite place?' she asked curiously.

'Well, of course, nowhere compares with my home . . .' he started, and she laughed.

'That goes without saying! But Chile and Argentina, California, New Zealand, Australia! You've circumnavigated the whole world.'

'I suppose I have, although only the parts of the world with extensive winemaking businesses.'

'Even so, you have been to a lot more places than I have. I haven't even left Europe – and not seen a fraction of that yet. So, what was your favourite place? Where was your heart broken and where did you break hearts? Any life-endangering escapades?'

'Yes . . . to all three.' His grin was so infectious, she couldn't help but return it. 'Let me see, my heart was broken by a no-nonsense Argentinian woman who thought I was nothing but a callow youth and treated me with contempt the entire time I was there, which only made me worship her more. In my defence, I was twenty-two and ridiculously romantic. Hopefully, I didn't break any hearts in return, although I did have to spend quite a lot of time avoiding the bored and much younger wife of a Californian millionaire. Luckily, vineyards are great places to play hide-and-seek, but I did end up having to lock my bedroom door. I don't know if I was more scared of her or the seven-foot-wide bodyguard her husband employed.'

'Ouch! Does that count as your life-risking adventure?'

'One of them. Add in white-water rafting in crocodile-inhabited rivers, some terrifying spiders – I soon learnt to check my shoes the whole time I was in Australia – an idiotic decision to go bungee jumping . . . That one was actually pretty safe, but there's nothing like plummeting towards a river from a great height to make your life flash before your eyes.'

'It all sounds amazing. Maybe not the spiders. Or the crocodiles. I like my wildlife less life-threatening, to be honest.'

'Me too. I was offered a permanent job in Australia but realised, amazing as the country is, it wasn't for me. Getting to New Zealand was such a relief. Nothing more deadly than a bee sting. Not that a bee sting can't be deadly.'

'Ah, so you're a Bridgerton fan?' she teased.

'My sisters are obsessed, so I may have seen the odd episode. I admit nothing else.'

'Don't worry, Luca, your secret is safe with me.'

It was nice when he let his guard down. More than nice, *easy*. Nora didn't feel that she had to be constantly entertaining or admiring or effortlessly cool like she did with Gabe. It was funny how two brothers could look so similar and yet be so different.

'OK, ready for more sightseeing or do you want to call it a day?' Luca asked.

'Absolutely not, unless you have things you need to do.' Maybe Luca had had enough of her. The thought was curiously disappointing.

'Always, but I am quite happy here.'

Their gazes snagged and held and Nora felt that same tugging feeling of recognition, of knowing. More, a flare of heat that started low in her belly and spread out across her whole body. Luca Catalano, she realised, was not just a very attractive man, he was a very sexy man, especially when he bent all his focus on her, looked at her as if she were the only woman in the world. He was also Gabe's brother, a man who clearly distrusted her and she *really* needed to get a grip.

'OK, then!' Nora could hear her voice was overbright, as though she was channelling her best children's TV presenter, as she sprang to her feet. 'What's next?'

'Don't you want to finish your drink?'

'Finish my . . .? Yes! Absolutely! My drink!' She sat down just as suddenly, rocking the table as she did so and sending both drinks flying. 'Oh no! I am so sorry!' Somehow she had managed to avoid getting touched by even one drop, whereas Luca was soaked through. Who knew such a little amount of liquid could spread quite so fast? His white linen shirt was soaked, getting more translucent by the second, clinging to hard, honed planes of muscle that Nora could not seem to tear her eyes away from.

What was wrong with her? Obviously her so-called romantic decision to wait to have sex with Gabe had turned her into some kind of voyeur, ogling any attractive man she saw.

Although not any man – so far, she had only been afflicted by Luca.

The sooner Gabe was here, and they got the sex part of their relationship out of the way, the better.

Luca muttered under his breath as he dabbed fruitlessly at his chest, Nora curling her hands into fists to stop her issuing an invitation to help. Ogling his muscles was bad enough, she really didn't want to actually touch them.

'I am so, so sorry,' she said helplessly.

'It doesn't matter,' he said, staring down at himself ruefully. 'My apartment isn't that far away. I'll go and change and then we'll get on with our afternoon.'

'I'm not usually so clumsy. Shall I wait here?'

'Really, it's no trouble. And my apartment is on the way to the cable car. If you're ready, shall we go?'

There was a brief tussle over who would pay the bill, which Nora narrowly won but only after promising not to tell any of the family as they would take mortal offence, and then she followed Luca out of the bar and down the street until he turned down a narrow cobbled alley, brightly painted two- and three-storey houses close together.

'You live in Taormina?' She looked around curiously. 'Of course, you do, you said your house wasn't far.' Stating the obvious like a pro.

'The warehouse and office are in Taormina, so it makes sense for me to be here.'

'Do you miss the countryside?' Polite conversation was the way forward, anything to distract her from the way his shirt was clinging to his chest.

'Sometimes, but it's not as if it's far away. Besides, there are more opportunities in the city for a single man.' His smile was sudden and wolfish, and Nora had to work hard to stop her imagination going into overdrive, her body tensing with an emotion she wasn't sure she wanted to name or acknowledge.

It was the heat. It was the only explanation for her sudden clumsiness, the way her mind kept going places it had no right to go. The heat and missing Gabe.

'This way.'

The barred door was almost hidden, set back from the street, and led into a tree-filled courtyard, balconied buildings on all four sides. Benches and a table and chairs were situated in shady corners, a central fountain bubbling away.

'How pretty.'

'I think so.'

Gabe unlocked another door which led into a wide hallway, a staircase rising up, a door on either side. He set off up the stairs, Nora still following behind like Alice with the white rabbit, not sure where she was going. There were two thick wooden doors set back on each landing, the vestibules showing some sign of the apartment owners' personalities, these potted plants, another an ornate hatstand, a third a statue. There was only one door when they reached the top floor, and in this case no sign of the occupant's interests, just a small wrought-iron bench. An open-shuttered window looked out over the courtyard.

'This is just perfect. It's like the quintessential Italian apartment.' Nora knew she sounded like an idiot, but how often did she see her fantasy apartment come to life in front of her eyes?

'I'm glad you think so. Come on in.'

Luca had the penthouse, a high-ceilinged open-plan space that easily combined historic vibes with modern comfort. Shuttered doors led onto a wide flower-filled terrace housing a comfortable-looking outdoor sofa and a bistro table and chairs. Inside, the space flowed from a serious-looking kitchen, with an even more serious-looking wine fridge, to a dining area to a large seating area, a TV in the corner. Shelves along one wall housed an impressive selection of books and family photos, and a mix of prints, originals and framed photos were displayed in an eclectic fashion on the walls. It couldn't be more different to Gabe's sleek stylish apartment, but Nora instantly felt at home in a way she never quite managed at Gabe's.

'Make yourself comfortable,' Luca said. 'I'll just . . .' He gestured at his shirt.

'Of course.' She could feel her cheeks heat as she looked determinedly away from him. The last thing she wanted to do was think about Luca getting changed.

Luca headed towards a door at the far end of the sitting area and Nora drifted towards the terrace. The apartment looked down the hill towards the sea and Nora leant on the balustrade for a moment taking it all in.

'Another stunning view.'

'What was that?' Luca called.

'Oh nothing, I just said stunning view.'

'*Mi scusi*, I didn't quite catch that.'

This was awkward, if only she had said something a little more intelligent. A thought about one of the pictures, or the many books in at least three languages filling the bookshelves.

'Honestly, not worth repeat . . . Oh.' Nora turned just as Luca emerged from the bedroom, shrugging on a fresh white shirt. His chest was broad, perfectly proportioned, muscles clearly defined, enhanced by a smattering of dark hair. She could see the start of his stomach muscles, smooth and toned . . . and oh dear God, she should not be looking. Staring. Lusting.

Not lusting. That would be wrong. Appreciating.

Still wrong.

'I was just admiring the view.' Was she sounding husky? And the view she was looking at was not the one she should admit to looking at. 'From your window! That view. Not that there is any other view.'

Luca's brows drew together in concern. 'Are you OK?'

It was a valid question.

'Never better! Maybe a little hot. From the weather. Obviously. What other hot could I be? Anyway! I'm ready to sightsee some more. Not that your flat isn't lovely, but did you mention the beach?'

'Yes, there's a cable car . . .' He was clearly a little puzzled. No wonder, she was confusing herself.

'Sounds perfect, let's go.' She needed to keep busy and be surrounded by other people, lots of other people, and then maybe she could forget that she had just been checking out her boyfriend's brother, and worse, how much she had liked what she had seen.

Hampsted, 15 April 1997

Dear Erik,

Our baby is one! We are so lucky – she is the smiliest and sunniest baby imaginable. All the neighbours adore her and when I walk on the heath, I get stopped by all her (usually elderly) admirers.

I still can't see much of you in her; her hair is definitely going to be strawberry blonde (not red, no matter what you say!) and her eyes are green, but she does have a dimple, just like you. I love that dimple

. . .

And I have news! Mum is retiring and has offered to look after Nora so I can start university this September. Isn't she just the most amazing mother ever? She told me the other day that in some ways she was relieved I got pregnant so young – she was over forty when she had me and she adores being a youngish granny! And I adore her. And you. And our delicious one-year-old.

Charlotte xxx

# Chapter Eleven

Nora felt vaguely guilty for the rest of the afternoon. It didn't help matters that Luca continued to be a considerate tour guide, both knowledgeable and funny. It had been easier when he was rude to her. Hopefully, this truce was temporary and they could go back to sniping at each other in the morning.

It was a relief to get back to the sanctuary of her cottage, where she could call on some help.

> *Nora: What is wrong with me?*

> *Ana: Are you really ready to have this conversation?*

Nora scowled at her phone. That felt *very* pointed. Ana still hadn't forgiven her, then. To be fair, Nora still hadn't apologised. But then again, neither had Ana.

> *Nora: Ha very ha.*

> *Grace: WHAT'S HAPPENED?*

> *Nora: I spent the day with Luca . . .*

> *Felix: The hot brother?*

Nora: I didn't say he was hot.

Felix: You said he looked like a brooding Gabe. From that, I deduce hotness.

Grace: Was he mean? Did he try to discover your intentions towards his brother? Warn you off? Pay you off?

Nora: No. I thought he would but no. He was nice. Really nice . . .

Felix: Uh-oh!

Grace: What am I missing?

Felix: Nora has feels for the Italian Heathcliff

Grace: Nora!

Nora: I don't! I just . . .

Nora is typing . . .

Nora is deleting . . .

Ana: ???

Nora: I just had a moment, OK? He was changing his shirt and I had a moment. It was probably because he looked like Gabe. But I feel so guilty.

137

*Grace: How hot was the moment?*

*Nora: You know I am near a volcano, right?*

*Felix: That hot? \*Fans self\**

*Nora: I am a terrible human.*

*Grace: I have got to meet him.*

*Nora: Not helpful.*

*Grace: Don't be greedy, you have your Sicilian. You can't have his brother too. That is seriously AITA territory. Or like one of those menage books. But usually the brothers are werewolves or something in those. They're not werewolves, are they?*

*Ana: And you a teacher.*

*Nora: I am not planning on having anyone but Gabe. I just want some reassurance that this is normal.*

*Felix: Normal in what way?*

*Nora: In a I am missing Gabe and got confused way.*

Ana: You keep telling yourself that.

Grace: Any news from Gabe
yet? Wedding confusion
cleared up?

Nora: Not yet.

Grace: Mama Catalano is
going to have you trying on
wedding dresses before you
know it.

Felix: Or has Italian
Heathcliff got you in a spin?

Nora: No. No spinning.
Gabe is the best thing that
could happen to me.

Felix: In that case, stay
away from the brother . . .

Nora: You're probably right.

Felix: I'm definitely right
– and you have to sort this
engagement confusion out!

Nora: I'll try.

Ana: Nora!

Nora: I will!

Ana: Report back. We are
doing this for your own
good.

*Nora: I know.*

*Nora: Got to go.*

*Felix: Keep us updated.*

Nora put her phone down, not sure she felt any better, especially as her friends were right. If Gabe wasn't going to sort this wedding business out, she was going to have to do it. And she needed to ensure she didn't spend any more time alone with Luca. Not until Gabe had returned and all was right in her world once again.

At that moment, her phone rang and, to her delight and relief, Gabe's name flashed up on the screen. She snatched it up.

'I miss you. Please tell me you're calling to say you are on your way here!' That would solve everything.

'Ah, *bella*.' Her stomach tightened at the regret in his voice. She knew that tone and what it meant. 'I wish I could say that, but I have to go to Singapore.'

'*Singapore?* Oh, Gabe.'

'I know, it can't be helped.'

'But you are supposed to be on leave, how can they keep ignoring that?' A terrifying thought struck her. 'You *will* get here, won't you? I'm not going to have to turn up at your Nonna's birthday party alone?'

'I promise that won't happen; I will be there as soon as I can.' Somehow what wasn't as reassuring as Gabe clearly meant it to be.

'I love your home and I got to see Taormina today, but it would be better with you.'

'Ah, Taormina. Did Nicoletta take you?'

'No.' Could he hear the guilt in her voice? 'Luca was very nice and showed me around. It was very kind of him of course, but he's not you.' Repeat *that* ten times every day. Maybe make it one hundred.

'Luca?' His voice sharpened. 'What did you talk about?'

'Well, it was mostly history and sightseeing.' Nora felt like she was lying by omission, but she really didn't want to recap the day to Gabe. 'I missed you.' That was true. Mostly.

'Me too. At least I know my family will take care of you, they know I love you.' He sounded his usual affectionate self again, which just intensified her guilt.

Speaking of . . .

'Gabe, look, you really have to tell them we are not engaged, it's getting embarrassing now.'

'Of course, I will. If that's what you want.'

Relief swamped her. 'That's great . . .'

'But do I need to? I mean, we *are* going to get married, aren't we, *cara*?'

'I . . . I guess so.' Why did she feel so uncertain? This was what she wanted . . . wasn't it? Her own happy ever after, and not just so her friends could tell Jake's family how she had clearly moved on, but because the universe had sent her Gabe just when she needed him. He was her soulmate.

'You deserve a proper proposal and you will get one, that is a promise. But we both know that we are going to get married, so what's the point in telling my whole family first that we are not engaged and then that we are? I want to spend my whole life with you, *bella* Nora. *Ti amo*.'

What Nora should do was gasp 'oh, Gabe,' and tell him she loved him too, but instead of the exhilarating excitement, the all-encompassing happiness she expected, she felt curiously numb. Instead of returning his extravagant compliments, all she managed to say was 'OK.'

Not that Gabe sensed her inexplicable transformation into Elsa. 'I promise, we will do this properly when I return.

*Ti amo, bella.*' And with that, he was gone, leaving Nora staring at her phone in some despair. Did this mean that they *were* engaged? Or engaged to be engaged? Was it wrong that Gabe was so very sure of her when suddenly she wasn't sure of anything at all?

For the next couple of days, Nora amused herself by helping out at the vineyard, assuring the family there was nothing more she wanted to do more. She enjoyed the easy routine of it. Breakfast with Chiara and Nonna under the lemon trees, a morning filling in wherever help was needed, from the fields, to the office, to the restaurant. Lunch was swift but taken seriously and then she would be shooed off to relax, reading by the pool, a free session at the spa, coffee and chat with Nonna, a walk around the estate as she began to figure her way around. Late afternoon, she would be back at the villa helping to prepare dinner – a long leisurely meal al fresco – before an evening losing at cards to Nonna. The gentle, soothing way of life was exactly what she needed. Oh, she knew she was seeing it through rose-coloured glasses, as an outsider – there were family spats and business worries, a missing invoice here, a cancelled booking there – but in the main the Catalanos seemed to have worked out a secret to a happy life. If you ignored the underlying tension between Antonio and Luca that was.

That day, she had spent some time walking around the vineyard with Antonio. She had felt a little shy of the older man at first but had soon realised that under his somewhat gruff exterior he was as kind as the rest of his family, and she had relaxed into an easy relationship with him, peppering him with questions about the vineyard and winery.

'I wish Gabe shared your interest,' he had said and she'd winced at the sadness in his voice.

'It's a shame, but I suppose I would never have met him if he had stayed here,' she had pointed out. 'He's equally passionate about his work, it's just a very different kind of job.' Although she did wish Gabe wanted to return to his roots; she understood winemaking, at least she understood the outcome, but she was still hazy about how international finance worked.

Antonio had sighed. 'I suppose you think I am old-fashioned, wanting to pass this onto my sons.'

'A little,' she had said as diplomatically as she could. 'But I'm an only child, so big family dynamics are not really my thing. But,' she had carried on daringly, 'I do see two young women full of ideas and enthusiasm, I love spending time with them, it's a real education.'

'And I should count my blessings?' He had looked thoughtful. 'Maybe you're right. But there's the wine itself. If only Luca . . .' He had stopped then and changed the subject, but the regret and sadness on his face was easy to read.

'Nora, you have barely seen anything of Sicily,' Antonio said at dinner that evening. For the third night in a row, Luca had not appeared for the meal and Nora was both relieved and achingly aware of his absence. 'You came here for a holiday, not to check labels on bottles all afternoon or file invoices or indulge an old man by keeping him company in the fields.'

'Hardly old! Besides, I don't mind,' Nora protested. And she didn't. It made her feel like she belonged. And how she wanted to. To her increasing panic, absence wasn't making her heart grow fonder where Gabe was concerned, the opposite, he felt more ephemeral, like a figment of her imagination, but she was falling harder for his family every day. Apart from Luca. She was not feeling anything for Luca. She was neutrality personified. Practically Swiss.

'I have the day off tomorrow,' Nicoletta said. '*And* I have childcare, thanks to Carlo's parents, so I was planning to go for a hike and a swim up in the gorges. Do you want to come?'

'Wouldn't I be in the way?' She knew between their two small children and the busy demands of the restaurant, Nicoletta and her husband got very little time together.

'Carlo is working in the day, so it's just me. Luca was supposed to come, but he's pulled out. It's a gorgeous walk, but the water is very cold, be prepared.'

'In that case, I would love to. Thank you.'

Luckily, Gabe had mentioned that Sicily was good for hiking and so the following day she packed some sports leggings, a vest top and her trail shoes, plus a lightweight rucksack, to which she added a swimsuit and towel, water, grapes (never in short supply at the vineyard) and some apples. Suntan cream and a baseball cap completed her outfit the next morning: with her hair pulled back in a high braid, she was ready for physical activity, she felt like a realistically proportioned Lara Croft, sartorially at least.

'*Buongiorno*,' she said as she headed around the corner to the terrace, where she had arranged to meet Nicoletta for breakfast before they set off, only to skid to a sudden halt. 'Oh! Hi, Luca.'

Luca was not only unexpectedly here, but he was also dressed in what could only be described as hiking-appropriate attire. Shorts – *do* not *look at his legs* – a T-shirt and light walking trainers that looked as high-tech and expensive as something Gabe would own.

'*Buongiorno*.' Nicoletta greeted Nora with the customary double kiss. 'Luca can make it after all, isn't that good?'

'Amazing.' Nora couldn't bring herself to look at Luca as she spoke. Instead, she set her rucksack down, poured herself a cup of coffee from the pot in the middle of the table and helped herself to some fruit, bread and cheese. 'But are you sure you want me to come along in that case? I won't be offended if you want some quality brother and sister time.'

'Don't be silly, of course we still want you to come, don't we, Luca? Besides, soon you will be our sister.'

Luca's expression tightened. 'Of course you are very welcome to join us.'

Nora was almost relieved to hear the hint of reserve in his voice. Had he gone back to distrusting her? That was fine by her.

'Have you heard from Gabe?' Nicoletta asked. 'Is he planning to actually come here and spend any time with you? It's been, what, five days since he left you at the airport?'

'Not the most romantic of fiancés,' Luca said blandly and Nicoletta elbowed him.

Nora ignored Luca, turning deliberately to Nicoletta. 'He only arrived in Singapore yesterday, what with flight times and time differences, so I don't see him getting here this week. Hopefully he'll be here the middle of next. Definitely by the party. He has promised no more sudden trips – the next plane he gets on will bring him here. Or to Rome anyway. But no firm date yet.'

'Is this how marriage will be?' Luca asked. 'Seems a little lonely – for you anyway,' he added in a low tone his sister didn't appear to catch but Nora did. As she suspected he had intended.

'We don't need to live in each other's pockets. I have my work, my friends. It's not like I'll spend every evening sitting in missing him.' But Nora didn't sound convincing even to herself. It was as if the moment she had laid eyes on Gabe, she had been caught up in a whirlwind, one that left her with no time to think or breathe, just be. But now she was able to catch her breath, doubts were seeping in. Doubts about her own behaviour, the way she had manipulated their meeting, the way she enabled Gabe to take her acceptance for granted by never making her own feelings clear, whether it was a small decision like what she wanted to eat in a restaurant to bigger ones, such as leaving her here without him.

'Nora!' Chiara bustled in and gave Nora a double kiss, followed by a quick, warm hug. Nora didn't think she would ever take for granted the genuine and yet unassuming affection. She wanted to inhale it, imprint every sight, sound and scent, so she could replay it back in Hampstead whenever the house felt too big and lonely. 'Did you sleep well? Have you had enough breakfast? Are you looking forward to today?'

'*Si*, *si* and *si*.' Nora returned the embrace. 'Well, I'm not so sure about the cold gorge part, but Nicoletta assures me the swim is worth any pain.'

'Totally,' Nicoletta said with a grin. 'But you will yelp when you first get in. It's impossible not to.'

'Can't wait!'

Luca sat, leaning, arms folded, eyes hooded, forbidding and remote, although neither his mother nor sister seemed to sense his dangerous mood. Maybe that was because it was directed solely at Nora.

'I was just asking Nora if she expected Gabe to continue to be so flaky when they are married,' he said casually.

'Gabe's not flaky!' Nora said with more heat than she intended. 'The opposite. It's not as if he went to New York or Singapore on a whim, it's his job. It shows how very responsible he is actually.' Nora scowled at Luca, not caring who saw it. This new opening of hostilities was a good thing. If Luca carried on being this obnoxious, she needn't worry about any inappropriate feelings towards him.

'Flaky?' Chiara's forehead was crinkled in query.

'Unreliable,' Nora said curtly as Nicoletta said something quick in Italian.

'Luca!' Chiara gave her oldest son a quick look of displeasure. 'I am sure Nora is quite able to manage Gabe without your help.'

'If you say so.' Luca raised his coffee cup to Nora, eyes gleaming with dark amusement. 'All I was saying was that she has been here nearly a week and her *fiancé* has yet to make an appearance.'

'Nora is welcome here at any time, with or without Gabe. I very much want her to feel that the villa is home. In fact . . . Nicoletta, do you have time to spare Nora for a few minutes before you set off?'

'*Nessun problema.* Take as much time as you need.'

Nora was relieved to have an excuse to get away from Luca's narrow-eyed appraising gaze. Clearly, Monday's truce was over.

'Are you sure you don't need me today?' she asked as she followed Chiara up the staircase. 'I can hike another time. With Gabe,' she added almost defiantly. 'I'm sure he will be here soon.'

'No, no, go walk and see the island. Spend some time with Nicoletta, she has too little time to see her friends, I am glad she has you. And ignore Luca. He always has to play the big brother, he can't help it. He and Gabe have always had a typical brother relationship. They argue, both like to win, but underneath they care for each very much. Luca stays with Gabe whenever he is in London, makes sure Gabe remembers big family occasions, such as Nonna's birthday. He has always looked out for his siblings.'

'Oh please don't worry. Luca and I understand each other very well.'

Chiara sighed. 'He misses Gabe, we all do, which is why we were delighted when he said he would be here for two whole weeks. We don't often get him for more than a day or two. Maybe he is embarrassed by his home.'

'Not at all,' Nora said, a little uneasily remembering how little Gabe had told her about his family and their lives. 'He was really excited to bring me here. He told me I would love his home and I really do.' She did, the villa had a real charm, with its parquet floors which showed the wear and tear of generations of families, the wooden window frames, sanded and polished and repaired time after time, the weathered stone, the eclectic furniture, a mishmash of styles and ages, the pictures on the wall chosen for love, not value. This was a house built to house generations, each of whom left their mark on it and that, she knew, was priceless.

Besides, Chiara had exquisite taste and that permeated every corner of the villa. No room was cluttered, the villa felt airy and light despite the sometimes heavy, dark old furniture. Vases of fresh flowers were arranged in corners and on mantels, rugs and cushions were chosen to complement the house's history, not fight against it. It gave Nora ideas about how she could start to introduce her own taste into her own home without losing the memories every piece of furniture, every paint colour, every scrap of wallpaper held.

'That is very kind of you to say.' Chiara's beam belied her modest words, she was justly proud of her beautiful home. 'Anyway, what I want you to know is that we would love it if Gabe came home more often, but we know how hard it is for him to do so. But we want you to feel you can come here whenever you want without him. To be part of the family, Nora.'

Nora swallowed. 'I would really like that too.'

'So. This is Gabe's room now.' Chiara opened a door and ushered Nora into a large room, the walls painted white, decorated with framed posters of mountains and oceans and a large map pinned up over the neat desk. The bed was made up with white linen, a blue blanket neatly folded on the top.

'How lovely.' Nora wasn't sure what else to say. The room seemed sparse somehow, in contrast with the rest of the villa and with Gabe's own immaculate and luxurious flat.

Chiara laughed. 'It is empty, yes? Gabe took some of his things with him when he moved to England, the rest he boxed up. It does make the room feel empty, but he prefers it that way. I was going to redecorate, but then I thought that with your marriage, it might be time to move into a new space. A space as much yours as his, especially as we may see more of you than him. I thought about redecorating these for you. Come . . .'

Nora followed Chiara out of the room, pausing on the threshold to look back at the room, unease niggling at her. There was something cold, uncaring about the space, as if Gabe didn't mind where he slept when he was here, knowing he wouldn't be here long.

Chiara led the way down the landing and opened a door at the far end. It led into a corner room, with double-aspect windows overlooking the pool and lemon groves on one side and the vineyard on the other. The sun beamed in through the unshuttered windows, dancing on the polished wooden floor and bouncing off the white walls. It was empty apart from one enormous bed and a large antique chest of drawers. A door in the far wall led into a smaller room. Behind Nora, another ajar door showed an en suite. She turned slowly, taking it in – the cornicing, the shutters, the golden wood of the floors. 'What gorgeous light.'

'I thought you could choose furniture, pictures, lights, everything you need to make this your bedroom – yours and Gabe's – and we could make this other room a little sitting room and study, so that when you stayed, you had somewhere to work and to be private. I can't always guarantee that the barn will be empty . . .'

'Oh, Chiara, I love it. I would love that.' Nora turned to survey the room once again. She could visualise it perfectly: a reading chair in that corner, a table with one of Chiara's gorgeous flower arrangements next to it there. She crossed to the open door and looked into the smaller room. She would put a sofa by the far wall, heaped with cushions, maybe a desk under the window, the perfect place to work . . . The only thing she *couldn't* quite visualise was Gabe agreeing to the simple colours and furniture which would best complement this space. But, then again, Chiara was probably right. The truth was, if Nora really wanted to spend proper quality time with Gabe's family, in all likelihood she would mostly do so alone.

'Maybe we could spend some time choosing colours and things together?' Chiara sounded uncharacteristically nervous as she watched Nora pace around the room, taking it all in.

'I can't think of anything I would like more.' She wanted these rooms to be hers, to be a real part of this family. Nora turned towards Chiara and impulsively seized her hands. 'Well, maybe there is one more thing. I need to talk to Gabe, of course, but I can't imagine anything nicer than getting married here at the vineyard. Do you think that would be possible?'

No more doubts. Gabe *was* flaky and could be a little self-centred at times, and could definitely be a better son and brother, but at the same time, he was fascinating and gorgeous and exciting and generous and he loved her. He wanted to *marry* her. And his wonderful, warm, loving family also wanted her, wanted to give her a room – or two – of her own and to make their home her home. How could she walk away from that? It was all she had ever wanted.

Chiara beamed. 'Oh, Nora, that would be wonderful. I would love that. Do you think Gabe will want to marry here too?'

Nora wasn't sure at all, but she knew without a shadow of a doubt that it was what she wanted. Gabe would understand that, wouldn't he?

'This is his home. I am sure he will, but of course we should check with him before making concrete plans.'

'This is the best news.' Chiara pulled her in for another warm hug. 'I am so glad that Gabe had the sense to choose you, Nora. It was a good day for all of us that he was there just when you needed him and that you found each other again. Fate knew what she was doing when she threw you together.'

Nora hugged her back. This was all she had ever wanted, a place where she belonged, people that were hers. It didn't matter how she had got here; she was where she was meant to be and that was all that mattered.

Hampsted, 17 July 2000

Dear Erik,

I haven't written to you for a while, I'm sorry about that. Not that I ever actually send these postcards, but still. I like to think that somehow you receive them, that you read them and smile as I tell you about how Nora is growing and her first ballet class and how she insists on wearing her wellies everywhere no matter what the weather. Maybe I just hope that I will be able to hand them over to you one day and you will know that you were with us the whole time, in our hearts at least.

I tell Nora all the time about her daddy, about the ice cream and how we talked and talked and never ran out of subjects. How you brought a building or landscape alive with just a few words. How you smiled with your eyes. How you made me laugh so hard I couldn't stop. I don't tell her how you kissed me like I was the only woman in the world. How you touched me and I fell apart. How we fit like we were made for each other. No one needs to know that about their parents — and she is only four! But I know. I remember . . . Do you?

I graduated last year (do you like the photo? Nora insisted on wearing my cap!) and have spent this year doing my law course. Next up is a training contract. Not international law after all, instead I have chosen probate and family law. I might not change the world, but I can make difficult times easier for some families. That counts a little. Doesn't it?

Are you designing beautiful buildings yet? Do you think you might design one in Hampstead, so that I will turn a corner and you'll be there? Do miracles happen twice?

Charlotte xxx

# Chapter Twelve

'Nicoletta! Luca! Such wonderful news . . .' Chiara practically skipped down the stairs before breaking into a jog and skidding into the kitchen, where the siblings were filling water bottles and sounded like they were bickering amicably.

'George Clooney has decided Lake Como is dull and is buying the vineyard next door?' Nicoletta suggested.

'Calcia Catania phoned and need me to step in as striker for their next match against Palermo?'

Nicoletta rolled her eyes. 'You wish.'

'I wish? *George Clooney?* He's old enough to be your father.'

'Maybe, but you know what, nine out of ten women aged between nineteen and ninety would pick George over you, isn't that right, Nora?'

'I . . . well, they don't call him gorgeous George for nothing.' But Nora was aware her voice lacked conviction and she could feel her face heat. Obviously, Mr Clooney had an appeal that transcended age, but it wasn't him she had seen half undressed the other day, it wasn't his dark eyes and sculpted body that had disturbed her sleep over the last few nights. But that had to stop, Luca was going to be her brother-in-law after all.

'Nora isn't interested in film stars,' Chiara said, beaming. 'She only has eyes for Gabe. And she is going to marry him here. At the vineyard.'

'If Gabe agrees,' she protested a little weakly, but her words were drowned out by Nicoletta's screech of joy.

'This is so exciting. Let me check the diary and see when we are free. We get really booked up, but you don't mind out of season, do you?'

'No, but I need to check in with Gabe,' she tried again, but Nicoletta and her mother were talking over her.

'September is beautiful.'

'But we have no free weeks in September for the next three years!'

'Three years seems about right.' Luca leant back against the kitchen wall, arms folded. 'A long engagement to give the bride and groom time to get to know each other.'

Nora glared at him. 'We know each other just fine, thank you.'

'Really?' Had he just raised *one eyebrow* at her? Who did he think he was? Mr Darcy? Who was the Italian Mr Darcy? Casanova? No, that wasn't right. 'Tell me his favourite football team.'

Aha, she knew that. 'The national team. *Sicilian* national team,' she clarified, folding her own arms as she squared up to her interrogator.

'Favourite music?'

'He prefers classical and opera but does like jazz.' Unfortunately. Opera and classical she could manage, although she was more pop and urban herself, but jazz made her want to stick her fingers in her ears.

'Favourite film?'

'I . . .' What was his favourite film? They had only had a couple of film nights so far and he had chosen something obscure and arty but, in the end, paid it little attention, spending most of the time on his phone. But before she could reply, Nicoletta elbowed Luca in the ribs.

'*Star zitto*, leave poor Nora alone.'

'*Wolf of Wolf Street!*' she said triumphantly. It had to be. New York, money, excess. By Luca's glare, she knew she was right.

'Sport?'

'To watch or to do?' she countered. This verbal sparring was turning out to be fun, especially as she was winning.

'Luca! Enough,' Chiara commanded. 'Nora, you don't have to humour him. So, we have found a week free in the middle of October!'

'October?' When she had suggested marrying at the vineyard, she had been thinking next year some time at the earliest. October was just four months away and she would have known Gabe less than six months. Would agreeing be ridiculously impulsive?

Luca shifted, still watching her closely with narrowed eyes, and she tilted her chin. Why wait? If it was right, it was right! 'October will be perfect. An autumnal wedding, how gorgeous.'

'A family wedding during the grape harvest?' Luca pointed out. 'I can't imagine Papà agreeing to that.'

Not for the first time, Nora realised how ignorant she was of the rhythms and traditions of this family. 'Oh, I hadn't realised. Maybe we should wait . . .'

'The vineyard is open for business during harvest. The restaurant serves, the cottages are let and we hold events,' Nicoletta said. 'And this is at the end of harvest. All will be well, Nora. It will give us even more to celebrate this year.'

'This is wonderful!' Chiara clapped her hands together. 'Nora, you can say no, but it would be a great honour to take you shopping for a dress.' Her smile dimmed. 'I'm sorry your mother isn't here to do it, and of course you might find something better in London, but . . .'

'I would love to,' Nora blinked hard. The thought of embarking on wedding planning and shopping without her mother was painful, but she knew that having Chiara there would lessen the blow and that the offer had been made with love. She turned to Nicoletta. 'And it would mean a lot if you and Violetta join us. If you want to, I mean . . .'

'I would love to, and I know Vi would too. Thank you, Nora.' Nicoletta hugged her.

'Touching as this is, don't we have hiking to do? It would be good to get started before the temperature hits boiling.' Luca grabbed his bag and water bottle and headed for the door in a way that meant business.

'*Si, si*, go. Oh, Nora, you make me very happy.' Chiara kissed her on both cheeks. 'I will make appointments at all the best shops. We will have the most wonderful day. And I was wondering . . .'

'Walk?' Luca repeated.

'Luca!' Nicoletta stared at him. 'What is *with* you?'

'I just want to get going.'

Nora wasn't sure she was hiding her smirk very well. There was something almost endearing about Luca being scolded by his family. No, not endearing! Satisfying!

'I was thinking that we should celebrate your engagement. All the family will be here for Nonna's birthday, we could hold a party then,' Chiara said.

'Oh, no,' Nora protested. 'It's Nonna's day, We couldn't, I couldn't . . .'

'She wouldn't mind. In fact, she suggested it. You could invite your friends for the weekend. A double celebration.'

'If she really doesn't mind, then that does sound lovely.' A party to welcome her into the family. What could be nicer? Especially if her friends could make it. This would be the perfect opportunity for them to finally meet not just Gabe but his family too, to see how happy Nora truly was.

'Lovely,' Luca echoed, but his tone made it clear he thought it was anything but.

Luca maintained his disapproving glower as they drove towards the Alcantara Valley and the car park that signified the start of their walk, but, to Nora's secret amusement, Nicoletta talked so much, it was barely noticeable.

'When I married Carlo, I was determined to be different, you know? Wear something short, maybe not even white. I am a modern woman. I was keeping my surname. But Mamma wanted me to try on more traditional dresses and so I went to several different shops to please her, and every dress just confirmed my decision. But then I tried on this dress, it was close-fitting silk with this little train, the most delicate sleeves, and I fell in love with it, almost as much as I loved Carlo . . . Violetta and Carlo's sisters wore silk too, a pale yellow because it was early spring. Nora, please don't feel you need to have Violetta as a bridesmaid, but I am sure she will try to convince you that you should.'

'I would love you both to be bridesmaids. Along with my friends of course,' Nora promised a little recklessly, but she meant it. She had always dreamt of a big family wedding and that dream was about to come true.

Hopefully Gabe was going to be happy with all her decisions. The vineyard and the imminent date. The fact that the wedding was no longer a hypothetical but a reality. It was a lot. Had she overstepped? This was his family, after all, and there were dynamics at play she was only just beginning to understand. But surely one of the positives of being on the outside was not being bound by pride and history?

Luckily, the walk was just gruelling enough to stop Nora dwelling on what she had just agreed to; breathtaking scenery across to Mount Etna and the mountains and down into the gorge making the hike worthwhile. It wasn't too far, just three or four miles, but with enough up and down in blazing sunshine to add some serious cardio to the walk. Nora was hot and sweaty by the time they reached their destination, her hair sticking to the nape of her neck, grateful for the baseball cap shading her face and that she had lathered herself in suntan lotion. It was pretty busy, with several organised walks passing them, and Nicoletta told her that it would only get busier as they headed into the full summer.

'This was once a locals-only spot,' she said a little wistfully. 'Now it's on all the must-see lists and there is a café and a water park for kids. All of which is great, but I kind of preferred it when it was more simple.'

'It feels wild enough to me.' Nora couldn't believe the incredible rock formations. 'So many beautiful birds and butterflies, as well as the water. Where do we swim?' She looked down the steep gorge at the water below.

Nicoletta pointed at the stone stairs leading down the deep, tree-lined gorge to a pebble beach, where a group in wetsuits were congregated. 'We take those steps. There are lifts you can pay for, but we never do.'

'Down there? Where do we change?'

'What were you expecting?' Luca sounded unnecessarily supercilious. 'A spa area?'

'No,' she protested. 'I wild swim a lot. Only at Hampstead, there are changing rooms.'

'And here you find a sheltered spot. Part of the fun!' Nicoletta was peeling off her top as she spoke, but she was wearing her bikini underneath. 'Oh, I brought you some water shoes. It gets painful underfoot.'

'Thank you. Sheltered spot. Right.'

'Just look out for scorpions.'

'Scorpions? Got it.' She had no idea whether Luca was joking or not, but if he was hoping for a hysterical reaction, he had chosen the wrong girl. Unless she actually saw one that was.

Gingerly, Nora picked her way through the trees until she found a place where she had a) space to change, b) was reasonably sure she wouldn't be overlooked, and c) wouldn't get stabbed by twigs. It also looked mercifully scorpion-free.

Changing wasn't easy. Her clothes clung to her sweaty body and she was trying to perform a modesty dance, not letting any more of her body be on show at any one time than necessary, just in case she had miscalculated the privacy element of her changing plot.

When had she got so timid? When she, Grace and Ana used to jump on a train to Brighton, she would change under a towel without a care. Conversations with her mother about the travels they would one day embark on would include dreams of wild swims in lakes and streams and seas. Now here she was in a popular swimming spot more Charlotte Bartlett than Lucy Honeychurch.

The thought made her giggle to herself and Nora felt much more confident as she stepped out, clothes in her backpack and the water shoes Nicoletta had given her in her hand. For a moment, she wished she had packed – that she owned – a bikini as gorgeous as Nicoletta's vivid green affair, rather than her sensible Lido-ready one piece, but all comparison was forgotten as Luca joined her.

'I thought you might appreciate being shown the way,' he said.

'Oh. Yes.' It was a struggle to get even two words out of her drying mouth. If Luca Catalano looked mouthwatering changing his shirt, he was practically ambrosial in nothing but a pair of low-slung shorts. Broad shoulders, muscled arms, really *really* capable-looking hands. Nora swallowed. She wasn't sure she had even noticed a man's hands before, not even Gabe's, but now she was somehow fixated on Luca's. But that was good because fixating on his hands meant she wasn't staring helplessly at the chest she had had such intriguing glimpses of the other day, nor the six-packing stomach overlaid with a narrow smattering of hair leading down and under those really rather indecent now that she was thinking about it (and she really shouldn't be, but God help her she had no idea how not to) shorts. Long, muscled legs completed a package she had no right to be noticing, let alone being hyper aware of, let alone overheating her until she had no idea what was sun and what was her own body.

What was *wrong* with her? Nora had never experienced such a visceral reaction to another human being before. It was wrong on every level. She was objectifying him! Worse, she was engaged to another man. Worse he was about to become her family. Whatever way she looked at it, she was in trouble.

Luckily, Luca didn't expect or make conversation as he led the way down the staircase to the small pebble beach. Nicoletta was waiting for them, her hair scooped up in a large knot.

'This bit is always the worst.' Nicoletta grimaced as she walked to the water's edge. 'It would be easier if you could just jump and get it over with.'

'Don't be a coward, show Nora how it's done,' her brother responded unsympathetically.

'Is it really that cold?' How could it be properly cold? With the volcano and the hot springs that created the natural spa at the vineyard, Nora had rather thought that 'icy' was a euphemism for 'not as warm as other natural water'.

'Try it and see,' Nicoletta invited.

Nora walked cautiously to the edge of the beach and extended a toe, only to jump back as she encountered water more akin to the Antarctic than a volcanic Mediterranean island.

'It's fast moving in the middle,' Nicoletta warned her. 'Be careful if you are going to do more than paddle.'

'Like this . . .' Luca winked at his sister and headed in, waded, teeth gritted until he was deep enough to dive under, emerging spluttering, pushing his hair off his forehead. He looked even more magnificent, water droplets shimmering on his dark olive skin, like some kind of god waiting to seduce innocent naiads.

Now Nora was even hotter. Maybe an icy river was exactly what she needed to get her temperature down.

'Every time,' he said, laughing. 'Every time I forget just what a shock this is.'

'OK.' Nicoletta looked determined. Like her brother, she headed straight in, wading out until she could swim. *Cavolo, fa freddo.*

'Swim,' Luca told her. 'It's the only way to warm up.'

'Come on, Nora,' Nicoletta said as she began a splashy crawl. 'Once you get used to it, it's . . . well, not lovely but bearable.'

Nora knew two things. One, she needed to cool down, and two, she was not going to be a coward in front of Luca Catalano, so, with a muttered curse and a prayer, she took a deep breath and launched herself forward.

She had been expecting cold, but this went beyond mere chill, it was icy, pure and fresh and painful and yet strangely exhilarating. The first shock made her catch her breath, but once she started moving, she could feel her blood pumping, her whole body awakening. She was alive in a way she hadn't been for longer than she could remember and she shouted out loud, a wordless expression of happiness and surprise.

It was all too short a swim, the temperature making it unwise to stay in too long, and far too quickly for Nora's liking they were back on the pebbles, drying off on towels, sharing the snacks they had brought. No one spoke much, all three content to lie in the sun. Nora choosing a spot as far from Luca as possible, her body a heady mix of hot and cold. After a while, she managed to get the energy to grab her suncream and started the serious business of reapplying it to her now dried skin, pushing her braid under her baseball cap to reach her neck and shoulders. But contort as she might, the vee made by her swimsuit was unreachable.

'Shall I?' Nicoletta offered, but as Nora gratefully accepted, the other woman's phone rang. 'It's Carlo. Apologies, Nora, I will not be long.'

'I'll do it.'

Nora jumped. The last thing she needed or wanted was suntan lotion rubbing in by Luca. 'Oh no, I am sure Nicoletta won't be long.'

'You're already turning red,' he pointed out, that annoying eyebrow raised.

'But . . .' *But this is too intimate. But I am already bizarrely, unhappily attracted to you and I need to make it stop.* But, of course, she couldn't say that out loud and she couldn't say no without seeming churlish and, really, it was just a little suntan cream on her back, she wasn't asking him to give her a tantric massage. And now she was definitely red all over.

'Thank you.'

Nora gritted her teeth as Luca took the bottle and moved around to her back. The cream was cold and made her jump, but his fingers were strong and sure, rubbing the cream in with efficient strokes. There was nothing about his approach to suggest Luca approached the job with anything but businesslike straightforwardness, but Nora was achingly aware of his every touch, the feel of his fingertips on her skin, the way he moved her strap aside to make sure every centimetre was protected.

'Thank you,' she managed as he finally sat back.

It took him a moment to reply and when he did, his voice was husky.

'*Prego.*'

Nora couldn't turn to look at him, she was frozen in position, her back still tingling, hyperaware of his proximity, it was as if the two of them were caught in a spell, until Nicoletta broke it, returning to the clearing, her usually sunny smile missing.

'What's wrong?' Luca asked.

'Oh, nothing. It's just Carlo's parents need to get back to the city so can't babysit after all. Carlo and I so rarely get an evening together, I'm stupidly more upset than I need to be.'

'Can't Mamma help?'

'She would, but tonight she and Papà have those theatre tickets and I am not going to ask her to give that up. She deserves a night off.'

'I'm sure Papà wouldn't mind.'

'Oh, I know *he* wouldn't, but she's been looking forward to it, even if he isn't.' The two siblings grinned at each other.

'Violetta?' Luca suggested.

'Covering for me in the restaurant. No, it's fine. We will make a nice meal at home instead.'

'I could babysit,' Nora offered.

Hope flashed across Nicoletta's face but faded as she shook her head. 'That's so kind, but the children don't speak English. Well, baby doesn't speak anything at all, but if Gianni wakes up and he can't understand you . . .'

'I could babysit with her.'

'You?' Nicoletta stared at her brother, shock on her face. '*Babysit?*'

'I'm sure I'll be fine . . .' Nora said quickly.

'Why not me?' Luca said. 'I speak pretty good Italian . . .'

'Ha ha,' his sister retorted. 'When have you ever changed a nappy?'

'Has Nora?'

'Plenty.' She flashed Luca a triumphant grin. 'I was the Hampstead babysitter of choice between fifteen and nineteen.'

Luca shrugged. 'There you go. The boys know me and Nora can work out nappies. We'll be fine.'

Nora didn't like that *we* at all. But before she could suggest that nappies were not exactly tricky and maybe this was the perfect time for some uncle-nephew bonding and she should just leave them to it, Nicoletta smiled gratefully.

'They shouldn't wake, but I would feel better if both of you are there if one did, or God forbid both,' she said. 'I'd postpone, but we've been invited to the opening of a new restaurant in Catania and Carlo is really keen to go and try it out. And I am keen to spend time with my husband when I am also not looking after a restaurant or children. Thank you both.'

Nora smiled weakly. What could she do but say 'you're welcome'? But just because she was going to spend the evening with Luca Catalano didn't mean she was going to let her guard down. Not at all. In fact, the best thing to do would be to pretend he wasn't there at all.

Hampstead, 1 September 2004

Dear Erik,

We've had the loveliest summer, two weeks on the Brittany coast with Mum and Dad, picnics on the Heath, a few days at the coast. I can't believe autumn is on its way and another school year is about to start. Nora is heading into Year 4. Isn't that the most ridiculous thing you ever heard?

She's small for her age and just looks so tiny, especially walking into the playground with Felix and Ana, who are both twice her size! She has brains though, our girl. Loves school, loves play and still, thank goodness, loves her Lego and dolls and isn't growing up too quickly. If I could freeze time right now, I think I would — but I say that every year!

So. I have news. I have met someone. Traditionally, no ice cream fails or moonlit walks involved, but then they do say lightning doesn't strike twice, don't they? He's a friend of a friend, they set us up and we have been decorously dating for some time. He's nice. I like him. He's not you, but then you are not here and you never will be, I do know that now. Know that it's time I moved on.

166

Have you met someone too? I want you to be happy, but oh I wish you were here to wave our girl off at the school gates with me.

Charlotte xxx

# *Chapter Thirteen*

Nicoletta and Carlo lived in a charming, converted cottage at the far end of the Catalano estate. Nora arrived promptly at half six as agreed – right at the same moment as Luca.

On reflection, she had decided that completely ignoring him would make her look slightly unhinged, so instead she was going to go for passive. Make no conversation, reply in mono-syllables and absolutely, definitely, no inappropriate ogling.

She'd dressed for the part, in her plainest skirt paired with a plain T-shirt, no make-up and her hair tied up in a knot. Somehow, Luca still managed to make her feel wrong-footed as he gave her an unsubtle once-over.

'You came?'

That was a promising start. 'I said I would.'

Nora did her best not to give Luca enough attention to be aware of him, but it was hard not to, he pressed on her consciousness, his hair a little softer, untamed, falling over his brow, yet another white linen shirt, unnervingly like the one he had pulled on back at his apartment, jeans that clung, in all the right – *no*, wrong, she reminded herself – places.

She touched her phone reassuringly. Once she was in the house, she would send a long loving message to Gabe. Her kind of fiancé. Her hero. The man she loved and who loved her. The man who didn't look at her as if he couldn't decide if she was dangerous, amusing, irrelevant or all three.

'So, are you going to knock on the door?'

Nora debated telling *him* to knock but caught herself in time. Polite but don't engage. Certainly, don't rise to him.

'I was just about to.' She paused. 'You know, I can manage by myself. I am sure you have many better things to do.'

'Better than spend quality time with my nephews?'

'Your sleeping nephews.'

'But you need a translator,' he reminded her sweetly. 'Honestly, Nora, you make it sound like you don't want to spend time with me.'

'What on earth gave you that idea?' Her smile was saccharine as she knocked on the door. It was going to be a long evening.

A couple of minutes later, she was ensconced in the high-ceilinged open-plan kitchen diner. Food had been left ready for them, an array of antipasti laid out on the kitchen island, a saucepan full of a delicious-smelling pasta puttanesca on the stove and a mouthwatering-looking lemon cake cooling on the side.

'I've opened a bottle of red to air, and there is some white in the fridge,' Nicoletta said as she fastened in an earring. She looked stunning in a green dress, hair up in an elaborate knot.

'Oh, no, not while I am babysitting,' Nora protested.

'I would be amazed if they woke up. Besides, I trust you not to finish the bottle.'

That was kind of Nicoletta, but while Nora was feeling so unnerved, she didn't trust herself.

'So, baby monitor here. There are nappies on the changing table in baby's room. If Gianni wakes up, he just needs a cuddle and his dinosaur.'

'*Si, si,* you told us in one of your twenty messages.' Luca picked up a piece of cheese. 'This looks delicious. Now go and have a wonderful time. Report back.'

'Oh, we will. Modern twist on the classics indeed, as if Carlo hasn't been doing that for years.'

'Are they going on a date or a reconnaissance mission?' Nora asked as the couple finally left. Damn it. So much for dignified monosyllables. Turned out she wasn't comfortable with a loaded silence after all, even a ten-second one.

'Both.' Luca nodded at the feast that had been left for them. 'Hungry?'

'Not just yet.'

'Sure I can't get you a glass?'

'Maybe later.'

Now what? She almost hoped one of the children did wake up. That would give her a purpose beyond awkward conversation.

Nora delicately placed a few nibbles on a plate and poured herself some lemonade before heading into the sitting room and taking a prim seat in a small armchair in the far corner, pulling out her phone. She still hadn't told Gabe that she had suggested they marry at the vineyard, that they marry this year, or about the engagement party his mother wanted to throw. Anxiety twisted her stomach. She had no idea how he would react, especially as they weren't *really* engaged, no matter his assurances. It was an unwelcome reminder how little she really knew about the man she intended to spend her life with.

'How's Gabe?'

How on earth did Luca seem to read her mind like this? 'Fine.'

'Excited about a vineyard wedding? I'm surprised, you *have* changed him, Nora. A black-tie wedding is more his style. Reception in an art gallery somewhere. When I was in London a few weeks ago . . .' He paused and his gaze flickered away from her, an unreadable expression crossing his face.

Nora had an idea why. 'When he told you he wanted to get back with Lily?' She wasn't the kind of person who was insecure about exes. Gabe was with her now, he had made his choice.

Although he and Lily did have a lot in common. From what Nora had gathered, the other woman was cultured, effortlessly cool and stylish. And she seemed to have had Gabe where she wanted him. There was no way Gabe would have got away with leaving *her* in a strange airport.

'We spent three days talking about it. About how and why it ended, his time alone, the changes he wanted to make. It was unlike Gabe to be so . . . open. Introspective even. That's how I knew he was serious. But obviously things have changed.'

'Yes, they have.' She had manipulated a meeting and changed things. Not for the first time, Nora felt a creeping doubt. For her actions, for the outcome. But, no, she had just gone for a coffee. In fact, she had left the second she had seen him. He had come after her, recognised her, asked her out. 'And there are two of us getting married, remember? It has to suit us both.'

'And you are not a black tie, art gallery type?'

'I didn't say that. Sometimes.' Never, unless she was with Gabe.

'How about mountain biking? Rock climbing? Yacht racing?' She mutely shook her head at each suggestion. 'No? What *do* you and my brother have in common?'

'I think it's healthier when people remain true to themselves,' Nora snapped.

Luca looked at her consideringly for a long moment before leaning back on the sofa he had sprawled all over and picked up the remote control. 'Shall we watch a film?'

'A film?' Nora felt thrown by the abrupt change in subject.

'You're not hungry, you don't want a drink and you don't seem interested in conversation. We could sit here in awkward silence for four hours or . . .'

'Fine. Yes. A film.' She sounded like a spoilt brat and tried to smile. 'That would be nice.'

'Progress. So, what do you want to watch?'

'You choose.'

'Oh no, Nora.' His voice was silkily soft. '*You* decide.'

What was this? Some kind of psychological test? Was he going to make some deduction about her character from the film she chose? That was it, she was going to choose the most intellectual, unintelligible, art house film she could find. One at least three hours long and preferably in black and white.

'Will I be able to find one in English?' she asked as she took the remote he handed her and perched gingerly at the other end of the sofa as far from him as she could get.

'*Si*, on this service they are subtitled rather than dubbed, so as long as you don't choose a French film, you should be OK.'

'Got it.'

Nora had no idea if Luca was purposefully making her feel like he was scrutinising every film and pre-judging her whenever she lingered on one, but it certainly felt that way. She doubled down on her decision to go long and boring when . . .

'Oh! *Sleepless in Seattle!*'

'Great. Fine. Finally.' Then, suspiciously: 'What is it?'

'What is it? Only the greatest romantic comedy ever made.'

'Not that one in Rome with the princess and every Italian cliché possible?' He sounded horrified.

'First of all, *Roman Holiday* is a classic. Secondly, is it a romcom when there is no happy ever after? Thirdly, the fact it's got Seattle in the title should be a clue it's not set in Italy. Actually, to be accurate, this is the greatest romcom of the *second* great era of romcoms.'

'The *what*?'

Nora snuggled into her corner. This was her *Mastermind* subject. 'My mother had a theory. She said that there was the first great era of romcoms, the Cary Grant and Audrey Hepburn-type years – you know, *Bringing up Baby* and *His Girl Friday*, those kinds of films.'

Luca didn't look like he knew what she was talking about, but he *did l*ook interested, not slightly bored like Gabe might have.

No, that wasn't fair. She really needed to stop thinking such negative things about Gabe. He just wasn't good at faking interest in things that didn't interest him. He was refreshingly honest that way.

She could hear Ana scoff as clearly as if she were really there. *Refreshingly honest or rude?*

'And the second era?'

'Late eighties and early nineties. Female-centred and witty character-driven films written by people like the great Nora Ephron.'

No man's smile should be allowed to be so charming. 'I assume the similarity in names is no coincidence.'

'Not at all.' Yet over the last few years, Nora had not lived up to her clever, fearless namesake. She'd allowed her tragedies to make her small, quiet, acquiescent. Funny how it took time away from your life to see that. 'My mother wanted to name me after someone she admired. A groundbreaking, fearless woman. In the end, she narrowed it down to Nora or Madonna.'

'She chose wisely. Are we still in this great era?'

'Sadly not. By the late nineties, romcoms had evolved into male-character-led gross-out comedies where the female lead was there to be a foil for the male and objectified, all the wit and subtlety and beauty replaced by slapstick and generic storylines.' Nora realised that during the conversation she had physically unwound, no longer huddling into her corner but taking up more space, closer to Luca and yet not uncomfortable, not exactly. Just suddenly aware of his proximity.

'And this film is an example of this perfect era?'

'It's the gold standard – and written by Nora herself.'

'OK.'

'OK what?'

'Let's give it a go.'

'Oh, no, I didn't mean for now . . .'

'You *don't* want to watch your favourite film?' Luca sounded confused.

'Oh, I always want to watch it, but I don't expect you to. We could find something we both want to watch.'

'Why wouldn't I want to watch the genre-defining film of the second great era of Romcoms?' He was definitely being ironic, but his half-smile took the edge off his tone, there was truth in the sarcasm. 'But I do want some pasta and a little more of this wine. Are you sure you don't want anything?'

Nora wasn't sure of anything except that a glass of wine would help after all. And maybe some pasta.

The pasta and wine were both excellent and she settled down as the familiar credits rolled, the old-time music comforting as the film opened with unspeakable grief before the tone lightened and Meg Ryan headed home for Christmas. To her horror, Nora found she watched Luca as much as she watched the film, alert for signs of boredom, but, to her relief, he was soon engrossed, laughing gently at times, a low, deep rumble that reverberated through her, at others quiet and attentive, especially during the sadder moments.

All too soon, Meg Ryan picked up a lost teddy bear and headed towards the lifts at the top of the Empire State Building.

The last scene played out and Luca gave a contented sigh as he leant back.

'That was tense, I thought they would miss each other.'

'Every time I hold my breath just in case,' Nora confessed.

'Have you seen the other film, the one they talk about all the way through?'

'An *Affair to Remember*? Oh, yes, of course. Not as many times as *Sleepless*, but plenty. My grandmother really loved Cary Grant and it was one of her favourites. Sometimes on a Sunday afternoon we would all watch it together, Grandpa pretending to hide behind his paper but as into it as the rest of us.' Nora smiled at the memory. It didn't sting the way it used to.

'It was just you and your mother, right?'

'Me, my mother and my grandparents,' Nora corrected him. 'We lived with them my whole childhood. I was really lucky. It was idyllic really.'

'What was she like, your mother?'

Nora glanced at Luca a little warily, but he seemed really interested, not looking for ways to discredit her. She stared down into her barely touched glass of red wine and tried to find the right words.

'Romantic, fearless, fun. My best friend in many ways. Being a teenage single mum wasn't her plan, but when it happened, she just ran with it. It didn't stop her doing anything. She went to university, she qualified as a solicitor, although she ended up in family law, not a barrister battling for human rights as she had planned. But she said she wanted

to be home for dinner and bath time and she always was.'
Nora tried to smile, but her throat was too tight.

'Your grandparents looked after you as well?'

She nodded. 'I was so lucky. My grandmother had always wanted a big family, but it didn't happen for her, so when I came along, she was just happy to have a baby in the house. She and my grandfather loved me and supported my mother. It wasn't the most conventional set-up, I suppose, certainly not in the UK, but families come in all shapes and sizes. And then, of course, as they got older and things became a little harder for them, we were right there. It's just . . . things got harder too fast.' She stopped, swallowed. 'They were so healthy and young-seeming all through my childhood, I thought they would live until they were a hundred, but in the end neither saw eighty. Then it was just me and Mum and then, well, just me.' It would never stop hurting and she wasn't sure she ever wanted it to, that sharp jab a reminder of love as much as loss.

'Your mother never met anyone else? Never thought about another relationship?'

'She dated, had a couple of relationships, but she took care to keep that side of her life private; she always said my stability was the most important thing. She was with someone for a few years, who proposed when I was ten, and I think she seriously considered it, weighed up what it would be like to maybe have more children for instance, but she said although he was very nice and she liked him, she couldn't imagine sitting up all night in the corner of a piazza sharing her dreams with him and that was her gold standard. She'd rather be on her own then settle. She said she knew what perfect was, even briefly, and she didn't want anything less.'

'And is that your philosophy too?'

'Absolutely.' There had been very little perfect in her recent dating life, too much compromising. Which was why she had given up dating only for the fates to deliver her not only Gabe, but his warm, loving family.

'And you never regretted she didn't marry, give you brothers and sisters?'

'Sometimes.' Especially now she was so alone. 'But I loved my grandparents, I couldn't imagine not living with them. And I had Felix and Ana close by, we knew each other from playgroup, Grace too when we went to secondary school. I spent my childhood running in and out of their houses; they are my family still. And there was next door, there were four of them and I was always welcome until . . .'

'Until what?'

'Until they moved.' She sensed that Luca knew that wasn't what she had been planning to say and carried on quickly, 'It wasn't conventional maybe, but it was idyllic. I was loved, I lived in a beautiful house in a beautiful area. Until I was eighteen, life was perfect. And it will be again.'

Luca didn't say anything for a while and when he did speak, she got the impression he had discarded the question he had wanted to ask. 'And you never found your father?'

'No. There wasn't any social media back when Mum met him, and although she asked around in some old backpacker groups later on, she didn't have any luck. I've tried of course. I've done as much googling as I can with a one-name clue, run her old photos through face recognition software, scoured alumni lists for universities in Sweden, architect lists, but nothing came of any of it. Of course, in the end he might not have become an architect at all, or not returned to Sweden. Maybe he is still in Florence, hoping that my mother will walk back into that ice cream shop. Or, more likely, he has forgotten all about her and is married with five children. I hope he is. I hope he's happy.'

'You have a photo of him?'

'I do.' Nora grabbed her bag and took out the small wallet she took everywhere. It didn't contain cards or cash but photos: her grandparents on their fiftieth wedding anniversary, her mother on her twenty-first birthday, a fat beaming toddler Nora on her knee. A photo of her friends on the heath building a snowman. And copies of two of the precious photos which proved Nora did have a father. She handed them over to Luca. 'He's handsome, don't you think? And look at the way he's staring at Mum. I think he was as besotted as she was, don't you agree? I look like Mum, everyone says, but she always said I had his chin and his dimple – see in that one where he is smiling?'

Luca was frowning as he squinted at the photo. 'I know this café,' he said slowly. 'Have you ever been to Florence?'

'No, Mum and I were going to do a grand tour after my A levels, but I think I told you that that was when things started to unravel and so it never happened.' Unravel. An innocuous word for the disintegration of a family for five sad defining years. 'But it's not as if I could go to that café and find out if they remembered him after all this time, is it?'

Luca shrugged. 'Why not?' he asked. 'What have you got to lose?'

Nora stared at him. 'I don't know. I just never thought of actually *going* there.' Which was ridiculous, she was supposed to be a professional at tracking people down. But then again, she had barely managed to travel for work the last few years, the thought of a solo trip abroad had been overwhelming. 'I mean, talk about a long shot. Wouldn't it make as much sense to go to Stockholm and ask every man of around fifty if they were my father?'

Luca laughed. 'That could be plan B.'

'Always good to have a plan B.' She stared at the frozen TV screen, the credits paused mid-roll. 'You know, Florence has taken on ridiculously mythic proportions to me. It's my Seattle, or top of the Empire State Building. It's where my mother's life changed, just like Lucy Honeychurch. I've always wanted to go, but at the same time my expectations are ludicrously high. I feel nervous, like being there would change everything forever. Is that silly?'

'Not at all. It's understandable.' Luca paused. 'Look, I am heading to Florence on Saturday. I'm actually going into Chianti to see a wine producer there but staying with a friend in Florence. You would be welcome to come with me.'

'Saturday? That's just two days' time.'

'Of course, I understand if you would rather wait for Gabe to go with you.'

Nora started. She had barely thought about Gabe over the last couple of hours. Guilt overwhelmed her. 'It's not that. If I wait for Gabe, I'll be fifty myself before I get there and probably end up going alone anyway.' She meant to sound teasing in a proprietary, mock eye-rolling *you know Gabe* way, but to her horror she just sounded a little sad. 'I just wanted more time to prepare myself. But that's silly, isn't it? If not now, when?'

'I fly out Saturday morning and return Sunday evening. The offer is open, but I understand if you want to stay here in case Gabe arrives while we are gone . . .'

Nora picked up her wine. 'We both know he won't. Look, are you sure? You're on a business trip, do you really want me tagging along?' And did she really want to tag along beside Luca? The attraction was one thing, the sparring between them another, but spending nearly forty-eight hours with him away from his family, in the city of her dreams felt dangerous and attractive in ways she couldn't, didn't want to, define.

'Not at all. Saturday afternoon is business, and you are more than welcome to come along or do your own thing. Sunday I had left free to do some tours of a few smaller vineyards before flying back late, but I can do that any time. Happy to be at your disposal.'

'Well, in that case, how can I say no?' And she didn't *want* to say no, Nora realised. Going to Florence with Luca might not be the most sensible decision she had ever made, but it felt right. 'Thank you, Luca. I would love to come.'

Hampstead, 10 August 2006

Dear Erik,

Tom proposed.

I'm happy, of course I am. It makes sense for us to move forward together. He offers me stability, he loves me and I do love him. It's different to how I felt about you. But that's to be expected, isn't it? I'm older. At least a little wiser (I hope).

You'll be glad to know that he is a really good man, and he wants to be a dad to Nora. He is kind and sweet and funny and I should jump at the opportunity, shouldn't I?

I know (no matter what my friends say!) that life is not a film, that I won't turn a corner one day and find you there. I know this and yet . . . I had the fairy tale once, for such a brief time. Is it wrong to want it again?

C x

# Chapter Fourteen

'Look! I have a room with a view!'

'And that's a good thing, I guess?'

'Well, obviously objectively, it's a good thing because the view is amazing. The Arno, the Ponte Vecchio, Florence herself!'

Nora drew in a breath that could only be described as rapturous – she didn't even know a breath could be so heady. She had felt herself get giddier and more anticipatory the closer they'd got to the famous city and now she was actually here, she was so filled with excitable energy she wasn't quite sure what to do with it. She couldn't remember the last time she'd been so excited. Even in the last few weeks with Gabe, her happiness had been underlaid with a faint anxiety that it was all too good to be true.

'But just as importantly it's a good thing because of the film! OK, book really, and a TV series, but for me and Mum, always the film.'

Luca didn't say anything but his puzzled expression spoke volumes.

'Helena Bonham Carter? Exploring without a Baedeker? The English Signorina?' She stopped, Luca quite clearly laughing at her.

'I thought my English was quite fluent, but you are making no sense to me at all right now.'

'Your English is perfect, but your film education is in need of some tutoring, Catalano.'

'Happy to be tutored by you any time.' The words themselves were innocuous enough, his tone teasing, Nora cleared him of meaning any double entendre, and yet as their gazes met and held, Nora's cheeks began to burn. And not just her cheeks. Her whole body was on fire.

'Tell me about it on the way to vineyard,' Luca said quickly. 'Unless you prefer to stay here and explore?'

Nora hesitated, torn. On the one hand, she couldn't wait to get out and immerse herself in the cobbled streets and inviting squares, and after forgetting herself and getting far too comfortable with Luca, some distance did seem like a sensible idea. But, on the other hand, she knew his contact was expecting her as well and when else would she get to see the Tuscan countryside?

'If it's OK with you I would love to come too. Thank you.'

Luca's friend had been called out of town and had left his key with a neighbour, instructing them to make themselves at home. Nora would have been quite happy to make the quaint apartment tucked under the eaves her forever home, enchanted with every detail, from the aforementioned legendary view to the tiny balcony and the winding stone staircase.

'I thought my apartment was the nicest you had ever seen,' Luca said with mock indignation as they made their way to the car he was also borrowing.

'So did I until I saw this one.'

'I didn't know you were so fickle.'

'There's a lot you don't know about me.'

He slanted her a dark gaze. 'That's very true. Just when I think I have you figured out, you surprise me.'

Nora's pulse was hammering so hard, she was sure it out-drummed the engine. 'Is that a good or a bad thing?'

'I don't know yet. But one thing I do . . .' He stopped abruptly.

'One thing you what?'

'No, it's not really any of my business.' All the light, teasing notes had left his voice, his posture stiff, face so carefully expressionless he had to be making an effort.

'You don't think I am right for Gabe.'

'I didn't say that.'

'You don't have to. You have made it quite clear from the moment we met you don't trust me.'

'Not from the moment we met,' he half muttered, so low she wasn't sure she had heard him correctly.

'The thing I don't understand is why?'

'Why what?'

'Why don't you think I am right for Gabe? What is it you dislike about me?'

'I don't dislike you.'

She laughed, unbelieving. 'Luca, you've been suspicious of me from the start. You've made it clear you think we are rushing into this, that Gabe could do better . . .'

'I do think you are rushing into this, people spend more time researching holidays then you and Gabe have spent together. And it's not that I think that Gabe could do better, it's just . . .' He stopped again.

*Just what?*

'I don't dislike you at all,' Luca said finally. 'I wouldn't have invited you along if I did. I don't know, maybe I shouldn't have. Maybe it complicates . . .' His voice trailed off.

Nora sat so still, so rigidly every muscle ached.

'I don't dislike you,' he repeated. 'And my whole family loves you. I just wonder if you've taken a couple of coincidences and turned them into something more. You said yourself your mother was a romantic, all your favourite films are romances . . .'

'Would you call Gabe a romantic too?'

'Gabe?' He laughed softly, but there was no humour in it. 'No. Gabe is ambitious and selfish. No,' he stalled her as she opened her mouth to interrupt. 'I love my brother very much, but I am not blind to his faults, and I don't think you are either. But if you see him for all he is, those flaws as well as his qualities, and love him anyway, then you have a chance. I just hope . . .'

'What do you hope?' Nora asked when the moment had stretched on almost unbearably long.

'I just hope he really sees you in return. That he doesn't take advantage of your romantic nature but nurtures it. That you are your true self with him and he loves you for that. There's no point pretending where marriage is concerned.'

'He does.' But Nora didn't look at Luca as she spoke. *Was* she her true self with Gabe, or was she who she thought he wanted her to be? A little more cultured, a little more easy-going. Who *was* her true self anyway? 'You sound like you know what you are talking about. You're what, thirty-two? Ever been close to being married?'

'Twice.'

'Twice?' Nora didn't know what to make of the sudden hot flash of jealousy that stabbed through her. 'What happened?'

'Distance the first time. I met Tania in New Zealand. Looking back, it was probably an extended holiday romance, but we did discuss marriage. In the end, I didn't want to move there, she didn't want to move here, and the Pacific proved too big a barrier. Then my relationship with Sofia ended a year or so ago. I liked her, she seemed to like me, we had fun, marriage felt inevitable, but I wasn't ready to propose.

In the end, she gave me an ultimatum and that finished it. I felt guilty for a bit, but she's now engaged to someone else and seems very happy, so clearly it was for the best.'

Engaged to someone else.

Like Jake.

Nora probed the thought, waiting for the usual flare of pain, but there was barely a twinge.

'I thought I would marry my first love,' she said before she could think better of it. 'He was literally the boy next door. I think, looking back, he had outgrown the relationship long before he ended it, but my mother was ill – who can finish with their girlfriend when she's going through that? I was absolutely broken-hearted. It took me a long time to be able to date again.' Luca didn't need to know about the bad choices that had followed once she had started dating. Nora was quite happy to airbrush those couple of years out of her history. 'Between losing Mum and Jake leaving me, I was paralysed for a long time, unable to think about moving forward with my life. But, of course, I would never have met Gabe if I had still been with Jake. Everything happens for a reason.' But she didn't feel the same certainty any more, that certainty that had propelled her through the last few weeks in a besotted haze.

'Tell me about the view,' Luca said abruptly.

'The *what*?'

'The view in Florence?'

Nora stumbled over the sudden subject change. 'The view from the apartment?'

'The film. What do you love about it?'

'Oh! *Room with a View*?' She glanced over at Luca, but he looked completely relaxed as if sudden subject changes weren't at all odd. 'Um. The scenery of course. It starts and ends in Florence, and then in one of those idyllic English

186

country villages in the middle. It's Edwardian, I think, pre-First World War, so big hair and amazing dresses for the women and floppy hair for the boys with striped waistcoats. It's really beautiful to look at.'

'Is it a love story?'

'Yes, but it's about growing up too. About being free of expectation, about daring to be yourself. About taking a risk.'

'Sounds like a good message.'

'Yes, it is.' Nora leant back against her seat and looked out at the green Tuscan countryside. 'That's why it was my mother's favourite, aside from the whole Florence looking glorious part.'

Her mother had never been afraid to be herself, facing up to her problems with integrity, her ready laugh still pealing out, even in the darkest times. Nora loved and admired her so much, wanted to be just like her, was never embarrassed by her, or at odds with her, even when her friends hit their teens and started pulling away from their families.

Charlotte Fitzgerald wouldn't have spent the last five years locked away in her grief, the last two dating patently unsuitable men just because she didn't want to be alone. Would she approve of this new spontaneous Nora and her whirlwind romance? Or was Nora just repeating the same old pattern? Letting herself be subsumed to hide how lonely she really was? But how could she turn back now she had experienced life in the heart of this warm loving family, when she was finally where she yearned to be?

*Nora: Guess where I am?*

*Grace: Drinking wine in some amazing hot spring and enjoying incredible views? Again.*

*Grace: Or a yacht?*

*Felix: In a tiny neighbour-
hood coffee shop drinking
incredible coffee?*

Nora grinned as she read the replies.

*Nora: Any more guesses?
No? I am in Florence on
this amazing terrace overlooking the actual bloody
Arno, with a glass of the
nicest Chianti, and all I
need is a long white dress
and a lot more hair.*

*Ana: They used hairpieces.
No one has that much hair.*

*Nora: Helena Bonham
Carter probably does.*

*Felix: Never mind Helena
BC's hair. Does that mean
Gabe is with you at last?*

*Nora: Not exactly.*

*Ana: You went on your
own? Oh, Nora, I am so
proud of you.*

Nora blinked. Pride seemed an odd response to a quick trip, but then again, when had she last left London before this holiday? There was always an excuse, even when she had the time and money to go anywhere she fancied.

She stared out at the famous river, mind heavy with unease.

> Nora: Not exactly. Luca
> had a business trip here and
> I kind of tagged along.

Felix: You are alone on
a minibreak with Italian
Heathcliff?

> Nora: It's not a minibreak,
> it's a business trip for him
> and a research trip for me.
> We are going to retrace
> where my mother met my
> father. It kind of made
> sense for me to come when
> he suggested it, but now we
> are here I don't know what
> I was thinking.

Felix: Luca suggested he
help you look for your
father? You did mention the
Swedish part?

> Nora: Track down the
> photo locations, try to get
> a clue. Long shot, I know,
> but nothing else has worked
> so far.

Felix: I've changed my
mind. He's not Sicilian
Heathcliff, he's Sicilian
Signor Darcy.

*Grace: How did you work
that out?*

*Felix: Because clearly there
is a good heart under that
aloof brooding exterior.*

*Grace: OMG. Felix, you
are right!*

*Ana: Be careful, Nora. I
hope you know what you
are doing.*

*Nora: Don't worry. I do!*

She just wished she was as sure as she sounded.

'Are you ready?' She hadn't heard Luca step onto the terrace and jumped at the deep rolling timbre of his voice.

'Yes, whenever you are.' She turned and smiled at him, the smile freezing as she took him in, Felix's Signor Darcy running through her mind like ticker tape. Luca was back in the beautifully cut designer jeans that showcased long strong legs (legs she had definitely *not* been hyperaware of when swimming) and a neat backside she had *absolutely* never noticed. Breeches did a lot for a man, but, on the right man, so did the right pair of jeans.

He had teamed the jeans with another of his seemingly limitless supply of white linen shirts, this one unbuttoned at the neck to show a deep vee of olive skin, rolled-up sleeves revealing tanned, strong-looking forearms. Signor Darcy before he dived into the waters at Pemberley. She was conflating books and film again and she really didn't care.

Oh God, she was in trouble. This wasn't a fleeting attraction due to Gabe's absence but one that seemed to deepen day by day. Worse, minute by minute. She didn't even look at Luca now and see the resemblance to Gabe, he was his own person. A person she was increasingly starting to like.

Things would change when Gabe came. They had to. Her happiness depended on it.

Neither spoke much as they left the apartment and headed down the street, which led to the river. In fact, conversation had been limited since the journey to the vineyard. Once there, Luca had switched into business mode, showing he could be every bit as charming and knowledgeable as his brother. Nora had enjoyed the tour and the wine tasting, using her recently acquired surface-deep knowledge to compare some of the practices to the Catalanos' own operation. Driving back, they had stopped at another couple of vineyards which welcomed visitors and discussing the wines tasted, the countryside, and Luca's job had kept them away from any more personal conversation.

But now they would be spending the evening together in the most romantic city of all. How businesslike could she keep the conversation? And did she even want to?

Luckily Florence proved a glorious distraction. The glimpses Nora had had of the ancient city had been enchanting, but nothing had prepared her for being in the heart of it. Gold weathered stone buildings melded into each other, around every corner was a winding cobbled street, a grand square, a fountain or an ornate church. Cafés and restaurants and gelaterias competed for business from the myriad tourists taking photos or queuing outside the museums and art galleries.

'No wonder my mother loved it here,' Nora said. 'I mean, she loved everywhere she visited. I found the postcards she sent Granny and Grandpa after she died, they read like a diary. She declared her intention of staying in Paris and renting a garret and becoming an artist, not that she could draw. Then it was Vienna that took her heart and then Berlin; she fell in love with every city and town and village she saw. Really, she was in love with life. Even at the end, she wrung the most out of every moment. It was a gift she had.'

'She sounds very special.'

'She was. I guess that's why I want to track down my father, even though it seems like an impossible task. Not just to know that side of my heritage, but to know someone who knew her at her peak happiness. Someone who knows how very special she was.' But it was also why tracking him down frightened her. What if that time hadn't been special for him? What if her mother was one in a long line of backpacking flings and he barely remembered her name?

'That makes sense.'

Luca's words were strangely comforting. Nora felt understood in a way she hadn't realised she needed to be, in a way she hadn't even known was missing.

'So,' Luca continued, 'do you want to go find the café in the photos now, or just enjoy Florence and look tomorrow?'

Nora hesitated. The city was intoxicating and it would be nice just to enjoy it. The café was unlikely to give her any real leads after all, and she didn't want the rest of her brief stay here to feel disappointing.

Of course, spending time with Luca with no real purpose might be, well, *confusing*, but not if she didn't let it. He was going to be her brother-in-law. Her family. He was kind and thoughtful and understanding, when he didn't act like she was some kind of gold-digger swindling his brother into marriage, that was.

'Don't you have plans for tomorrow?'

'I have some notes to write up, some emails to send, but otherwise I am all yours.'

Nora shivered involuntarily at the image this presented but scolded herself quickly. 'In that case, what do you suggest?'

'Well, I have been doing some research about the city and I thought you might want to start here.'

Nora looked around. *Here* was a spot by the Ponte Vecchio overlooking the Arno. It was beautiful of course – everywhere was – but what was so special about it? 'OK . . .'

'Recognise it? This hotel was the pensione run by the Cockney Signorina.' His brows drew together. 'What is a cockney?'

'An East Londoner. My grandmother was a cockney because she was born within the sound of Bow bells.' She laughed at his confused expression. 'So, this is the pensione? Of course! How did you find it? You hadn't even heard of the film stroke book a few hours ago!'

'I asked Davide, whose apartment we are staying in. Apparently, it's pretty famous.'

'I might have mentioned that.'

'And he sent me this route which takes in the most famous locations from the film. According to this, the actual view is on the other side of the river, but the rest of the route is this side.'

'I see . . .' Her chest was tight. Had Luca really organised a walk based on her favourite film?

Luca paused. 'Do you not like it? We can do something else if you want.'

'No, I love it. I'm just . . . Nobody has ever done something so thoughtful for me before.' As she said the words, Nora realised two things. One that they were true and second that they shouldn't be.

Gabe was fun and over-the-top romantic. He showered her with flowers and gifts and amazing five-star experiences. Life with him was like a perpetual holiday, champagne and Michelin stars. But would he listen while she told the plot of a film she loved, find out more and plan an activity around it?

She knew the answer. She just wasn't sure what it meant. And she didn't want to think about it either. In fact, she *wasn't* going to think about it but rather enjoy this moment.

'OK! Where's next? And, of course, the main question is, if I am Lucy Honeychurch, which I intend to be, are you Charlotte Bartlett or Eleanor Lavish? Of course you could be Mr Bebe.'

'I have no idea what you are talking about. Is Mr Bebe very handsome?'

'Erm . . . he has his own charm.'

'Do I not get to be the hero?'

Nora had a sudden vision of her and Luca walking through a field, music swelling and then . . .

*No.* She was not going there.

'Mr Bebe is very heroic,' she said firmly. 'OK, where's next?'

Although it was evening, it was still light and so Nora got to appreciate every step of the tour, from the Piazza Santissima Annunziata to the grandeur of the Basilica di Santa Croce and the Piazza della Signoria. She tried to explain the plot to Luca as they walked, but by his politely incredulous look, she knew she was doing a terrible job.

'You'll just have to watch it!' she said at last.

'You are definitely educating me in films, but to make this fair, I think the next time it should be my turn to choose.'

'What's your favourite film?'

'Now that is a question. I'll need to think about it.'

'I get that. There are lots of films I love, but I'd find it hard to pick a definitive favourite. Narrowing it down to ten is hard enough!'

'Anything after 1995?' he teased.

'I do love *Mamma Mia* . . .' She laughed at the horrified expression on his face.

'No wonder you get on so well with my sisters.'

'They are easy to get on with. OK, I think you deserve an amazing dinner after planning this. My treat.'

'Not at all, you bought the drinks in Taormina.'

'I didn't know we were keeping score. And it's your friend's apartment we are staying in and you only invited me to Florence because . . .'

'Because I wanted you to come along.' He spoke so low that she thought she'd misheard him.

Nora had no idea how to respond, how to deal with the pleasure that spread from her toes all the way up, the butterflies taking flight in her stomach. There were so many things she could have said, wanted to say, but instead all she could say, the only thing, was: 'Fine, we'll argue about the bill after dinner. But I warn you, if you insist on paying, I'm having steak.'

'I'd expect nothing less. It's a Florentine speciality, best served with a nice Brunello di Montalcino.'

'I love it when you talk wine at me.'

She did. In fact, she enjoyed every part of their conversation, whether they were sparring or getting along. Spending time with Luca, finding out more about him, opening up to him. It was dangerous and she needed to put a stop to it. And she would. As soon as this trip was over.

Hampstead, 1 December 2006

Dear Erik,

Advent is here, the nativity scene is up and Nora's sustainable Advent calendar (so Hampstead, darling) is filled with chocolate and hanging on the wall ready for her to build her nativity scene.

I love this time of year. We have all these traditions — Christmas carols and the crib service, a pantomime with Dad and The Nutcracker with Mum (lucky Nora and I do both), putting the tree up the weekend before Christmas, decorating it with baubles spanning all our lifetimes, a Fitzgerald family history on one tree, making mincemeat, drinks with neighbours, a Christmas morning walk on the Heath. I wonder how different it would be if you were here? We'd have to be part Swedish, with Christmas Eve a big deal, and those frankly dangerous-looking candle crowns!

So, Tom and I broke up. It was inevitable, I suppose, from the moment I said no. And I did say no. Did I do the right thing? Is kindness and respect and attraction enough for marriage? It's more than so many people have. But then I look at my parents. They know each other bone-deep. Those twenty-odd years they wanted

children and it didn't happen tested them so deeply,
but they had each other and they made that enough.
Is it wrong that if I marry, I want that? That I want to
see and be seen, understand and be understood?

Sometimes I wonder if we really had perfection for
a short while or whether I have romanticised a brief
fling? Either way, I don't want to be alone forever, but
I would rather be alone than lonely in a marriage.

C x

# Chapter Fifteen

Nora barely slept that night, but whether it was the fault of the rich food and excellent wine, the hope she couldn't quite dampen down that tomorrow she would actually get a clue to her father's whereabouts, or the knowledge that every moment she had spent with Luca had been both very right and very *very* wrong, she wasn't sure.

Her plan to remain friendly but impersonal had melted away the instant she had found out that he had researched a walk themed around *Room With a View*, just because he thought she would like it. Dinner at a tiny restaurant near the Ponte Vecchia had threatened her resolve even further, thanks to the intimate atmosphere, delicious food and even more delicious wine and the easy, interesting, fun conversation. They had, by unspoken accord, kept the conversation light, no discussion of past relationships or personal revelations, but chat about films and books and food, favourite childhood memories, Luca carefully keeping Gabe at the forefront of every tale, a reminder of why they were here and what their relationship to each other was.

But try as she might, the meal had still felt meaningful, every story, every disclosed like or dislike peeling off another layer. It was hard to shake off the feeling that she knew Luca better than his brother.

Or that *he* knew *her* better as well.

Nora stayed lost in her thoughts as she drank her coffee the next morning and got ready for the day ahead, for once dressing mechanically, not with any thought about the history or the story of the outfit.

Luca was also silent until they left the apartment.

'How are you feeling?' he asked at last.

There was no way Nora was going to confess to the conflicting, whirling, overwhelming emotions, so many she could barely name them. Especially not to Luca, who completely unwittingly had provoked so many of them.

'Like this is the longest of long shots,' she said instead. 'But I guess I get to see an important part of my history whatever happens. The actual spot where my parents met, where my mother fell in love.'

'How did they meet?'

Nora was grateful for the gentle line of questions, walking and talking relieved some of the pressure twisting her stomach. 'According to my mother, it was the day after she arrived in Florence. She was exploring; she wasn't a fan of guidebooks or maps, just liked to wander the streets to get a real sense of a place, and part of her sightseeing was trying as many different gelateria as she could. She had ordered a triple scoop and was so busy admiring it, she didn't look where she was going as she left, bumped straight into my father and it went flying. He insisted not just on replacing it but on buying her coffee and they ended up in the café next door and didn't leave for twelve hours.' She sighed. She had heard the story so many times, she could visualise it as perfectly as if she had been there. 'Then they went for a midnight walk around the city; she had no idea how long they had been out until she realised it was dawn.' She smiled. 'My mother said that they didn't run out of conversation, but at times the silence was even more comfortable.' She could see her mother now, sitting on Nora's bed as she retold the story, her gaze far away, as if back in Florence.

'At some point that night, their hands brushed against each other and that was it, they held hands for the rest of the night, but no more – not that night anyway. They went back to their respective hostels to get some sleep and arranged to meet on the steps of the Uffizi. She said she was walking there the next morning, wondering if he would even show, not sure *she* should because it felt so big, so life-changing, and then she rounded the corner to hear a busker playing a violin concerto and she saw him leaning against a pillar. They just walked towards each other and that was that.' It was achingly perfect.

'That's quite a lot to live up to.'

'What do you mean?'

Luca frowned as if trying to find the right words. 'Not many people have those perfect meeting moments, do they? Most relationships start as a conversation at work or at dinner with mutual friends or eye contact in a bar, they are a building up of time together, not an instant connection. Do you think it would have been the same if they had met in, oh I don't know, some grim industrial city, or a tiny village where the only café closed at eight? Or do you think the setting made it feel more than it was?'

Was he asking about her parents – or about the connection the two of them patently shared? The one they were both working really hard to ignore?

'But that's what makes it so perfect. They met *here*. It was fate, it was supposed to be.'

'You believe that? That their meeting was fate. Like you and Gabe?'

Nora looked up at Luca quickly, but he didn't look sardonic or disbelieving, just thoughtful.

'Yes. I mean . . . Yes.'

She did, she had to. If only she didn't feel so guilty. Tracking him down had felt so innocuous; after all, everyone researched their potential dates, stalking social media for clues before meeting. But she had gone that step – or two – further. And if that didn't fill her with guilt now, there was Luca and her complicated feelings for him. Nothing in her mother's stories had prepared her for this confusion.

'We're here,' Luca said as they turned a corner.

Nora looked eagerly at a scene she had imagined a thousand times if not more. On the surface, it was no different to any café in any Italian city – a small interior with a curved bar and small round tables set with two or three chairs, standing room only for patrons to gulp down a coffee and a breakfast pastry, bigger tables with umbrellas in a roped-off area in the square outside. The menus were leather-bound, a blackboard advertising the specials of the day.

But it wasn't just *any* café. Nora stared at it for a long, long moment, at her photo come to life. She could see her mother, a decade younger than Nora was now, laughing and talking and falling in love for the first, perhaps only, time. It was harder to picture Erik, the photos showed floppy dark blond hair, a narrow face with a determined chin and high cheekbones, a shy smile, but she didn't know him in 3D. Didn't know the movements of his face, his body, the timbre of his voice.

'What do we do now?'

'Get a coffee?'

'Right. Yes. I guess.'

She was shaking, she realised – nerves and adrenaline and hope and fear mingling. Being here felt like proof. Proof that Erik had really existed, ridiculous as that was.

She took a seat outside while Luca went to the bar, trying to control her still-trembling hands, looking out at the same view her parents had seen. That ice cream shop there might be *the* gelateria, or maybe that one, both inviting tourists inside with their tempting window displays. They would have seen that fountain, that small market in the far corner, colourful with fresh fruit and veg and flowers.

'Nora?' She startled as Luca strode over to her. 'There's a wall in there, a wall of photos, you should go and look and see if your father is there.'

'Really? That's a good idea.' But she didn't stand. 'Do you think I'm being . . . I don't know. Do you think this is pointless?'

'Not at all. Go and look.'

On unsteady legs, Nora walked into the dim inside, breathing in dark roasted coffee overlaid with the sweetness of pastry. The photos Luca mentioned were easy to see as they took over the entire back wall; there must have been hundreds pinned up, overlaying and obscuring each other, some so faded they must be at least . . . at least twenty-eight years old, if not more. Nora started to scan them all, this pictorial history of customers of all ages, all ethnicities, all sizes, but nearly all smiling as they posed with their coffees or drinks. The poses got gradually more and more practised, a social history in the advance of digital cameras and smart-phones, an advance her mother had always bemoaned, trying to convince Nora of the romance of waiting for a film to return in the post with no knowledge until you received it of how blurred a photo might be, if eyes were closed or a thumb obscuring the lens.

And then . . . 'Luca?'

He was there almost instantly.

'*Sì?*'

She pointed with trembling hands. 'Is that him?' Older than in her own treasured photos, on his own, smile less wide, almost – unless she was projecting – wistful . . .

'Where's your photo?'

'Here!' She fumbled through her bag, but she didn't need to open it to know. There was the same pointed chin, the shadow of a dimple, the same lively intelligence in his expression. A few wrinkles around the eyes showing the shift in time, his hair shorter, reflecting the change in fashion. 'It's him! He came back, Luca!' Nora wasn't sure why she was so excited. A return visit to a place that held fond memories was a normal thing to do, but it felt like more. 'Do you think it's a sign?'

'Maybe. Look there, is that him again? And there . . .'

They scoured every photo, finding five, each a little older, the last showing a handsome man in his late forties.

'It's like he's leaving a message for us,' Nora breathed. 'Do you think they know anything here?'

'Only one way to find out.' Luca strode off towards the bar and Nora waited impatiently, studying each of the photos in turn, trying to learn them by heart before taking a picture of each one. He looked kind, she wanted to shout to the room, wanted confirmation that yes, he did.

She turned and watched Luca as he spoke to the man behind the bar, wishing she could follow the rapid flow of Italian, but she could tell by Luca's final nod that it wasn't good news, although he slipped his card and a folded note over the counter.

'He doesn't know him?' she said as he returned to her.

Luca shook his head. 'He inherited the bar from his uncle a few months ago. You're lucky, he was planning to redecorate before the season started but ran out of time. If you had got here just a few months later, these might not be here at all. I asked him to check with his uncle, any other long-serving staff, to see if anyone knows who this is. He will but did warn us not to expect any kind of answer, apparently people would pin their own photos up.'

'Oh well, we knew it was a long shot.'

'I'm sorry, you must be disappointed.'

'No,' she said slowly. 'I'm not. Not really. Because this shows he thought about her too, don't you think? He returned here not once but several times. He left a photo, like a message for her. It makes it feel like it was real. I mean, *obviously* he existed, I am proof of that, but I mean my mother's faith in him, in what they shared. It was real and that means more than I . . .' She stopped, throat suddenly thick with myriad emotions. 'Thank you, for suggesting we come here, for helping me. I'll never forget it.'

Luca looked at her steadily. 'Come on,' he said. 'Our flight isn't for a few hours yet. What do you say we go for a walk in the countryside?'

'Yes,' she said. She could do with the space. 'I'd like that.'

Much as Nora had fallen in love with the city, it was nice to be back out in the rolling, Tuscan countryside. They parked up, before following a trail through a wood, taking them high up into the hills.

'Are you OK?' Luca asked after a while, and Nora realised she had barely said a word since they had left Florence.

'I'm sorry, I am being dull company. It's all just a little overwhelming.'

The sun beamed down through gaps in the tree canopy and she was glad of the shade of the trees as they walked along the brow of the hill, breathing in the pine-scented fresh air.

'I can imagine,' Luca said and then corrected himself. 'That is a foolish thing to say. How can I imagine something so different to my experience?'

'It's not just the past, not just the search for my father. It's like . . .' Nora had been struggling to make sense of the tumultuous feelings since they had left the café. 'It's like I'm free finally. I can't really explain it.'

'You don't have to explain anything to me,' he said softly – so softly she barely heard him.

'I hardly understand it myself. You see, in many ways, my life stopped five years ago and somehow I never got it restarted.' Nora thought back and shook her head. 'No. I suppose it stopped long before then. I know my family set-up was a little unconventional, but I had a brilliant childhood, I really did. So much love and laughter and three parental figures who believed in me, supported me. At eighteen, I felt unstoppable. But then my grandparents died, I lost my way, failed my exams, didn't go to university and as for Mum . . . That winter it was like her light went out and I couldn't help her. Grace and Felix were at university, Jake, my boyfriend, was at university, Ana was travelling all over the world modelling and I was in stasis.'

'From everything you have said, that sounds like the last thing your mother would want for you.'

'Oh, she said the right things, tried to smile while she said them, but she was lost herself and although she knew she should make me do something with my life, she was secretly relieved, I think, when I said I needed more time. Then, finally, we started to come out the other side. We didn't get over it, of course, grief and loss isn't something you just get over, but we learnt to live with it, to find space for it, to see joy in the small things again. I'd started to work with one of Mum's contacts who specialised in tracking down heirs to estates and I was good at it, enjoyed it. We started to look forward. This time an around-the-world trip. A renewal. Time for me to figure out what I really wanted from life. What my Plan B was. Only then . . .' She stopped. 'Only then she went to the doctor for something small and came back with an emergency referral and our lives flipped again. I don't regret a moment of it,' she said fiercely. It was important somehow that he knew that. 'I will never regret staying home to be with her, supporting her through every treatment, every setback, the amazing days and weeks and even months when we thought it was going to be all right. I didn't want to be anywhere else. But afterwards I felt like I had no one and nothing. My friends tried, my boyfriend for a while, but I was lost. I had my grief, I had my work, I had no interest in anything else. No wonder Jake . . .' She sighed.

'No wonder Jake what?'

'Couldn't wait to get out of the country.' She tried for a smile but knew it was more of a grimace. 'I wasn't a fun girlfriend for a really long time.'

'Love isn't about fun though, is it? It's about the dark times too.'

'There has to be a balance. Anyway, he went off abroad and I sort of stumbled along and then lockdown happened, and you know what? It was a relief. I had every excuse to stay home and mope.' She grimaced. 'My friends soon put me to shame. Grace was working, somehow teaching online and in person and being all round brilliant. Ana and Felix both used lockdown to reset their lives. Ana couldn't travel and was bored of modelling anyway, so she threw herself into volunteering, took some business classes and when the world started to open up convinced her agency to give her a job as an agent, while Felix quit his job and started to sell coffee from a bicycle cart, to his father's absolute horror. Six months later, he had his own coffee shop, six months after that he married Dai. And you know, I was jealous. I wanted that certainty, a path forward.' She bit her lip. 'I have never told anyone that before. It was so petty, I am still ashamed. I thought a new relationship might fix me, so as the world reopened, I threw myself into dating. I was on every app, I went to singles night at the bookshop and gym, at the little organic supermarket and the music shop, although I can't play any instrument. I did the whole saying yes thing, and I went on a million awful first dates and a hundred awful second dates and had some awful relation-ships. And I still wasn't moving any further forward and I was definitely not happier. I decided I was done. I was going to leave my future to fate, just like Mum always said. No more trying. And that was the night I met Gabe.'

'I see.' His tone, his expression were totally unreadable.

'Being here' – she wanted to say *with you* but knew she shouldn't, mustn't – 'I feel like me again for the first time in the longest time. Your family, they make me feel whole again.'

'I'm sorry. That you lost so much so young.'

Nora nodded. 'Me too. But I'm gradually beginning to be glad for what I had. For the memories. For my friends of course. They were there for me always, no matter how much I hid myself away, or later how many truly awful dates I introduced them to.'

'How awful is awful?' Nora could hear the smile in his voice.

'Unimaginably awful.' She shuddered to think of how low her self-esteem must have been to have turned up for a second date, let alone a third, with some of them. 'Which is why . . .' She paused.

'Why what?'

'Why Gabe swept me off my feet. How about you?' she said, wanting to change the subject. 'I know you've been nearly engaged twice, anything else you want to share to make up for *my* chronic bout of oversharing?'

She *had* overshared. Her friends knew or guessed most of it, but Nora had always kept her feelings, her loneliness and grief locked away. This was the first time she had allowed herself to articulate just how she had felt for most of her adult life, allowed herself to look back and see just how lost she had been. If only past Nora could have known that one day she would be here, in this glorious countryside, in this glorious sunshine with this glorious . . .

With her brother-in-law-to-be.

'You want me to tell you a secret?' Luca was looking amused now and her heart lifted. She was growing fond of that half-smile, the warmth in his eyes. She liked it when that smile was directed at her. Liked it too much.

'Yes, did you used to steal Gabe's toys or tease your sisters until they cried, or harbour a secret wish to be an astronaut?'

'Um, did you know that Gabe and I were in a band in high school?. Has he told you about that?'

'No!' She was instantly charmed. 'What happened?'

'We split up over creative differences.'

'Very Noel and Liam of you. What else?'

He shrugged. 'I'm not really a secrets kind of man. What you see is what you get.'

Nora was not going to look and imagine getting anything thank you very much.

'I guess there's one thing.'

'You don't have to,' she said hastily. 'I was just joking. Two overshares don't make a, well, anything.'

'I was wrong to walk away from the family vineyard but have been too proud to admit it to my dad or to anyone.'

'Oh.' Nora stopped walking and turned to face him. 'Oh that's . . .'

'Ridiculous?'

'No, a real shame. I'm sorry.'

'There's been a . . .' He gestured, clearly trying to come up with the right word. 'There's been a barrier between us ever since I returned from abroad. At the time, I thought he was the proud one, too set in his ways to see that I might have knowledge he didn't. Now I think I was probably arrogant, dismissive of all he achieved. But we don't talk any more, not properly, and I don't know how to tell him I wish things were different.'

'Luca,' she said gently, 'you should say all this to him.'

'It's too late.' He shrugged. 'My sisters have plans for the vineyard, the last thing they would want is me muscling back in.'

'Have you asked them? I agree they wouldn't be thrilled if you wanted to take over and push them out, but it's a big place, growing all the time, I'm sure they would be happy for you to be part of it. I know your dad would. He misses you, it's obvious every time he looks at you. And when you look at him.'

'Maybe.'

'Sometimes an outsider can see things clearly. This rift between you is breaking your mother's heart, that's obvious, and you and your father miss each other. Talk to him, talk to your sisters. Believe me, you don't want to leave things unsaid. Family is too important. I wish Gabe . . .' She stopped.

'You wish Gabe what?' His voice was low.

'Oh, I'm just being silly. But I love the vineyard, being with you all. I wish it was part of Gabe's future, but we both know that will never happen.' Maybe that was the reason her chest was so tight, the reason for her inexplicable sense of loss.

'No.'

'Besides,' Nora tried for a smile. 'Your sisters might be happy for one brother to get involved but maybe not two. Especially two with a history of creative differences. Talk to them, Luca, what have you got to lose?'

'Maybe.' He smiled then – a serious, sweet smile that made her heart contract. 'You are very wise, Nora Fitzgerald.'

'It's much easier to see clearly when on the outside – and even easier to dish out advice than to take it! But it does feel good to unburden yourself, doesn't it?'

What would he say if she confessed the biggest secret of all. That she couldn't stop thinking about him, that she was attracted to him in a way that frightened her, that she was confused and conflicted and scared. That she desperately wanted Gabe to be here and for things to go back to normal and at the same time wanted this day to go on forever.

'Come on,' she said instead and headed out of the woods at a fast pace, only to come to a stop, words of awe dying on her lips. A field stretched out before her, carpeted with a profusion of flowers, the Tuscan hills framing it like a perfect painting. 'Oh,' she managed at last. 'Oh how . . . No. Beautiful doesn't come close. It's just everything, isn't it?'

She turned to smile at Luca, but he was closer than she had realised and she was looking right at him, so close she could see the gold flecks in his long-lashed eyes, the stubble on his chin, the hollows in his cheeks. She could trace the curve of his mouth, no longer smiling but danger- ously slanted.

Nora couldn't breathe, couldn't think, she was nothing but sudden overwhelming need. She wanted to press herself close and never let go, to taste that wicked-looking mouth, to run her hands over him, unbutton the white linen shirt, an object she was in danger of fetishising every time he wore one.

She wanted him more than she had ever wanted any man in her life. And he wanted her too. She knew it.

Just one step. That was all it would take . . .

But she was practically engaged to his brother.

Nora took a sudden step back, and as she did, her ankle turned, the same one she had injured the night she met Gabe, and she staggered. Immediately, Luca was there, holding her as she let out a small cry of surprise, murmuring reassurance in low-voiced Italian, and as she looked up into his familiar gaze, Nora was hit with déjà vu. They'd been here before, she knew it.

But if she was right, then that changed everything.

Hampstead, 20 July 2007

Dear Erik,

I saw Tom yesterday, holding hands with someone else. He looked really happy, she looked really happy, there was this glow about them. Which made my decision not to marry him feel validated, I guess.

It made me think. About you and me. About myth versus reality. It's easy for me to put what we had on a pedestal because it was brief and it was perfect and it was unmarred by real life. What if I had done the sensible thing and got your number and address? Would you be here and part of our lives or would you be an absent father? If you were here, would I still find your absorbed silences charming or would they get on my nerves? Would you still love my absurd prattle or would I irritate you every time I opened my mouth? I'll never know. In my head, we lived happily and compatibly ever after, and that's why it's hard for any man to really measure up.

C xxx

212

# Chapter Sixteen

> *Nora: Were there two men*
> *there that night?*

*Felix: Hello to you too. And*
*I'm a happily monogamous*
*married man, I'll have you*
*know.*

*Felix: Nora that was weeks*
*ago!*

> *Nora: Just think.*

*Felix: Let me check with*
*Dai, he was the first to see*
*you needed help.*

. . .

Nora watched the cursor flashing by Felix's name, her nerves completely on edge. Had she tracked down the wrong brother? How *could* she have? Gabe had recognised her almost immediately, she was sure he had . . . Only hadn't there been recognition in Luca's gaze that first evening at the villa as well? His voice was exactly as she remembered, he felt right, dependable and solid and safe, whereas Gabe was many – many – good things, she reminded herself fiercely, but he certainly wasn't dependable.

*Felix: Dai says yes. There was a taxi waiting and he saw someone sprint towards it, grab a case and jump in, and then saw Gabe crouch down by you. Dai came out, they had a quick chat and he handed over his card and then we all came out and he had gone.*

*Nora: I see.*

*Felix: Are you OK? What's all this about?*

*Nora: Fine. Nothing. Thank Dai for me.*

Nora stared at her phone and reread the conversation. It clarified nothing. Luca might have been there, he might not. If he had, then maybe he had been the one to act, maybe he hadn't. The real question was, did any of this matter?

She was attracted to Luca and that was shameful and bad and no one must know, but she *loved* Gabe. Not because of what he may or may not have done on a rainy night, but because of the whirlwind courtship that had followed, because he had swept her off her feet – only maybe not literally after all. Or had she wanted to love him so badly she had refused to consider that she may have made a mistake? Had she refused to see flaws because she needed him to be perfect? But a relationship was loving someone *for* their imperfections. Wasn't it?

She should tell him she was having doubts. As soon as he arrived.

But if she called off the almost-engagement, then that would be it. No more card games with Nonna, chats over coffee with Chiara, approving smiles from Antonio when she remembered something he had shown her. No more laughter and friendship with Nicoletta and Violetta. No more Luca, although maybe that was for the best. No more being part of a family. Back to Hampstead and a house too big for one. A house full of memories of all she had lost.

She couldn't do it. She needed to see Gabe and remind herself why she loved him. Why all this was real.

And she needed some space. Time away from Luca. She needed to stay away from Luca Catalano until Gabe arrived and restored sense to her disordered world.

'I was thinking,' she said as they returned to the apartment to get their bags before their flight back. 'Now I've started to follow in my mother's footsteps, I'd like to continue. Maybe not come back to Sicily tonight.'

Was it her imagination or did Luca look slightly relieved? Was it because he was aware of the tension between them, or maybe it was because any tension was purely one sided and he was glad to get rid of her and her obvious inappropriate crush? 'You want to stay in Florence? I could see if my friend is happy for you to stay another night . . .'

'Actually I thought I might head to the train station and get a fast train to Rome.' Just saying the words felt bold, brave. Adventurous. It was a long time since she had been so spontaneous. 'I might even meet up with Gabe there if he gets an earlier flight.'

'Roma?' Luca didn't hide his surprise. 'Now? Do you have anywhere to stay?'

'Well no, but that's the point. After all, my mother didn't have anywhere to stay when she arrived in a new place either, she just found a hostel—'

'There was no internet or Airbnb when your mother travelled,' Luca pointed out. 'Are you sure? I could recommend some places.'

'It's less than two hours on the train and not even mid-afternoon, I'll be there in good time. I appreciate the offer, but I'm sure,' she said, more firmly than she felt. 'I want to arrive there the same way she did, to a city full of possibilities.'

Luca clearly wasn't convinced, but he didn't try to dissuade her, instead he sent her a list of places to avoid and insisted on walking her to the train station. It was good of him, but Nora was ready to be on her own, to try to figure out what, if anything, she had learnt, how she felt about Gabe in light of it, about Luca. What it all meant. She couldn't do any of that cocooned in the heart of the Catalano family, when in close proximity to Luca.

The train was fast, whisking her through the country at breathtaking speed and before she knew it, Nora had arrived at the bustling Roma Termini.

While on the train, she had rethought her idea of heading to the nearest tourism office and finding a hotel there, booking online instead. Luca was right, finding a hotel on arrival was just making things more complicated than they needed to be. After all, if her mother was backpacking now, she would be doing so with apps and reservations.

The city was everything she had dreamt it would be, loud and busy, imposing and beautiful. Nora clung on as her taxi careered recklessly along the busy roads with scant regard for pedestrians, who treated the traffic with equal disdain, muttering a brief prayer of thanks when they pulled up outside her hotel unscathed.

She'd treated herself to a small boutique hotel in the Trastevere district. Check-in was quick and friendly and she soon found herself in her pretty room with a balcony overlooking the internal courtyard. Luckily, Nora had over-packed for Florence and had a couple of clean tops, a pair of lightweight jeans, a dress and enough underwear to last her for the impromptu trip. She quickly showered, changed into jeans and a vest top and then stood irresolute in her room. It really was a *very* nice room, with a comfortable-looking sofa and an inviting room service menu. She could stay in and . . .

*No.* What would her mother do? Anything but skulk in a hotel room, that was for sure.

'I wish you were here,' Nora said aloud. 'Not just to kick my butt and get me out but to talk to. I'm in such a muddle and I don't know where to start.'

She could imagine what her mother would say: *It doesn't matter where you start as long as you do start.*

And, as always, her mother was right. She was in Rome. A whole city waited to be discovered and she could either go out and do just that or she could sit here and overthink. Put like that it wasn't much of a choice at all.

Her time was limited, so Nora made no apologies for heading straight for the most touristy spots. The hotel had recommended she pre-book the Forum and the Colosseum for the next day, and for the Vatican the morning after, before her flight back to Sicily, and she took their advice, using this first evening to wander the fabled streets. Her hotel was just over a mile from the centre and she enjoyed the walk, crossing the Tiber on the lively Ponte Sisto bridge, filled with artists, musicians and street sellers.

Just like Florence, there was an immediate sense of recog-nition. Here was the Pantheon, the Trevi Fountain, the Piazza Navana and Campo de' Fiori, all familiar and yet completely new. No picture or film could fully prepare her for the sights, sounds and smells of being here in real life.

Prepare her for the feeling of thousands of years of history combined with a modern thriving city.

If Luca were here, he would steer her to a little trattoria only locals knew – but he wasn't and that was absolutely fine with her thank you very much, and so Nora headed to a cheerful-looking ristorante with views out over the Piazza Navona and a spacious outside eating area, where she ordered pizza, salad and an Aperol spritz, taking a photo of her drink and sending it to her friends.

*Nora: Guess where I am now.*

*Grace: It's Sunday night, I am marking. This is hardly fair.*

*Felix: Is that Rome?*

*Nora: First prize goes to Felix.*

*Felix: Is hot Italian Mr Darcy with you?*

*Nora: a) Please stop calling him that, and b) no actually, I am here by myself. It was a spontaneous decision.*

*Grace: Nora, that's brilliant. I am so proud of you, babe!*

*Nora: I know it's really short notice, but did you get the invites? Chiara said she was emailing you over the* weekend. I don't expect any of you to actually trek all the way to Sicily for just a couple of days fyi.

Felix: Trek to Sicily for a couple of days of wine, amazing food and sun? I think I can take the hit. Dai and I have booked flights and cannot wait.

Grace: I was going to be sensible, but then three children threw up on Friday. THREE. So I came home and booked my flights before I had showered off the lingering smell of vomit. I will be there.

Felix: Always up for a celebration, even if it's a party for an octogenarian I have never met. It's nice of them to ask us.

Nora: Well actually . . .

Grace: Actually what?

Nora: It's kind of also an engagement party . . .

Felix: A WHAT? How? When? WHAT?

*Grace: Nora! I thought you were going to clear this all up.*

*Nora: I was, but then Gabe said . . . well, he said we were going to get engaged one day anyway so why upset everyone by saying we weren't and then things just snowballed.*

*Felix: Nora!*

*Grace: Nora!*

*Nora: Honestly, it's all fine, you'll see when you get here. I'm happy, guys. The Catalanos are amazing, it feels like I belong already. Oh, my food is here. Better go xxx*

She clicked out the chat with a sense of relief that she wouldn't be quizzed any further, although it was no wonder they were surprised. After all, she had handed over her friends' email addresses for Chiara to send invites but not warned them that rather than sorting out any engagement misunderstanding she was taking it, running with it and looked like completing the course. How could she explain it to them when she couldn't explain it to herself? Especially when the whole situation was made more complicated by her growing feelings for Luca, by the possibility that *he* had actually rescued her that night.

She also couldn't help noticing that Ana hadn't responded, although the blue ticks indicated that she had read every message. She could really do with her friend's no nonsense insight right now, but at the same time, wasn't sure she was ready to admit just how confused she was.

Tourist trap the restaurant undoubtedly was, but the pizza was delicious, as was the glass of red wine she followed up with, before she headed out into the evening to soak up the sights and walk enough calories off to allow room for an ice cream. Her wanderings led her to the Spanish Steps, and she stopped to take a selfie in the same place where her parents had had their photo taken all those years before.

Nora knew how lucky she was to have been so close to her mother, but her father had always been an elusive figure, a story and photo, far away. But today he had solidified, become real and she felt connected to him for the first time. Felt like she was following in his footsteps, as well as her mother's.

She wandered back to her hotel, enjoying the thrum of life all around her. Groups of families out for strolls, the smartly dressed locals a contrast to the more casual tourists from pretty much every country around the globe. Cafés and bars were full, queues in most ice cream shops and someone was taking a selfie in every direction she looked.

Nora stopped at a gelateria and, after some deliberation, ordered a lemon and forest fruit combination which was served in a bowl, garnished with a freshly made vanilla wafer. She sat at the window as she savoured every bite.

Look at her! In a strange city, exploring, ordering in Italian – OK the server had replied in English, but even so! If she hadn't met Gabe, fallen for Gabe, then she wouldn't be here, she'd be back in Hampstead, her life confined to her friends and work, hoping that Prince Charming would ride across her path someday. That first meeting might not have been exactly as she remembered it, but it had led her here and that was something she couldn't, mustn't forget.

Nora knew that she had forgotten how to live during the last few years, and when she did force herself back into dating, she used the lives of the men she'd dated as a substitute for her own. Ana was right, she had lost herself along the way. What were *her* dreams? Her hobbies? Her plans? It was time she stopped drifting, had agency.

Which reminded her . . . She pushed the empty bowl away and picked up her phone.

> *Are you ignoring me?*

Nora waited and finally saw a reply.

*Ana: I'm busy. Not everyone
is on leave, you know.*

*Ana: I'm not ignoring you.*

*Ana: I just don't know
what to say.*

> *Nora: Tell me what you're
> thinking.*

*Ana: Nora, you really don't
want me to do that.*

> *Nora: Try me.*

*Ana: OK, then. I think you
are crazy. What on earth
are you doing inviting us
to an engagement party for*

*someone you're not actually
engaged to????*

*Nora: I'm not not engaged*

*Ana: And just as impor-
tantly, more even, why are
you celebrating this not not
an engagement when you
have clearly developed feelings for someone else?*

*Nora: I haven't developed
feelings for anyone.*

OK, not strictly true, but she didn't want to have developed
anything. That had to count surely?

*Nora: I know you don't like
Gabe . . .*

*Ana: I don't know if I like
Gabe or not. I don't know
him and neither do you.
Not really. How can I trust
you when you don't trust
yourself? When you are
relying on fate and signs
rather than your heart?*

*Nora: So you're not coming?*

*Ana: I'll be there. Whatever
happens, you need support.
But it doesn't mean I
approve. Of any of this.*

Nora knew that Ana was only saying what her other friends were thinking, what Nora herself thought in her less certain moments. How she wanted that utter certainty back, the certainty that had propelled her into that first lunch, into coming to Sicily. The certainty she felt whenever she was next to Gabe. If he was here, none of this would be happening. She would be on polite terms with Luca, nothing more.

But Gabe wasn't here. She had to figure out her path on her own.

The next day, Nora set about sightseeing, glad that her hotel had warned her to pre-book. Both the Forum and Colosseum were packed, with huge queues at the entrances, but even the crowds and noise didn't take away from the awe, the sense of history she felt as she looked around buildings which had stood for over two thousand years. It wasn't just ancient history she was remembering either. Her parents had wandered through the Forum together, her father full of stories about the past and her mother full of myths. In some alternate universe, maybe they would have brought her here to relive that first trip, all three of them together.

She stopped and watched a small family. A little girl of about eight posed for a photo in front of a temple, before skipping over to take her father's hand, her mother taking her other, the three moving as one. As they moved on a young couple took their place, a baby in a sling strapped to its father's chest, a sunhat carefully covering the fragile head.

Nora smiled as the father carefully adjusted the small sunhat. This could be her future. A future so close Nora could visualise it, taste it. She would make Gabe come back to Italy more often, explore all the cities and regions, bring their children here to the Forum and bring history alive, tell them their grandparents had travelled here.

Another family group stopped next to her, the grandfather stooping down to explain something to a serious-looking boy of around six and her heart squeezed. She'd had the best grandparents in the world, but she knew Antonio and Chiara would be a close second best. If she married Gabe, she would have sisters-in-law she loved, cousins for her children to play with, in-laws who already made her feel like she was at home. Her children would be wrapped in love.

At that moment, her phone rang. Gabe, as if her thoughts had conjured him.

'Gabe? You're not in Sicily, are you?'

'Hello, *bella*. I'm still in Singapore, why?'

'Because I'm in Rome and I would hate to have missed your arrival, because I miss you.' It was true. She wanted the certainty he gave her.

He laughed. 'My family too much for you?'

'Not at all,' she protested. 'I was just thinking how much I love them already. But I was in Florence . . .' She stopped, cheeks suddenly hot, guilt twisting her stomach. 'Luca was there on business,' she said as airily as she could. 'He suggested I go too and do some sightseeing. You know, because it's where my parents met.'

There was a pause at the end of the phone and she squeezed her eyes closed, the guilt intensifying.

'Just you and Luca?' Was that suspicion in his voice?

'It was really kind of him, wasn't it?' she said, avoiding the question. 'Anyway, I thought why fly back with him when I could just jump on a train and come to Rome and here I am. It's a great city, I love it, but I wish you were here.'

'Soon, *bella*, that's what I was calling to say. I am nearly done. I'll be in Sicily in plenty of time for the party as promised.'

'That's great. You know your Nonna wants to make it into an engagement party, don't you? Your mother has even invited my friends. I didn't know how to say no without offending everyone, and, really, if you had just told your family straight away that we weren't engaged this wouldn't even be an issue.' She stopped, not sure what point she was trying to make, what reassurance she wanted. 'It's a lot, I know. I don't want you to feel ambushed.'

'A party to celebrate us sounds wonderful, Nora. I am so happy my family loves you the way I do.'

It wasn't just the party waiting to ambush him. She should mention the October date pencilled in, the plans his family were making for the wedding he didn't know was so imminent. But there were other things she needed to clear up, Luca's words and Ana's reservations playing on her mind.

Nora leant against a wall and summoned up all her courage. 'Gabe?'

'Hmmm?'

'Luca said something that I can't not ask you about . . .'

Gabe's voice sharpened. 'What is it?'

'He said the last time he saw you, you were talking about getting back with Lily. That he thought you were still in love with her.'

Gabe muttered something in Italian she didn't quite catch.

'He wasn't stirring,' she added hurriedly. 'He was just . . . surprised. By me, by how fast we are moving. The thing is, Gabe, I've been the rebound girl before. I don't want to be her again. If that's what this is . . . if now you've had some time away . . . I mean, we jumped all in, didn't we? Is it too soon to be even talking about an engagement, let alone having a party with all our family and friends?'

'What are you saying, Nora? That you don't want to get engaged?'

226

'No . . . I'm asking if the speed of our relationship is about you and me or about you not being over your ex. I'd rather know, Gabe.'

'When I see that brother of mine . . .' Gabe sighed. 'Nora, Lily and I, we have been over for months. Maybe I did think about trying to reconcile, but that was before I met you. It's you I love, you I want to marry. Nora, fate has put us together twice, who am I to argue? What is this? Are *you* having doubts?'

Of course she was. Ana was right. It was all going too fast, she didn't really know Gabe, not the way she should know her fiancé. She should speak up, put a halt to the not an engagement that was heading inexorably to an actual wedding, get to know Gabe properly, as a man, flawed like all humans, not a hero from her dreams, and put Luca out of her head. It didn't matter who had been there that night in Hoxton, who had done what. Luca was Gabe's brother. There was no future there for her. Besides, all he had offered her were a few kindnesses and here she was weaving an entire romantic daydream around him. No, it was time to live in the here and now, and in reality she was with Gabe, he loved her and he was offering her all she had ever wanted. Offering her the family she craved.

She looked across at the big extended family again, at the children with their grandparents, the parents hand in hand. This could be her future. Gabe, the Catalanos, Italy. Or she could go back to Hampstead alone. Again.

How could she choose that when she could have love and family?

'I just miss you,' she said. 'Hurry home.'

2 March 2008

Dearest, dearest Mum(my!),

Happy Mother's Day!

Do you remember that year Nora had to draw a picture
at school of all the things she loved about me for
Mother's Day and she drew me in a bikini, drinking wine
on the Heath and dancing. I cringed every time I spoke
to her teacher that year! As if being a teen single
mother (and in Hampstead, darling) wasn't enough!

I still have that picture. I have all the pictures. And I
know you do too. Anyway, I am not going to draw you a
picture, I think we will both be relieved about that, but
I am going to write you a list of all the things I love
about you. It's not exhaustive, how could it be? Just
the start . . .

1. The way you get so lost in a book you don't hear us
speak to you . . .

2. Your sense of style (and that you don't mind me
borrowing your clothes)

3. Your Sunday roasts (and your lemon drizzle cake)

4. The way you listen . . .

228

5. The way you loved Nora from the moment I told you I was pregnant

6. The way you love me

7. The way you still hold Dad's hand . . . and the way the two of you danced at Lucy's wedding, like it was just the two of you in the world

8. That neighbourhood kids still want to talk to you about their favourite books and you always want to hear

9. For introducing me to Cary Grant

10. For being you

Nora, Dad and I are so very very lucky to have you.

Your ever-loving Lottie xxx

# Chapter Seventeen

Nora was taken aback by the rapturous reception when she returned to Sicily, with the family treating her as if she had been away for weeks rather than a few days. She was also taken aback by her own feelings as the taxi turned in at the villa gates. She felt as if she had come home.

The little cottage was needed for a guest, but Nora didn't mind vacating. Luxurious as it was, it was a place for couples, not solitude. She moved into the bedroom Chiara had picked out for her. Chiara had cleaned it thoroughly while Nora had been away, the floors polished to a warm golden shine, and Nora impulsively offered to get started on the decorating, assuring Chiara that she could quite happily furnish the sitting room with spare pieces from the house and didn't need anything new. She was aware Gabe might not be so impressed with an eclectic mix of preloved items, but she also knew that it was far more likely she would be the one spending time here.

'Of course, you can get started,' Chiara agreed. 'I'll help you tomorrow, but there won't be time on Thursday. The girls and I are taking the day off and I have booked us an appointment at the wedding dress shop!'

The older woman was clearly so excited that Nora had no choice but to push all her misgivings and worries to one side and assure her that she couldn't wait. But as she began cleaning the walls in preparation for a simple whitewashing, she couldn't help but reflect that things were rushing away from her.

Before Florence, it had seemed simple. Gabe was happy for them to be engaged, she loved being here, she loved Gabe. But now, despite the decision she had made in Rome to concentrate on Gabe, she still didn't know if she was doing the right thing, if she could trust her own heart.

Spending the next day decorating with Chiara and Antonio didn't help. They were clearly delighted that she wanted to make herself at home in the villa, reiterating that she was welcome to come and stay whenever she wanted. The future they so casually offered her reminded her of how much she had to lose if she did walk away.

It was clear the Catalanos took wedding-dress shopping very seriously indeed. All three were up bright and early, made up as if they were heading out for a fancy lunch, hair shining and blow-dried into three almost identical glossy manes. Nora took one look at them and fled back upstairs to replace her casual sundress with a flowing maxi dress and add some more bronzer to her pale face. Her half-braided hair would just have to do.

The shop was on an exclusive street in Taormina, an attractive boulevard of high-end boutiques and fancy-looking restaurants and cafés. The bridal shop had a double frontage filled with some of the frothiest and laciest dresses Nora had ever seen and she stood there for a moment unable to move, visualising herself in one of the ornate confections. She would look like a wedding cake covered in extra doilies.

'Don't worry,' Nicoletta murmured. 'There are some much nicer dresses at the back. But Mamma will definitely want you to try on a couple of these hideous things before we get to the good stuff. Just humour her, will you? She's been so excited.'

'Of course!'

Once inside, it was like setting foot onto the set of a reality television show, everything vaguely familiar and yet new, from the racks filled with satin, silk, lace and tulle in shades ranging from the iciest white through to warm golden creams, accessories shining and twinkling from shelves and display units in pearls and rhinestones and crystal. The overall effect was one of sparkle and gleam, it was almost overwhelming.

A cream velvet sofa was arranged in a semicircle around a pedestal, a huge mirror on one side, gold thread curtains looped back revealing a huge changing room behind. Coffee, iced water garnished with lemon and tiny pastries were set up on a polished bronze coffee table.

They were greeted like old and beloved friends in a mixture of Italian and English. Nora found herself under immense scrutiny, her hair and skin exclaimed over, and measuring tapes whipped around her so swiftly she barely registered the two polished women of indeterminate age who owned the boutique scribbling numbers and notes in a notebook as they did so.

'They think ivory or cream,' Violetta translated in a low voice. 'Because you are so pale, they think white will wash you out.'

'They're not wrong.' Despite assiduous use of suncream, Nora had gained some colour over the last ten days, but it had merely moved her one place on the redhead skin colour chart.

'Possibly with warm gold accents, to bring out the colour of your hair, which they very much like by the way.'

Panic gripped Nora as she looked around the huge room, each enormous dress looking like it would turn her into a doll with no will of her own. 'I don't have to choose today, do I?'

Nicoletta regarded her in surprise. 'No, of course not, but October is not so far away. If you did order from here, then it will be a rush job and the same will be true in London – they often want six months' notice. But, of course, you might already have a dress? Your grandmother's perhaps? You wear a lot of her clothes.'

Nicoletta was right, that *would* be the most obvious choice. Her grandmother's dress had been carefully preserved. 'My grandmother got married at a registry office in this gorgeous knee-length dress with a really full skirt and a little matching jacket and hat. It's adorable and very much of its time, but maybe not really suitable.' It gave her a pang to say it. Once upon a time, she *had* imagined getting married, wearing her grandmother's dress, but that vision belonged to her past. 'Gabe isn't a big fan of vintage dressing. I want him to love what I wear.'

'Well, he won't approve of that,' Nicoletta said drily as she nodded towards a huge ensemble of tiered silk and tulle with a ruffled bodice being picked out by Chiara. 'I love Mamma, but where wedding dresses are concerned, she loses all sense of proportion and taste. You are far too small for that dress.'

Nora agreed with Nicoletta, but it made no difference, she couldn't resist Chiara's pleading expression and allowed herself to be pummelled and laced into the dress. For a moment as she smoothed the shining folds, she almost hoped that she was wrong and she would turn to the mirror and see a princess, but what she actually saw was a dress so big she looked like an ornate snowball, some kind of glittering Christmas bauble. The barely repressed laughter her future sisters-in-law didn't hide from her confirmed her fears and she glared at them as they all started to take pictures.

'Oh we can blackmail you with these for years,' Violetta said happily. 'I still have yours, Nicoletta! Do you remember that one that looked bright yellow on you? You looked like a big feathery chick.'

'I have two words for you,' Nora told her, with a mock-glare. '*Bridesmaids' dresses*. Don't think I won't truss you up like a Bavarian barmaid in the most unflattering colour I can find, because I will.'

Chiara took some persuading to see that Nora didn't actually look lovely but maybe a little overwhelmed and Nora proceeded to the second and third of Chiara's picks – dresses equally big, equally unsuitable and equally unflattering. The last, which involved long lace sleeves, a high neck and sweeping train, made her feel as if she were being consigned to a nunnery, and even Chiara admitted that it was probably a *little* too much lace.

It was a relief to turn to the sisters' picks, although once again none of them tallied with her own taste. Violetta favoured skintight scraps of silk, more negligee than dress, while Nicoletta chose a selection of severely elegant dresses with cowls and dropped backs which would probably fit Gabe's aesthetic but made Nora feel like she was dressing up. She was just too short for such pared-back simplicity. But when asked to choose some styles of her own, she froze. The problem was she didn't know *what* she wanted; in fact, she couldn't visualise the day at all. When she thought about it, she just felt scared.

No, not scared. Numb.

But either she was a great actress or the Catalano women were too swept away by the occasion and fun of playing dress-up-Nora to notice that although Nora obediently tried on every gown they suggested, smiled and said how lovely, she didn't pick out any as a favourite or at any point show any signs of finding the one. There were several that might do – the most restrained of Chiara's picks, a very pretty sheath Nicoletta loved and a boho-inspired dress Violetta was rooting for – but she couldn't say with any certainty that, yes, this *was* her dress. But she allowed them to take photos of her from all angles, tiara and heels on, and left the shop with a shortlist, the attendant promising to email her the prices including alterations and lead times.

'This is just the first look; it would be unusual to find the perfect dress in the first shop. Go take your friends and look in London. Then you can either come back for a second try of any of these gowns, or if you do definitely decide on one, then you can always order from London. They have your measurements. Whatever you choose, you will be beautiful,' Chiara said, not seeming in the slightest bit disappointed but more than ready to do the whole thing again.

'It's too much to expect you'll find it on the first try,' Nicoletta agreed. 'I must have visited every shop on the island and I eventually found mine in a tiny shop over in Palermo. I did have more time though. I started looking a year before the wedding and was only really humouring Mamma – but just like men, when I knew I knew.'

'I know October isn't that far away.' It really wasn't and yet Nora still felt numb rather than pressured. The whole thing was so unreal.

They had spent more time in the shop than Nora would have thought possible and everyone apart from her declared themselves hungry. Nora was swept along into a very chic café, where a series of antipasti and Prosecco was ordered and a passionate conversation about the forthcoming wedding started.

'Sunset,' Violetta insisted. 'There is no more romantic time.'

'But then everyone is hanging around all day and the meal is rushed,' Nicoletta objected. 'Mid-afternoon is better.'

'Fireworks at midnight,' Chiara said. 'Maybe along with a roasted pig?'

'After a full sit-down dinner? Who will want roast pig?'

'Dancing makes you hungry,' Violetta interjected. 'Besides, maybe Nora doesn't want a full formal sit-down dinner?'

'You're not suggesting a buffet?' Chiara couldn't have sounded more scandalised if her daughter had suggested each guest forage for their own supper. 'For a party, yes, a wedding, no.'

'Carlo will organise the menu with Nora and Gabe. I agree something to round off the evening is nice, but maybe not quite such a production as a full roasted pig. What I want to know is colours.' Nicoletta smiled at Nora. 'With your hair, how about soft gold? Very fitting for the time of year as well.'

'I thought green,' Violetta said.

'Why? Because she's a redhead?' Nicoletta couldn't have sounded any more scathing. 'Show some imagination.'

'Green suits her and it looks good on us as well.'

'True, but so does gold.'

It didn't seem to occur to any of them to ask what Nora wanted. She knew them well enough now to know that it wasn't because they didn't care but that they expected her to shout out with any ideas. She just didn't have any ideas. Besides, Nora was enjoying listening to them discussing her wedding with such passion and enjoyment. The ease of their acceptance, the way they had welcomed her into their family so eagerly, warmed her through, would never ever be something she would take for granted. She would quite happily go along with every single suggestion if that was what they wanted.

'You are forgetting one important thing,' Violetta cut into Nicoletta's plans for the evening entertainment, which

236

involved a local covers band and a playlist for which every attendee would be invited to submit a song.

'What's that?'

'Gabe.'

'*Gabe?*' Nicoletta rolled her eyes. 'He's just the groom – everyone knows weddings are women's work. Unless it's two men getting married, obviously.'

'This is Gabe, not Luca. Luca would quite happily do whatever made Nora happy, well, not Nora obviously, but whoever he was marrying.'

Was she red? She must be scarlet, just the casual coupling of their names enough to undo her.

'But Gabe will have definite ideas.'

Nicoletta groaned. 'Black and white and some dreary jazz band.'

'Tiny food that looks amazing but tastes of nothing,' added Violetta.

'Spiky flower arrangements with leaves that catch at you if you are not careful.'

'Oh, Nora, don't let him. You need to manage Gabe from the off.'

'He is very lucky to have you, don't let him forget that.'

'I'm the one who is lucky to have him.' And she meant it. She *did*. And she didn't deserve him, all these doubts and intense emotions for another man. It had to stop. She was going to marry him and be a Catalano and belong, and if Gabe wanted jazz and spiky flowers and intricate food, then that's what he would have. Well, maybe not the jazz. There was only so much making up to him for her doubts she could do.

Her phone buzzed and Nora glanced at it automatically, her pulse speeding as she saw the name – guilt and a little fear mixed with hope and excitement. *Gabe.* Once he was here, everything would return to normal. He would sweep her along in his certainty and confidence as he had from that first and she would be happy to be swept once again.

Hands shaking, she pressed on the message, read it, and then read it again disbelieving. 'Oh my goodness.'

'What is it? Nora?'

'Not bad news?' Chiara asked.

'No, not at all, the opposite.' But she didn't feel joyful, the numbness was back. 'Gabe is back. He's at the airport. He's here.'

'Great! The wedding planning will start properly.' Chiara clapped her hands.

'And we can celebrate your engagement!'

'Let's hope he stays until the weekend this time.'

'Violetta!'

'Mamma, you are thinking the same.'

'I am thinking we are all going to be together.' Chiara laid her hand on Nora's. 'The whole family together. It makes me so happy.'

Nora hoped her smile didn't look as fake as it felt. She *was* happy.

At least she would be.

She just needed to see Gabe and all would return to normal.

It had to.

Hampstead, 22 August 2012

Dear darling perfect Nora,

Am I allowed to say that or will you roll your eyes at me and walk away with a toss of your head in that haughty way only teenagers can really pull off?? I used to be good at that too, you know. But of course you don't. No teenager can imagine their parents as anything but old, even mothers as scandalously young as me! Friends are only just having their first babies, or starting to think about trying, and here I am with a teenager. And I hope you know I would never want it any other way.

So, GCSE results tomorrow. I meant what I've said all along. No one was ever defined by a two-hour exam. It's what you do with adversity that counts. Not that I want you to ever face any adversity. I want you to stay as fearless and confident and untouched by sadness as you are now. I'd take that over all the As in the world.

But whatever tomorrow brings, I am so very proud of you.

All my love,

Mum(my) xxx

239

# Chapter Eighteen

As the car drove through the vineyard gates, Nora was aware of every detail as if she were watching the scene, not taking part in it. The sun was high and hot, bleaching the colour out of the vivid green landscape, the air thick with pine and lemon and heat and expectancy. It seemed to take forever, then no time at all, to reach the villa. Chiara had, of course, wanted to head straight for the airport, but Gabe had already hailed a taxi, so instead they had paid for their food and left the restaurant quickly, Violetta bemoaning her uneaten lunch loudly and pointing out that this time Gabe would not be going anywhere.

'Even he wouldn't be so selfish,' she'd said. That *even he* reverberating around Nora's mind as they made their way back.

Gabe's family loved him, of course they did, but they didn't understand him. They saw his ambition and love of making money and the finer things in life as arrogant, his way of sweeping you up in his wake as selfish, but Nora hadn't thought any of these things until she had got here. The Gabe she had fallen for had faded away replaced with their version and in his absence it had been hard to challenge their views. It wasn't right or fair, she needed to reestablish him as hers, to find that certainty she had been drawn to . . . to stop thinking about Luca. Her place here depended on it.

They beat him back to the house, where Antonio and Luca were waiting at the end of the drive. It was the first time Nora had seen Luca since he had dropped her at the train station and she was instantly aware of him. The way his hair fell over his forehead, his rolled-up sleeves, his gaze intent on her.

'Hi,' she managed somehow, her knees annoyingly weak, her voice high and strange.

'He's made it back, you must be happy.' His voice was as unreadable as his expression.

'I am. Very.' She knew she sounded almost defiant and tried to smile.

At that moment, a taxi pulled up and there he was. Gabe. Chiara and his sisters fell on him, all shrieks and kisses and exclamations, but Nora hung back, instinctively moving closer to Luca as she took in his brother, for one startling second no longer familiar and safe but a stranger. Gabe looked different here, what seemed so polished in London now almost too much. His suit so formal, hair so perfect even after travelling, his good looks burnished, like a movie star trying to blend into normal life. Nora found herself retreating, unsure how to approach him.

'*Bella!*' Gabe clearly had no such reservations, striding towards her, his eyes narrowing as he took in her proximity to Luca, before he smiled, scooping her up, whirling her around like a returning soldier. 'I missed you.'

'I missed you too.' But as she returned his embrace, she was all too aware of Luca, leaning against the corner of the house, arms folded, mouth set. His presence made her clumsy, as if she had forgotten her lines as she let Gabe pull her in close.

'I am so sorry, *bella*,' he murmured as he kissed her. 'I have a lot of making up to do.'

241

'I've been fine. Your family are . . . well, they are wonderful, they have made me feel very welcome.'

Now he was here, holding her, looking down at her, her emotions were more conflicted than ever. It seemed crazy that she had been so apprehensive about his return. He wasn't some unknown quantity, he was *Gabe*, tall and solid and certain, that same expensive sandalwood scent, the same handmade suits and shoes, the same appreciative smile in his eyes, dimming slightly as he looked her up and down and she remembered she was wearing a 1970s paisley maxi dress that he certainly wouldn't approve of. Guilt that intensified as she remembered that she had been wedding-dress shopping for a date he hadn't agreed to, in a place he might not even want to get married in.

Nora touched his cheek, still acutely aware of Luca watching them. 'I have a lot to tell you.'

'And I have so much to show you. Some friends of mine are on a yacht near Taormina and they have invited us for dinner. Get changed and let me introduce you. You'll love the yacht. We should consider getting one, I'll make a sailor of you yet.'

'What now? You just got here.'

Gabe looked faintly surprised. 'But I slept on the plane.' His smile grew tender. '*Bella*, it's so like you to be concerned.'

'No, that's not what I meant – although obviously I am glad you aren't too exhausted. But, Gabe, it's your first night back. You can't go out! Your parents will be so upset. They've been really looking forward to you getting here.'

His brow creased; he looked a little annoyed but mostly surprised. It wasn't often, Nora realised, that she had said no to him. 'They won't mind.'

'They'll tell you they won't mind, but they will. Honestly. It would be lovely to see your friends, but some of your extended family and my friends are arriving tomorrow; this is the only opportunity for your parents to have you to themselves.'

He hesitated. 'If it means that much to you, then of course we'll stay.'

'It'll mean that much to them and that means to a lot to me. Thank you.' She reached up to kiss his cheek, but he turned his head and she ended up kissing him properly instead. It felt . . . strange. There was no sense of familiarity, no feeling of coming home, more like kissing a stranger than the man she loved. Where was the dizzying rush of blood? The addictive swoop in her stomach? It must be nerves. She just needed to get used to him again. 'Come on, let me show you where we are sleeping.'

'I know where my bedroom is, *cara*.' But he followed her obediently, up the stairs and past his usual room.

'Ta-dah!' she said as she opened the door. 'These will be our rooms from now on. They're not finished,' she added hurriedly.

With Antonio's help, Nora had managed to put the first coat of fresh white paint on the sitting-room walls the day before and had hunted through the some of the lesser-used rooms to add a pair of occasional tables to serve as nightstands, a small armchair and a rug into the bedroom, and a desk and chair, a small sofa and a coffee table to the sitting-room. She'd hung up a couple of pictures on the sitting-room walls and added vases of flowers in both rooms. They looked fresh and welcoming even half finished.

'We still need blinds or curtains and the walls need finishing, of course. Oh, there's a wardrobe from your old room to be brought in, but there was only so much borrowing of the farmhands I could do. What do you think?'

Gabe didn't speak for a moment. 'I don't understand. Why are we not in my room?'

'Your mother thought it might be nice to have a bit more space when we are here on longer visits. Look, there's a desk here either of us can use, and we could add another into the bedroom as well . . .'

His smile was indulgent. 'I know we came on a long visit this time, but I only really come back once or twice a year, for a weekend at most. There really was no need for my mother to go to so much trouble.'

'I don't think it was trouble, she wanted to do it, and so did I. She wants to make us feel at home, for *me* to feel at home. And I do, Gabe. I love it here and I love your family and I want to spend proper time with them regularly, not just a weekend here and there. These rooms are one of the nicest things anyone could ever give me.'

'Nora, you are so very sweet. I am sure I can give you something better than a couple of disused rooms. But if they really make you happy . . .'

'They do,' she assured him. 'They really do.'

'Then of course I am happy too. You really have made yourself at home here.'

She wasn't sure if the thought pleased him or not. 'I can't tell you how much. Obviously, I've missed you, but I have had a lovely time.' Nora bit her lip. She should tell him about Florence, about the photos, about spending so much platonic time with Luca, but somehow the words wouldn't come. In fact, there was a great deal she needed to tell him before his family did. 'Gabe . . .'

'Hmm?'

'Look, I shouldn't have agreed without you here, and it's not too late, we can do something else . . . but actually, it would be lovely.'

'Nora, darling, I have no idea what you are talking about.'

Nora took a deep breath. 'Your mother would really like us to get married here, at the vineyard. And so would I. There's a space in October and we are pencilled in. But it's really soon and we are not even properly engaged yet and we can postpone. Maybe we should postpone.'

Of *course*, they should postpone! They hadn't even slept together yet! What had she been thinking, prancing around in a wedding dress with no engagement ring and still (practically) a virgin? Maybe her mother should have called her Madonna after all.

'Here? Get married *here*?' That had got his attention. 'Oh, *cara*, let me deal with this. You are too nice, that's your problem.'

'No one pressured me into anything if that's what you mean. I love it here. I can't imagine anywhere nicer to get married than right here.'

'*Here?*' Gabe repeated, looking confused. 'I thought we would get married in London. At Somerset House, or the Serpentine. How about a country house if you wanted to be out of London?'

'They all sound wonderful.' And expensive! 'But this is your *home*, where you grew up. What could be more romantic? We don't have to get married in October obviously, but can you think about it? Please? For me?' She hated the wheedling tone in her voice, but it seemed to do the trick as Gabe just smiled at her indulgently, pulling her in for an embrace and kissing the top of her head.

'I can't resist you when you look at me with those big eyes,' he murmured. 'So let's stay in for dinner and let's have a think about the wedding venue. We could always have a celebration afterwards in London.'

'Yes, we could. Thank you.'

'I've missed you,' Gabe murmured. 'We had such plans

for this fortnight.' He moved closer, his hands light on her arm, eyes darkening with intent.

Nora felt frozen in place as Gabe ran a hand lightly down her body, coming to rest on her hip, his mouth moving slowly over her ear, down to her neck. She really, *really*, wasn't in the mood. She should be. She should throw him on the bed and get this first shag over and done with and take the pressure off both of them. Forget her doubts and inconvenient sudden lustings over someone else in a good old-fashioned sweaty bout. They had waited so long. But she couldn't will her body, or her mind to respond. Just under two weeks ago this was all she had wanted.

'Is that someone calling us?' she managed to say through a throat thick with tension and slipped out of his embrace. 'I think your mother mentioned drinks on the terrace. Come on.'

She could tell Gabe was a little puzzled, but he just laughed as he took her hand. 'I am looking forward to some real alone time with you.'

'Yes! Me too.'

It wasn't a complete lie. She *wanted* to look forward to being alone with him. She just needed to get used to him again. It was engagement jitters, that was all. The sooner she conquered them, the better.

Nora had no idea how Chiara had managed it with so little warning and having spent most of the day away from the house, but she'd pulled all the stops out for dinner and the table was groaning under the weight of food and wine.

The whole family was there, including the children, and Nora started to feel more like her old self again, watching Gabe play with his nephews, holding the baby with a natural ease which was absurdly sexy. She was relieved that she had broached the subject of an autumn wedding with him as it was the subject of much discussion and, to her surprise, he didn't demur or object but joined in with interest, mostly quizzing his sister about the food and decor choices.

'We tried to get Nora to think about colours today,' Nicoletta told him. 'But she was undecided.'

'Nora isn't interested in that kind of thing,' Gabe said. 'You had better leave the theme to me.' He winked at Nora. 'I'll make sure we don't get stuck in the past. Just *one* something old, not an entire vintage theme.' He laughed.

'I love Nora's vintage look.' Violetta scowled at her brother. 'She *does* have a quirky style, true.'

Nora looked down, her cheeks flushed, the brightly patterned fifties swing dress she was wearing feeling garish and over the top. When she looked back up, she saw Luca staring at her, his expression totally unreadable. There was no sympathy, or understanding, that she could decipher, which was a relief – either would embarrass her more – but there did seem to be a hint of regret, and maybe something close to anger.

The evening passed quickly. Gabe had evidently decided to make the most of his decision to stay and was at his most charming, dominating the conversation, teasing his sisters and grandmother. Luca, on the other hand, was uncharacteristically quiet.

Eventually, Nonna turned in, proclaiming that with just two days until her party, she needed her beauty sleep, while Antonio and Chiara disappeared to deal with some last-minute extended-family changes of plan for the next day, leaving the younger members of the party sitting around the table, open bottle of wine and platters of fruit in front of them, Nicoletta's children fast asleep in their pram and pushchair.

'So, Gabe,' Nicoletta stood up and refilled all their glasses, 'when did you know that Nora was the one?'

'Yes!' Violetta chimed in. 'What made you fall in love with her?'

Gabe sat back, his arm casually along the back of Nora's chair. 'It's easy to see why I love her. Look how beautiful she is.'

'Yes, but *when* did you know?' Violetta asked. 'Was it love at first sight like it was for Nora?'

Nora stared at her plate. Hearing Violetta parrot the words she had so artlessly uttered just a few days ago made her feel exposed, absurdly naive.

She felt Gabe shift and, looking around, saw him exchange a defensive gaze with his brother. She touched her phone, lying in front of her, and thought of her exchange with Felix. Her certainty that it had been Luca, not Gabe, that rainy night. But she had no proof and she wasn't exactly Miss Honesty herself. She needed to let it go, all of it. Look forward, not back.

'It was fate,' Luca said. 'Wasn't it, *cara*?'

'Yes.' Nora tried to smile. 'Fate.'

'What's the expression?' Luca asked. 'Fate goes in strange ways?'

'Fate moves in mysterious ways,' Nora said.

'That's it. Mysterious and yet very convenient, wouldn't you say?'

'I for one am glad it does.' Gabe clearly hadn't clocked the taut undercurrent in his brother's tone, but Nora was preternaturally aware of his every shifting mood.

'It's great that fate brought two such compatible people together,' Luca continued. 'I know. Let's play a little game. What's Nora's favourite book?'

Gabe moved his arm to Nora's shoulder, pulling her tight to him, his gaze steady on his brother. 'She's always reading, aren't you, *cara*?'

'Not always.' Nora's smile felt more and more forced. 'But I do like a good book.'

'Well done on noticing her hobbies.' There was no humour in Luca's voice at all, and the two brothers continued to stare at each other as if they were dogs with hackles raised. She could almost hear growls. 'But I asked what her favourite book is.'

'Luca.' Nora glared at him. What was he playing at? '*I* don't know what my favourite book is from one moment to the next! I'm not sure I could pinpoint my favourite *ten*, it's an unfair question.'

'OK, then, name one of her favourite films. Any of her top three will do.'

Gabe laughed, although clearly puzzled. 'What has got into you?'

'No, this is fun!' Violetta said; she clearly hadn't picked up on whatever weird vibe there was simmering between the brothers.

Nicoletta nodded. 'It's only fair. Nora got all her questions right.'

Gabe's eyes narrowed. 'You questioned Nora about me?'

'Don't change the subject,' Luca said. 'Her favourite film. Come on, Gabe. I said top three.'

'How am I . . . Oh! I know. The one you made me watch. I fell asleep.'

'Yes!' Nora was almost ridiculously relieved. She wasn't going along with whatever stupid game Luca was playing, but at the same time, she hoped Gabe would win and show Luca that whatever point he was trying to make was wrong.

'Yes! That old film! The romance one.'

'That's right.' She couldn't resist throwing a triumphant look at Luca. Stir up trouble would he?

'With Julia Roberts. There was a bookshop.'

249

'*Notting Hill*,' Nora said flatly. 'Yes, you did fall asleep during that.'

'I knew I was right,' Gabe said smugly. 'You said you loved it!'

Had she? She might have said 'I love this part' or 'I love his shop' or even 'I love Hugh Grant'. But had she said she loved the film? She *liked* the film, but it wasn't top three or ten or even probably top one hundred. But Gabe seemed so pleased with himself and Violetta and Nicoletta were looking so expectant, all she could do was smile and say, 'I do love that film!'

The party broke up soon afterwards. The next day would be busy as some family and Nora's friends arrived, and they would start preparing and decorating for the birthday party the next day. Nora had tried again to shift the engagement celebration focus away from the party itself, arguing that it was Nonna's night and she didn't want to take away from that, but Nonna had insisted that nothing would make her happier than to announce the engagement on her birthday and what could she do but say she couldn't wait?

Nora and Violetta started to carry things through to the kitchen, sending Nicoletta away home with her sleeping babies despite her protestations that it wasn't fair not to help. Luca roused himself from his brooding and started stacking the dishwasher. Gabe, she couldn't help but notice, pleaded emails and sloped off upstairs.

Upstairs. To the bedroom they would share. With the one bed.

If only she hadn't thought it was romantic to wait! Who was she? Lizzie Bennet? Cher from *Clueless*? She was *twenty-eight*. She'd slept with men she didn't even really like and then here came fate and she went all abstinence and now she wasn't sure she wanted to go there at all.

With her own actual fiancé.

The man she loved.

The man she was marrying.

It was ridiculous. She just needed to get over *it* and onto *him*. It was the only way.

And it would be tonight.

No more delaying tactics. Mind made up, she looked at the cleared table to make sure there was nothing else to be done and turned, only to walk straight into a broad chest. She almost fell back, but a strong hand shot out to grab her arm and haul her back upright.

'Oof!' was all she managed before clocking Luca. 'What is it with you? I am always falling over when you are around.' She flushed, her certainty that it had been Luca that night resurfacing.

He looked at her grimly. 'What was that?'

She glared up at him. '*"I'm sorry, Nora, I didn't mean to bump into you and send you flying." "That's okay, Luca, I know you didn't mean to send me flying."*'

Her sarcasm was completely lost on him as he folded his arms, towering over her. 'Well, obviously. But you didn't answer my question. *What was that?*'

'What was *what*?'

'Why did you cover for Gabe back then?'

'Why did I *what*? The real question is what was going on with you! Why did you get so intense? Put him on the spot like that? Asking him questions that you knew . . .' She stopped.

But Luca obviously knew what she was going to say. 'Questions I knew he didn't know the answer too? Questions he *should* have known the answers to?'

'Firstly, we have only known each other a few weeks – ask the Mr and Mrs questions at our golden wedding celebration. Secondly, he's not a details guy, I know that and I am fine with it, so why are you interfering? He's here and we are planning a wedding and your whole family is excited. And *I* am excited. I want to be here, to be part of this so please, just . . . don't.'

He watched her for a moment. 'Your favourite film is *Sleepless in Seattle* . . .'

'Well, yes, but you know that because we just watched it and I gave you an entire lecture on why it's the greatest film of all time so . . .'

'And you never gave Gabe the same lecture?'

'I . . .' She had tried but he had fallen asleep.

'Your favourite book is *Pride and Prejudice*.'

'I am a romantic twenty-something, of course that's my favourite book!'

'Your favourite colour is green, and not just because it brings out the red in your hair. Your favourite flavour is anything citrus and tart, ideally lemon, and your favourite music is Taylor Swift, specifically *Speak Now* or her *Folklore* era . . .'

'Again, I am a romantic twenty-something and Taylor Swift is the bard of my generation.'

'Does Gabe know any of that?'

She couldn't answer that honestly. She would have told him all these things – her impassioned theory on why *Speak Now* was the greatest album of the early twenty-first century was so well honed it could be a PhD thesis. But she knew that Gabe often tuned out what he indulgently called *her chatter*. He was convinced she would grow out of her youthful passions and into the sophisticated tastes he preferred and she loved the vision of the woman he thought she was, she could be.

*Had* loved. Now she wasn't sure she wanted to fit into that narrow box of his expectations at all. Was it too much to ask that someone loved her because of who she was, not because of how she bent herself into being what they thought she should be? She pushed the thoughts away. She had made her mind up to marry Gabe, she wouldn't allow any doubts or negativity.

But she did have a question of her own.

'OK, Mr, let's be honest, why didn't you tell me it was you that night?'

She didn't need to specify which night. She could tell by the way Luca paled that he knew exactly what she meant.

'You let me babble onto everyone about how it was fate and how Gabe saved me and you knew all along it was you. Thank you, by the way,' she added. 'But you still should have told me.'

'I think you're asking the wrong person.'

'What do you mean?'

'Why aren't you asking Gabe why he *didn't* tell you? After all, what difference would it make? It was still a staggering coincidence you bumped into each other so soon afterwards in a city the size of London, right? Still love at first sight? Still a perfect romance?'

'I . . .' How could she ask Gabe when she was as guilty of subterfuge as he was, but she couldn't say that to Luca. Nor could she say that she had heard a voice that seemed as familiar to her as her own, looked into eyes that seemed to promise safety and happiness and she had projected that memory onto Gabe. Because then he would know she was talking about him. That she had fallen for *him* at first sight.

The realisation hit her and she almost staggered under the weight of it. She had fallen for Luca that night and she was falling still. No wonder she didn't want Gabe to touch her.

But her friends were flying in the next day, his family joining them to celebrate her engagement to *Gabe*. An engagement which would give her everything she wanted. Which would make her part of this family. She just had to stop falling. Remember what was important.

'Nora . . .' Luca stopped. They were so close, as close as they had been on the Tuscan hillside, and her whole body was lit up with awareness. With want and need and knowledge. His scent, his nearness, the dark expression clouding his eyes, the set of his mouth, everything was so familiar and yet so intriguing, she wanted to know all of him, to explore him. For him to know all of her.

She meant to take a step back, to put distance between them, but instead she moved slightly forward, so close they were almost – *almost* – touching.

'Do you think I should marry Gabe?' As soon as she said the words, she wanted to snatch them back. They were so exposing, especially said like this, standing so close, looking at each other as if no one else existed in the world.

'He's my brother, Nora. That's not for me to say . . .' He paused. 'You have to do what's right for you.'

'Yes.' If only she knew what that was.

He turned, started to walk away and then stopped, hope flaring up sudden and disastrous as he turned back to her. 'In Florence, you said being part of this family made you feel whole.'

'Yes.' It was like being naked, her words repeated back to her in all their need and loneliness.

'*This family*, Nora. Not Gabe.'

And then he was gone leaving Nora standing even more alone than ever.

Hampstead, 10 July 2014

Dear Daddy,

My heart is too full, my throat so sore from crying, there is so much I wish I had said, so much I hope you know.

No girl could ever have had a better father. I'm not sure I've said that enough, said it at all. I have spent my life in awe of your cleverness, your kindness, your ambition, your sense of fairness. I always wanted to grow up to be just like you. That's why I became a lawyer. Following in your footsteps felt like the best thing I could do.

Watching you with Nora has been like reliving my childhood, that same patience, that same sense of humour, those same fantastic stories (I always said you should have written them down). I never worried about her not having a father figure thanks to you, the very best man there is. Thank you for loving her as you loved me, unconditionally and completely.

Your love for Mum has been a template of what marriage should be — respect and laughter and love and equality. I always knew I couldn't settle for

255

anything less. Thank you for being the perfect role model, the perfect father. Even when you listened to cricket all day . . . I never did learn to appreciate it. I wish I had tried harder.

Thank you for never showing by a word or a look that you were disappointed with my choices. I am sure you must have been, at first anyway, but you always made me feel like I could achieve anything, and you made my success possible, giving me a home, helping with Nora, showing me what grit and determination could do.

You will leave a huge gaping chasm in our lives and I have no idea how we will negotiate it. I'll look after Mum, that I promise.

And I will love you forever.

Your Lottie xxx

# Chapter Nineteen

Friday morning dawned bright and sunny. Ana was the first of Nora's friends to arrive, choosing a morning flight rather than a Friday evening one 'full of mini-breakers and hen nights'.

Nora took a taxi to the airport to meet her, curiously shy. The words they had exchanged just a couple of weeks ago still rankled, especially as she wasn't sure that Ana was wrong after all.

To her horror, she felt herself tear up as the familiar tall, elegant figure strutted through Arrivals as if it were a catwalk, heads turning as she passed by. Ana always knew how to make an entrance.

Conversation was a little stilted on the way back to the villa, mostly focusing on the countryside and views, easing as they reached the villa and Ana met the family, all furiously working to get things ready for the following day. Nora's offer to finish preparing rooms or to start on lunch were waved away with an admonition to get her friend settled in. Chiara had been joined by couple of sisters-in-law and several nieces and nephews and was marshalling her army of helpers so calmly that only a keen observer would spot signs of stress and Nora was glad to be able to escape the hot, if aromatic, kitchen, directing Ana to her room.

'OK, I hope you and Grace will be comfortable in here. They are put-up beds, but they seem pretty solid.' Ana and

Grace were to share the sitting room adjoining Nora's room, with Felix and Dai in Gabe's old room. 'Although maybe you should have the bed and Gabe and I can be in here.'

'Not at all. You can't celebrate your engagement in two single beds! This is gorgeous; if I was you, I would never come home.' Ana wandered over to the window and leant out. 'Although that volcano really is close, isn't it?'

'You do get used to it. Not that it's been too active so far. I might not be quite so calm if there were flames.' Nora waited for Ana to stow her bags and then directed her to the small en suite. 'The only problem is that you have to go through our room to get to the loo.'

'That will dampen the celebrating. Maybe we can do some kind of exaggerated knock to give you enough time to stop doing whatever X-rated things you are doing.'

'So far we haven't made it past PG.'

'What? Still?' Her glance was far too assessing.

'Gabe has been gone most of the time I've been here,' Nora pointed out. 'And last night he was fast asleep when I got to bed.' To her intense relief, as she was still shaken by her encounter with Luca.

'What about the middle of the night? Or the morning? I think I prefer morning sex anyway. It makes me energised. Better than morning yoga any day if done right.'

'This morning, we were all up and cleaning and bedmaking from seven.' Well, she had been. Gabe was still recovering from jetlag and had still been asleep when she'd headed to the airport.

'Hmm.' Ana stood back and surveyed her critically. 'Maybe the enforced celibacy is the reason you're not glowing.'

'The reason I'm not *what*?'

'Do you remember when Felix told us he and Dai were engaged? He was . . .' Ana shook her head as she searched for the right words. 'He was luminous. He was so happy that it shone through him, and *you* are not shining.' She bit her lip. 'I'm sorry, Nora. I know I haven't been the most supportive friend recently, but you still can talk to me about anything. I promise not to judge any more.'

'Everything is fine . . .' Nora started automatically and then she sighed, sitting down on the bed and looking down at her hands. 'Only I lied.'

'About what?'

'About running into Gabe. It wasn't some huge, amazing coincidence, the truth is that I cheated, I tracked him down. He gave his card to Dai and I used it to find out his routine and make sure I was in the right place at the right time. It wasn't fate or an amazing coincidence. I made it happen.'

'I know.'

Nora looked up at Ana incredulously. There was no judgement or scorn in her clear gaze, just amused warmth.

'Nora, you track people down for a living. Of *course*, you engineered a meeting; we all guessed that was what happened. That's not cheating, that's having agency.'

'Maybe, but I got it wrong. It wasn't even Gabe that night in Hoxton. It was Luca.'

Ana whistled. 'Hot Signor Darcy? That makes sense.'

'Does it?'

'It's just that from the very little I know of him, Gabe doesn't seem the type to notice an emergency going on under his nose, that's all.'

'That's not fair!' Although Nora had to concede that Ana had a point. 'Maybe. But that doesn't change the facts, does it? I engineered a huge coincidence, dressed it up as fate and . . .' She nearly said *got the wrong brother* but managed to stop herself in time. She couldn't allow herself to think that way. Luca might be attracted to her, but he had made his feelings plain last night, Gabe was his brother and that was more important than whatever spark was between them. Nora just needed to do her best to extinguish that spark, to concentrate on her feelings for Gabe. And she did have feelings for him, intense and real and all consuming, she just needed to find them again – and quickly.

'The only question is why does any of this matter?' Ana asked.

'Why? Apart from the fact I lied to my fiancé and his family? The fact that Gabe has misled me in turn? Oh, Ana, if Gabe wasn't responsible for helping me and if I didn't run into him by chance, then is any of this real? Are we meant to be?'

'Nora!' Ana sat down beside her and pulled her in for a hug, before leaning back and looking at her searchingly, Nora shy under her scrutiny. 'You're worrying about things that don't matter at all. The only real question is do you love Gabe enough to marry him? Is he the first thing you think about when you wake? Do you obsess about jumping his bones? Does he make you feel safe and wanted and respected and seen and heard? Because if the answer to all that is yes, then none of the rest is important.'

'I just wanted a sign. I got it wrong so often.'

'That's dating. You have to wade through a swamp of frogs to find someone whose ribbit isn't quite so irritating and who is an acceptable shade of green. No one said it was fun or easy, Nora. Life isn't a film . . .'

'I know that!'

Ana squeezed her hand. 'Do you? I loved your mother's stories as much as anyone, but you know that what she had with your dad, it wasn't real life, don't you? She didn't have to wake up one morning to realise he's started to grind his teeth while he sleeps, or he can't put his socks in the

260

laundry basket, that he doesn't rinse the sink out. They had a perfect few days and that's a romance, but a love story is a life together. Like your grandparents.'

'They had a romance too,' Nora objected. 'My grandfather used to come into her library every day to study, and they used to look at each other, and then one day they left at the same time and he held the door open for her and their hands brushed and he asked her out for coffee. They had a perfect romance and the perfect happy ever after.'

'Nora, that story could have ended one of a million ways. He might never have got up the courage to ask her out and every now and then wonder if she was the one who got away. He might have stood her up, on accident or on purpose, and never set foot in that library again. She might have turned him down because someone else asked her first. They might have had nothing to talk about and had no second date. What your grandparents had was a love story. They fell in love and made a life together. They stayed together through all those years when your grandmother thought she couldn't have children, they laughed and cried together, got on each other's nerves sometimes but cared enough to make it right when they went through a bad patch. I always loved how he made her a morning cup of tea even though he drank coffee, and she would always ask about the cricket score even though she had no interest in it herself.' Ana laughed. 'It was so funny watching her do her best to look interested when he got carried away and took her through every over and she never once tried to change the subject. She cared because he did. That's couple goals right there. That's what I want.'

Nora had never heard her friend say any of this before. Ana's parents were rich Russian expats who had moved to London in the early nineties, and who coexisted in their big

Hampstead mansion in between international travel and long working hours. There was no warmth, no companionship she could see in their high-powered marriage. Ana's life had been luxurious but rather lonely – no wonder she had preferred to hang out at Nora's smaller, shabbier, warmer home.

'I guess you're right.'

'You know I am. And that kind of love story takes a lot of work. It takes compromising and forgiving and putting your pride second. But that's what we should all aim for. If that's what you have with Gabe – really have – then I will happily apologise on bended knee for doubting you and cheer as loud as anyone if an engagement is announced. But, Nora, don't mistake romance for love. That will only lead to heartbreak.'

Nora leant against her friend, glad of her strength. 'You never need to apologise for looking out for me. When did you get so wise?'

'There's a lot of time to think on photo shoots,' Ana said drily. 'OK, I was promised a glass of wine and a look around. I didn't travel all this way to stay indoors.'

Nora took Ana on a tour of the vineyard as promised, her mind whirling as she showed off the sights. She had always thought of her mother and father's meeting as the perfect love story. But Ana was right. A meet wasn't the end goal, it was the beginning. It was what happened after the credits rolled that mattered. What did that look like for her and Gabe? Was there respect and compromise and love in her future no matter what tests came their way?

She wanted to believe it was true, but doubts gnawed away at her as much as the memories of Luca's gaze, his words of the night before. The way he'd looked at her as if there was so much he wanted to say but couldn't. *Wouldn't.*

'Where *is* Gabe?' Ana asked as they walked through the kitchen, snagging a roll warm from the oven and a handful of grapes as they did so.

Violetta rolled her eyes. 'He's gone to see those friends of his, didn't he tell you, Nora?'

'The ones in Taormina?' Nora said, shocked. 'Today?' When there was so much to do? Luca had taken the day off and was helping his father set up the terrace, turning it into the perfect party venue, Carlo was prepping like mad for the next day. The only idle hands were Nora's and she had put in a good few hours bedmaking and dusting earlier, only stopping because the family insisted she spend time with Ana.

She pulled out her phone and, sure enough, there was a brief message from Gabe. A profuse apology alongside a wish she had a good day with her friend, and he would see her that evening, followed by a protestation of love and a line of kisses. But the extravagant compliment failed to move her, and the kisses left her cold. He knew she wouldn't approve, that was why he had disappeared while she was at the airport.

'Oh well,' she managed to smile, 'you know what he's like, he'd only get in the way. Better that he's not under our feet.'

The rest of the day passed quickly. After the tour and a quick dip in the hot spring, Ana and Nora helped decorate the terrace with more fairy lights, placing tall candelabras in corners, covering long trestle tables with white cloths and bright flower arrangements.

More and more guests turned up during the day, the villa and gardens buzzing with chat and work. The sun was hot, the air even more aromatic than usual, lemon tinged and full of fragrant herbs and pine. Nonna held court in the formal sitting room, in use for the first time since Nora had come, clearly thrilled to have all her family around, despite her protestations that it was too much fuss, looking even more glamorous than usual and ten years younger than her eldest daughter. Antonio, quiet and determined, a hammer in one hand, a measuring tape in his pocket, a pencil behind his ears, was effortlessly tweaking and creating, turning the back garden into a perfect party venue. Chiara was clearly in her element, ruling her kitchen with a steely calm, pausing only to consult with Carlo, who was running service as usual in the restaurant that day but had all sorts of things simmering in preparation for the next day. Violetta was helping her father and brother clad in a tiny pair of denim shorts and a sports bra, an outfit which bought comments from her aunts and uncles which she bore with a good-natured smile that said she had heard it all before. Nicoletta, baby in a sling, was seemingly everywhere at once.

Nora's heart squeezed. They had taken her in, accepted her, made her one of them. And it was all right there for the taking. She could listen to her doubts and lose everything or she could celebrate her engagement and then in October she would be back here, becoming one of them officially, with her own rooms, a permanent space in the heart of the family. It was perfect, she couldn't let a few jitters derail her. Surely everyone had doubts when the rest of their life was on the line?

But whenever she convinced herself she was doing the right thing, she would catch sight of Luca, jeans low slung, bare chested, hair wild, a broad grin on his face. Up a ladder, hammering or sawing or planing a piece of wood that ten minutes later would become part of a bar, or a new table. He worked seamlessly alongside his father, although they only communicated in grunts and monosyllables, and her heart ached, for the estrangement both were too proud to bridge, and for him. She couldn't tell him how conflicted she was, couldn't ask him if he wanted her, couldn't come between two brothers because she was needy and had tried to manipulate fate. It wasn't right or fair. She had to take these inconvenient feelings and wanting and attraction and lock them all away. It was Gabe or no one, there was no other choice.

And she couldn't go back to no one. So she had to concentrate on everything she loved about Gabe.

Her friends were the last of the guests to arrive that day, their taxi pulling in just as Gabe drew up in his father's car. Nora suppressed a surge of irritation that he hadn't offered to pick them up, that he had spent the day sailing and relaxing while his family had been so hard at work, but she hid it as she greeted him with a kiss, reminding herself that just yesterday he had been on a long-haul flight, that he had been working while she had been relaxing in the sun and they had a long weekend ahead of them. But all her worries were forgotten as she embraced Grace, Felix and Dai.

'You're here! I can't wait to show you around.'

'I can't wait to look around. Do you know that Ana sent me a photo of her lounging in a hot spring while I was doing maths catch-up with Table Six?' Grace shook her long braids decisively. 'No, I am not going to think about maths and I am certainly not thinking about Table Six all weekend.'

'Would a glass of wine help?'

'I thought you would never ask. Look at this, Nora! A real vineyard. You get to marry a hot rich man and his family own a vineyard! If you wanted to one up Jake, you have succeeded. I can't wait for his wedding now, I'm going to casually drop this into conversation with absolutely everyone.'

'I don't care about Jake.' And she realised with some astonishment that it was true. 'I just wish him well, that's all.'

Grace nudged her. 'Of course you do, from your amazing villa with natural hot springs and its own vineyard.'

After quick introductions, praying she wouldn't forget any of the extended family's names, Nora took her friends up to their rooms to freshen up. 'It's a kind of buffet this evening,' she said. 'Pasta and salads, that kind of thing. Chiara assured me that she is only serving the most simple of meals tonight, but I have been in that kitchen and her definition of simple and mine are very different things.'

Felix grinned. 'That's because, my darling, you think a baked potato is a fancy meal.'

'They were hasselbacks, heathen, and they took me hours. Anyway, come down when you are ready. Ana is all settled in, I would say I can't believe she hasn't come to say hi, but last I saw her, she had found a handsome lawyer cousin and was busy terrifying him into submission.'

'A girl needs a hobby,' Dai said.

Felix followed her to the door. 'You look well,' he said, searching her face. 'Sicilian air suits you.'

'I am well.' And she was. These stupid doubts would be forgotten and she would be sure and happy again, happier because she would belong somewhere.

'And this is really it? You're engaged?' His gaze dropped to her still bare left hand.

'Looks that way. There's a party tomorrow and everything.' But she couldn't hide the waver in her voice and she knew he had heard it. 'Look, Felix, that message the other day. About the accident . . .'

'None of my business. But your happiness *is* my business, Nora. We have been friends since we were four. You're like a sister to me. I just want you to be happy.'

266

'I am.' And if she said it enough, it would be true. 'Thank you for being here.' But she couldn't meet his kind, steady gaze as she kissed his cheek and walked away.

An hour later, Nora stepped out onto the terrace, showered, her hair a gleaming mane of silk thanks to Ana and her box of tricks. Her friend had also worked her magic with her brushes, elongating Nora's eyes into Taylor Swift-like cats' eyes, painting her mouth a redder shade than usual. Nora had hesitated between a deceptively simple and terrifyingly expensive white sheath dress Gabe had brought her back from New York and one of her mother's slip dresses, this one a soft green edged with cream lace, but the white felt too bridal and so, almost defiantly, she chose the slip, although she knew Gabe would be expecting her to wear his gift. The silk settled around her, comforting and familiar, and as always Nora could smell her mother's perfume, although she knew full well the dress had been cleaned several times and any scent was just her imagination.

Her friends greeted her with wolf whistles.

'You look stunning, Nora, and is that a real tan?' Dai asked.

'I am officially off-white rather than corpse bride,' Nora told him proudly, comparing her arm to his.

'I am still Celtic pale,' he sighed, sounding more Welsh than ever.

'Two words, Dai. Fake tan,' Ana said and watched his struggle to reply with obvious amusement.

'I can't fake tan, I play rugby,' was his only rejoinder.

'You'll never get on *Strictly* with that attitude.'

And then Nora was borne away by Chiara to be introduced to some friends who had joined them for the evening. The terrace was full of people, chattering and laughing, the tables groaning with huge bowls of food, music filled the air and fairy lights twinkled in the trees and from the beams. The evening felt festive and celebratory; it was hard to remember that this wasn't even the party, just the warm-up event.

'I love your dress,' Violetta gasped as Nora joined the family.

'You are always so unique, Nora,' Nicoletta said. Gabe had said the same words several times, but from Nicoletta it sounded approving.

'You look beautiful.' Luca's voice was so low that Nora almost thought she had wished the words into being, but when she looked up at him, she saw only appreciation. 'Doesn't she, Gabe?'

'Always.' Gabe took her hand and kissed it. She slipped her fingers through his, holding on tight. He was here and he was real and he wanted her and she was the luckiest woman in the world. Just look at him, tall and gorgeous and perfectly turned out in a white suit that on any other man might look ridiculous but on him looked effortlessly stylish. '*Bella.*' He slipped an arm around her waist and steered her away from the family group. 'Come, my friends are here. They are longing to meet you.'

Gabe's Sicilian friends were similar to his London friends, rich and cultured and fashionable, and Nora felt on the outside of a clique she had no idea how to infiltrate. They spoke mostly in Italian, occasionally apologising to her, before heading straight back into the conversation, and she stood awkwardly, aware of her aching feet and calves in her too-high heels, a fixed smile on her face, sipping her Prosecco and wondering when she could politely leave and make her way to a more convivial group.

'Nora!' To her relief, Violetta appeared flanked by a group of teenagers. 'Come meet my cousins! Maria loves your dress, I told her you have lots more just like it.'

With no little relief, Nora turned to the group and was soon swapping stories of vintage finds with the terrifyingly stylish teen. It was no surprise to find out that she lived in Milan, sister to the cousin Ana was once again deep in conversation with.

Eventually, the youthful group drifted off and Nora turned to head to the bar for a refill, only to walk straight into a tall, solid figure. Of course it was Luca. She had managed to spend twenty-eight years never falling over or bumping into anyone, then along came Luca and her sense of balance totally disappeared.

'Having fun?' he said, steadying her, then snatching his hand back as if he didn't want to touch her for any longer than was strictly necessary.

'Of course,' she said, her smile as bright as she could make it. 'My friends are here, Gabe is right here . . .' She couldn't help looking over at the tight circle around him, despite knowing that Luca followed her gaze.

'Gabe is here *now*. Did you miss him today? Seems strange that he has been gone for nearly two weeks and yet didn't want to spend today with his fiancée.'

'Not every couple need to be joined at the hip. Gabe understood that Ana was arriving today and I wanted to spend the day with her, just as he wanted to see his friends,' she defended but wasn't sure whether it was Gabe or herself she was standing up for. 'Besides, I wanted to help . . .'

As soon as she said the words, she knew they were a tactical error.

Luca's smile was cynical. 'And Gabe wanted to do anything rather than spend the day on chores.'

'He has been working the last two weeks, he had a gruelling flight and deserves some downtime.' She stepped away, further from Gabe and his friends, not that any of them seemed to be taking any notice of her or the conversation. 'What are you doing, Luca?'

He rubbed a hand wearily over his face. 'I don't know. I just . . .'

'Just what, Luca?'

What did she want him to say? That he was attracted to her too? That he didn't want her to marry Gabe because he wanted her for himself? In a film, that might seem a realistic and even romantic scenario, but in real life it was the stuff of soaps, a headline on a supermarket magazine. *I ran off with my fiancé's brother at our engagement party.*

There was no happy ever after in that scenario.

'I just want to make sure you're happy,' he said finally in a low voice.

Nora refused to acknowledge the stab of disappointment shooting through her.

'I am fine,' she snapped. 'It's a beautiful night and I am with the man I love and who loves me. My friends are around me and I am arranging a wedding which will give me companionship and security and a family. Who are you to ask me about happiness, Luca? You have everything a man could want: you have a wonderful life, and a family who adores you and a father who misses you, but you let pride keep you away. You could be here, every day, part of it all, but you choose not to because you don't want to say sorry, to admit you made some mistakes, that you are not Mr Perfect. So don't worry about my happiness, take care of your own first.'

Nora had no idea where the bitter words came from. Luca was her friend and ally, and that early suspicion (warranted admittedly) aside, he had been nothing but kind to her. He had seen her at her most vulnerable, understood her and she was in love with him—

270

She was *what*?

But of course she was in love with him. Not because their eyes met in a moment of crisis but because of the man she had got to know.

But he wasn't in love with her, and even if he was, his pride and honour wouldn't allow him to act on it, which was probably, definitely, for the best. Everything was tangled enough as it was.

'I have everything I ever wanted right here,' she said, hating the pleading note in her voice. 'I can't just throw it away without . . .'

Without what? A sign? A word from him? She didn't even know herself, but whatever she needed, Luca was clearly not able or willing to supply it, his face was expressionless, his eyes shadowed and all he said was, 'You are right,' before he turned and left.

Nora stood for a moment, tears trembling in the corners of her eyes, thickening her throat, resolutely swallowing them back.

She turned back to Gabe, who was watching her and Luca, his expression unreadable. She sauntered over with a smile, and slipped a hand through his arm. She had made her bed and she was going to enjoy lying in it. No matter what.

Hampstead, 15 April 2015

Dearest Nora,

Nineteen today! An adult for a whole year — and the same age I was when you were born. A sobering thought, and yet in some ways you are so much more mature than I was. That's grief, I think, it accelerates the growing-up process. I feel like I have aged a decade in the last year. And as for you . . .

Oh my best and only girl, you should be in your first year at university kissing unsuitable people, sleeping in and rushing into lectures in last night's clothes, figuring out who you are away from me and London and the safety net of home. And I should be wandering around the house, sitting on your unnaturally tidy bed in your unnaturally tidy bedroom and missing you in ways I will never admit to you.

I am truly devastated that you're not out living your best life, but at the same time, I am (selfishly) so glad you are here. I'm not sure I am ready to be alone in this house. Only you feel the same unbearable loss. Only you miss them so much that it feels impossible to carry on. If misery loves company, grief needs it, I think, but only the company of someone who really understands. I can't be selfish forever and at some point soon I know I need to nudge you out of this nest. But not just yet.

xxx

# Chapter Twenty

Chiara clapped for attention and announced that dinner was ready, served buffet-style from the kitchen for hot food; salads, breads and drinks heaped on the long wooden table outside. Everything looked and smelt incredible.

Nora mechanically filled her plate with salad, a perfectly cooked arancini, crisp, hot calamari, pasta tossed with aubergine and other delicious food, but she didn't feel hungry despite her busy day; the wine was tasteless, the laughter and chatter overwhelming. But she pasted on her game face, slipping into a seat next to Ana, whose plate was piled high and who was busy continuing her flirting with Alessandro, one of the Catalano cousins.

'He works in Milan,' she said as Nora sat down, a small smile playing around her perfectly made-up mouth. 'He says I should look him up when I am next there.'

'Where's my hot Sicilian fling?' Grace set her glass on the table and looked around. 'It's not fair, I want a Signor Heathcliff too.'

'There will be plenty more tomorrow, I'll look one out for you,' Nora promised. It was good to have her friends here – beyond good. They were safety, anchoring her back in the real world, not the heady place where she had been romanticising and dreaming as if she was the heroine in a film, not Nora Fitzgerald of Hampstead.

She looked around for Gabe, hoping he would join

them, but he was at another table with his friends. When she caught his eye, he smiled and held up his glass to her in a silent toast and she mirrored the gesture, filled with relief. They would be OK. Better than OK, they would be perfect. Absence had shifted her perspective, just as spending all her time with him had. He was neither the charming prince of those first weeks nor the feckless adventurer she had started to see him as but, like most people, somewhere in between. OK, he could be a tad self-absorbed and occasionally selfish, but she had her foibles too. Ana was right, marriage was learning to love each other's flaws. Not expecting perfection.

Antonio stood up and said a few brief words in Italian, which Alessandro translated for them. 'He says that tomorrow is the time for speeches, tonight is for food and family and friends.'

'Amen,' Felix agreed as everyone stood and held out their glasses in a brief toast before tucking into the delicious food.

Nora found she was hungry after all, her busy day leaving her little time to eat, and the wine slipped down just as easily.

'I am so happy we are all together,' she said after they had finished the main course and replenished their plates with fresh fruit and home-made cannoli. 'Thank you all for coming on such short notice.'

'Wouldn't miss it for the world,' Dai assured her.

Felix nodded. 'Obviously it's a terrible chore to be sitting in a Sicilian vineyard eating gorgeous food with a day of sightseeing, beaches and swimming tomorrow, followed by a party which promises even more free-flowing wine and delicious food, but sometimes friends need to make sacrifices.'

Nora grinned at him. 'You are so selfless, Felix, that's what I love about you.'

'I'm a giver,' he agreed. 'Nora, my darling, you know we think this has all felt very fast.'

'It feels it because it *is* fast,' Grace chimed in, and Felix swatted her.

'Shush, I am making a heartfelt point,' he said. 'There is no set time for love,' Felix continued. 'Look at us: Dai and I were married six months after he asked me out and that was the best decision I ever made. Well, that and leaving banking. What I am trying to say is that if *you* are happy, *we* are happy. We celebrate with you, just as we have grieved with you, laughed with you, cried with you. That's what friends do. That's what family does, and you are – my family, that is. Ever since the day you stormed over to Peter Fotheringham and threatened to beat him up.'

'I can still see it now,' Ana laughed. 'Pint-sized Nora, hands on hips, her red hair practically flaming.'

'Strawberry blonde,' Nora corrected automatically, knowing it made no difference. This was one battle she had lost many years ago.

'And then you joined her.' Felix blew Ana a kiss. 'Although, in your case, not so pint-sized. And you said to him, *If you hurt my friend, either of them, you had better watch out. I will come for you.*'

'How old were you?' Dai asked, grinning.

'Five,' Ana said. 'Nora was still four.'

'My dad wanted me to be more like my brothers, tougher, sporty, into rugby,' Felix said and shuddered.

'At least you married a rugby player.' Dai kissed his cheek and Felix grinned.

'True, marrying you is the one thing I did he's ever approved of. The truth is, I felt like a disappointment, an outsider at home, but I always felt free at your house, Nora. Your grandmother's cakes on the table when we got home from school, and the way your grandfather would talk to us like we were people, you know? And your mother so funny and kind and impetuous, always thinking of the best adventures for us. It was a home in a way my house never was.'

Ana nodded. 'Me too. For me, my childhood was nanny after nanny and never seeing my parents, alone in that big, cold house.' There was a reason Ana had a flatmate although she could afford to live alone, had given Grace so much free rein with the decoration. Nora knew how much she liked to return from a trip to a busy, lived-in space. 'I begged my parents not to send me to boarding school because I didn't want to leave you guys. Leaving the friendliness and love of your home and returning to that mausoleum of a mansion was always a wrench. I love your house, Nora. It's all the best bits of my childhood right there.'

'I wish I had gone to primary school with you all,' Grace said. 'I'm devastated that I missed out on being on the Felix protection squad.'

'You've always been on my squad,' Felix assured her.

'You were so cool,' Ana remembered. 'I couldn't believe it when you spoke to me in form that first day in Year Seven.'

Grace scoffed. '*I* was cool? You were this terrifying, glamorous creature who already looked like a supermodel. And then there was Nora, aways with a cause and a petition and a placard and all that fire and determination . . .'

'It's a long time since I made a placard.'

'I've missed that fire, Nora, but it feels like it's started to come back,' Grace said quietly, and Nora nodded.

'Maybe it has. I was so ground down by everything for so long, but it feels like I'm figuring out who I am again. It's about time, I know I haven't always been easy.'

'Well, if a volcano can't reignite a fire, then nothing can,' Dai joked and they all laughed.

'I don't know if I have ever thanked you enough, for the last ten years. For sticking by me. At times it felt like I was in stasis, you know? But you never gave up on me, never let me wallow. Always there, even when I didn't realise I needed you, told myself I didn't need anyone.'

'Of course we were there,' Ana said. 'That's what families do. And I know it feels sometimes like it was all dark, that you lost a lot, Nora – I mean, you *did* lose a lot – but there has been a lot of fun and happiness, even when your mother was ill.'

'That time she made us sneak cider into the hospice so she could relive her school prom,' Grace said.

'That trip to Brighton when she was so weak but insisted on swimming,' Ana added. 'I was so terrified she would get swept away, but she was in her element, remember?'

'The texts she would send. Remember the soap opera she made up about the staff. Her poor doctors. It was totally libellous. Brilliant but libellous.'

'It hasn't been a one-way street, Nora. I would never have had the courage to start the café without your support,' Felix said, smiling at her.

Ana nodded. 'You always put my ridiculous job into perspective. That awful time at Paris Fashion Week when I called you from the loos, crying because the outfit was so hideous and you told me to strut like no one had ever strutted before.'

'The way you always listen. Table Six always feels much more manageable after one of your pep talks,' Grace added.

'You made me so welcome,' Dai laughed. 'You were so protective of Felix, but ready to give me a shot, although it was very clear that if I messed him around, I would have to answer to you.'

'Nora Fitzgerald, protection squad since the Year 2000.' Felix's expression was full of affection.

Nora looked around the table at the dear, familiar faces. Faces she had known almost all her life. People who had been there for her at her lowest, and who were always ready to celebrate her triumphs no matter how small. People who had never judged her, whether it was a whirlwind engagement or failing her A levels. People who wanted nothing for her, or from her, but her happiness.

All this time she had been grieving for the loss of her family, Jake's family, now here she was trying to find a family in Sicily. But she *had* a family, one brought together not by blood but by love. Her friends were her brothers and sisters in every way that counted. They knew her inside out. Had held her hair back when she had drunk too much of her mother's cider that night in the hospice, and comforted her as she had sobbed out all the fears and grief she had kept from her mother. They had allowed her to moon over Jake and dried her tears when he left. They never judged her, but sometimes they nudged her, and they were always, *always* on her side.

Her eyes filled. 'I am so lucky to have you all.'

'Damn right,' Grace said. 'You can thank us with regular long breaks at your in-laws'.'

'Hear, hear.' Ana held up her glass in approval as they all laughed, only for the laughter to die away as Gabe got to his feet, clinking his glass for attention.

The wine soured in Nora's mouth and the laughter turned to dread. Whatever Gabe was plotting, she was sure it had something to do with her, and she hated public scenes.

'*Attenzione,*' he called, his voice breaking through the low buzz, and the courtyard silenced, everyone looking at Gabe expectantly. 'Nora.'

Gabe looked larger than life, his smile warm and full of adoration, hair perfect, eyes alight with happiness, the white suit enhancing his good looks, a fairy-tale prince come to life, gorgeous, strong and ready to take care of her. So why wasn't she filled with anticipation and happiness as he gazed at her in a besotted fashion that had his aunts whispering in admiration and his friends throwing her envious glances?

'Nora Fitzgerald, please join me.'

What could she do but obey? Gabe's family were laughing and clapping, her own friends were clearly half amused, half horrified, knowing how much Nora had always preferred a role backstage rather than being in the limelight, how any kind of public declaration made her squirm with embarrassment even when she was just spectating.

This wasn't *really* public, she reminded herself, this was a space full of friends and family, people who loved them – and Gabe's sophisticated friends who all looked irritatingly amused, except for one very elegant woman who just looked sour. Nora pulled herself up and tottered towards him on wavering, shaky legs, wishing she had swigged her glass of wine first. She needed Dutch courage – or Italian courage, or English, or any kind of international courage she could find or drink.

'Gabe,' she half whispered as she reached him and he raised her hand to his lips. 'What are you doing?'

He didn't answer, too intent on his audience.

'Tomorrow, we celebrate my wonderful Nonna.' He beamed over at Nonna, who lifted her hand in a very regal wave. 'And we also celebrate my engagement to this amazing woman. But, let me tell you a secret. I haven't formally proposed yet, which means Nora hasn't actually officially said yes.'

His tone, his smile, both made it clear that he had no fear that this extravagant gesture might backfire, that this was another romantic story to add to their history. And why not? After all, Nora had confided her fears to her friends, to Gabe's own brother, but not to Gabe himself. Some not-fiancée she was.

'So it's time I corrected that.'

Nora could only stare at him in mute shock as Gabe took both her hands in his, no kneeling in that suit, she thought, half hysterically.

'*Bella*,' he murmured, and with sudden cold clarity Nora realised that he was really going to do this, that he was going to propose to her right here in front of all these people – and that she had no idea what she was going to say. It was one thing to keep heading blindly in a set direction because the alternatives were too unknown but quite another to set off anew.

'Gabe, can we . . .'

'*Ti amore*,' he continued as if she hadn't spoken. Maybe she hadn't, maybe she was too paralysed by fear and shock. 'You tell people I swept you off your feet . . .' She couldn't help but glance at Luca, despite her determination not to; he was thin-lipped, staring at his brother, mouth twisted. 'But the truth is that you swept me off mine.'

'Gabe,' she tried again and was pretty sure that this time she had definitely spoken aloud, but either he didn't hear or took it as a sign of encouragement.

She looked at her friends. Ana had her hand over her mouth, whether in horror or to suppress her laughter, Nora wasn't sure, Grace looked as pained as Nora felt, while Felix and Dai were holding hands tightly as if watching some terrible accident unfold. Which in a way they were.

'I know we have known each other for a short time, but nothing, no one, has ever felt so right. I love you and I want to spend the rest of my life with you. Nora Fitzgerald, will you marry me?'

The hush was so expectant that Nora could hear it breathe as she stared at Gabe in agonised indecision. It would be so easy to say yes. She *wanted* to want to say yes. To go back two weeks to when this would have felt like the perfect happy ever after to their whirlwind romance. But Ana was right. A proposal wasn't the end goal, it was the beginning, and she wasn't sure she and Gabe had built the foundations they needed to start out, not yet.

She looked over at his family. Gabe's mother and sisters smiling expectantly, tears already welling in the older woman's eyes, Antonio proud, nodding at her warmly. If she said no, then this would be it. No home at the vineyard, no ready-made family to step into. How could she walk away now she knew what it was like to belong?

Her gaze moved on to Luca, looking fixedly at his hands, but just as she started to tear her gaze away, he looked up and met her eyes and for one second she could have sworn his heart was in his eyes, that he was saying everything he had been so careful not to say, showing everything he had tried not to show, and she knew. There was no going back. She only had now.

'Gabe.' She clasped his hands tightly, familiar and comforting and oh so tempting. 'This is . . .' She tried to find the right words. 'This really is everything you promised and more.' She could feel the crowd relax at her words, the slight tension she'd sensed as she searched for words dissipating. 'Which is exactly what I'd expect from you.' Low chuckles and her breath came more easily. The last thing she wanted to do was hurt Gabe, especially not publicly. 'But I prefer to be a little less centre stage. Can we go somewhere more private?'

For a moment, his expression wavered, the certainty fading, then he winked at their captivated audience. 'The lady wants to get me alone. We will be right back.'

Nora half-pulled him around the corner, to the moonlit glade of citrus trees. The stars were so bright in the sky overhead, they didn't need lights, the air was warm, even more lemon-scented than usual. The beauty of the scene hurt her heart. Could she really walk away from all of this? Walk away from the man who wanted to lavish her with love and romance?

She took a deep breath. 'Gabe, why do you want to marry me?'

He looked unsure for a moment and then his smile was more expansive than ever. 'Bella, of course I want to marry you.' It wasn't an answer to her question, but typical of Gabe to see it in that light.

'I just want to know what it is you love about me.' Her hands were shaking. 'Why you think we are ready for marriage after such a short time. After all, you aren't keen on the way I dress, you're not really interested in my friends or the things I enjoy. I don't think you even know what I do for a job, do you? And that kind of goes both ways,' she admitted. 'Gabe, I hate jazz and I have no idea what a hedge fund even is, except that hedges aren't actually involved, no shrubbery at all, in fact.'

'Nora,' Gabe just looked confused, 'what do these things matter? What matters is how we feel.'

'Yes, that's true. And I feel that we need more time. I think we need to know each other properly, good and bad, before we get married, or even engaged. I think we both need to be sure that this is love and not infatuation. That we like each other and respect each other, that we are friends as well as lovers. That we can be our worst selves and know we are still understood. We are not anywhere near that yet.'

'But, *cara*, we are fated to be together, what difference will more time make?' His smile faded. 'Don't you want to marry me?'

Nora reached up and touched Gabe's cheek, wishing with all her heart that this was the romantic moment it was supposed to be, the beginning and not the end she feared it was. 'I think we both wanted it to feel fated, don't you?' She didn't want to tell him that she knew he had lied. For him to think that was the reason for her decision. 'I was so lonely, Gabe, and you were the answer to my prayers. You swept me off my feet in every way, swept me out of my comfort zone and into a new, more glamorous, fun-filled existence. You made me feel more – more beautiful and more desired and sophisticated than I have ever felt before and I am so grateful for that. But I think to stay in that life, I need to change, to try to be the woman you see, not the woman I am, and I don't think that's right. I need you to love me for me. And I need to do the same. I need to love you, Gabriel Catalano, not because you dazzle me, but because of who you are, and I'm not sure I know that man yet.'

Gabe took a step back. 'You don't want to get married.'

'No. Not yet at least.' OK, she had complicated feelings for Luca, but she owed it to Gabe, to those giddy few weeks they had shared, to try to see if they could salvage this relationship. 'But we could start again, be more real, more open and see where that takes us?' The offer was honestly meant, but as he shook his head, she knew his answer had never been in doubt. Gabe didn't want honesty and openness; he preferred the show.

'It's too late for that. It's now or never, Nora.' He reached into his pocket and brought out a box, flicking it open to show her the contents. Inside was a ring, a huge pear-shaped diamond on a diamond-studded platinum band. It was clearly very expensive – and as about un-Nora as a ring could be. 'I bought you this. I want you to wear it, Nora. Now, not one day.'

'It's beautiful.' She wasn't lying. Many women would think it utterly gorgeous. But Nora would prefer something smaller, less ostentatious, a ring with history behind it, and if Gabe didn't understand that, then he really didn't know her at all. But then again why would he when she had hidden herself from him from the start? 'It's beautiful,' she repeated. 'But I can't accept it.'

Even though she knew it was the right choice, the only decision she could make, it still hurt to see the words land, to see the warm glow replaced by hurt and shock, to feel that she had played him, even though her every move had been in good faith.

He was still for a moment, like an actor who had forgotten his lines.

'Then this is over.' Gabe stood tall, proud, but there was a little break in his voice that nearly undid her. She was pretty sure she hadn't broken his heart, not after such a short time, not when he didn't really know her at all, but that didn't mean she hadn't wounded him. Or that she wasn't hurting too.

'Yes. I think so. I'm really sorry, Gabe.'

'Me too,' he said quietly. 'Me too, Nora.'

He stood looking at her for one long moment and then he pocketed the ring, turned and was gone, leaving her standing all alone once again.

1 January 2016

Darling Nora Florence,

Happy New Year! It's 2016, a brand new year, and it is time for you and I to live again. I can't help thinking just how cross Mum and Dad would be if they could see how we have been over the last year or so. We will always miss them, but we need to move forward, to start to remember them with love and laughter as well as tears.

So, how about this for a resolution — let's resurrect our backpacking plan but make it bigger and better and longer and further and see the whole world? At some point, you, my darling, need to figure out exactly what you are going to do with your life, and at some point, I need to do the same! But no one said we can't figure it out while having adventures, did they? So here is a travel planning book, a special New Year present for you. Let's pick five places each and make an itinerary and who knows where we will see in 2017?

Love Mum xxx

# Chapter Twenty-One

'Don't leave, Nora, you should still stay for the party, Nonna would want you to, we all do.'

Nora smiled at Chiara gratefully. 'Thank you,' she said. 'Thank you for the offer and thank you for last night. For being so understanding.'

Nora had no idea how long she had stayed alone in the glade after Gabe had left, sick and trembling, knowing without doubt she had done the right thing but dreading the fallout. She'd just about got the courage to return to the villa and creep up to her room to pack, with no idea what to do next or where to go, when Chiara had appeared. The older woman had asked no questions, just reassured her that Gabe had left with his friends, nobody was talking about her (no doubt untrue, but Nora decided it was easier to believe it anyway), and swept her into the kitchen for a large glass of wine, telling her to make no decisions until the next day.

But now it was the next day and decisions had to be made. One thing was clear, her Sicilian dream was over. She was no longer part of the family, but an ex-girlfriend once again, and she couldn't outstay her welcome. She certainly couldn't stay for the party, no matter what Chiara said. It was a family occasion – Gabe needed to be there, not her.

'No understanding needed,' Chiara said. 'Marriage is too serious a business to rush into. Of course I wish that things were different. But I hope you know that you will always be welcome here, Nora. Any time.'

'Thank you.' Nora doubted she would ever take up the invitation, but she was genuinely moved by it. 'I can't tell you how much I've loved being here, loved getting to know you all. I've been made to feel so at home, it really has been the best two weeks. But after last night, I think the best thing to do is see if I can get a flight home today.' Nora cradled her coffee cup close. 'I just don't know what to do about my friends, they came all this way. There's no reason to drag them back with me, but you can't be expected to put them up either. Maybe I can find an Airbnb or something.'

They were all still sleeping off the night before, to Nora's relief, but she hadn't been able to fall asleep and after a fitful night had been up with the dawn. She had expected to have the kitchen to herself after such a late night, but Chiara had already been up and busy, looking as refreshed as if she had had a full eight hours sleep.

'How about my apartment?' Nora jumped as Luca strode into the kitchen. She hadn't seen him since Gabe's public proposal and found herself unable to meet his eye now, although she couldn't help but notice, despite her sudden preoccupation with her drink, that he looked unfairly fresh and alert.

'Your apartment?' she half mumbled into her coffee.

'I won't be using it as I am staying here and, as you said, there seems no need for your friends to cut their weekend short.' He paused. 'You are of course very welcome to stay as well. I am sure they would rather you were there.'

'I guess I could. I have a flight booked for tomorrow night anyway.' As did Gabe, but she would worry about that tomorrow. Today seemed enough effort right now.

'Then why not book your friends onto a vineyard tour for the morning, the restaurant for lunch and then into the spa for the afternoon and I can deliver them into Taormina later today?'

'That's too much, you have all your relatives here. I'm sure they can get a taxi.'

'And *I'm* sure I'll be glad of an hour's respite, there can be too much of a good thing when the whole family get together.' For a moment, as they exchanged grins and Chiara swatted her son affectionately, it felt normal, like this was still somewhere she belonged. But the moment faded all too soon.

'In that case, thank you. But I won't wait around. I think, for everyone's sake, I had better pack and leave as quickly as possible. I know,' Nora insisted as Chiara started to object, 'I know you don't mind, but this is Nonna's day. The last thing I want is people talking about me when they should be celebrating her. It's not fair on Gabe either.'

'I'll take you into Taormina as soon as you have packed. Make sure you have everything you need at the apartment.'

Nora opened her mouth to object and say taking her friends was more than enough, she really *should* just get a taxi, and then closed it again. She didn't have the strength to argue, and it did make sense for Luca to take her if she was using his apartment. She also couldn't deny that she wasn't quite ready to say goodbye to him yet, to any of them.

'I will miss you all so much.' The words were said before she could think better of it. 'I wish things could have been different.'

'If Gabe had just come home sooner,' Chiara burst out. 'If he had stayed home yesterday with you rather than heading off to those fancy friends of his, then we might be celebrating today as we planned. That boy never recognised a good thing when he had it.'

'It's not Gabe's fault,' Nora said quickly. 'No, the truth is, if it's anyone's, it's mine. I filled my head with fairy tales and romantic films. I let myself get swept along and didn't listen to any doubts or let myself notice any of the signs that said maybe it was all too good to be true. I should have put a stop to any marriage talk at the start, but I wanted it to be real so very badly.' Her voice broke a little and she stopped, afraid she might cry for the first time since it had all fallen apart.

'Gabe can be very persuasive,' his mother sighed.

'The irony is that in the end it wasn't Gabe keeping me in the engagement, it was you.' To her horror, Nora realised she was looking straight at Luca – and that he was looking straight back at her. Her heart stuttered and she felt her cheeks, her entire body, heat as she snapped her gaze away. 'All of you,' she quickly amended. 'I was infatuated with Gabe, I know that now, but I really fell head over heels in love with you. You're the family I have always wanted and I loved being part of you, helping in the office, or folding towels in the spa, setting the table for dinner. Listening to you all tease and bicker and laugh.' She stopped then, her throat too full to speak. 'It's been so lonely the last few years,' she half whispered. 'And then I came here and there was so much love and you shared it with me so unconditionally. I didn't want to walk away from that. I wanted to belong so badly that I refused to see what was right in front of me, that Gabe is amazing, but we weren't at all right for each other. Because if I walked away from Gabe, then I would have to walk away from you.'

Nora allowed herself to look back at Luca then, drinking him in, knowing that this morning would probably be the last time she would see him. Memorising the unruly fall of hair, his expressive eyes, the curve of his mouth, the hollow in his throat. 'You were right to be suspicious of me. I'm sorry I gave you a hard time over it.'

Luca half smiled, the crooked tilt of his mouth she loved to provoke. 'You didn't.'

'Can you tell your sisters how sorry I am? I really love them both. I just hope in time they forgive me, that you all do, especially Gabe.'

'I'm sure his pride is hurt more than his heart. Not that his heart wasn't . . . I mean . . .' Despite the complete awkwardness of the situation, Nora couldn't help enjoying Luca's clumsy attempt to salvage his faux pas.

'No. We both saw what we wanted in each other. You realised that before I did. You're right, I suspect he was trying to prove he was over Lily and I was in the right place at the right time. Anyway,' she said quickly, aware that Chiara was looking at them with sudden keen curiosity, 'all that matters now is that I really am sorry and all I want is for Nonna to have an amazing party and for everyone to forget about this as soon as possible.'

Much as she wanted to get a chance to apologise to Gabe's sisters in person, Nora also thought it politic to get away as quickly as possible, for all trace of her to be cleared before Gabe returned.

In the event, she was packed before any of the family or her friends were awake. It took just a few minutes to gather her things, her heart clenching as she turned to look at the room she had started to decorate with such hope and happiness, a room that was no longer hers. All too soon, Luca was loading her suitcase into the car, while Chiara gave her a much warmer goodbye than Nora knew she deserved and then she was twisting back in the passenger seat, watching the villa gates receding into the distance, knowing her all-too-brief time as a Catalano was at an end.

She was aware of Luca shooting her a not unsympathetic glance, but he didn't say anything as the car wound its way towards the city. Nothing really had changed. She might no longer be engaged to his brother, but Luca felt more unreachable than ever.

Their journey to Taormina was mostly silent, Nora remembering all the journeys they had taken over the last two weeks. The understanding they had found in her first visit to the Sicilian city, an understanding that had deepened in Florence.

'Are you sure you have room for us all?' Nora said as they reached the outskirts, unable to bear the silence, or her thoughts, any longer. If this was the last time she would spend with Luca, she needed to say something.

'Of course. There's a pull-out bed in the study, my room and a sofa bed; it'll be a squeeze, but you'll be fine for one night. For what it's worth, I think you are doing the right thing, leaving the vineyard, giving the gossip a chance to die down.'

Was that why he was helping her? Because it meant she left nice and early so everyone could forget about her? It felt good in a way, to torture herself with the negative thoughts. 'Thank you. And for tonight as well, it's really nice of you and it does make everything easier. I know I don't deserve your kindness, but—'

'Don't say that, Nora.' Luca's voice was harsh and Nora gripped her seat, shocked at how much the tone hurt, far more than Gabe's disappointment last night. She probably didn't deserve forgiveness and Luca hadn't always been on Team Nora, but she wasn't used to harshness from him. 'We all make mistakes. It's not about deserve or blame, it is what it is. We just have to live with the consequences.'

Was he talking about them? Not that there *was* a them; in fact, there wasn't much proof that her connection to Luca didn't exist solely in her head. A few glances, some tense moments, some chronic oversharing. She could have misread the whole thing completely.

But she knew she hadn't.

'It's ironic, don't you think?'

She didn't know she had spoken aloud until Luca responded. 'What is?'

What the hell, if she couldn't be completely honest now . . . 'I felt this connection, the night my shoe got stuck, I'd never felt anything like it before. It really did feel like . . .' Oh God, was she really going to say it? 'Like I'd fallen in love at first sight.' There, she'd done it. 'So I tracked down Gabe and manufactured this perfect meet. But if I had just called him to thank him, then he might have told me it was you who had helped me instead. I might have reached out to you and then . . .'

'Then what?' His voice was low and husky, vibrating through her.

'I don't know. Just we could have got to know each other properly. Or maybe we wouldn't. But trying to manipulate fate never works out. Look at Oedipus. At least we're not related. Not even by marriage now.' *Oh God. Please stop talking.* But at least her babbling had broken the awkward tension, Luca letting out a surprised jolt of laughter.

'What I don't get,' he said after a moment, 'is why you think tracking Gabe down was so bad?'

'Because I meddled with fate! Like Oedipus!'

'Oedipus tried to outrun fate, that's a whole different thing. Look, I sat with you less than a week ago to watch a film you assure me you have seen at least one hundred times. Did that woman . . .'

'Annie?'

'Did she sit on her hands hoping that Tom Hanks would just walk around the corner one day?'

'No,' she said in a small voice.

'No, she used some kind of nineties internet to stalk him, turned up at his house, wrote him a letter, walked out on her Valentine's Day dinner. I mean, he could have taken out a restraining order, maybe he does in the sequel, but she at least did her best to grab what she thought would make her happy. You just tried to do the same.'

She had, but for the wrong man. But she didn't want to say that out loud. She'd already made herself vulnerable and he hadn't responded. There was nothing more to say.

Finally, they reached Taormina, Luca navigating the narrow steep hills expertly, pulling into a garage a short walk from his flat. He won the tussle over who would carry her suitcase, Nora secretly relieved as he manoeuvred it up the several flights of stairs.

'There's milk, cheese and bread in. Fresh sheets and blankets in the cupboards. Make yourself at home. What are your plans, do you think?'

'I'll probably get some beach time in today until everyone arrives. Dinner out tonight, a little sightseeing and swimming tomorrow before we fly back home. I was always heading back tomorrow.' She hoped Gabe had rearranged his plans, it would be super awkward if they flew back together. 'Do you want us to clear out early?'

'No, no, I probably won't come back until Monday morning. Use the apartment for as long as you need.'

'Thank you.' Nora could barely manage to say the words. If leaving the villa had been difficult, this was Herculean. This really was goodbye. No more possibilities or if onlys, just a thanks for everything and a closed door. 'I mean it, thank you, especially for Florence. That was just . . . Anyway, can you tell Nonna I am sorry to miss her party, and everyone else . . .' Her voice trailed off. She'd left messages enough with Chiara. What else could she say?

'Hey.' Very gently, Luca tilted her chin so that she met his gaze. 'It was an honour to go to Florence with you. And I should be thanking you, my film knowledge has expanded by knowing you.'

'Happy to help,' she said hoarsely. She wanted him to keep touching her, to keep looking at her with that mix of longing and regret and amusement forever, but his hand dropped and he stepped away, her chin still tingling from his touch.

'I hope you find whatever it is you are looking for, Nora. Especially your father.'

'My new plan is to move to Florence and stake out that café until he appears.'

'That could work.' Oh how she loved that half-smile, the wry twist of his mouth.

'And I hope you find a way of talking to your father, if that's what you want. But I really shouldn't have said what I said, I was lashing out and that is unforgivable. But to an outsider, it's obvious how much you miss each other. You don't want to have any regrets, Luca. Family is too important to let pride get in the way.'

'I know.'

Nora held out her hand. 'Goodbye, then.' She tried not to shiver as he took it, his own hand cool and strong, his fingers closing around hers gently.

'Ciao.' He leant forward and brushed her cheek with his lips and she shivered again at the gentle caress, her fingers tightening on his.

Nora had no idea who moved first, but suddenly his mouth was on hers, her hands gripping his shoulders as if she might float away without him to hold her down. She had never allowed herself to fantasise about kissing Luca Catalano, but if she had, then her fantasies would have come up short because this kiss was more than she had ever imagined a kiss could be.

His mouth slanted on hers as if it were made to fit, his hand possessive on her hip, in her hair as she clung even harder onto him. Neither made any move to deepen the kiss at first, to press closer, to touch and caress, and yet Nora's whole body was alive and standing to attention, whimpering for more, her knees weak, her thighs jelly, her breasts, the pit of her stomach aching for him.

Luca half growled as she leant closer into him, his mouth tightening on hers, his hand splaying over her hip nudging her closer, his other hand positioning her head just where he wanted it, where she needed to be. It was like the climax of a movie, she could almost hear the swell of the score, see the fireworks, but somehow she still kept herself in check, much as she wanted to explore his body, to feel his hands on her bare skin, to finally rip that white shirt off his chest, she knew there was a line they couldn't – shouldn't – cross.

Just as she couldn't have said who made the first move, she couldn't say who broke away first. She stood there swaying, dizzy, cold, staring up at him. He looked almost winded.

'Nora. That—'

She couldn't let him finish. 'Please don't say that should never have happened. I'm glad I don't have to go home wondering what it would be like to kiss you.' She would be going home wondering what it would be like to shag him, but some things she really didn't need to share.

He looked at her then – really looked at her, unleashed, no more politeness, or reserve or holding back, his eyes filled with heat, the curve of his mouth all wolf, and every nerve stood up to attention, her knees barely holding her up. 'I was going to say that was incredible. You're incredible.'

For a moment, hope flared in her, that maybe there was a way they could salvage something from the whole mess, but that hope died away as he walked past her, careful to keep a clear distance between them.

'I want you to know that I felt it. In London.'

'Felt what?' she whispered.

'A connection. I felt it too. Take care, Nora Fitzgerald.'

And then he was gone and Nora knew he wouldn't return.

Hampstead, 15 April 2018.

Dear Erik,

I haven't written to you in a long, long time. There came a point when I thought it's time to accept that these postcards would never be sent. Miracles didn't happen twice. I wasn't going to turn a corner and see you standing there and it would be just like that afternoon in Florence, with the violin soaring and the world stopping and the first kiss to end all first kisses. I still dream about that kiss at night.

I thought the internet might bring you to me, all those backpacker Facebook groups and reconnecting with old acquaintances and do you remember whens. But you still eluded me. Maybe I could have tried harder. I didn't return to Florence or visit Sweden (not that Sweden is exactly small!). Part of me always hoped it might still happen for us one day. But I don't think I have that many one days left.

I've been ill, Erik. The kind of ill where all the talk is of battles and fights and winning, but every day feels like an endless slog instead. It's our girl's twenty-second birthday today and I will be putting on my most colourful scarf and dancing with her all night long, even though she and I both know I will pay for it tomorrow. But if this illness has taught me anything, it's that I need to take every opportunity to dance.

The truth is, I don't know if I will be here for her twenty-third. And that hurts more than anything else, knowing she will be left alone. I wish I had tried harder to find you, for her as much as me. I wish she had you for the days that lie ahead. I wish I could see you one last time. But, Erik, I am so grateful for what we did have! For every second of our time together, and for our brilliant girl. Thank you for everything you gave me.

C xxx

# Chapter Twenty-Two

Nora stared at her kitchen table and then over at the huge backpack on the floor. Huge it might be, but surely the laws of physics wouldn't allow *all* the items heaped in piles on the kitchen table to fit in and, if by some miracle they did, for her to ever actually carry it.

She looked over at a framed photo of her mother just as she set out on her life-changing trip, hair in plaits, a rucksack half her size by her side, excited grin taking up half her face and blew it a kiss. 'I need your help, Mum,' she said. 'Tell me I can do this.'

But she already had her mother's help. The travel planner her mother had surprised her with over eight years ago lay open on the table. Throughout her mother's illness, they had planned and refined, put together the perfect itinerary, researched routes and trains and trips and potential jobs. The work had been done. All Nora had needed to do was update it and book it.

'I still can't imagine it,' she said to her mother's photo. 'It seems impossible that in just two weeks' time, I'll be stepping off a plane and I'll just *be* there. In *Bangkok*. That I'll be sleeping in a hostel and meeting new people and doing all those things we planned. I know once I get started, I'll be fine, but the getting started part honestly terrifies me. How did you *do* it? There wasn't even internet back then! But right now, even getting to Bangkok seems impossible unless I can pare this lot down by at least half!'

She surveyed the table again, hoping that some solution would miraculously occur to her. Everything was sorted into piles: summer clothes, thin gauzy layers, scarves and sarongs, bikinis and flip-flops; waterproofs and warmer layers, all packed into little bags; hiking boots and socks, bulky but necessary; a medicine bag, including water tablets and flat rolled-up water pouches; two hammam towels, lightweight and quick drying; a case for cables and plugs; her toiletry bag; her Kindle, plus her well-thumbed guidebook and the precious planner.

It had taken her just over two months to get to this stage. Nora had allowed herself one week to mope when she had returned from Sicily before sitting back and taking a long, hard look at her life, and she hadn't been too keen on what she had seen. Yes, there had been tragedy, but she had allowed it to overwhelm her, had spent too long standing still instead of moving forward. She had let down everyone who loved her. Rereading the travel planner, it was as if her mother was back with her, advising her, pushing her, believing in her. Loving her. Seeing her sprawling hand-writing, laughing at her annotations and observations, made it feel as if Charlotte was here planning the trip with her.

'I don't have to pack it all now,' Nora said to the photo. 'It's not that I use the kitchen table for eating on most of the time anyway, and I still have a fortnight. I just wanted to do some test walks. If I am going to topple over like an overloaded turtle, I'd rather do it here in the privacy of my own home!'

It didn't matter that her mother couldn't reply. Just talking to her was enough.

'You're no taller than me and you managed.' Nora picked up the photo, only to put it down as the doorbell sounded, a long peal that aways made her jump, despite living with it for twenty-eight years. She glanced at the clock. She wasn't expecting any parcels, and her friends would all be at work. 'Jehovah's Witnesses, window cleaners, a surprise bouquet from a secret admirer?'

She was still laughing to herself as she stepped into the hallway and started to walk towards the front door. A tall figure was visible through the frosted glass and her pulse instantly started to race.

*You are ridiculous*, she scolded herself. *You can't react every time you see the outline of someone who vaguely resembles Luca.*

Was this how it had been for her mother? Had she spent her life catching glimpses of the man she had loved and lost?

Nora allowed herself one secret moment of hope before opening the door, preparing her 'Not today' speech – unless it was a bouquet from a secret admirer of course.

'Hi . . . Oh! Luca.'

For all the hope and the pulse racing, she hadn't actually *expected* to see him there. To see him at all. He looked just as good as she remembered, irritatingly – she had hoped that over the last few months she had embellished him, burnished him, but no, if anything, he was more mouthwatering than she remembered. Not that her mouth was watering or her stomach was dropping or her knees were weakening or her throat drying or any kind of physical reaction at all. It was just the shock of seeing him that had her clinging onto the doorpost like it was the mast of a ship and he an unexpected storm.

Luca was more tanned than she remembered, the dark olive highlighting the gold flecks in his eyes, the stubble on his chin emphasising the razor cut of his cheekbones, the sensuous slant of his mouth. She tore her gaze away, not allowing herself to linger on his mouth or to think about that one explosive kiss. Damn it. Now she was thinking about it. Remembering it. Reliving it.

'Um, come in?' Her voice was too high, the invitation sounding more like a question, standing aside awkwardly and still holding onto the door for dear life as he stepped inside.

'This is nice.' The low thrum of his voice reverberated through her as her body reacted to the slight rasp that had resonated so strongly with her that very first night.

'Thanks, it's nothing special, but it's home.' Every piece had been there since before she was born, the old bench rescued from a church against the wall, the antique hat and umbrella stand by the door, the original floor tiles and cornicing. Luckily her grandparents had spared the house the usual mid-century improvements, keeping all the original features intact. 'Do you want a cup of tea?' Wait, did he even drink tea? 'Or a beer? Wine?' She thought rapidly, what else did she have? 'Milk?' *Milk?* Was he five?

'Water will be fine.'

'Right.' She tried to hide her disappointment. Water was a subtext for *I won't be staying, this isn't a social call.*

'The kitchen is this way.' She started to lead the way. 'So how is everyone? Nonna? Your parents? Sisters?' She paused. 'Gabe?'

'You haven't spoken to him?'

'No.' She winced. 'For a couple on the verge of getting engaged, our lives were very separate, he had left nothing here and there was nothing of mine at his. I messaged, asked if he wanted to chat, apologised again, but I didn't hear back. I don't blame him.' The more time went on, the more clearly she saw how shallow their relationship had been, no friendship underpinning it, nothing tangible to hold on to, to miss now it was over.

'Everyone is good.' He didn't elaborate and she didn't press, although the scant detail left her hungry for more. But they weren't her family, and she had no right to demand details. She had exchanged messages with Nicoletta and Violetta for a couple of days after she had left, sent an extravagant bouquet of flowers, but the contact had soon petered out, Nora not really knowing what to say.

'I'm sorry about the mess.' Why had she brought him into the kitchen? Last night's dishes were still piled up in the sink as she hadn't unloaded the dishwasher yet, the large table heaped with her belongings.

Luca stopped and picked up the guidebook. 'You're going somewhere?'

'In a couple of weeks. This is all here waiting for me to figure out how to cram a year's worth of stuff into one bag that I can actually carry. I'm finally doing the round-the-world-trip my mother and I had planned to do,' she added, almost shy as she said it out loud.

'Amazing, that's brilliant, Nora.'

'Is it?'

'You know it is. Are you going alone?'

'Partly. Ana did consider coming for the whole lot but in the end didn't want to take so long off work, but she and my friends will all join for stages, some longer than others.'

She filled the kettle almost automatically. Stressful situations and visitors before six always required tea; after six, tea and wine or gin. She didn't make the rules, but she always followed them. 'Oh, you wanted water.' She added some ice cubes to a glass, a sprig of mint and filled it, handing it to him and then busying herself with making her tea, glad of a task.

'Thanks. So how did you decide where to go without a wine-making industry to pin your trip on?'

'Through this.' She touched the journal. 'I don't know if I ever said that before she got sick my mum and I were planning an around the world trip? Well, the New Year after my grandmother died Mum bought me this, so we could plan. We both had to pick five places we wanted to visit. We kept adding to it, refining, researching the whole time she was sick. I figured it was time I put all that work to use.'

'Good for you. Where are you starting?'

'Flying into Bangkok, for a month of trekking through Thailand, Vietnam and Cambodia. Then Australia, via a couple of nights in Bali. I'll land there early November and stay until January – Grace is joining me in Sydney over Christmas. Then New Zealand for a month before I head to South America. Ana will meet me there and we are going to spend six weeks trekking across Chile, Peru and Brazil before spending two weeks in Costa Rica and Paraguay. Then she goes home and I'll drive up the west coast of the States to Vancouver, where Felix and Dai will meet me for Easter. I'll head across Canada for about a couple of weeks which takes me into May and home again. I might interrail across Europe once back but will see how I feel. It might be good to save that for another year!'

'Very nice. Will you be working at all? I can sort out some introductions to vineyards if so.'

'I'd like to. Obviously, some things are set in stone – flights and organised treks are all booked – but there's lots of time to just see where the road – or train or bus – takes me, and to do a few days' work here and there as well.'

'Email me your plans and I'll see what I can do.'

'Great.' Her tea was ready and she curled her hands around the mug, grateful for its warmth, trying to find a way to ask what he was doing here without shutting down the unexpectedly easy conversation they had fallen into.

'I'm sorry for just turning up like this, but there's something I wanted to tell you in person,' Luca said abruptly and Nora froze, scenarios streaming through her head at warp speed. Nonna was ill, Violetta had dropped out of school, someone had died. He had met someone.

'Tell me what?'

'Can we sit down?'

'Of course.' She sank into a chair, setting her mug carefully in front of her and made herself breathe. Luca took the seat opposite and put his untouched water on the table. 'What is it?'

'The café called.'

'The café?'

'The café in Florence. They know who your father is.'

It was the last thing she was expecting him to say.

Nora just stared, she had no idea how to react. 'You found my *father*?'

'Apparently, he's not an architect but an artist, a professor, but he does live in Stockholm, so your Plan B might have paid off in time. I have a name, a workplace, everything you need to contact him. Here . . .' He took a piece of paper out of his pocket and held it out towards her, and when she made no move to take it, laid it carefully on the table. 'Erik Larsson. He teaches at the Stockholm Institute of Art.'

'Erik Larsson,' she repeated. Larsson. The missing piece of the puzzle. 'That's . . . that's a good name.'

'Are you OK?'

'I think so.' She should jump up, thank him, hug him, call her friends, scream, cry, but she was utterly numb with disbelief. Nora reached across and picked up the paper. It was just a torn-off piece of A4 with handwritten notes scrawled on, but it was one of the most important documents she had ever seen. 'I just don't know what to feel, to do.'

'I don't think there's a set response here. You can do whatever you want, whenever you want to. Email him, write to him. Head to Stockholm to see him.'

'Go to Stockholm? Just like that?'

His smile was tender. 'Nora, you are heading off around the world. Sweden is just an hour or so away.'

'I could. I could go to Stockholm.' She tried to read the piece of paper again, the letters jumbling in front of her eyes, feeling almost disembodied, like everyday tasks and thoughts were impossible. Her pulse was too fast, her heartbeat so loud she was sure it must reverberate around the room, the rush of blood in her ears making her dizzy. 'What if he doesn't remember my mum? What if she got it wrong and he isn't my father at all? What if he doesn't want to see me?'

She wasn't really aware she had spoken any of this aloud, until Luca laid a comforting hand on her arm. She couldn't help leaning into his touch.

'Breathe. Maybe I should have called first, obviously this has been a shock. Look, you don't have to go straight away, take it slow, write to him, email him. You've got plenty of time.'

Nora stared almost unseeingly at the table, piled high with clothes and towels and maps and waterproofs, walking sandals and boots and flip-flops. 'I'm going away for nearly a year, if I don't do it now . . .' Her voice trembled. She knew more than anyone that time couldn't be taken for granted, that she couldn't rely on everything being the same tomorrow. 'No.' She sounded stronger, felt stronger. 'I want to go to Stockholm and see him in person, see for myself that he is real, not a picture. I have no idea what, if anything, happens after that, but I should go. I have to go.' She looked at Luca pleadingly. 'Luca, thank you for coming here and letting me know. I appreciate it more than I can say, and I know I have no right to ask anything else from you, but I really would like you to come with me.' She had had no idea she would ask until she spoke, but she didn't want to recall the words, or hide from them. She did want Luca with her. 'I wouldn't be here without you; it feels in some way that this journey is yours too.'

Luca didn't answer for a long moment. She couldn't tell what he was thinking, his face utterly inscrutable, but at long last he nodded. 'Of course. When do you want to go?'

'Really? You will? As soon as possible, I guess. I only have a fortnight and I'm not working right now so happy to fit in around you.'

'I can book flights for tomorrow, does that work?'

*Tomorrow?* Her already erratic pulse sped even more, the blood now galloping around her body. She was so close to answers. 'Yes. That works.'

'Good. I'll text you the details.' He stood, the visit clearly at an end, and she got clumsily to her feet. 'I'd better go.'

'You're welcome to stay for dinner. I'm not sure what it is, but—'

'No. I don't think that's a good idea, do you?'

'Maybe not.' It was clear that although he had agreed to come with her, the past still lay between them. She had to clear the air, otherwise what was going to be an emotional trip already was going to be ten times more difficult. 'I really am sorry, you know. For everything. I didn't mean to cause such a mess.'

He didn't move, his expression as unreadable as ever. 'You don't need to apologise. Gabe doesn't come out of this brilliantly. Nor do I,' he added, his voice low. 'As far as I was concerned, you were my brother's fiancée, I had no right to . . .' He paused, tantalisingly close to saying something Nora really wanted, needed to hear.

'To what?' she prompted him.

He looked at her then, emotion raw in his eyes, and she shivered. 'To get so close to you, to start to care about you.'

'I care about you too,' she whispered. 'All that time, I thought I was falling in love with Gabe, I was falling in love with you. With you all,' she hastily added. Maybe she was a coward, but she couldn't make such a raw declaration, not when they were heading to Sweden together, not when she had planned a step into the future, not when she had spent the last few weeks working hard to stand on her own two feet, to try to get over him.

'Everyone misses you, Nora.'

'Except Gabe, probably. I wish I had a chance to put things right with him.'

'Gabe is back with Lily.' His eyes were fastened on her face, searching for a reaction. 'They reconciled pretty much straight after the party.'

'Oh.' She waited for a moment to test her feelings, but all she felt was relief. 'I'm pleased for him, for them. How does your mother feel about it?'

'Resigned. But, of course, she just wants Gabe to be happy. We all do.'

'Of course.' She wanted to ask, was he, Luca, happy? But she didn't have the courage.

'I'd better go, get things sorted.'

'Of course,' she repeated, she seemed to have lost all vocabulary. 'I'll see you out.'

They headed back into the hallway.

'I spoke to my father,' Luca said abruptly as they reached the door. 'The day after you . . . the day after Nonna's party. I told him I was sorry. That I hated the distance between us. That I missed him. That I like my job, but it doesn't mean I can't be involved with the vineyard as well, in whatever way he needs me.'

'You did? Oh Luca, I am so proud of you! What did he say?'

'It was more what he didn't say. I can't quite explain it; he looked ten years younger, like he'd found something he didn't know he'd lost. I'm not making sense.'

'No, no you are. This is brilliant. Well done.'

'It made me feel guilty for taking so long. Thank you for pushing me into it.'

'For interfering, you mean.'

'For being right.' His eyes were warm, his mouth tilted into the half-smile she couldn't resist and for one almost unbearable moment her whole body ached with painful longing. How was she going to manage a whole trip away with him? Was she making a terrible mistake? She could manage on her own, but it would be so much easier with him by her side. She would allow herself this trip, but she just had to be careful not to read anything more into his kindness. He had made his stance quite clear. Whatever had been between them, her status as his brother's ex meant there could be no future. She respected that. She had to.

'Mamma thinks that now we are getting along, I am coming to live back at the villa, but I'm not planning to give up my apartment. I'm used to my own space.'

'And you do have the perfect apartment.' Her gaze caught his and she knew he was thinking, as she was, of that last time they had been alone there, of the kiss, of that moment when everything else was forgotten but the way they felt. If she could go back, she would undo so much, but not that, her only regret was ending it when she did.

She couldn't look away, and nor seemingly could he, the air charged, her whole body hyperaware of his every tiny movement, every breath, until he stepped back, breaking the spell, and before she could react, he was gone.

23 April 2019

Darling Nora,

I've been putting this one off, hoping against hope I
would never need to write it, but I guess now I'm in the
hospice I need to accept that I have to say goodbye.
I hope there is time to say everything I need to say
and thank goodness we have never been one of those
repressed types of families with a million secrets and
I love yous to divest ourselves of before it's too late.
I hope you have always known just how very loved you
are.

So, my amazing girl. I want you to know that I loved
you from the moment I found out you were on the way
and have only loved you more with every day since.
You have brought me nothing but sunshine and joy
and laughter, and if I had to do it all again, there is
nothing I would change (except getting your father's
address).

I want you to be happy. I know you have been through
a lot. You have been my rock these last few years, but
it's time for you to be selfish now. Go dance all night
and kiss strangers and take the road less travelled and
swim in the river and wear your best clothes every day

and eat the cake and play your music and live! Take all
that every day has to offer and wring every moment
out of it. I did and I regret nothing.

Keep your friends close. What an amazing group of
young people they are. Tell Felix to follow his heart,
Grace to keep being brilliant and Ana that it's OK to
be vulnerable. Tell them they have made me laugh so
much the last few months, even on days when I have
been in such pain and so scared, laughter felt like an
impossible dream. Tell them I love them.

Life is a journey, my darling, and we don't always end
up where we think we will and that is part of the fun
of it. It's those twisty alleyways and wrong turns and
diversions that make it worthwhile. Explore every one,
Nora Florence! I hope your journey brings you as much
happiness as mine has.

Mum xxx

## Chapter Twenty-Three

'What a beautiful city!' Nora drew in an ecstatic breath. 'The air is so fresh, just breathe it. And it's so blue. A lot colder than London, but blue! And clean. Isn't it clean?'

It seemed impossible that just a few hours ago she had headed out into London's grey September mugginess and now, a short flight and a train ride later, she was in the heart of Stockholm. There was water everywhere, she hadn't really expected that, rivers and sea mingling, the city itself spread over bridge-linked islands. It was a definite few degrees colder than London – crisp autumn very much in the air, fresh and sharp – the cooler temperatures suiting the elegant stone buildings in various shades of grey and gold, or painted cheery pastels. This was a city made for boots and hats, scarves and gloves, as much as sandals and shorts, and Nora wanted to experience its every mood, every season.

They dropped their bags off at the hotel Luca had booked, a centrally located anonymous chain overlooking the harbour, then Luca insisted on taking her to one of the many bakeries for something to eat.

'You look like you might pass out, have you eaten anything today?' he asked and she had to admit she hadn't.

Nora wasn't sure she *could* manage anything, her nerves dialled right up with the thought of the impending meeting as well as the reality of Luca's company, but the excellent coffee, which even passed muster for the picky Sicilian, and the even more excellent cinnamon bun tempted her and before she realised it, she had picked at every last crumb.

She sat back with a contented sigh. 'Thank you, you're right, I did need that. And thank you for organising everything, you'll have to let me know how much I owe you. I'm not sure we need to stay over though. Do you think it's tempting fate?' Would she want to stick around if her father rejected her, or was away?

'It seems a shame not to do some sightseeing while we're here.' Luca picked up his coffee. He was calmness personified, as he had been all day, solid and strong, a soothing force every time her nerves threatened to spiral out of control. 'This place is part of your DNA after all.'

'Allegedly. I guess we'll soon find out. Not that I think Mum was lying or mistaken, and we have the photos,' she added hurriedly. 'It's just I thought I might feel something, you know? The ghosts of my ancestors, a sense of belonging. Like the way you all feel about Sicily.'

'But we were born and raised there, fed on local produce and stories of our history. This is all new to you. Did you think you'd set foot on Swedish soil and suddenly be fluent?'

'Not really. Maybe a little,' she confessed. 'But it's not just the language. It's everything. The customs, the food, the history, all those things that make a person belong to a place. They are all new to me, different. I'm an outsider, whatever a DNA test reveals. I wasn't expecting that. I wish . . .' She stopped, feeling disloyal, but Luca seemed to know where she had been going anyway.

'Why didn't your mother ever bring you here? From all you have said, she seems like the kind of woman who would have wanted you to have a sense of your heritage.'

'She did to a certain degree. Foodwise, there was a lot of herring, and mackerel and dill salad, that kind of thing, and when the whole Scandi noir kicked off she was right there, watching every series, although she was indiscriminate about countries, she didn't really care if they were Danish, Swedish or Norwegian! Also, don't forget that when I was really small, she was a student and then a trainee, and then we always holidayed with my grandparents and that meant visiting France or Scotland usually. She talked about us coming here, but I think she was as nervous as I feel now. It would be making myth reality and that's not easy. And even if she had, I would still have visited as a tourist, on the outside.'

It was hard to explain the bittersweet twist of emotions the beautiful old city evoked. The curiosity and interest of a tourist combined with a melancholy sense of loss, a childhood unlived. Even if her parents had not stayed together, if Erik had known about her, then maybe she would have spent summers here, long light days in a cabin by a lake, lingonberries and meatballs, winter visits for the Saint Lucia ceremony, Swedish customs and tradition weaving through her memories and experiences, anchoring her here. Even if her future included a relationship with her father, a Swedish passport, she would never be able to get that time, those memories. The sense of loss was almost unbearable and for one weak moment she wished she hadn't come.

But that was cowardly, she scolded herself, and she had had enough of missing out because of fear or because she didn't know how to move on. No more regrets, or passively watching her life go by, no more daydreams instead of living. In two weeks, she would be on another plane and she would absolutely, unequivocally be a tourist, a stranger when she landed, but one ready to soak in the sights and the sounds, and there was no real reason why this should be any different.

'OK,' she said resolutely. 'I'm ready. Let's do this.'

'*Bene.* You are going to be fine, Nora.' Luca's smile was slow and sweet. 'OK, the Institute of Arts is not far.'

'Then what are we waiting for?'

Despite her nerves, Nora couldn't help but enjoy the walk. Their destination was on one of the many islands and their walk took them along the boat-lined waterfront and across a pretty footbridge. 'I love Hampstead, but I think we need more rivers and bridges and a lot more boats,' she said as they stopped so she could take a photo. The exercise, fresh air and different sights and sounds all helped to calm her, and at times Nora couldn't help but feel that she really was on a minibreak rather than a life-changing mission and noted several other places to visit: the Viking Museum, a boat museum and, to Luca's evident horror, the ABBA museum all at the top of her list. It felt good to make plans for later, as if this destination was just a tick on her itinerary, not the moment she had been dreaming of all her life.

All too soon, they reached the Royal Institute, an imposing building overlooking the water. As they climbed the stairs up to the front door, her hand found Luca's as if by its own volition and, after one long second, his closed around her, anchoring her. 'OK?'

'I think so. No, yes. I am.'

And she was, she realised. Of course, she wanted the next few minutes or hours or days to go well, but this moment didn't define her, this place didn't and Erik Larsson didn't. The only thing that mattered was how she managed the outcome from whatever happened next. Sicily had woken her up, reminded her that she had agency and purpose. Luca had woken her up.

'Do you want me to speak to her?' Luca asked as they reached the reception, where a terrifyingly cool-looking woman sat behind the desk.

Nora squeezed his fingers gratefully. 'I think I need to,' she said. 'But thank you.' She let go, missing the feel of him, her hand suddenly cold, and stepped up to the glass screen. 'Hi,' she said, glad that so far everyone in Sweden seemed to speak intimidatingly perfect English. 'I'm looking for Erik Larsson. Is he in today? If so, I wonder if you could let him know we are here to see him.'

'He might be teaching,' the woman displayed no interest in who Nora was and why she was looking for Erik. Why should she? She didn't know that Nora was here to hopefully change her life. 'Who shall I say is here?'

'Nora Fitzgerald.' She inhaled and clarified: 'Can you tell him Charlotte's daughter?'

'One moment. Please take a seat.'

Nora and Luca retreated to the uncomfortable if stylish bench and obediently sat. Now that they were here, her nerves had wound back up again, taut and almost unbearably tight. The moments ticked by unbearably slowly and by the time the woman beckoned her over Nora had convinced herself that Erik didn't want to see her, that he was abroad, ill, dead . . . Why had she just shown up here without doing any research of her own? She hadn't even googled him, checked his hours, found a photo or a Wikipedia page or anything.

'He says he will be down in a moment.'

'Great!' Her voice sounded high to her own ears. He was here. He was coming to meet her. This was it.

Time slowed even further. Every atom was tense, anticipatory, her stomach a labyrinth of nerves, breathing shallow as adrenaline flooded her system.

Luca stood, clearly as wound up as she, pacing a few steps before standing behind her, his hand solid and warm on her shoulder.

Nora started as a man trotted down the stairs, her heart giving a painful leap, but he jogged on by with without even noticing her. She jumped again as a lift chimed and the doors opened, but it was a young couple who tumbled out. A group walked by, leisurely talking, and still she waited. Finally, another chime, doors opening and there he was, still recognisable from her mother's photos despite the intervening years. Tall, hair still a dirty blond, the temples greying slightly grey. Piercing blue eyes, wrinkles at the corners emphasising the colour, a firm chin, a little pointed, just like Nora's. Slim, almost lanky and real. She stood up on shaky legs, managing a smile as he halted in front of her.

'Of course you are Charlotte's daughter. You look just like her.' He looked around, eyes eager. 'Is she here?'

Nora's stomach dropped. In all her imaginings, the one thing she had maybe purposefully avoided envisioning was the scenario in which she told Erik that Charlotte was dead.

She swallowed. 'Is there somewhere we can talk?'

He studied her for a moment, then nodded. 'Of course, follow me. What did you say your name is again? I didn't quite catch it when the receptionist phoned.'

'Nora. Nora Florence Fitzgerald.'

She saw his eyebrows rise at her middle name, saw him take her in properly, his expression keen and alert, and she knew that he understood who she was and why she was here.

'Lovely to meet you, Nora. Let's find somewhere private. I think we have a lot of catching up to do.'

Nora's hands were still shaking as she finally inserted her keycard and almost fell into her hotel room. She wasn't drunk, or even tipsy, although she had consumed a fair amount of wine over the day and evening finishing off with Swedish schnapps which had left her whole head ringing. But she was on a high of pure emotion, giddy with happiness.

'I have grandparents! And cousins!' She twirled around. Luca stood in the door of her room, eyes amused and tender. 'I spoke to them and I am going to meet them tomorrow! They seemed nice, didn't they seem nice? Oh, Luca, it was better than I dared even hope. He didn't once question whether I was telling the truth. And he felt just the same way. He really did fall for her, he even said she was the reason he never married, that he was always searching for that same feeling he had with Mum but never found it. Thank you.' She reached for him and pulled him into the room, the door closing slowly behind him, enfolding him into a hug. He stood, stiff and unyielding until, almost with a sigh, he gave in, his arms holding her close, and she swore he dropped a light kiss on the top of her head. 'Thank you,' she said again, muffled against his cashmere jumper.

She felt his chest reverberate with amusement. 'You don't have anything to thank me for.'

'Oh, I do. You suggested I went to Florence and took me on the tour and spoke to the café owner, so his uncle got in touch. You came with me today and made me feel safe and supported when I was ready to head back home convinced it wouldn't work out. I'm the one who has spent the last decade reuniting families, but I couldn't have done any of this without you.' She pulled back and cupped his face. 'You've saved me several times now.'

'It was my pleasure.' He took her hands in his, held them for one second and then stepped back.

Nora dropped down onto her bed and grinned up at him. She didn't know what to do with all this adrenaline. She felt like she could run a marathon, dance all night long. The last thing she wanted to do was sleep despite the late hour.

Luca leant against the wall, hands in his pockets. She did like that jumper on him, although she missed the ubiquitous white shirt. 'So, you're staying on for a while?'

'Yes. My dad suggested it – do you hear what I said there? My dad! After all, all I really need to do at home is brief the house-sitter and finish packing, there's no reason to rush back and so many reasons to stay. There's still so much to say, to learn. And I want to just be as well, you know? To have some comfortable silences.' To cram a lifetime into the next few days.

'It makes sense.'

'Can you believe that he – that we – have family in Australia? That I can visit them when I am there, and Erik will join me? That he wants to take me to Florence next summer?'

'I really am very happy it's all worked out for you, Nora. It's wonderful. But it's late and I was thinking I should go.'

'Go?'

'Back to my room, to get some sleep and change my flight tomorrow to get back a bit earlier. You've got this, Nora, you don't need me.'

'You're right,' she said slowly. 'I don't need you.' She took a deep breath. 'But I want you, Luca.'

'Nora . . .' She didn't know if it was an entreaty or a warning.

'And I think you want me too.' OK, maybe she was tipsy after all. Or maybe it was just the happiness running through her veins, the endorphins and dopamine making her bold and daring.

She stood up and took a slow, deliberate step towards him. He didn't move, either to meet her or in retreat, but stayed still, his eyes fixed on her, amusement and something hotter flickering in their gold-flecked depths.

'I've been thinking, Luca,' she said. Another step. 'You could have sent me my father's details in several different ways.' Another step. 'You could have emailed them or texted them, put them in an envelope and posted them. Or you could have dropped them at my door and left. But you didn't.' Another step. 'And here you are. Still here.' Final step. Now she was up close and personal, although not quite personal enough. She splayed a hand on his chest, a light touch, the cashmere soft under her fingers in contrast to the hardness of the muscle underneath. 'You have been by my side every step of this journey. I think it's because you belong there.'

She felt him inhale, exhale. His eyes were almost pure gold, his mouth a wicked slant.

'Four months ago, we had a moment. You felt it too, you admitted it. You said we had a connection.'

'I did. We did . . .'

'But things got so tangled, went so wrong, I started to doubt myself. I knew I had feelings for you when I left Sicily, but it was hard to disentangle what I felt for you from my yearning to be part of your family. It took Gabe asking me outright for me even to admit that I shouldn't marry him. How could I trust in the way I wanted you?'

Luca didn't answer, but she felt his breathing speed up. His heart beating faster under her palm.

'I had to consider whether it was real at all. Whether I took a moment and created a whole narrative out of it. Whether my mother's tales of love at first sight were just that, tales. But today I realised that she was telling me her truth. It's like Erik gave me her magic back today, her belief. Because I did fall in love that day, with you.'

He quivered under her hand. Nora kept her gaze firmly on him.

321

'In some ways, I think I realised the moment I first met you in Sicily, and I think that you knew it too, that's why you were so off with me, so suspicious. Not because I'd withheld some details and manipulated a meeting, but because you knew I was with the wrong brother. You knew I was meant to be with you. But you had too much honour, too much respect for your family, to act on it. You still do. But you can't keep away. And that's good because I don't want you to. I want you right here with me. Always.'

Nora held her breath as Luca stared at her, conflicting emotions passing across his face like clouds in a summer sky – denial, regret, loneliness, but also hope, desire and something she thought, she hoped, might be love.

She took a deep breath. 'I love you, Luca. I've known all along but didn't want to admit it to myself. It was embarrassing after being so adamant I was head over heels about Gabe. But that wasn't love, it was infatuation, the need for my narrative to have a hero in it. It wasn't based on anything solid, anything real. But the way I feel about you . . .' She could barely say the words, her voice almost a husk, her heart beating in time with his, faster and faster, her pulse racing, matching the speed of his. 'The way I feel about you is based on more than our eyes meeting on a rainy night and you playing the hero. It's based on your integrity, and your kindness, on your ability to sit through a romcom and enjoy it because you know it means something to me. It's based on how you make me feel safe and wanted and yet confident to go out and do anything because I know you'll support me. It's also based on the fact that I really, really fancy you and I want to kiss you so badly, I can't think of anything else, even on a day as momentous as this.'

His mouth twitched, just slightly, but enough for desire to roll through her, knowing he was imagining, contemplating kissing her right now.

'I nearly reached out so many times, but embarrassment, fear stopped me. But I am not embarrassed to feel like this, and I am not afraid any longer. We get one shot, Luca. I don't want to waste mine.' She stopped, almost trembling with adrenaline, unable to believe all she had said, how exposed she had left herself, but she also knew that if Luca walked away and she hadn't said it, she would regret it forever. 'My father has spent his life missing the woman he lost; my mother died never seeing him again. I don't want to follow in their footsteps. I want to reach out and grab my chance at love with both hands.' She paused. 'I've done a lot of talking,' she said with a shaky laugh. 'Are you going to say anything?'

'I think,' he said slowly, his voice a rasp. 'I think you've said it all, except this. I love you too.'

And then he was kissing her, hard, not slowly or sensually or seductively, but with an intent that took her breath, all conscious thought, away. A deep, claiming kiss, pulling her close, no holding back this time, touching her, exploring her as she finally – *finally* – slipped her hands under the cashmere sweater.

'I've been wanting to do this since you changed your shirt in Taormina,' she said against his mouth. 'Every time you wore one of those bloody white shirts, I wanted to tear it off you.'

'I know,' was all he said, and as she gasped at the audacity, he slipped her cardigan off her shoulders and unzipped her dress, one fluid movement leaving her in just her underwear. 'And I've been wanting to do this since I found you banging on your front door in just that little towel.'

'Pervert.'

'Voyeur.'

She laughed at him. 'Where you are concerned, always.' She eyed the jumper. 'I am not going to rip that off. Next time, I insist on one of those white linen shirts.'

'Next time?' He raised a brow. 'You seem very sure of yourself.'

'I am. Now take that jumper off before I forget cashmere needs careful handling.'

'I like it when you talk dirty at me.' But he obediently pulled the jumper off. Standing there bare chested, just as toned and delicious as she remembered. 'Anything else you want me to take off?'

'Mmmn, let me think. Luca?'

'Mmm?' His eyes were glazed, his expression pure intent.

'I mean it. I do love you. I don't want to just sleep with you tonight and then that's it. I want this to be the first of many, many times. I know I am heading off and I know it's complicated and—'

He cut her off with a kiss. 'You, Nora Fitzgerald, think too much. I think we need to do something about that?'

'Oh? What did you have in mind?'

His smile made her whole body quiver. 'Come here and let me show you. I love you, Nora, and I am not going anywhere and I am happy to prove that to you as many times as you like.'

She smiled back, holding his gaze. 'That sounds like fighting talk, Catalano. Game on.'

31 May 2025

Dear darling Mummy,

Luca bought me a travel journal to match the planner and here I am, on the last page, on the plane heading back to London. It's amazing to flick back through the pages and relive my adventures. There have been plenty of times when I have been too hot, too cold, really uncomfortable, more than a little scared, lost, as well as exhilarated, awestruck, giddy, spellbound, and really, really happy, but whatever I felt and whatever I have done, sharing it with you in this book has been really special.

I worried about being lonely, that stepping away from Hampstead would just make me miss you all the more, but thanks to the planner, it was like having you with me wherever I was. And in the end, I actually spent hardly any time alone! Obviously Grace, Ana, Felix and Dai were always going to join me for some parts, but Erik came out to Australia for several weeks and I met his family (my family, Mum!) in Perth and on the Gold Coast and Luca joined whenever he could — a couple of weeks at the beginning, New Zealand, some of the treks through Peru and Chile (as did Alessandro! You know

325

what, I think Ana is smitten and I never thought I would write those words).

Luca was with me the last weeks in Canada. And guess what, Gabe and Lily joined us in Vancouver for a couple of days! They were there doing some terrifying adventure sports. It was odd, awkward, Lily definitely will never be my biggest fan, but it was lovely to see the brothers together, to see Gabe as a person, not a hero or a mistake, just a human. We tacitly agreed to pretend the whole relationship never happened. Sometimes it's better not to talk things out!

You'd like Luca, you'd really like him. I might be smitten myself. I am smitten.

He's gorgeous, obviously. Clever and knows a lot about wine (see, told you you would like him), a problem-solver but not in a smug takeover way, but a good person to have by your side in a crisis — as we found out in the Andes. He's kind. He cares about me. He makes me laugh. He's a good son and brother (he's Sicilian, family is important). He respects the second great era of romcoms. He loves me. And he found Erik for me.

Mum you chose so well! I have loved every moment of getting to know him. We're (that's me and Luca!) spending some of the summer at his cabin by a lake in Sweden (so wholesome) and meeting more family and hearing more tales about you. We're also heading to Florence, so he can show me all the places you visited together. He really loved you too — loves you still — and finding someone who cares about you as much as I do is almost as amazing as having a father.

326

A father! I still haven't got used to those words. I gave him the originals of all your postcards to him, last September in Stockholm. I figured he was the right person to have them. They were meant for him after all. We cried and laughed over them together. He's hungry for every detail of our lives and reliving them makes me feel like you are still here.

So what's next for me? I haven't got it all figured out the way I hoped I would. Too busy doing to plan! But that's OK. Because you were right. Living is about the journey, not the destination, and I intend to enjoy every step, especially as I really think (I know) that Luca and I are in it for the long haul. That might mean me moving to Sicily for most of the year, but I think I could definitely live with that. As long as we go to Florence every so often and have a drink at your café.

I am thinking about university and that English degree I never did, maybe with the OU. The world is full of opportunities and I can't wait to explore them. I want to learn more about wine making — and I know the perfect people to teach me. Luca's family welcomed me back so warmly, I video call his mother and sisters every week, I can't wait to see them again.

So much has changed in the last year and it all started when, just like you, I fell in love at first sight.

Your ever-loving

Nora xxx

# Acknowledgements

I promised my daughter Abby (who refuses to read my books) to acknowledge her lovely friends who do. Romance is having a much-deserved renaissance right now and much of that is thanks to Gen Z and BookTok. So this is for you Tilly, Daisy, Lottie and Molly! I hope you enjoy it.

It's been a long, wet and extended winter so huge thanks to Charlotte Mursell and Sanah Ahmed for giving me the opportunity to spend most of it in Sicily, even if only in my imagination, and to the rest of the team at Orion, especially Jade Craddock for another careful, detailed copy-edit. As always any mistakes very much author's own.

Thanks also to Katie Fulford and everyone at Bell-Lomax for taking me on and, after over thirty books, steering me towards a much-needed business-like approach to writing.

Writing is a solitary pursuit which makes the friendships we forge with other writers especially important. Love and thanks to Christy McKellan, conference partner in crime (literally when we hit Harrogate!) and duet partner Sophie Pembroke for sanity-saving chats, messages and meet-ups. Thanks also to Abby Green, Susan Wilson, Heidi Rice Fiona Lucas and Iona Gray for parties and catch-ups and an awful lot of getting caught in the rain.

As always, the first draft of this book was mainly written on the 7.46 train. Second drafts need more time and space and I took myself off to Gladstone's Library for a week of writing and contemplation. Thank you to all the staff there for making me feel so welcome. I could quite happily just move in and spend all my days in those beautiful reading rooms.

Writing, working full time and commuting doesn't leave me with an awful lot of leisure time, so thank goodness for Rufus and Clover whose daily walk deadlines are far more important than my writing ones. And thank you to Rose for weekend reminders for walks, luring me out from my study into the fresh air.

And finally love always to Dan and Abby.

# Credit

Jessica Gilmore and Orion Fiction would like to thank everyone at Orion who worked on the publication of *Love at First Sight* in the UK.

**Editorial**
Sanah Ahmed

**Copyeditor**
Jade Craddock

**Proofreader**
Marian Reid

**Audio**
Paul Stark
Louise Richardson

**Contracts**
Anne Goddard
Dan Herron
Ellie Bowker

**Design**
Rachael Lancaster

Loveday May
Nick Shah

**Editorial Management**
Charlie Panayiotou
Jane Hughes
Bartley Shaw
Tamara Morriss

**Finance**
Jasdip Nandra
Nick Gibson
Sue Baker

**Marketing**
Lauryn Embleton

**Publicity**
Frankie Banks

**Production**
Ruth Sharvell

**Sales**
Jen Wilson
Esther Waters
Victoria Laws
Toluwalope Ayo-Ajala

Rachael Hum
Anna Egelstaff
Sinead White
Georgina Cutler

**Operations**
Jo Jacobs
Sharon Willis

'Sunny, sexy and gloriously escapist. The perfect beach read' **ALEX BROWN**

Indi Drewe is turning thirty and is *exactly* where she wants to be: she's on the cusp of a promotion, lives in her gorgeous London flat and is sure her perfect-on-paper boyfriend, Will, is about to propose...

Only, on the night she'd hoped Will would present her with a sparkling diamond ring, she finds out that her younger sister Jade is getting married to a man she's known only for a few weeks!

Worried her sister is about to make a terrible mistake, she immediately flies out to visit her sister in Greece - and is shocked to discover she's sharing her villa with a far-too-handsome (and perpetually shirtless) stranger, Mikhos.

Indi and Mikhos might be each other's worst nightmare, but together, they only have days to stop the wedding before it's too late! Yet with so much love in the air on this paradise island, will they be able to resist falling for each other, too?

# Help us make the next generation of readers

We – both author and publisher – hope you enjoyed this book. We believe that you can become a reader at any time in your life, but we'd love your help to give the next generation a head start.

Did you know that 9 per cent of children don't have a book of their own in their home, rising to 13 per cent in disadvantaged families*? We'd like to try to change that by asking you to consider the role you could play in helping to build readers of the future.

We'd love you to think of sharing, borrowing, reading, buying or talking about a book with a child in your life and spreading the love of reading. We want to make sure the next generation continue to have access to books, wherever they come from.

And if you would like to consider donating to charities that help fund literacy projects, find out more at **www.literacytrust.org.uk** and **www.booktrust.org.uk**.

THANK YOU

*As reported by the National Literacy Trust